MIDNIGHT
IN THE
PENTAGRAM

MIDNIGHT
IN THE
PENTAGRAM

Edited by Kenneth W. Cain

www.silvershamrockpublishing.com

Table of Contents

Foreword by Ronald Malfi 1

"The Corn Maidens" by Brian Moreland 9

"Father MacLeod" by Tony Tremblay 33

"Opening the Door" by Kenneth McKinley 51

"The Other" by Laurel Hightower 69

"Legion Cast Forth" by Robert Ford 83

"Angel Dust" by Shannon Felton 97

"What I Wouldn't Give" by Chad Lutzke 107

"Hellseed" by Tim Curran 115

"Devil's Ink" by Mark Towse 131

"Baby Teeth" by Azzurra Nox 141

"My Body" by Wesley Southard 155

"The Red Butcher of Wrocław" by Graham Masterton 173

"Dog Eat God" by Kenneth W. Cain 187

"The Oubliette of Élie Loyd" by Catherine Cavendish 195

"Discovering Mr. Jones" by Cameron Ulam 211

"The Gods of Our Fathers" by Todd Keisling 225

"I Know He Loves Me" by James Newman 245

"Second Sight" by Allan Leverone 251

"Family Reunion" by Stephanie Ellis 267

"A Night Above" by John Quick...283

"Brujeria" by Michael Patrick Hicks 293

"White Walpurgis" by Tim Meyer 309

"Family Business" by Charlotte Platt.....................................323

"Flaking Red Paint" by Armand Rosamilia 339

"Diminishing Returns" by P.D. Cacek....................................351

"The Story of a Lifetime" by JG Faherty 369

"The Furious Pour" by Amanda Hard.....................................383

"A Virgin Birth" by William Meikle 399

"Complex" by Jason Parent 411

"Black Jar Man" by Mark Steensland.....................................421

"Babylon Falling" by Brian Keene 435

"Express" by Edward M. Erdelac..465

"Witches' Night" by Owl Goingback 475

"Dispatches From a Pandemic: A Foreword"

by Ronald Malfi

"We are all going to die," says the guy on the news, or at least that's my interpretation. I'm writing this smack in the middle of August, in this century's most un-august year—2020, that is, for any readers who may be perusing this text decades from now, whose grasp on history might be wanting. For the most part, my family and I have been holed up in our house since mid-March, watching with the medicated stupefaction of the soul-shocked as life as we knew it seemed to be grinding to a halt. We all know the deal, right? Businesses shuttered. Deaths skyrocketed. Facemasks appeared. Politicians became even more political. Where the hell was the world headed?

Not to sound like an asshole, but I was built for this. No, I'm not some doomsday prepper, but I've eked out a profession over these past two decades that affords me the luxury of solitary confinement: I'm a writer. In fact, just a few scant years earlier, I'd written a novel called *The Night*

Parade about a fictional disease that now seems every bit as enigmatic as COVID-19. At the time, I spoke with epidemiologists and staff at the WHO to gather intel, such as what sort of death-rate numbers would the world need to see from a disease that would ease polite society toward the brink of extinction. They essentially gave me COVID numbers. Truth in fiction, right, kids?

But my point is, the fact that I've been pretty much confined to my house has had little effect on my mental wellbeing. As long as I don't pay too much attention to the news—something I've forced myself to do these past few months—it's pretty much been business as usual for me. My wife, not so much—the kids are home and driving her nuts, and to cope with the ennui, she's undertaken renovations in the home where the results, on occasion, have reached such proportions that, upon walking into a room, I do a double-take to ensure I'm actually still in my house. (My wife will deny this—she's of the belief that I wouldn't notice if a tractor-trailer bulldozed its way into our living room, and for the most part, she's not wrong.)

I've gotten some good work done during this time: I've completed a novel, wrote a script for a TV show pilot, and banged out about two dozen songs for my band's sophomore album, which we had just started recording weeks before the pandemic shepherded us all back into our homes. I also received quite a number of requests to write forewords for upcoming publications during this time—novels and anthologies and the like. Generally, I turn these requests down; I just don't have the time to read as much as I'd like to, and I hate making a promise to do so when I fear I may ultimately fail to come through.

When Ken McKinley asked if I'd be interested in writing a foreword to *Midnight in the Pentagram,* I was struck by that familiar concern that I might not have the time. But Ken's a swell guy and I dig Silver Shamrock Publishing, and, shoot, when he said the anthology was about demon possession, devils, and all facets of the occult, I felt him successfully reeling me in. So he sent me a copy of the book.

Immediately, I was taken by the incredible lineup of authors assembled in this collection—authors I both admire and, in some instances, am fortunate enough to call friends: Armand Rosamilia, Wesley Southard, Brian Keene, Robert Ford, Brian Moreland, and a handful of others with whom I've become friendly online.

What do you do to relax as the world comes to an end? You read a bunch of short stories about various breeds of possession, of course. So that's what I did, starting with relative newcomer Cameron Ulam's deliciously unsettling story, "Discovering Mr. Jones," wherein a group of junk haulers experience an otherworldly, er, *homecoming*, during one of their gigs. With an assured, confident voice, she's a writer to watch.

The body as a home vulnerable to some foreign entity is echoed in Tony Tremblay's "Father MacLeod," a twist on the traditional exorcism trope. Ulam's and Tremblay's tales about things *coming in* were juxtaposed by Mark Towse's "Devil's Ink" and Charlotte Platt's "Family Business," stories about things *coming out*, so to speak. And all of this got me   thinking. [1]

I'm a sucker for stories built on legends, whether those legends are fictions from our real lives or fictions within fiction (like little storytelling nesting dolls), so Mark Steensland's "The Black-Jar Man" hit all the right spots for me. Next, the aforementioned Wesley Southard and Armand Rosamilia deliver a one-two punch with the tales "My Body" and "Flaking Red Paint," respectively. (And if you're ever fortune enough to sit beside the Rosamilia family during a convention, well, then you're fortunate, indeed.)

Is there a better title than James Newman's "I Know He Loves Me (He Just Has a Funny Way of Showing It)"? This tale explores the aftermath of a teenage girl's possession, with a brilliant twist on the trope, and it's probably what *Exorcist II: The Heretic* should have been.

Great titles are, well, great, but I love a good opening paragraph, so I bow to the opening of Jason Parent's "Complex." I'm generally unimpressed by gore for gore's sake—it seems a shyster's game to me—so I applaud Parent's opening to this tale, which is well-crafted and slips in the mention of a dead child as effortlessly as sliding a piece of bread into a toaster. It perfectly sets the stage for the main character's temperament and the tone of the rest of the story, and when the end comes, it's swift and satisfying.

Azzurra Nox's "Baby Teeth" dips its toe back in the possession pool, where a woman is confronted by a psychiatrist about murdering her infant daughter. It also serves as a frightening metaphor for postpartum depression. (WARNING: Do not read while holding an infant.)

The first thing I read by Tim Meyer was his short story collection, *Worlds Between My Teeth*, which I thought was very good. I followed this up by reading his short novel, *The Switch House*, which was truly excellent, and highly recommended. His tale herein, "White Walpurgis," continues the trend of chilling his readers to the bone.

If I created a character called Graham Masterton, my editor would say that name is too on the nose. But he's a true master, and someone I've been reading since forever. One of my first professional sales was to a fiction magazine in the UK called *Peep Show*, edited by Paul Fry. When I received my contributor copies, I saw that Masterton also had a story in the same issue. For me, this put a stamp of authenticity on my own achievement, a whisper in the ear that said, *See? You're a real writer now, right there next to none other than the author of* The Manitou. Reading Masterton's story in this collection, "The Red Butcher of Wrocław," was like reading a letter penned by an old friend, since I've become so accustomed to his body of work.

With all the creeping around the devil typically does, Chad Lutzke plops him in an armchair in his protag's living room at the beginning of his story, "What I Wouldn't Give," like Old Splitfoot's about to be interviewed by Barbara Walters. It's a tongue-in-cheek story with some rock n' roll references that'll summon a devilish grin to your lips.

If Stephen King is the self-proclaimed literary equivalent of a Big Mac and fries, then Brian Keene is a bottle of Knob Creek wrapped in a Batman comic that smells vaguely of cigar smoke. His story, "Babylon Falling," dumps us in the parched, war-torn terrain of Southern Iraq, then he continues to dump his characters into literal Hell.

Laurel Hightower's "The Other" starts with an almost *Jolly Corner*-esque premise, before turning the reader on their head. This is a tale of the *other self*, the part of us that lurks in the periphery of ourselves, literally presented here as an intrusion. But who exactly *is* the other self?

"Brujeria," by Michael Patrick Hicks delivers one of my favorite conceits in dark fiction—the "lost film" now found—and is delivered with all the glamour of a modern-day Hollywood house party. It also contains one of the best bits of dialogue in this anthology. [2]

I've read a number of Tim Curran's novels lately, so reading "Hellseed" was like hearing a familiar voice whisper a dark "devil birth" story in my ear.

When you introduce your character as Cletus Estep and have him popping open a can of Bud in your story's first sentence, you're painting a pretty precise picture. Robert Ford's "Legion Cast Forth" does just that. Add to that a hotline direct to the Vatican, and you've got Ford's inimitable, delightful, blue-collar brand of off-kilter fiction.

Ah, Shannon Felton, brave soul that you are, you've employed one of the most prized narrative chestnuts in all of short fiction—the present-tense, second-person narrator. What is it about "Angel Dust" and, by extension, all second-person narratives that make you instinctually and immediately distrustful of the narrator? Is it because you don't necessarily trust yourself? Are you over-thinking things? Have you had one scotch too many? Did you deliberately write this paragraph in second person? How meta...

If you're going to save one story for Halloween, I'd suggest JG Faherty's "The Story of a Lifetime," which will check all your witchy, autumn boxes. Similarly, William Meikle's "A Virgin Birth," with its frozen duck ponds and gloomy inns, might be best savored in front of a hearth at Christmas. Warm mug of spiced rum cider optional.

Catherine Cavendish's tale of a woman's guided tour of a gothic castle, "The Oubliette of Élie Loyd," is expertly written, but for me, the most chilling (and beautiful) sentence is also the most seemingly innocuous, as our heroine watches her ex-lover leave their room and slam the door behind him. [3]

In Todd Keisling "The Gods of Our Fathers," a tormented child invokes an otherworldly presence to enact revenge. It serves as a nice companion piece to Stephanie Ellis's "Family Reunion," which presents a variation on family and devotion to dark religions. Completing the triptych is Brian Moreland's offer, "The Corn Maidens," featuring a female child ousted by her male family members in the beginning of the story. It's written like a fable and is effective in its reach. These three tales together showcase strong, terrifying female characters. They ring true.

Oh, what these eyes have seen! could be the tagline for "Second Sight," by Allan Leverone, the story of an organ donation gone horribly awry. If you're a pupil of ocular horror literature, look no further. (See what I did there?)

When you're an author who opens your story describing the sensation of whiskey searing down someone's throat, chances are I'm going to Google you and see if you live close enough to grab a drink. Amanda Hard doesn't live close enough, but her tale, "The Furious Pour," sated my desire (momentarily) for a sip of the hard stuff. [4]

I was born in 1977, which ostensibly makes me a child of the eighties, yet the teenage protagonists in Owl Goingback's "Witches' Night," which takes place in 1974, were wholly relatable. I'm even pretty sure my friends and I used to lie to each other about seeing horror movies, too—everything from *The Exorcist* to *The Texas Chainsaw Massacre.*[5]

"Express," by Edward M. Erdelac gave me some unexpected chuckles while "Diminishing Returns," by P.D. Cacek, punched me in the gut with its opening salvo about Alzheimer's. [6] Finally, "Dog Eat God," by Kenneth W. Cain, posits the curious request of a parishioner to a dirty-minded priest that he should kill her possessed dog, which goes to show that just when you think you've seen everything, you really haven't.

And that's that, folks. It's still August of 2020, we're still roiling in the depths of a pandemic, and I'm launching this dispatch to you in part to praise this delightful collection, yet in hopes that this serves as some sort of anchor to all of you, a lifeline to the real world. Not just from me to these specific authors—(Can you hear me, Keene? Still ordering those T-shirts, Wes? Say hi to the family, Armand!)—but from me to you, the reader, the student, the teacher, the head-case. This year has forced a possession on us all, altering our behaviors and perhaps even modifying our views of the world. I peer out a window and see people in masks walking dogs. I go to the grocery store and stand in line behind a friend whom I don't recognize beneath his face covering, as if some devil has come and inhabited his body, physically altering his appearance.

We're all a little possessed right now, is what I'm saying.

So be kind, read on, and I'll catch you all in another life.

— Ronald Malfi
Annapolis, Maryland
August 2020

---

[1] I look around the house, see our freshly-painted walls, the bookshelves my wife diligently assembled while I watched, sipping a cup of coffee, my kids' toys strewn about, and think, *Home as home, but body as home, too. The body is a home, ripe for break-ins.* Shudder.

[2] "Andi, this is Madeline. Don't be a cunt."

[3] "I stared at the closed door while an inexplicable twist of panic threatened to strangle me."

[4] I'm a liar. This story will make you salivate for a glass of single malt Macallan.

[5] Erol's Video was our local rental joint when I was a kid, and I had a buddy whose mom would let use rent pretty much any horror movie the place had to offer, with

one caveat: she insisted on being in the room while we watched it. If there was too much language, she'd make *tsk-tsk* noises from the couch. Too much violence, and she'd utter a comment under her breath. A pair of perky 1980s tits bouncing across the screen, she'd make my buddy hold an afghan quilt in front of the TV until the scene was over. But still—Erol's fucking Video, man!

[6] Which forced the thought: what is Alzheimer's if not some form of possession, or de-possession, if you will? Something formidable and *there* being irrevocably replaced by something equally as formidable yet invisible, changing who we are at our core?

The Corn Maidens

by Brian Moreland

There is a story told among the crows. A dark tale about a misunderstood girl. One old crow knew Hannah Creed all too well; the bird witnessed her plight firsthand. The girl's story began in late July 1933, in a barren patch of South Nebraska. Crackling heat shimmered across the sun-baked wheat fields. The crow's flock, perched on a white church roof, squawked and watched a ruckus happening in the farm town. A mob of men and women shouted, as two men dragged a fourteen-year-old girl in a faded-blue dress kicking and screaming down the road...

"No," Hannah cried. "*Please.*"

She resisted her father and uncle as they roughly took her to the edge of town. Just beyond the painted sign that read "Providence Fields, Pop. 42, The Lord Saveth the Righteous," the farmers dropped Hannah hard on the dusty dirt road.

"Go on. Get!" her papa yelled.

Her eldest brother, Ezekiel, pulled her pet billy goat by a rope. "Take your damn goat and don't come back." He gave its tail a swift kick. The big-horned goat bleated and took refuge behind Hannah.

In tears, Hannah looked from her brother and uncle to her father. "Papa please!"

"No child, not after all you've done. I never want to see your face near our town again." He spat on the ground by her feet.

The three men walked away, leaving Hannah crying in the dirt, and joined a wall of angry townspeople standing at the town's border. Folks she'd known all her life, her family and neighbors, gripped pitchforks and hoes and shouted for Hannah to leave. Pastor Brooks, his Bible open, spouted verses from The Book of Daniel. "'That you be driven away from mankind and your dwelling place be with the beasts of the field, and you be given grass to eat like cattle and be drenched with the dew of heaven...' "

Heartbroken and terrified, Hannah got to her feet and found her mother in the crowd. "Mama!" she pleaded.

Her mother held up a cross and prayed with the other women. The expression Mama wore was far from the loving mother who had read to Hannah when she was younger and patiently taught her to play hymns on the piano. Mama's God-fearing eyes looked at her daughter with disgust. When Hannah defiantly walked toward town, the crowd stepped back. Her brothers and cousins threw stones at her. One pelted Hannah's arm. Another struck her forehead. The ground spun as she stumbled backward. Blood dripped into her eyes, turning the townspeople red. She screamed with all her fury at the mob and they retreated in a panic. They stopped twenty yards within the town limits and reformed their human wall—pitchforks, hoes, and crosses pointed at Hannah.

"Curse every one of you!" she yelled. In a tearful huff, she grabbed her goat's rope and headed down the road.

The girl and goat walked on and on in the dry heat of the afternoon. The sweat-soaked fabric of her dress clung to Hannah's skin, and her long damp hair stuck to her neck. Her forehead throbbed where a bump had formed around a cut. Dried blood crusted in her eyebrows. What ached most was the pain in her heart from being banished by her family. *How cruel of them to send me away.* She had no food or money, just her farm dress and shoes. At least she still had her goat. Flies buzzed around Samson, who stopped occasionally to chew on kernels of wheat.

Hannah petted his coarse fur. "You're the only family I've got."

Samson *bahhed* and flapped his tail at the flies. The black and white billy goat had been a gift from Papa when Samson was tiny with nub horns. Now he was full grown with curved horns. She tugged the rope. "Come, Samson, we have to keep moving. Maybe we'll find some kind folks who will feed us."

After another hour of walking through the desolate landscape, the drought-ruined wheat fields changed to lush green cornfields. High stalks formed leafy walls on either side of the road, reducing visibility to the narrow stretch ahead. Every so often, she passed a scarecrow with a burlap face that loomed down at her. Hannah had always hated the hideous straw men, with their stuffed shirts and bony stick fingers. Her brothers had mocked her fears and spooked her even more, telling her scarecrows were made from dead people, that underneath the burlap masks and tattered clothes were human skeletons. Even though Papa had sworn that wasn't true, that her brothers were just teasing, Hannah still felt uneasy. She couldn't shake the feeling that the scarecrows' hollow eyes were watching her. She hugged herself and kept her attention on the road. She'd never been this far from home. While she'd eaten corn brought in from distant farms, she'd never seen where it grew. The dense stalks, teeming with plump corncobs, seemed never-ending. The cornfields made her feel like an ant walking through high grass.

A cloud of dust approached from up ahead. A motor coughed and groaned. A rusted pickup truck drove by. The back bed was jam-packed with men, women, and children with forlorn faces. The passengers looked emaciated in their drab, dirty clothes. Hannah had seen pitiful folks like these before. Groups of them had wandered into Providence Fields, hoping to find work, food, and shelter. But these were hard times. A severe drought and dreadful year for crops had made the townspeople overprotective of their farms. There was not enough food and shelter to go around, so desperate folks like these were turned away, with pitchforks, shotguns, and the Lord's book, if need be.

Hannah had hated seeing hungry people suffer and voiced her concern to the patriarchs. But she was just a girl on the cusp of womanhood and women had no voice in Providence Fields. The fears and desperation in her holy town had grown so bad that blasphemous members of their own community had been made pariahs and forced to leave.

As Hannah continued down the road, she wondered where she and Samson would go? Who would take them in? She had not seen so much as a farmhouse. She prayed for a miracle.

The sun steadily arced toward the horizon. She feared being out here among the corn after dark. She picked up her pace. Up ahead, a flock of crows pecked at something black on the ground. Hannah cried out and waved the birds away. They flew up in a black whirl and perched on the stalks. A dozen, maybe more, watched her with beady eyes.

Lying on the road was a dead crow. Holes dotted its neck and breast. Black feathers were scattered around its corpse.

Hannah looked at the dark flock in anger. "Curse you, eating your own!"

Her eyes moistened as she picked up the lifeless bird. "Oh, you poor thing." *None of God's creatures deserved this.* Her tears dripped on its butchered body. Caressing its head, Hannah whispered, "Wake up, crow. Come back to the living."

At first, nothing happened, and Hannah wondered if she had lost her gift. Then the half-eaten crow's beak slowly began to move. The light of life filled its dark eyes. The bird flapped its wings, flew up to a cornstalk, and looked down at her.

Hannah smiled. "Welcome back."

The resurrected bird tilted its head and crowed at its savior. It flew to the tops of the stalks and cawed at its flock. The other black birds cawed back in a loud chorus. Then, in a spiral of black wings, they followed the half-eaten crow into the sky.

At dusk, the sun glowed across the tops of the cornstalks, casting the dirt road in gray shadows. Hannah's legs had grown tired and her feet ached. Beyond hungry, she tried eating a corncob from a husk, but the raw kernels made her stomach cramp. Hannah bent over and retched the grain bits back up. She could feel herself becoming weak. Her parched throat yearned for water, but she hadn't seen a creek since leaving wheat country.

As she continued following this uncertain road, the last vestiges of sun faded. The twilight sky dimmed to a purple-gray and the stars came out. A near-full moon rose over the cornfields. The stalks, blade-sharp in the silvery light, made Hannah nervous as darkness clotted the narrow spaces between the rows. Hearing things stirring in the corn, she quickened her step, pulling Samson against his goatly urge to gnaw on the abundant leaves and husks.

A rumble vibrated the ground beneath Hannah's feet. The *clip-clop* of hooves sounded from the direction she had just come. A single-horse wagon was approaching. On a bench sat a man and woman who looked as if they'd ridden in from another age. The man wore a tall black hat and burlap shirt. He had shoulder-length hair and a bushy beard. The woman looked foreign in her gypsy dress and hooded cape that exposed only her pale face. Behind the man and woman huddled other hooded figures, mere silhouettes in the moonlight.

Unsure about these migrants, Hannah ducked into the stalks and tried to pull her goat with her. But Samson resisted and bleated in protest.

The wagon pulled up even with the billy goat and stopped with a clack of wooden axels and wheels. Samson, who didn't like horses, stood on his hind legs and shook his horned head. The frightened horse backed up.

"Whoa, easy, easy." The bearded driver steadied his horse.

The woman aimed a lantern at Hannah's hiding place. "The girl went in there."

In a panic, Hannah let go of Samson's rope and crouched deeper within the corn. The stalks pressed in close, rubbing their leafy blades against her. Her back felt vulnerable to any creatures that might live within the darkness of the corn. Her mind conjured an image of a skull-faced scarecrow climbing down from its post and creeping up behind her. A clawed hand reaching for her neck. Shuddering, she shook the imaginary fear away. Her real worry was the strangers on the road.

The man shouted, "That's our fields yer trespassing on."

"Shush. Ye'll frighten her." The woman then called out, "No need to hide, girl. We mean ye no harm. Ye can come out."

Hannah stayed put. She listened to them whispering. A moment later the wagon rode past a short distance and stopped. Someone wearing a long skirt hopped out of the back, approached carrying a lantern, and knelt at the edge of the corn.

The figure lowered their hood, revealing a girl, no older than fifteen, with long golden braids. She smiled and spoke softly. "Hello in there. You seem far from home. Are you lost?"

Hannah shrugged.

"Please, don't be afraid. You must be parched. Here's some water." The girl tossed a canteen.

Hannah drank from it greedily.

Samson gently nudged the girl, making her wobble on her knees. She giggled, petting his back. "Your goat's a might friendly. Reminds me of a billy we have on our farm."

That Samson seemed to trust this girl eased Hannah's fear. "He usually doesn't take a shine to strangers."

"Well, animals love me. My grandmother says it's 'cause I smell like sweet corn." The girl pulled a cob off a stalk and fed it to Samson. "My name is Maewyn. But everybody calls me Mae." She pointed to the wagon. "That's my *Mamaí* and *Dadaí* along with my sisters."

Hannah ventured to the edge of the stalks and peered out. A group of girls wearing matching dresses and hooded capes stood in the back of the wagon. There seemed to be a religious uniformity to their clothing.

"Are you nuns?" Hannah asked.

"Nothing like that." Mae laughed. "We're just farm folk. We're headed to our village up the road. Supper will be ready by the time we get there. Are you hungry? You're welcome to join us."

Hannah's empty stomach gurgled at the mention of a meal. Were these the kind people she prayed would take her in? She remained within the stalks, uncertain. She remembered how cruelly her family had mistreated her and Samson. "What about my goat?"

"He is welcome to stay in the pen with our goats."

Samson *bahhed* as if he approved.

Mae offered her hand to Hannah. "Come. Our family always has room for more."

With nowhere else to go and too afraid to sleep out here, Hannah took Mae's hand and followed her to the wagon.

On the night ride through the corn, beneath the roving moon and stars, Mae introduced her three sisters—Arwen and Bronwen, redheaded twins with freckled faces, and Mary Katherine, a short-haired girl who didn't look or talk like the others. She seemed American, while Mae, Arwen, and Bronwen had foreign accents.

"We came over from Wales," Mae said. "In our village, there are six large families. We aren't all akin, but all the women and girls call each other sisters." She squeezed Hannah's hand. "Maybe you could be our sister too."

Hannah had never had sisters, only four older brothers. Even her cousins were all rough and rowdy boys. The thought of having sisters sounded delightful.

Her thirst finally slaked, Hannah offered the canteen to the other girls. They all shook their heads, and Mae insisted Hannah drink the rest. "You need it more than we do."

"Thank you for picking me up." Hannah felt grateful to have encountered such kind folks. She longed for a hot meal and warm bed to sleep in.

The covey of girls were all giggles as they asked Hannah question after question about who she was and where she came from. She didn't tell them much, other than her name and that she'd left home in search of a better life. If they knew she had been banished for sinning, would these people exile her too? *The less they know about me the better,* Hannah decided.

She was eager to know more about them. She found it peculiar that the girls wore matching capes and dyed green dresses with ornately stitched patterns. Instead of a cross necklace, each girl wore a burlap rope with a figurine woven from dried husks.

As Hannah was about to ask what the pendants were, she yawned, suddenly feeling quite sleepy. Less than a mile from where they'd found her, the wagon turned down a narrow road that carved between high cornstalks.

The woman riding up front hushed the chattering girls. Beyond the creaking wagon wheels and clopping horse hooves, Hannah heard more stirrings in the corn. She yawned again and struggled to keep her eyes open. Mae gently lowered Hannah's head into her lap and stroked her hair while singing a lullaby in some strange language. The moon and stars overhead grew blurry then sharp again. Wakefulness and dreams seemed to mesh as scarecrows appeared at the periphery of her awareness. Before Hannah surrendered to the darkness of sleep, she thought she saw winged shadows fluttering above the cornstalks.

In dreams, she found herself alternating between two places: inside a cellar, hands tied above her head, her body dangling from a hook; then walking in the nave of her church. The congregation of families sat in pews with their heads bowed. Pastor Brooks prayed the gospel. With each sinful step down the center aisle, Hannah felt the sting of her father's lashings against her back. Yet, Papa was seated in the front row next to Mama and their four sons.

Trembling in pain, Hannah stepped closer to the area beyond the pews. Her grandmother's open casket was on display. Gramm's side profile, gray hair done up in a bun. Eyes copper coins, bloodless cheeks withdrawn in death. Hannah reached into the open coffin, held Gramm's cold, ash-white hand.

Inside the cellar: Hannah flinched at more lashings from Papa's belt. When she refused to repent, he switched to the buckle end. Blood seeped from fresh agonies on her back.

Hannah awoke to the sound of tapping. A fog clouded her head, like the time she'd drunk her eldest brother's mash whiskey and suffered the Devil's wrath the next morning. Now, she cracked her eyes open wider. Above, a bouquet of dried roses hung from a slanted ceiling. A fly crawled over the wilted blooms.

Where am I? She remembered not a thing since Mae sang her to sleep on the wagon ride. Somehow, Hannah had ended up in an attic room lined with single beds. The other four were empty and neatly made with a husk doll propped against each pillow. A similar doll, against Hannah's headboard, had a yellow-corn face, brown-leaf dress, and smelled of crop fields.

Tap...tap...tap...

A shadow fluttered at a sunlit window shrouded with white curtains. The ornate patterns, the cotton material matched the nightgown Hannah now wore. Where was her blue gingham dress? She sat up fast. *Where's Samson?*

More tapping against the window pane.

Hannah hopped out of bed and pulled the curtains aside. Her view overlooked part of a farm village. Beyond a weathered barn, cornfields stretched forever. She spotted Samson eating hay in a goat pen, right where Mae had promised.

Children's laughter drew Hannah's attention to the ground below. Boys and girls skipped around a boy wearing a bearded mask and wicker crown. The children teased him with sticks while singing a nursery rhyme. At the chorus, they shouted "John Barleycorn! John Barleycorn!" and poked the boy. As Hannah wondered about their peculiar game, a black bird struck the window pane, startling her. The crow perched on the outer sill. Its half-eaten breast was missing feathers, its rib bones exposed: the bird she had brought back.

"What are you doing here?" Hannah spoke through the glass.

The bird squawked loudly.

Hannah grew nervous. "You shouldn't be here, crow. Go away."

It flapped against the window, wanting inside.

Hannah knocked on the glass and waved the bird away. "Leave! Go back to your flock."

The crow flew off.

Relieved, Hannah backed away from the window. On a nightstand, someone had left a basket of muffins. Famished, she devoured three sweet cakes, thankful no one was around to see her ill manners.

Exploring the attic, she curiously studied a wall covered with framed mosaics made from corn and grain seeds that featured groups of farm girls holding hands. The girls had yellow-corn faces and different colored hair. Touching their braids, Hannah realized the hair was real. One red braid fell off. She chided herself in her mother's voice, *Clumsy girl, look what you've done!* Hannah tried to stick the twist of hair back on the picture, but it wouldn't stay. She set the braid atop the frame and hoped no one would notice.

A dyed-green dress with white embroidery hung from a hook on a wall. A little note pinned to the skirt read "For Hannah." She changed out of the nightgown and put on the green dress and a pair of well-worn leather shoes that fit just right.

From below came the boisterous hen-chatter of girls. Hannah walked down a staircase to an open room. The four "sisters" she had met last night sat around a table threading needles through cuts of yellow fabric.

Mae looked up. "Good morning. How'd you sleep?"

Hannah yawned. "Like the dead."

The girls snickered. Hannah half-smiled. She dared not mention her horrific dreams. The atrocities would require explanation. She worried that whoever had undressed her last night had seen the scars on her back. She prayed none of the girls would pry for answers. She rubbed her eyes as she ambled over to the sewing circle. "What's that you're making?"

"Dresses for the harvest festival," said one of the redheaded twins, Arwen or Bronwen. It was hard to tell them apart.

"We're this year's corn maidens," the other twin said excitedly.

"Corn maidens?" Hannah asked.

Mae said, "Why, they're only the most important roles of the whole festival after the Corn Queen. Each year a few lucky girls are chosen by the elders. We get to dress up all fancy and everyone treats us like princesses for a day. It's heaps of fun."

"This will be my first time," said Mary Katherine, the soft-spoken girl with a southern accent. "I've only lived here a month, but I'm looking forward to the celebration."

"Mary Katherine came all the way from Kansas," Mae said. "She's a talented dressmaker. Her embroidery is by far the best."

Mary Katherine blushed. Neither girl explained how a Kansas girl with a Catholic name had wound up in rural Nebraska.

Hannah admired their yellow festival dresses. These were fashioned with green-hemmed sleeves and immaculate threadwork on the bodices depicting various harvest scenes—a woman swinging a scythe, arms wielding sickles, a basket of corncobs—all inside a border of stalks.

More than their needlecraft, Hannah envied the bond between these girls. "I used to sew dresses with my Gramm. I'd be happy to help."

"Sorry, only corn maidens can make the dresses," one twin said.

"It's a strict tradition," said the other.

Hannah felt the familiar sting of not belonging. "Perhaps I should get back on the road."

"Absolutely not," Mae said. "We want you to stay." She grabbed Hannah's hand. "Come. It's time you met the Corn Queen."

She took Hannah outside. High corn-stalk walls enclosed the village like a fort stockade. Six wooden houses, a barn, sheds, and animal pens encircled a well. All around was a bustle of activity. Men with thick beards raised posts and hammered nails. While children fed and watered livestock, the women and older kids decorated the common areas around the well. Every ornament seemed made from materials garnered from the fields—cornhusk streamers, sheaves of cut grain stalks standing like teepees, and baskets filled with squash and pumpkins.

Mae led Hannah to a tall elder woman who was gruffly telling the others how to decorate. Mae said, "Wilda, this is Hannah."

The old woman turned and eyed Hannah up and down. "Aye, the girl who walks the road alone," she said in a thick Welsh accent. "Ye got a home somewhere?"

Hannah shook her head. She felt small under Wilda's strict gaze.

"Well, if ye stay with us, you earn yer keep like ever'body else. We don't allow sluggards in our village."

"I like being of help," Hannah said, grateful not to be sent away. "I'll do anything you ask, ma'am."

Wilda nodded without smiling. "Mae, give her some chores." Then the elder turned back to instructing the others.

The next two days, under Wilda's watchful eye, Hannah worked and worked. Mornings, she fed the chickens, goats, horses, and pigs, cleaned their pens, and added fresh hay. Afternoons, she followed Mae and the other girls into the fields and helped pick ripened vegetables. Observing the farmers swinging sickles and scythes, Hannah understood the scenes embroidered on the yellow festival dresses. These folks loved their land as much as they loved each other. They treated her like one of their own. Hannah worked among them until her hands were blistered, and after eating supper with the whole village, she and her newfound sisters fell hard asleep in their beds.

The day before the festival, Wilda let Hannah help decorate. The women hung cornhusk chains and streamers from the central well to every house like spokes on a wheel. Beneath a trellis wrapped in brown vines, Hannah, Mae, and the other three sisters sat at a table and glued yellow kernels onto green wooden masks. The corn filled in the face around cutouts for eyes, nose holes, and a slit for the mouth. While the girls chatted, the men erected a tall statue made of brown stalks. The faceless figure matched the figurines everyone wore around their necks.

"Who is the statue of?" Hannah asked.

"The Harvest God, *Lugh*," Mae said, bowing her head and squeezing her necklace idol. The other girls did the same. When she looked up, Mae continued, "We worship Him to bless our fields and keep us protected from the outside world."

"We owe everything to Lugh," Arwen said reverently. "He is the reason our crops are so bountiful. He brings us rain while other farms suffer drought."

"He fends off locusts," Bronwen added. "And keeps diseases away from our animals."

"Tomorrow's *Lughnasadh* festival is to honor the Harvest God," Mae said. She placed a yellow mask over her face. "As corn maidens we serve Lugh in the most honorable way of our village."

Hannah neither believed in nor disputed their crop god. She knew enough about religion not to question what others believed. She knew all too well the dangers of going against the grain.

At dusk, while everyone retreated to their houses, Hannah went to feed Samson his evening meal. He stood at the fence by himself. All the other goats were at the opposite side of the pen, keeping their distance. The flies around Samson had gotten worse. He smelled of rot. Thankfully, the goat pen was next to the pigsty. She gave Samson a carrot and petted him. "Stay among the living," she whispered. "I couldn't bear to lose you." She breathed fresh life into his face. His dull eyes brightened with color and his cold body turned warm again. She put her forehead to his and tugged his beard. "And play nice with the other goats. I want us to fit in here."

Samson backed away as if spooked.

When Hannah turned around, Wilda was standing nearby, watching. "Ye got kinship with that goat, eh?"

"Yes, ma'am. Samson's been with me since I was little."

"Somethin' foul about that billy. Draws more flies than our pigs." Behind Wilda, the half-eaten crow landed on the harvest god statue.

Hannah's heart clenched. *Don't make a sound*, she told the bird with her thoughts. Hoping to distract the elder woman, Hannah fed Samson another carrot. "I promise to bathe him."

"May take more than a bath to scrub out that stink."

The crow hopped along the straw god's arm. Cawed loudly. Wilda whirled and motioned with her hand for it to leave, but the defiant bird only squawked back.

"Damn crows! A bloody menace, they are." The elder woman transfixed her hot gaze back on Hannah and Samson. "I'd be careful gettin' too attached to livestock. Our kinship is with Lugh and the crops He delivers." With that, the old woman disappeared into her house. Hannah didn't know what to make of the warning. As she walked back to the girls' bunkhouse, a dozen more black birds landed on the harvest god's statue beside her resurrected crow. Its flock looked down at her.

"You can't keep following me." She shooed them with her arm. "Go on. Leave."

The black birds squawked loudly and flew away.

Looking over her shoulder, she saw Wilda's shadow at her window. Worry gnawed at the pit of Hannah's stomach. What if the crows damaged their crops? What if Wilda's clan found out what Hannah was capable of?

When she arrived at the girls' bunkhouse, her four sisters were all giggles as they tried on their yellow festival dresses. Each costume included a corn mask and green crown made from woven stalk leaves. Hannah admired the corn maidens as they pranced about the room. She tried not to let it, but their close-knit bond made Hannah feel left out.

Mae removed her mask and looked at Hannah sympathetically. "This seems a might unfair, doesn't it?"

Hannah shrugged and tried to smile.

"Don't be sad," Arwen said. "Not every girl gets to be a Harvest God's maiden."

"We have to prepare something for the ritual," Mae said. "Close your eyes, Hannah."

She did as told. Heard shuffling and whispering, then Mae said, "You can open your eyes now."

The four girls stood lined up in front of the table. They grinned as if trying to contain a secret. Mae reached behind them and picked up a yellow dress. She offered it to Hannah. "The elders have chosen you to be our fifth corn maiden."

Mary Katherine and the twins clapped their hands and bounced excitedly. Hannah, shocked, held the dress. Embroidered on the bodice was a girl walking a cornfield road with a goat. She was speechless, her eyes damp with gratitude. She'd never felt so accepted back home.

That night after changing into their nightgowns, Mae, Arwen, Bronwen, and Mary Katherine gathered around Hannah's bed. Mae sat behind Hannah, braiding her long hair to match the others. Hannah felt so at peace, so at home, as she and her new sisters chatted well past bedtime. At one point, the tone changed, and the other girls looked at Hannah with concern.

"We've all seen your back scars," Mae said. "Tell us what happened, why you left your home."

Hannah shook her head. "I can't." Once they knew why, they'd become afraid of her.

Mae touched her arm. "Sisters don't keep secrets. We share our burdens."

"You can tell us anything." Arwen and Bronwyn leaned forward.

When Hannah hesitated, Mary Katherine said, "I'll share mine. Before I came here my life was hell. My pa lost his job when the cotton mill shut down. He drank until his fists got mean. Took his frustrations out on me and my siblings. Every time he beat me, Pa said I was nothing but a useless mouth to feed. So I ran away, hopped on a train to Omaha. If Mae and Wilda hadn't found me at the rail station…" Tears choked up Mary Katherine's voice.

"I'm so sorry." Hannah hugged her.

When Mary Katherine was done crying, the girls pressed Hannah to share her burdens. Sighing, she looked at the wall. "My father was a monster too. Not just him. My whole town." She told them about Papa's belt whippings in the cellar. How Hannah's hands had been tied to a hook above her head, the back of her blouse ripped open. Mama, their neighbors, and Pastor Brooks were often there with their Bibles open, shouting scriptures while Papa tried to whip the Devil out of her. "Sins aren't taken lightly in Providence Fields," Hannah told the girls.

Mae touched Hannah's forehead and mocked a preacher's voice. "Well, confess your sins and be free, sister."

Hannah shook her head, tearing up. "You'll hate me if I tell."

The girls encouraged her to continue.

"I've always been different…" Her mouth quivered as she searched for the right words. "I can touch those I don't want dead, and if my grief is strong enough, my dead loved ones come back."

She told them about the time she was six and found a dead sparrow in the backyard. When the bird flew out of her hands, her youngest brother, Elijah, screamed and ran into the house to tell her parents. The resurrections happened other times, with a pet rabbit, two of their dogs. She'd even made a wilted rose bush bloom again, only to evoke her parents' holy terror.

Stop doing the Devil's work, Mama had said hysterically.

Papa had scolded Hannah, *Reversing what God intended is a sin.*

But what if it's God performing miracles through me? she had challenged, but such blasphemy had earned another thrashing in the cellar.

"My greatest sin happened with my grandmother," Hannah told her sisters. "Gramm was the only person who ever loved me. When she died, I couldn't let her go."

Esther Creed had been a respected member of the community. The whole town mourned her loss. Hannah had thought the God-worshippers might appreciate witnessing a miracle, that maybe her family would finally accept Hannah as she was. At Gramm's funeral, while Pastor Brooks gave a eulogy before the congregation, Hannah took her turn to say goodbye at the open casket. Gramm looked so pale and shriveled. Her closed eyes were weighted with copper coins.

The pain in Hannah's chest had been unbearable, her tears endless streams. She had gripped her grandmother's hand and whispered to her. Gramm's body convulsed, then sat bolt upright. The coins flew to the floor, rattling. A communal gasp had issued from the congregation as Gramm's head slowly turned to face them. Her eyes had remained half shut. She moved her jaw, struggling to speak. What came from her throat had sounded like crackles of wind-strewn leaves.

Every parishioner fled the church screaming. Everyone except Hannah and Pastor Brooks. The preacher's face had turned ashen. Hannah had been overjoyed.

With stiff creaking bones, Gramm had climbed out of her casket. Her dry hand caressed Hannah's cheek. Then, like a sleepwalker, Gramm left the church. She had wandered into a wheat field. Stood in one spot for two straight days.

Hannah had wanted to visit her, bring Gramm back more to life, but her parents locked Hannah in the cellar. She learned from Elijah what had happened. Rising fears at the church spurned several men to venture out to the field with axes. They chopped Gramm into many pieces, then buried her in as many graves. Not long after, their crops died.

"Farmers blamed me for bringing a scourge to their fields. Mama swore the Devil cursed her womb. Papa called me Satan's spawn. Everyone in town was afraid and angry. They all made me leave. Perhaps they had good reason. I don't know what I am. Good or evil. All I know is I can't bear losing anyone or any animal I care about. Gramm said I have a gift to give life back and that it's my birthright to use it."

The girls stared with heavy silence. Hannah held her breath and waited for them to react like her parents and brothers. She expected them to run tell others about the Devil girl in their midst. Blame her for any drought, disease, or crows that killed their crops. Chide her then drag her to the road.

Mae, in tears, gripped Hannah's hands. "You poor thing. How dare they treat you so cruelly."

Hannah felt tears coming on. "You aren't afraid of me?"

"Of course not." Arwen shook heard head.

Bronwen did too. "Never ever."

"You're too sweet and kind," Mary Katherine said.

Hannah wiped her eyes and laughed, trying hard not to cry.

Mae said, "In our village, we believe there's power in our blood. It can be used to make magick and serve the Harvest God. That's what you are to us, Hannah Creed. You're magick. You should be proud to have such a gift."

The dam broke then and Hannah cried as her four sisters embraced her.

August 1ˢᵗ, Festival Day

At the sunrise ceremony, Wilda preached to the village. "Lughnasadh is a time to be thankful and show O'Mighty Lugh we are ready for the harvest. The celebration honoring our Harvest God will last all day until midnight."

Hannah and her four sisters, excited about their big day, held hands as Wilda lit the morning pyre.

After breakfast, the competitions began. The men raced each other down cornrows and rolled barrels around stooks of grain, while everyone cheered. The women and girls competed in three-legged races and hopped in burlap bags. Laughing children chased baby pigs. Hannah loved the game where she passed eggs from between her chin and neck to Mae's neck and down the chain to Arwen, Bronwen, and Mary Katherine, who placed them in a basket. They were about to beat their mothers' team, when Bronwen dropped the last egg on the ground.

At midday, the corn maidens donned their yellow dresses and crowns and walked in a parade behind the Corn Queen and King. The village folk threw flowers and placed golden kernels in the maidens' baskets for harvest blessings. Feeling buoyant after receiving so much adoration, Hannah visited the goat pen and fed Samson handfuls of corn. "We are so blessed to have found this village, Samson. I've never been happier." She kissed his forehead then rejoined her sisters in another game.

As sunset cast a radiant orange glow over the cornfields, the whole village sat around the long table for a supper feast. Wilda, the Corn Queen, sat at one end of the table. Her docile husband, the Corn King, slouched quietly at the opposite end. Wilda blessed the food and surrounding cornfields. She raised her wine cup to the stalk statue and thanked Lugh for His skills and a bountiful harvest.

After supper, stars sparkled the night sky and a bright full moon hovered above the cornstalks. The elders played spirited music on drums, flutes, and fiddles. Revelers danced beneath the streamers. The five corn maidens held hands and danced in a circle, round and round, 'til Hannah was giggling with her sisters. Never in her life had she experienced such joy, such belonging. Men picked up the maidens and carried them on their shoulders. Riding above the dancing crowd, Hannah noticed elders leading Samson and other goats into the cornfield.

She called out to Mae, "Where are they taking my goat?"

"To the ceremonial grounds," was all Mae said before the man whose shoulders she rode upon whisked her away.

When the last song ended, Wilda waved a torch and the festive music gave way to a slow, tribal rhythm. Hannah followed her sisters as the corn maidens lined up at the edge of the stalks. Mae, at the lead, accepted a reaping tool taller than she was—a scythe with a long curved blade. Arwen, Bronwen, Mary Katherine, and Hannah were handed sickles and billhooks.

Mae looked back at her sisters. "Brace yourself, maidens. Our moment to serve the Harvest God is nigh."

Arwen and Bronwen raised their sickles and let out a shout.

Gripping the billhook's wooden handle, Hannah inhaled. All her senses were heightened, her nerves jumping. She whispered to Mary Katherine, "What are we about to do?"

"Whatever Wilda tells us." The girl from Kansas looked nervous too.

Wilda spoke in Gaelic as she covered each maiden's face with a yellow-corn mask and tied its strings tight. The wooden disguise itched and smelled of grain. Hannah peered through the eyeholes as she followed the other maidens into the stalks. The moonlit night darkened beneath leafy shadows. Sharp foliage and ripe husks brushed Hannah's body. Others walked parallel down the cornrows, beating drums and hollow sticks. All the leaf rustling, *pum-pumming* and stick *clacking* sent a flock of crows flying from their roost. Somewhere in the corn forest an elder woman screeched. Others screeched back, causing Hannah to keep close to Mary Katherine, who stayed on the heels of the twins and Mae.

Firelight flickered ahead, casting Hannah's sisters in rippling silhouettes. Their procession led from the stalks to a circular clearing where a crowd of adults had gathered near a pyre. The women, young and old, wore hooded capes. The men, shirtless, had smeared red muck on their upper bodies that stank of fresh slaughter. Their slick skin glistened in the sweltering heat. The crowd parted to let the corn maidens pass through to the clearing's center. The blazing bonfire, the glowing moon illuminated a large pattern on the ground made from corncobs—a mosaic of an upside-down star inside a circle. At the star's five points stood T-shaped posts draped in dried corn leaves. Atop each post loomed a skinned goat skull.

Hannah's breath caught in her throat. While walking through the corn, an apprehension had harrowed her nerves; now deep-burrowing fear took root and spread tendrils of dread beneath her skin.

The drumming and stick clacking picked up tempo.

Mae led the maidens around the wide circle and stopped. Each masked girl stood in front of a horn-headed T-post, gripping their reaping hooks like warriors. Hannah looked around at her sisters nervously. Mae and the twins stood perfectly still. Mary Katherine was shaking.

The drums and sticks hushed.

The Corn Queen emerged from the stalks in full costume: hooded cape, wicker crown, and corn mask. Her gray hair stuck out in wild tufts. She wore no dress beneath the cape, only a fur skirt. The vile nakedness of Wilda's blood-smeared breasts made Hannah's stomach turn. Wilda raised a wooden staff. A severed goat's head was mounted on its pike: Samson's head. Lifeless, tongue hanging out.

Hannah screamed. An uncontrollable convulsion shuddered through her body. Just like it had when Papa shot her favorite goat with his shotgun. An unspeakable sorrow had shaken her to the core as she had cradled Samson's dead body. She had felt the knife-gut of betrayal then as she felt gutted now. Hannah's eyes filled with hot tears. "Samson!" She tore off her mask and started for Wilda. "*What have you done*? What have you—"

Before she could reach the old woman, Wilda's followers mobbed Hannah. A dozen hands restrained her. Pulled her back against the leaf-draped post. She kicked and fought as they bound her wrists to the arm planks. They placed the corn mask back on her face. The mob backed away, leaving her to fight against the ropes. The queen, the other corn maidens, the wild-eyed men and womenfolk all watched Hannah sob and wail until her voice gave out. She lay back against the post, whimpering.

Wilda motioned with her staff. Two men pushed her husband into the center of the star. He was shirtless, hands bound behind his back. He dropped to his knees before the gathering. His wicker crown hung crookedly on his head.

Wilda smiled down at her husband then shouted, "In honor of Lugh, we celebrate the ceremony of John Barleycorn. To prepare for the harvest, it is tradition we kill the Corn King."

"Kill the king!" the crowd shouted.

His wet eyes told Hannah he was piss-drunk and afraid.

The slow drumbeats and stick clacks started up again. The remaining four corn maidens, clutching sharp reaping tools, circled the king on his knees.

Wilda shouted, "We till the Corn King's flesh and gift his essence to the soil."

Mae, Arwen, and Bronwen sliced his skin, drawing blood. Taking her sisters' cues, Mary Katherine joined in, little nicks at first, then giddy slashes as the Kansas girl got into the spirit of this barbaric game. Hannah watched in speechless horror at the merry-go-round of hacking blades. The masked maidens opened the poor man's body with a latticework of seeping red wounds.

As the maidens continued to till flesh, Wilda crouched with her palms on the ground. "The blood of John Barleycorn nourishes our fields and ripens the fruit of our crops."

The villagers chanted, "John Barleycorn! John Barleycorn! John Barleycorn!"

The lacerated king moaned in pain. Hannah felt every cut, every torment of his flesh. The scars from Papa's lashings flared up with remembered agonies. When the blood-soaked king reached the verge of toppling, the twins gripped his arms and held him upright. Mae, wielding the Grim Reaper's tool, swung her scythe with all her might. The curved blade stabbed through the Corn King's belly and out through his back. He coughed up blood. His eyes bulged the moment death took him. As the king slumped against the scythe, the worshippers rejoiced, applauding the corn maidens. The four girls, pretty yellow dresses now blood-spattered, curtsied.

Again, the Corn Queen motioned with her staff. The manic crowd grabbed the four maidens. It was Mary Katherine's turn to scream as the mob tied her to a T-post. Mae, Arwen, and Bronwen leaned back against their posts, allowing their wrists to be fastened to the beams.

With a wave of Wilda's staff, the riled up crowd became quiet. A frail, wrinkled woman stood at the circle's edge and began playing a haunting tune on her violin. Mae, Arwen, and Bronwen sang the Celtic song. Though Hannah didn't understand the lyrics, her sisters' sorrowful voices brought fresh tears to her eyes. The reverent audience joined in, humming the chorus with the girls.

Wilda picked up a sickle and carved the air as she walked in a circle, eyeing the bound girls. A deep sadness betrayed her commanding voice. "As corn maidens, ye serve Lugh with the highest honor. Yer youthful blood giveth our fields its drink so our village may live on in good health. We thank thee, brave girls for ye sacrifice."

With the curved blade, Wilda sliced open Mary Katherine's throat.

At the sight of her sister's gushing blood, Hannah screamed. More waves of revulsion coursed through her.

Mary Katherine convulsed as the lifeblood flowed out of her. Her masked face lolled forward. Two men untied her limp body from the post, then tipped her forward, allowing her neck wound to drain onto the ground.

While Hannah grappled with the loss of Mary Katherine, the maidens continued to sing with tears in their voices. In two quick swipes, Wilda slashed the twins' throats. Their voices cut short mid-song. In the crowd, their mother wailed and collapsed against her husband.

Hannah, a mess of tears and snot beneath her mask, couldn't stop trembling, nor could she look away as the life drained out of Arwen and Bronwen.

Mae's singing faltered.

Wilda struck Mae's post with the sickle. "Keep singing!"

After the twins' bodies were tilted to quench the soil's thirst, the Corn Queen stood beside Mae. "Maewyn, my *garinion*," her grandmother lamented, "I wish thee eternal youth in the Otherworld, *Annwfyn*."

"No." Hannah fought against her bindings. "Not Mae!"

Mae choked up but continued to sing in her lilting voice. Wilda harmonized with her granddaughter. Their mournful voices, sung through their corn masks, seemed to channel ghosts from some ancient otherworld. After the last words were crooned, Mae cried audibly behind her mask. She begged her grandmother, "No, *Nain*, please, I don't want to die!"

"Sorry, child, yer blood's been promised." Wilda's sickle blade slowly split open Mae's neck and set free the red fountain of life.

Her *Mamaí* and *Dadaí* tearfully shouted, "Bless our child, O'Mighty Lugh!" as their daughter's blood poured into the earth.

Hannah, shaking against the post, felt trapped somewhere between terror and grief. *How could these wretched folk slaughter their own? My sisters!* The immensity of her loss awakened a fury within she hadn't known was there. A deep chasm of roiling anguish and pain. Rage rose hotly from her core. She gave a guttural scream that turned all heads.

The Corn Queen walked across the circle, bare feet traipsing through the blood of her slain granddaughter and husband. She pointed her reaping hook at Hannah. "Yer blood is most powerful of all." Wilda rubbed the marbled pelt around her waist. Samson's fur. "I've seen what magick ye can do, Hannah Creed. Seen it twinklin' in yer eyes. Seen ye frighten off the crows. Yer a true gift delivered to us by Lugh Himself."

Wilda pressed her sickle against Hannah's neck and slashed a shallow cut that burned like fire. Hannah cried out.

The queen took off her mask and licked Hannah's blood off the blade. "Ah, sweet as honey."

Hannah shook her post and growled. She wanted to claw Wilda's face and make her shrivel into a corpse. Since she had a life-giving force, might she also wield its opposite? Reaching deep into her bottomless well of rage, Hannah hissed. "I rot your flesh. I send you to the grave!"

Wilda retreated, alarmed. Her followers backed away from the circle.

Several seconds passed. Nothing happened.

The old woman grinned. "Lugh protects us from yer magick." She approached again, pointing the sickle blade. "May yer sacred lifeblood feed the roots of our corn. May yer marrow bring us a bountiful crop for harvests yet to come."

Hannah shouted, "I curse you! I curse you all!" She unleashed another scream so loud Wilda and her followers covered their ears.

The night sky echoed back Hannah's fury with a clarion of caws. Black-winged shapes landed on the stalks. A palpable fear filled the air. The men and women cowered as the army of crows descended. More and more joined their ranks until hundreds of birds perched in the stalks around the clearing.

Wilda observed the cawing crows with a slow turn of her head. Then her fearful eyes stared back at Hannah. "How dare ye bring dark magick into our fields. With the might of Lugh, I cut thee down." Before she could swing the blade, the flock swooped into the clearing and attacked the Corn Queen and her followers.

Birds lancing their heads and shoulders, men and women ran screaming into the cornstalks. In seconds, a swarm of flapping-pecking crows covered Wilda from head to toe. She fought and screamed from within the whirling black tempest. Beaks stabbed out her eyes, opened a thousand cuts across her body. She stumbled backward and collapsed beside the Corn King's corpse.

A butchered crow with mottled gray flesh landed on Hannah's arm. Its eyes shown bright with devotion. Her resurrected crow squawked and called others from the flock. They pecked at Hannah's wrist bindings, setting her free. She rushed to the ground where her four dead sisters lay like broken dolls. She touched their slashed throats and spoke into their ears. "Come back to the living. Come back!"

Nothing changed. Her sisters remained limp. She feared they had been dead too long. Hannah went to each girl again, shaking her body, calling forth every ounce of power within, pleading for her sisters to return.

At last, one by one, their bodies jolted with life. All four sisters rose to their feet. Hannah hugged each one, crying tears of joy. Then Mae picked up her scythe; the twins retrieved their sickles; and Mary Katherine, her billhook. Without a word, Hannah's sisters dashed off into the stalks. Not long after more screams echoed from the cornfields.

Hannah picked up the queen's staff and petted the mounted goat head. "Come back again, my beloved Samson."

His mouth moved, but made no sound. His third life brought less of him back, but what little of Samson shone in his eyes, she still loved.

From a black circle whirling overhead, crows continued to dive into the frenzy on the ground. Hannah's dark-feathered rage relentlessly pecked and clawed Wilda's corpse, feasting upon her until there was little left but bloody hair and bone.

After all the screaming in the cornfields ceased, the crows and maidens returned from the slaughter. The black birds gathered in the surrounding stalks. The masked girls had more red stains on their yellow dresses and blood dripping from their harvest tools. Mae, Arwen, Bronwen, and Mary Katherine stared in silence. As Hannah broke down, her sisters closed in and held her while she cried. They no longer had breath or heartbeats or voices. Like others she'd brought back, they weren't the same as before. But her sisters had returned. And they were hers. Perhaps once her anger subsided, she would breathe more life into them. Her sisters raised their reaping tools and knelt around Hannah. The crows sang from the cornfields. Hannah looked upon her flock—alive and not quite dead—and accepted that this might be the only family that would ever love her back.

At dawn, the five corn maidens paraded down the dirt road, gripping their billhooks, sickles, and scythe. Hannah Creed led the way with her goat-headed staff raised high. Above them, flew a dark-winged legion. Their caws a battle cry. The parade marched toward the wheat country. Toward retribution. Toward Providence Fields.

Father MacLeod

by Tony Tremblay

Father MacLeod held his breath and closed his eyes. He clamped his lips shut. The priest grimaced from the stench as he attempted to pull away, but the boy's hold was too tight. An extra inch of distance between their faces was the most he could manage.

His nephew had been laying on the bed, restrained, arms at rest by his sides. As Father MacLeod stood over the boy's bedside taking measure, he'd bent at the waist for a more detailed inspection. The boy's hands had flown off the bed, gathering the fabric of the priest's black suit coat in his small fists. In the time it took to register what was happening, the cleric was snared. The boy had sat up, their noses almost touching, and MacLeod had breathed in the possessed boy's foulness.

"How long you been at me, priest? Four? Five weeks? I am still here, cocksucker. Your chants and holy words are not working. They will not work. I am taking this boy. His suffering now will be nothing compared to his time in Hell." His nephew's scabbed and bloody lips delivered the lines in a guttural bark.

Desperate to hide his fear, MacLeod peered deeply into the black pools that swallowed the boy's blue eyes. The demon smiled, and the priest knew he had failed.

The priest averted his gaze downward and noticed the shredded leather straps that had bound the boy's arm to the side rails. The twelve-year-old was emaciated, the outlines of bones pressed through his thin skin. He shouldn't have had the strength to lift his limbs, never mind tear through the restraints.

Fire erupted in MacLeod's chest. Pressure forced him back, away from the boy. Held in place by his nephew's clenched fists, the priest prepared for a jarring stop, instead, he continued to sail backward—the hold on his suit coat had vanished. The priest jettisoned his arms to his sides for purchase, but his fingertips slid over the sheet. Before he could form a claw to dig in, the muscles in his lower back screamed as he came to an abrupt halt. The cartilage in his neck stretched and popped as his head ricocheted. Dazed, he inhaled deeply to acclimate to the pain. It took a few moments for him to focus.

He was in a sitting position, level to the bed, but somehow, a couple of inches past its end.

Something's not right.

Lowering his gaze to the floor, he saw there was nothing but air between him and the concrete.

I— I'm floating!

Astonished, he lifted his head to the boy. A whimper escaped MacLeod's throat. His nephew was on all fours, the boy's face, once again, inches from his.

The demon cocked the boy's head. "What's the matter asshole, scared?"

"Who the hell are you?" MacLeod demanded.

"Fuck you, you are not getting my name. There is no way you are getting power over me."

The priest shifted his head to avoid the stench of decay. He knew he would not beat this demon. He had given it everything he had, yet the foul beast grew stronger. The exorcism rituals had failed, there was nothing left to do. How would he face his mother, his brother, when the boy died and his soul was dragged to Hell?

"Thinking about how you are going to tell your family that you fucked up, priest? I can see you have given up. Well, I will give you a way out of this."

MacLeod turned his gaze back to the demon. "You're full of shit."

The boy levitated off the bed and lowered himself onto his haunches. "Let's make a deal, priest."

"What kind of deal?"

"You want your nephew back so badly, you not only have to make it worth my while, you have to give something up."

MacLeod shook his head. "Fuck you. Your kind twists words. Lie. Any deal I make with you would wind up not only biting me in the ass, it would make everything worse than it is now."

"This deal is pretty straightforward, priest. If you agree to it, you will see the results right away. You have nothing to lose by hearing me out."

It took a few moments before MacLeod nodded his head.

"I will give you the boy back, in return, I want two others. They can be anyone of your choosing. You deliver me two souls, priest, and you can have your nephew."

The priest reared back. "You want me to give you two people to drag to Hell? Are you crazy?"

The demon said nothing. He peered at MacLeod, letting his offer sink in. Finally, it spoke. "It takes time, energy, to possess a single person, but if someone is sacrificed, it cuts all that out. A soul sacrificed is as good as a soul possessed." It paused to let the words sink in. "This vessel is ripe, priest. He will be mine soon. You have two hours to make your decision."

The boy rose, straightened, and descended flat on the bed. His eyes closed, and he was still.

Father MacLeod fell to the floor.

The priest stood, rubbed his ass, and gave the boy one final glance before he walked to the door. After pressing a code into the keypad, he stepped through and addressed a nun who was stationed outside the room. "Sister Bernice, please send a team down to replace the restraints on Cory."

The nun gasped, made the sign of the cross, and replied that she would.

"I will be in my office. I don't want to be disturbed."

"Father MacLeod, your mother and brother are upstairs waiting for you."

Closing his eyes, the priest shook his head. *What the hell am I going to do?*

Anger. Recriminations. Insinuations The worst of it was when they accused him of being responsible for the boy's possession. "You were targeted," his mother said, and his brother reinforced the accusation. He understood they were acting out of fear, desperation. In his heart, he knew their words might not have been far from the truth.

As an exorcist for the Catholic Church, he was party to events no man should ever witness, let alone participate. The filth he cleaned from his garments, the visions that haunted his waking hours, the perversions he had been exposed to—they all left no doubt that supernatural evil was genuine. Demons walked this earth.

He wasn't so sure God did.

What kind of God lets government deny human rights to its citizens? Who is this savoir who can't be bothered to stop a hospital fire, a train derailment, a tsunami? How could anyone in their right mind worship a magic man who allows Ebola, AIDS, and cancer to not only exist, but to proliferate? To bring this closer to home, why would a supreme deity let a young boy be possessed?

There was no arguing the good in the world. There *were* kind people to be found, love and pleasures to be had. The success he had in the past with the exorcism rituals also proved there was an opposing force to counter the shit he faced. Whatever this force was, it was evil's opposite, though it appeared to be unfocused and seemingly random. Father MacLeod wasn't sure when he stopped believing in the single creator myth, but his lack of faith may have been a factor in his failure to exorcize the demon from his nephew. Did this insight, his doubt in the existence of God, leave the door open for this demon?

No matter the reason, his nephew was possessed and on the brink of death. He had to decide if the boy's soul was worth damning two others. MacLeod pulled open the top drawer to his desk and removed a bottle a quarter-full of Glenmorangie. By the time he had made his decision, the bottle was empty.

"So, have you made up your mind, priest?"

The boy was restrained. Metal cuffs had been shackled onto his wrists and ankles, chains stretched across his torso. MacLeod glanced toward the door, ensuring it was closed and secure before answering. "How do I know you'll keep your end of the deal?"

"If you agree, I will relinquish my hold over the boy as soon as you give me your word. You must also swear to your God you will uphold our bargain. At that moment, you will see the change in the boy. He will be weak, but he will recover quickly. Throw some holy water on him if you want to be sure."

MacLeod remained silent. *What if I refuse to do what it asks after he leaves Cory?* There had been no record of a demon repossessing someone after they had been exorcised—well, none he had heard of.

A tongue, creviced as weathered leather, pocked with sores oozing puss, licked his nephew's lips. "I can read you like a book, priest. You are thinking of agreeing and then not keeping your part of the deal. I tell you this; I can reenter him, and when I am done with him, I will possess your mother. If you think what I am doing to this boy is an abomination, just think what I could do with a woman vessel."

He fought an image of his mother suffering at the hands of this demon. The priest curled his fists and raised them. He lowered his head until his chin rested on them. He squeezed his eyes tight, struggled not to gag. He didn't know how long he battled this vision, but he eventually regained control.

The demon picked up where he left off. "If you agree, I will need to know how and when you plan to make these sacrifices to me. Remember when I said you will have to give something up?"

MacLeod *had* forgotten.

The demon's black eyes swirled. "Give me a piece of your soul, priest, just a sliver. I will fill the space created with a small portion of mine."

The priest's reaction was immediate. "You're crazy! Out of your fucking mind."

"It will allow me to watch you, be there when you bring me the sacrifice. I must be present to claim the soul. It will not hurt. You will not change in any way other than having a feeling I am nearby. After you deliver the second sacrifice, we will exchange the small bits back."

"How do I know you will keep your word?"

The lips on the demon stretched wide. "You have no choice other than to believe me."

"Fuck you. No way am I doing this."

His nephew's right arm jerked. The fingers on his hand straightened. The bed trembled, rose an inch, then crashed down. Blood blossomed around the cuff, running off the boy's wrist. Demonic laughter, loud and sustained, echoed in the room. The arm jerked with more force, straining against the metal restraint. The cuff buried itself into the boy's flesh.

"No!" MacLeod screamed as he rushed forward to pin the arm.

He was too late.

From his wrist to the shoulder, his nephew's arm flew into the air, his hand remained inside the cuff. MacLeod recoiled as the boy's fingers wiggled, clawing the sheet. Blood spurt from the stump on his arm, leaving crisscrossed patterns of crimson across the boy's body and bed. The priest wasn't spared from the splatter. He froze at the sight, trembling, unsure what to do.

A low rumbling laugh shook the boy's chest. The demon raised its voice and spoke to the ceiling. "He has got one more arm, priest, and two legs. When I am done, I could leave him and let him live the remainder of his time strapped to a chair. You will be wiping his ass for him the rest of his life."

Violent shakes replaced the priest's trembles. "Oh God, oh God," MacLeod whispered. He repeated the phrase, over and over. His nephew's blood splashed on his lips, the taste releasing him from his affright.

"Okay, okay," the priest, pleaded, "I will make the deal. He'll bleed to death, stop the blood flow!"

The boy's arm fell. MacLeod's eyes widened as the skin at the stump knitted, sealing the wound. He stepped away from the bed, walked to a corner in the room, and vomited. The back of his throat burned from the scotch.

"You ready to do this, priest?

Bent over with his hands on his knees, drool hanging from his mouth, MacLeod nodded.

Dressed in his collar and black suit coat, MacLeod stood at the corner of Elm and Lowell Streets in Manchester. It was two o'clock in the morning. For what he had to do, leaving the confines of his office in Haverhill, Massachusetts and crossing the border into New Hampshire was his safest bet.

Manchester had a homeless population which was uncomfortably visible, and large. Men and women slept in public view during the day— often with confiscated shopping carts by their sides filled to the brim with meager possessions. Evenings were when these poor souls were most active.

Fortunately for MacLeod, only the main thoroughfare, Elm Street, bathed in the glow of streetlights. Roads running perpendicular possessed no such illumination. He took advantage of a shadow in the entrance of a drug store on the corner and blended in. As he waited for a prospect to appear, he replayed his last exchanges with the demon.

After he agreed to the demon's deal, it had provided instructions. When MacLeod was ready to procure the first sacrifice, the priest was to visit his nephew. The demon would then leave the vessel and accompany the priest. The slivers of soul they would exchange would enable it to communicate with him.

Once MacLeod had a plan figured out, he approached the demon in its holding room. The transfer *was* painless, and he did not detect its presence. As the demon mentioned earlier, the priest did note an immediate change for the better in the boy's physical condition.

Unsure how much control the demon had over him, or if it could read his mind, MacLeod directed his thoughts only to the task at hand as he left the building and journeyed to Manchester. The demon had remained silent during the drive, and since.

The sound of footsteps, a lone walker, snapped MacLeod back to the present.

A man dressed in a filthy sweatshirt, worn sweat pants that were at least two sizes too big, and sneakers with a loose sole that snapped as he walked, shuffled past the storefront and onto Lowell Street. MacLeod gave the man a ten-foot lead before he left the shadows of the entrance and followed. Almost immediately, the man stopped. The motion was too abrupt for the priest to follow suit and the sound of his own footsteps betrayed his presence.

MacLeod came to a halt, anticipating his prey to either run or scream.

The man did neither. Instead, he turned to face his pursuer. "Are you following me?"

"No," the priest stammered, "I mean, yes. I-I want to ask you something."

The man's right hand slid into his waistband. Moments later, he pulled it out. Even from this distance, the priest knew it was a knife, pointed his way.

"I have maybe three dollars and some change on me," the man said. "Enough to buy a cheap breakfast. I worked all night for this, and you're not taking it from me."

MacLeod was taken back by how clear the man's voice was. It lacked phlegm, and wasn't slurred. The words were enunciated in a weary tone, but not hurried or frightened. His sentences were articulate, leaving the priest to believe the homeless man was at least moderately educated. Also surprising was the pitch of the man's voice—that of a young man. He assumed a homeless man would be older.

The priest tugged at the hem of his buttoned suit coat. "I'm not going to take your money. In fact, I had the opposite in mind. How would you like to make fifty dollars?"

The homeless man approached him slowly. "Fifty dollars? What do I have to do for fifty dollars?"

"Suck my cock."

The man hesitated, eying the priest.

"Suck your cock, huh? Fifty bucks for that? I don't understand. You could get it for free around the corners at Billy's. You married or something? Don't want your wife to know you're gay?"

MacLeod unbuttoned the top of his suit coat and pushed the lapels to the sides. He stepped forward allowing the homeless man to see the collar.

"A priest." The man thought for a moment. "Makes sense now. You from around here?"

"No."

"Yeah, that makes sense, too." He continued to appraise the cleric.

An awkward silence ensued as the homeless man passed judgment over MacLeod. Unsure of the next step, the priest lowered his eyesight to the man's crotch, hoping it helped to allay any doubts and imply urgency. The man took the bait.

"Fifty bucks is a lot of money. I won't lie; I could use it. I know you're a priest and all that, but I want to see the money first before I agree."

MacLeod removed his wallet. He stepped closer to the man and pulled out a wad of bills. With his head cocked, he said, "If it's good, there could be more." He placed the wallet back into his pocket when the man's eyes lit.

"Okay," the homeless man said, "where you want to do this? Your car?"

There is a park two blocks down the street, under the bridge. Tell him you will go there. MacLeod flinched at the thought. The demon had made its presence known.

"There's a park a few blocks down, behind you at the bridge. It has trees and bushes. We won't be seen there."

The homeless man nodded. "I know it. I've slept there a few times. Could be some others are sleeping there now."

The priest smiled. "Let's find out. If there are, we can go somewhere else."

As the two walked to the park, his victim engaged in conversation. "You know, I've never done this before, but I really need the money. It's my kid's birthday next week. This will be my chance to buy him something nice."

MacLeod's back stiffened. "You—you have a family?"

"Well, I did. Jim's my name, by the way. Lost my job first, then my wife. Can't blame her for leaving me and taking Erick with her. I couldn't pay the bills and we lost everything. Me, I was so depressed—so convinced I was a loser that I made things worse. If you couldn't tell, I still think that way." He paused. "They—my wife and kid—live up in Maine now, with her folks. Haven't seen Erick in over two years now. Guess it's better that way. I wouldn't want him to see me like this. Wouldn't want him to know I was giving blowjobs to priests so I can buy him a present."

The pit of MacLeod's stomach turned sour. He wondered what the hell he was doing. This guy had a family, and he was not only leading the man to his death, he was condemning him to an eternity in Hell.

Ha. This guy is good, priest. His name's not Jim, it's Charlie. He was let go of his job for stealing and sent to prison. Yeah, his wife left him, but it was because he was a thief. And so you know, he's sucked cock before.

The demon took delight in exposing the man's past. MacLeod didn't know if the demon was telling the truth, but in some weird way, he hoped it was.

Priest, I don't care if you believe me or not. All you have got to remember is that I have your nephew. If you do not do this, he'll suffer a lot worse than a missing hand. And, I promise your mother will, too.

He silently asked the demon how it knew about the man. There was no answer. He tried another tact; silently asking it what was expected of him when they arrived at the park. Again, there was no answer.

Jim, or Charlie, whatever his name was, chatted until they reached the edge of the park. When they stepped off the walk onto the grass, the man pointed. "Over there, behind that bench is a cluster of bushes under the bridge. Let's go over there."

When they arrived, the priest stopped and surveyed the area. When he was satisfied no one else was around, he walked behind the bench and into the tall greenery. Though it was dark, he noticed a small clearing in the brush. He stood in the middle and heard the man following.

Jim approached, stood before him, and asked, "Are you ready?"

Tell him to get on his knees.

The priest followed the demon's instructions and the homeless man sunk down. On the ground, the man shifted left to right to get comfortable. Once settled, he stared at the cleric's crotch. "You want me to pull it out?"

MacLeod didn't have an answer. How far was he supposed to go? When he thought up this ruse, he never expected it to get this far. The demon could take the homeless man any time now, yet, it hadn't. It must be playing with him, reveling in the situation. But this was going to end *now*.

"Get up," he said to the man on his knees, "I changed my mind."

The homeless man shook his head. "What's going on?"

MacLeod reached to his back pocket and pulled out the wallet. "I'm not doing this, but I'm going to pay you, anyway." As soon as he finished the sentence, the demon mocked him.

You are no fun. When Father Gabriel did this, he went all the way before I stepped in. I think he wanted to. He came, too.

"You've done this before with a priest?" asked MacLeod aloud.

The homeless man shook his head once more. "No, I told you, I never did this."

What? You think you thought this ploy up yourself? I put the suggestion in your mind when we exchanged little pieces of ourselves. Now, stand back.

MacLeod paid the man, placed the wallet back in his pocket, and stepped back.

Jim grabbed the money out of the priest's hand before the guy changed his mind. He had no idea why the priest backed off at the last minute, but it didn't hurt Jim's feelings. He was telling the truth when he said he had never done this before, and he was happy he didn't have to add cocksucker to the long list of things he was ashamed of.

After placing the money in his front pocket, Jim wanted nothing more to do with the priest. He took two steps back with the intention of turning around and getting the hell out of there. On the second step, he hit something solid, but he didn't remember a large tree or an obstacle when he walked into the clearing. A chill rippled through his spine. A sense of darkness, wrongness, helplessness, invaded his thoughts.

Two heavy weights, one on each shoulder, shoved Jim forward, thrusting his neck back. The weights curled into clamps and squeezed. The pain shot down his spinal cord and spread through his upper body. His face contorted, and a high-pitched cry escaped his mouth. The pressure forced his back to arch; he stood on his toes in an attempt to twist out from the grip. A blow to the back of his legs forced his knees to shoot forward. His feet lifted off the ground. The clamps on his shoulders dug in tighter. On each side of his neck, the collarbones snapped, punching through his flesh and spewing blood.

As bad as the torture to his shoulders was, it dwarfed the pain in his legs as he was slammed to the ground. Both kneecaps shattered on impact. Small pieces of bone punctured nerves and muscle, sending lightning strikes through his body. The agony was so overwhelming, he was on the verge of losing consciousness.

"Oh, God," Jim moaned. He pleaded aloud to the priest, "Help me."

On his stomach, with his face in the dirt, Jim raised his head as high as the pain would allow. The priest's shoes came into view, but they vanished in an instant. His sight blurred as he was turned over with a violent yank.

Now on his back, he could see his tormentors.

Three men stood by his feet. There was enough light to see they were thin—sickly thin—with skin so taut it didn't seem possible for the flesh to hold their bones and insides together without tearing. Not one of these three appeared to have the strength to lift a small stone, never mind crush his shoulders and slam him to the ground. Jim lifted his gaze to get a look at their faces. He froze. *It's not possible. Those guys are dead.* All three were homeless men who passed away last year on the street. "Squeaky, Nashua, Buffalo," he whispered their names. They bent forward and reached for him. Jim responded the only way he could. "Please, stop," he implored them, "you're killing me. I hurt so bad." Jim closed his eyes.

When he reopened them, the dead stick-men were gone.

Jim's mind was cloudy, shutting down from the incessant hammering of pain. Exhaling, his body relaxed in preparation for a deep sleep. He could feel his awareness slipping away.

No, there will be no escaping. Those days are gone. Forever.

Jim was jolted to consciousness. The voice in his head was loud, the words echoing in his skull like a trapped insect attempting to find its way out of a screened window. Fully awake, the pain in his legs and shoulders was excruciating as wave after wave of fire-like pain washed over his body. His ability to talk was compromised by his suffering, but he did manage to mouth a question. "Why is this happening to me?"

The priest who led you here willingly scarified you in self-interest. You are going to Hell, and your suffering has only begun. There will be plenty of time for you to dwell on why, but first, let me give you a taste of your fate.

A vision appeared in Jim's mind. It was his wife, spread out naked on a bed, orally servicing a man. Like a photo app, the visions changed like snapshots, rapidly but slightly different—with a new man each time. The visions progressed from oral sex to sadomasochism and much worse.

Jim's scream was low and prolonged. The exertion ratcheting up the anguish of his physical pain.

You failed her, forced her into this. Her parents died. They had no money, and she was left to fend on her own. The sex paid the bills for a while, but it is not the worst thing she had done. It was not what led her to us. Broken, riddled with disease, she could not sell herself any more. Nobody wanted her. Despondent, with no money and a mouth to feed, she made a decision.

The vision in Jim's mind was clear, focused on a bare-bones room. He had no trouble recognizing it as the same type of flophouse room he had slept in when he had enough money to pay for one. The view narrowed to a bed. On it lay his wife, and Erick. The mattress they were on was gray, spotted with mold at the fringes. A single yellow-stained sheet prevented contact. Erick was nestled in his wife's arms, his son's surrounding her waist. The boy's eyes were wide, frightened. She was humming a song to him, something she often did to soothe the child to sleep after a nightmare. With one hand, she smoothed his unkempt, dirty hair. In the other hand, she held a kitchen knife. His wife stopped humming, and she asked Erick to close his eyes.

When his wife slid the blade over Erick's neck, Jim's body went slack. His physical pain receded, as did the awareness of his surroundings. His brain numbed, and for the moment, he was empty.

Oh no, we can't have that.

Jim's pain slammed back. He gasped at the impact. His body jerked, intensifying his agony.

This is merely a taste of the suffering you will have in Hell, and it will last an eternity. It's time to go. Have you any last words to the man who sent you to me?

Jim angled his neck toward the priest. He was confused by the expression on the cleric's face. The priest's eyes were wild, his mouth stretched wide with fear. The man's arms were raised, shaking, with his hands clenched into fists. Jim had expected the priest to be some kind of demon—gleeful, celebrating the fruits of his sacrifice. Something wasn't right. He wondered if the priest had been caught up in this similar to how he had. His thought process was cut short when spikes of thunderous agony tore through his body. He did manage to find enough strength to speak. It was one word. A question.

"Why?"

If the priest answered, Jim never heard it.

"Why?"

The homeless man's question burned like hot coal in Father MacLeod's mind.

Jim's head collapsed to the ground, and the man exhaled. The skin on his face yellowed. Sores burst through, filling in between rapidly appearing wrinkles. Blood spewed from his ears, nose, and mouth, at first a deep red, then a black hue. What sounded like gravel under foot accompanied the man's skull imploding.

MacLeod jumped back from the sight, doubled over, and dry heaved into the brush.

You have fulfilled half of your promise, priest. Was it not worth saving your nephew from a similar fate?

MacLeod silently screamed his reply, "You fucking asshole!"

What, no pithy response?

Reminded that the demon might not be able to read his thoughts, the priest repeated the statement out loud.

You clergy have to come up with a new invective. That one has been around since Theophylactus. He used it on me three times, for all the good it did him. Unless you have another sacrifice for me, we will now return to your nephew. If you have any thoughts otherwise, I will find the boy again, and I will make his suffering in Hell legendary. Then, when I am finished with him, I will go through your family, starting with your mother.

As he exited the clearing, Father MacLeod averted his gaze from the dead man. The trip to his car and the one back to his office were uneventful, and the demon did not communicate. The priest was grateful as it gave him time to think. By the time they arrived back in Haverhill, MacLeod had made enough mental notes to begin some research, but first, he had phones call to make.

Startled, Sister Bernice jumped in her seat when Father MacLeod appeared. The priest noted she was reading a copy of Vanity Fair, which she sheepishly placed next to a box of facemasks and a bottle of rosemary oil on the table in front of her. While the box and bottle used to combat the odors inside the holding rooms were well used, the magazine's cover was fresh, glossy. He couldn't help but comment. "Preparing for vespers, I see."

The nun gathered herself quickly. "It's a diversion, Father, something to help me pass the time." She paused. "It's unnerving down here. I don't have to tell you that. What goes on in those rooms is the stuff of nightmares. Sometimes, I hear those poor unfortunate souls. They scream, laugh, chortle, mock God. To have someone so young go through this is the worst kind of blasphemy." She appraised him. "Where have you been? It's been three days since you last performed the exorcism rites. What's in that plastic bag you're carrying?"

Ignoring the questions, he asked, "How's Cody doing?"

"Not well. After you left and we sedated him, he was doing better for a day or so. Some of his color returned and his ravings stopped. More's the pity it didn't last, as he got worse. When I check on him, he calls for you. Sometimes he yells your name, other times he singsongs it. He has not been kind to you, Father."

MacLeod inhaled deeply. "I understand this has been hard on you, Sister Bernice. Thank you for keeping an eye on him."

The nun did not respond.

Father MacLeod pressed the password into the keypad and entered his nephew's holding room.

The boy lay prone on the bed. The restraints on him now included a leather strap that traversed his neck. The priest walked to the head of the bed and gazed down.

The demon's eyes widened, and what passed for a smile crossed the boy's pulpy lips. "Just when I thought you had decided to abandon our deal, you show up. Your timing is good, priest. I was going to take this boy to Hell with me soon."

MacLeod squared his shoulders. "I'm here. Let's get this over with."

"You have thought up another sacrifice? Good. Where are we going this time? A playground? An old-aged home? A daycare?"

In lieu of an answer, Father MacLeod reached into the bag and withdrew a large bottle. He unscrewed the cap and went to the nearest corner of the room. He poured the contents on the floor. Following along the walls, he emptied the bottle along the entire room.

"What the fuck you doing, priest? That's holy water. I can feel it from here. You going to try to exorcize me again? You've just sealed your nephew's fate."

Father MacLeod took up his position again at the head of the bed. He removed a cross from his left back pocket and placed it on the boy's chest. From the bag, he retrieved his book of exorcism rituals.

"You fucked up, demon. Twice," the priest stated. "The first was when you mentioned Theophylactus. The name was familiar to me, so I looked it up. It was the birth name of Pope Benedict the Ninth. Seems you've been around for a long time, since 1012, at the least. I researched everything I could find on him. When you said he called you an asshole three times, I knew I had the right guy. After he lost his reign for the third time, he documented his encounters and deals with a demon. Man, you really are a piece of shit."

The boy's body tensed. It struggled against the restraints.

"You also spoke of a Father Gabriel. That one took some time to track down. I managed to trace him to a retirement home in Maine, close enough for me to pay him a visit. You did quite a number on him, demon. He's a broken man, wracked with guilt. Spends his days in a wheelchair, staring at the woods outside the home. He opened up to me. We compared notes. When we were done, I was sure I had the information I needed. It seems you couldn't keep your mouth shut around him, either."

The leather restraint around the boy's neck split in two. His head lifted, and it spit at the priest. "I'm going to kill this vessel. Now!"

Father MacLeod opened the book of rituals. He recited a short passage in Latin. He then switched to English when he shouted, "IN THE NAME OF OUR LORD, JESUS CHRIST, I COMMAND YOU, DEMON, TO LEAVE THIS BOY! GOD, SEND THIS ABOMINATION BACK TO HELL WHERE IT WAS SPAWNED! VACATE THIS CHILD AND

NEVER ENTER A HUMAN SOUL AGAIN! THIS I COMMAND YOU…ASMODEUS…IN THE NAME OF GOD!"

The cross he had placed on the boy's chest illuminated. As it glowed brighter, rays of light shot into all corners of the room. The boy's body trembled violently, and the priest heard more of the restraints snapping. His nephew's mouth opened and a roar mingled with anger and pain pierced MacLeod's ears. The priest repeated the ritual, word for word. A dark fissure appeared in the air above the boy. A howling wind emerged, slamming into the priest. He continued with the exorcism while he fought to keep his balance. When he finished the ritual for the fifth time, he took his eyes off the book to glance at his nephew. The boy was now sitting up, and once again, his face was inches from the priest's.

The priest smiled. "Not this time, demon."

Father MacLeod flipped the pages of the ritual book to the middle. A small pocket had been carved out of the pages to the back cover. Nestled inside was a bottle. He pulled the brass stopper off, and then shook the clear liquid into the boy's face.

The skin split where the water landed. Black steam hissed from the wounds as the demon screamed. His nephew's body shook, vibrating at an unnatural speed. Panic slammed into MacLeod as he wondered if the boy would survive this. He had doused the demon with water from Lourdes, consecrated by Pope Francis in the hopes it would cause the demon to flee. What he hadn't counted on was the demon destroying his nephew in the process.

MacLeod raised his head to the ceiling. "Saint Francis, I don't know if you can hear me, but if you can, I need some fucking help here!"

The boy froze.

The wind vanished, and the room went quiet.

The priest couldn't take his eyes off his nephew. For what seemed like an eternity, the boy remained still.

A dark shadow emerged from Cory, and it floated over the boy. His nephew collapsed onto the bed.

You have won, but you will not be rid of me that easily. You still owe us one soul, and we will collect. We will meet again, priest.

MacLeod rushed to his nephew and checked the boy's pulse. It was weak, but it was there. The cuts and fissures on the boy's face were either sealed or healed. His color was close to normal if not a bit pale, and the bruises and swelling were gone. Aside from his missing hand, Cory would be okay physically, but they would have to wait and see if there was any psychological damage.

If the ritual worked, Asmodeus would be unable to inhabit another human soul. The priest hoped that went for the small bit of the demon's soul that had been placed inside him. But its final words rested uneasy with Father MacLeod. After shaking his head and walking to the door, the priest paused. Looking up the ceiling, he said, "Fuck you, Pope Francis, for taking your time."

While punching in the password, MacLeod recalled he was out of scotch. He would pick some up after meeting with his mother and brother. The corners of his mouth rose. He'd heard of a brothel in Nashua, New Hampshire. This evening might be a good time to check it out.

Opening the Door

by Kenneth McKinley

The rusty padlock stared at the two from its perch on the vacant lake cottage's back door. Logan produced an equally rusty key and attempted to insert it. Years of oxide didn't make the process easy. He stuck his tongue out in concentration between his teeth as he worked on the lock, exhaling in a huff to get his dishwater blond bangs out of his eyes. He slammed the corroded Yale against the wood frame of the door in disgust. Faded white paint flaked off and fell to the floor of the back porch like dirty snowflakes.

"Fuck it, dude! This thing is going to snap the key off before it'll open," Logan said.

Tyler stepped forward and produced a black, canvas bag.

"No problem. You just need to have the right tool for the job."

Tyler Brooks may have been a few inches shorter and more than a handful of pounds lighter than his companion, but this wasn't his first rodeo. He came prepared.

He unzipped the bag and pulled out a long, red-handled implement.

"Step aside and let an expert handle this."

Logan scoffed at the remark, but yielded his space so Tyler could do his thing. With a quick snip of the bolt cutters, the lock fell into two pieces on the porch by their feet. A couple of slams from his muscular shoulder and the boys were in.

The cottage belched out a wave of stale, musty air as they entered into the back mudroom that hadn't seen a visitor since Reagan was in office. Boxes upon boxes were stacked as far as the eye could see, all under a thick layer of dust. Logan wrinkled his nose and waved a hand in front of his face, causing the dust motes to change their path of flight in the stagnant air. Sunlight attempted to illuminate the room but was compromised by the dirty film on the windows.

"Damn, dude. How long has it been since anyone's been in here?" he asked.

Tyler looked at his clipboard, trying to find the answers from the bank's paperwork.

"It looks like the bank and the attorneys controlled the property since 1987."

"1987?" Logan asked incredulously. "That was forever ago!"

The two made their way deeper into the cottage. At first, the house appeared like many of the other bank jobs they'd cleaned out together previously owned by hoarders. But upon further inspection, this place was different.

Most hoarders' houses were of a various level of chaos. Layer after layer of junk piled to the ceiling with no rhyme or reason. It was just mountains of stuff. But not the cottage at 289 Nottawa Lake Road. No, this place had an underlying order to the stacks of clutter.

"Where do we start?" Logan asked.

"Let's do a quick once through and see what big ticket items we have that'll be an easy sell. Look for antiques. Quality pieces. Anything old."

"You're kidding, right? Take a look around. Everything here is older than my parents!"

It was true. The kitchen had a Kelvinator refrigerator humming away in the corner that looked like it came down the same assembly line as a Packard sedan. Right beside it sat a white porcelain behemoth of a gas stove that appeared to weigh as much as the Titanic. Tyler ran his fingers across the chrome nameplate that said Magic Chef.

The living room was filled with quality, old pieces under the weight of boxes of all shapes and sizes, and even construction. Most were made of cardboard, but as you progressed further into the house, it was like you were going back in time. More and more wooden crates were under the thick layer of dust.

Logan pushed his bangs out of his eyes again, as he let out a low whistle.

"It looks like we'll be here for a while."

"That's why we brought the Ryder truck," Tyler said, pointing to the yellow beast of a box van parked in the driveway with its roll up door yawning wide open next to the back steps.

Tyler had been "picking" since his sophomore year at Covington University. Watching the History Channel's numerous programs gave him the idea to turn his passion, his major in history at Covington, into a way to pay for college. Besides, it sure beat washing dishes.

His professor, Dr. Forsythe, took a shining to Tyler and his enthusiasm toward his class, and made some calls to a few of his friends in the banking and realty industries. That landed Tyler his first property to clean out. Not only was he a good student, but also a hard worker, and word quickly made its way through the channels that Tyler was a dependable option you could count on to get the job done and on time.

That's how it started. He quickly developed a keen eye for what items had value and what ones needed to head to the landfill. By utilizing various online auction sites, Tyler Harris began padding his savings account to the point where he not only could pay for next semester's tuition, but he no longer had a problem paying for drinks at the campus watering holes.

After two days and numerous trips to the landfill, Tyler and Logan were making a dent in the endless stacks of boxes. Their deadline was a week away. An investor had purchased the house not for its contents or charm, but for the valuable lake front property where it resided. As soon as the old cottage was empty, it was to be razed and cleared for what Tyler believed would be a lake home worth millions. Nottawa Lake was loaded with them, and it didn't take much of a trained eye to see that this property, sitting all by itself on the northern point of the lake, was a developer's dream.

A strong breeze blew off the water, the scent of possible rain in the air. Both boys looked to the sky in search of storm clouds.

That's just what we need. A damn storm to slow us down!

"C'mon, Harris. Move your ass! I don't feel like getting soaked to the bone like the last pick."

Tyler chuckled. Logan was a good friend, and an equally hard worker. A difficult combination to find among the student body. They quickly hit it off their freshman year in the dorms, and when Tyler got the idea of starting a business cleaning out properties, Logan was the only one he considered asking to help.

"Well, if I wasn't always picking up your slack all the time, we'd be done already."

Logan threw his head back and brayed loudly. "Shhiiiittt!!"

As the boys steadily made their way back toward the far bedroom, the contents became more interesting...and more valuable. Lead crystal decanters and glasses, a rosewood chess set with what looked like hand carved ivory and ebony pieces, a mahogany cigar humidor, a thirty-inch globe of the world resting on a walnut floor stand. It was hard for the boys to take it all in. There was so much to see, their heads continually rotated back and forth, as if on a pendulum.

The door to the bedroom was slightly ajar. Tyler slid boxes out of the way, so he could shove the door open to see what treasures lied behind it. As he put his weight into it, the door creaked on rusty hinges, dust motes fluttered up into his nostrils. Holding back a sneeze, his eyes opened wide at the wonders the room beheld.

"Holy shit! Holy shit! Holy shit!" he stammered.

From the other room, "What is it?"

"Dude! You aren't going to believe what I just found!"

Logan tripped over the clutter on the floor, which caused him to stumble into Tyler, knocking them both forward and down on their knees. The duo's mouth dropped open in wonder at what they saw.

The room was filled with World War II memorabilia: firearms, uniforms, and crates of gear occupied the far corner. Maps and stacks of yellowed papers littered a walnut roll top desk to the left. Above the desk was a Japanese katana, an actual Masamune from the 13ᵗʰ century.

Pictures hung on the wall. They were black and white photographs of famous leaders and celebrities from the first half of 1900s, along with the same dark-haired man with an angular jaw and high cheekbones smiling an infectious grin back in each. There were pictures of him with FDR, Winston Churchill, General Eisenhower, Charles Lindbergh, Henry Ford, Howard Hughes, and Albert Einstein, a proverbial who's who from The Greatest Generation.

Tyler was in awe. Obviously, this man was the original owner of the house, but who was he? Being a history major at Covington, how could a gentleman of such importance escape his knowledge? He searched through the papers and discovered a name that seemed familiar.

"Carter Langston? Langston? Why does that name sound familiar?" Tyler asked.

"There's that building on campus named Langston," Logan offered.

Tyler's eyes lit up, and he snapped his fingers. "Of course! Langston Hall. How could I be so stupid? Logan, do you have any idea whose house this is?"

"Umm…Carter Langston's, I would imagine," his friend quipped.

"No shit. I mean, do you know who that is?"

Logan pondered for a moment and then admitted defeat. "I feel like I should, but I don't know. Who is he?"

"He was a professor at Covington University. Both his parents were too. In fact, his mother was a chemist that discovered some process to make a glow in the dark paint. They made a ton of money for the college. Anyways, Dr. Forsythe told me about this Carter. Rumor has it, he traveled all over the world, hunting down ancient artifacts and doing all sorts of undercover stuff for the government."

Logan looked at the man in the black and white photos.

"You're telling me that we're picking the house of some real-life Indiana Jones?"

Tyler shrugged. "It would appear so."

"Well, how come I never heard of this guy? You'd think if he was this big celebrity, everyone would know about him."

"That's just it. I think he was more of a secret agent than anyone knew. I mean, look at these pictures. He definitely hobnobbed around with the world's heavy hitters, yet was able to stay under the radar while living here in Covington."

"And now we are picking his house. I can't believe no one knew all this stuff was here, especially if this Carter guy was so important," Logan said.

"If he really was an undercover agent, I'm sure he had to keep a lid on it. I bet no one around here knew, and the people that did are dead now. That was a long time ago. Anyways, I'm not looking a gift horse in the mouth," Tyler said, rubbing his hands. "This place looks like it's going to be the mother of all honey holes!"

The boys worked tirelessly all week, and by Friday, had made a noticeable dent in clearing out the contents of the lake cottage. Whoever made the decision to have the house cleared and demolished, obviously never set foot inside. Every time the two would remove a layer, they discovered one full of antiques hidden underneath.

While working on the bedroom, Tyler pulled out first editions from Faulkner, Fitzgerald, and Hemingway, along with books and journals written in a multitude of foreign languages with maps and charts of destinations from all over the globe. He was thumbing through these when he heard a loud rapping from the adjoining bedroom.

"What the hell are you doing over there?" Tyler asked Logan.

"I think I found something."

Tyler set the journals down and peered in the other room. A grandfather clock stood rotated away from the wall where it normally resided. His friend was on his hands and knees behind it knocking on a wall panel with his knuckles, as if listening for something.

"What are you doing?"

Logan kept tapping the wall and listening to the sound it made.

"I was moving this clock when I heard a groan come from behind this wall."

"A groan?" Tyler asked, bewildered.

"Yeah," Logan said, still tapping. "It sounded like the house let out a big sigh. I think there's something behind this panel."

Tyler had a smart-ass comment for his partner, who continued to fiddle with the wall. Suddenly, there was an audible click and a small panel swung away, as if on a hidden door hinge. The two looked at each other in excitement. Behind the panel was an iron latch. Logan gave it a tug and a section of the wall rotated inward revealing a staircase that descended under the house into inky blackness.

The excitement in the air was thick enough to cut with a knife. Logan launched himself over furniture like a jungle cat as he sprinted out to the truck to get a flashlight. The dank air wafting out of the opening smelled like a freshly opened tomb, and Tyler could hardly contain his excitement as he wondered what riches might be buried here.

Logan returned with the flashlight, panting like an old dog while trying to catch his breath. The two made their way through the entrance, running their fingers on the opening. Whoever built this knew exactly what they were doing. The panel blended in perfectly with the wall, and it was only sheer luck that Logan stumbled across the secret door.

Down the steps they went. Decades of cobwebs brushed against their faces as they made their way below, causing them to spit and sputter as they slapped the strands away. The walls were rough fieldstone, and a hook fastened in the mortar held a cobweb covered Coleman Quick-Lite lantern. Tyler made a mental note to grab the valuable trinket before they were done with the pick. The two came to the bottom of the stairs to a hard-packed dirt floor. When Logan shined his light across the room, Tyler forgot all about the lantern.

The flashlight quivered in his hand. What laid in front of the two was almost too incredible to fathom. It was as if they had stepped through a time warp and were now back in a 1940s underground military bunker. There were all sorts of ancient electronic equipment: a shortwave radio, a telegraph, an ancient radar screen. If Tyler wasn't hallucinating, he would swear that was a genuine Enigma encryption device, used to decode secret messages in World War II, surrounded by maps and documents all stamped "Classified."

Logan finally broke the silence. "Holy... Shit... Dude!"

All Tyler could do was nod with his mouth open. Finally, he swallowed, blinked repeatedly, as if emerging from a trance. "Exactly," he whispered.

For the next hour, the two dove headfirst into the contents of the cellar hardly coming up for air. While working on an alcove, Logan found a large standup locker with a huge padlock that looked more suitable for an ancient jail cell than the locker door.

"Are the bolt cutters still in the van," he asked.

"Yeah, should be in back, in the bin by passenger side door. Why?"

Logan playfully flipped the padlock, showing his friend, and replied, "I can't imagine what could possibly be in here that warrants a padlock like this."

Tyler grinned from ear to ear and said, "There's only one way to find out. I'll go get them."

A couple of minutes later and the aged iron lay in two pieces on the dirt floor. The locker door groaned open on hinges that hadn't seen oil since Glenn Miller's orchestra was at the top of the charts. The door opened up into what looked like a recessed closet in the rock wall. Inside were wooden crates of various sizes stacked on top of each other. A heavy layer of dust covered the boxes, obscuring any writing or stamps identifying its contents.

Tyler used his sleeve to wipe away the layer of grime on the first crate. It revealed a stamp that said United States Antarctic Service Expedition. Other crates had markings for expeditions in the Bahamas, Siam, British Guiana, and the Belgian Congo. He inserted a screwdriver under the lid of the crate marked Belgian Congo, and the aged wood squealed in protest before it succumbed. The first item staring at him atop of the packing material was a British Pith helmet. His eyes lit up like a kid opening gifts at Christmas, and he plopped the helmet on his head before digging to see what else was in the crate.

From behind the crates, his friend let out a jubilant war cry. "Check this shit out!"

Tyler, still wearing his newfound helmet, peeped around the corner of the box to see what all the commotion was about. Logan appeared from out of the dark recess holding a leather-bound case with strange writing and symbols embossed in the covering.

Still studying the case's contents, Logan looked up at his friend. "Nice hat. Livingston, I presume?"

"I'll have you know this is a genuine Pith helmet, not a hat," Tyler said.

Logan rolled his eyes.

"What did you find?" Tyler asked.

"I'm not sure. I found another crate all padlocked up like it was Fort Knox, so I took the bolt cutters to it, thinking there was something valuable inside. But it looks like it's nothing but some old records," Logan said, while pulling out one of the black discs to show him.

The disappointment was apparent in Logan's eyes. Ever since they started picking together, Logan was struck with gold fever. He was convinced the two would eventually discover a pirate's chest full of doubloons and jewels or maybe a safe full of crisp one-hundred-dollar bills. Tyler imagined the look he was seeing on Logan's face was exactly like the ones worn by California prospectors in 1849.

Tyler stood and took the record, turning it over and carefully examining the album. Strange and archaic looking writing adorned the paper label in the middle, in what appeared to be several ancient languages and symbols. The only words he could make out were *A. Crowley 1926*. The record was heavy in his hands, weighing at least a couple of pounds and approximately a half inch thick.

"If I had to guess, I would say these are the master recording of something. I can't read the label. You took Latin, didn't you?" Tyler asked.

Logan shook his head. "Nope. Two years of Spanish in high school. How about you?"

"Yeah, me neither. Not until next semester."

Upon further inspection of the leather case, Logan discovered what looked like a journal with erratic handwriting scrawled in faded ink on its yellowed pages. He handed it over to Tyler to see what he made of it, while he pulled out the other records. There were a total of six in all, each with the same strange symbols and language.

Meanwhile, Tyler studied the notes in the journal, sounding out the odd writing. It wasn't like anything he had ever heard. He wished Dr. Forsythe was back from his seminar. Not only was he Tyler's mentor and resident expert at Covington on ancient languages, but he would be excited to know they were picking the late Carter Langston's house.

A few of the things that stood out were that the records were numbered one through six in Latin. That much he could decipher. The other thing that struck him was the name *A. Crowley*. Could this really be the recordings of the late English occultist, Aleister Crowley? The year 1926 made sense. Tyler knew that was the time period he was alive. But what could possibly be on these records, and why would Langston have them in his possession? Especially under lock and key.

He looked at his phone. 6:02 p.m. Damn, they had been down in this hole for hours. His empty stomach growled, as if to reinforce the realization. "All right, dude. Let's call it a night. I'm starving."

A look of disappointment crossed his friend's face.

Tyler itched to know what was on the records and in the journal as bad as he did. All of a sudden, a thought crossed his mind. "Hey. I haven't seen anything to play these on, have you?"

Logan looked around, as if a gramophone would jump out from the shadows. "No. As a matter of fact, I haven't."

"Damn. I sure wish we could listen to see what's on these, but you need something old enough for 78 RPMs."

Logan snapped his fingers as an idea came to him. "Wait a second. My Aunt Irene."

"Your Aunt Irene?"

"Yeah. Well, she's not my real aunt. She's my grandmother's sister. We call her our aunt. Anyways, she has this big wooden thing on legs in her dining room called a Victrola. She keeps plants on it, but I think it still works. Would that play these things?"

Tyler punched his friend in the arm. "Hell, yes, it will. Do you think she'd let us use it?"

"Psh. Are you kidding? She loves company. In fact, she won't let you leave without eating. She's a hell of cook, and never happy unless you're waddling out of there."

A grin stretched across Tyler's face. He couldn't wait to hear what was on these records, and he never turned down a free meal.

"Let's go!"

His Aunt Irene lived in a two-story Craftsman over on Buchanan Street, near the high school. Logan told Tyler on the way over that she had worked in the school cafeteria for forty years before she retired, and had always taken a shining to Logan. When her husband died during Logan's senior year, he made it a point to stop in often to make sure she was doing okay. The visits always made Aunt Irene smile and tonight was no exception.

"Logan!" She gave him a big hug and an old lady peck on the cheek.

He gave her a sheepish grin. "How are you doing, Aunt Irene?"

"Oh, just fine. Just fine. My gout's been acting up a bit, but I'm too ornery to let it get the best of me." She laughed. "Come in. Come in. Who's your friend?"

"Aunt Irene, this is Tyler. Tyler, this is my Aunt Irene."

"Very nice to meet you, ma'am," he said, extending his hand for a shake.

She looked down and scoffed. "Please. Call me Irene, and we don't shake around here. We HUG!" And with that, she gave Tyler a big squeeze.

She ushered them into the kitchen where she had pulled an apple pie out of the oven right before they got there. The fragrance of hot cinnamon filled the room, and Tyler's stomach grumbled in response.

"Why, you boys must be hungry. I can heat up some fried chicken and mashed potatoes for you."

"Oh, we didn't come over here to trouble you ma'am...err, I mean Irene," Tyler said.

Irene's brow furrowed at this. "Nonsense. Growing boys like you can always eat. Now, you two go out in the garage and get yourself something to drink out of the refrigerator. I'll heat you up some food." When the two didn't move fast enough for her liking, she said, "Go now. I'm not taking no for an answer."

The boys finished off three helpings of fried chicken with all the trimmings. Tyler couldn't help but wonder how a widowed woman of Irene's age happened to have a full chicken dinner in her refrigerator big enough to feed a small battalion, as if she was waiting for them to show up. He chuckled to himself, noting that it must be something with that generation. His grandmother was the same way.

In between bites of fresh apple pie, Logan asked, "Aunt Irene."

"Hmm?"

"Does that Victrola in your dining room still work? We found some old records at a house we've been cleaning out, and we'd like to see what's on them, but it takes an old 78."

"Why, I think so. At least it still did the last time I tried it."

The two finished their meal and washed their dishes to Irene's protests. When they were done, they made their way into the dining room with the leather case. They set up the Victrola and tried one of her records as a test run. The sound of Benny Goodman emitted from the speaker.

Irene closed her eyes and smiled, as she tapped her foot to the beat. "That was always my momma's favorite."

After the record finished, Logan pulled out the first album with *A. Crowley 1926* on the label. He set the needle down on the black shellac and strange chanting erupted from the Victrola. It sounded like a drunken band of Tibetan monks. To Tyler's untrained ear, it sounded like Latin, but only to the point where he could recognize an occasional word here and there.

"My goodness! I don't know what they're saying, but there's nothing to keep a beat to," his Aunt Irene remarked.

She was right. The chanting was more mesmerizing than musical.

Tyler leafed through the journal and racked his brain to recall what Latin words he could make out. He downloaded an app for his phone, but it was slow going trying create any type of coherent sentences. It appeared the writing was some sort of code that used multiple languages, many of which weren't recognized by his app.

"So, did you figure any of this stuff out?" Logan asked.

"Yes. No. Well…some of it, I think?" Tyler said.

"Well, that clears it all up. Thanks so much." Logan rolled his eyes.

"Screw you. I don't see you cracking this code, Mr. Rosetta Stone," Tyler replied.

"Hey! You're supposed to be the brains of this operation. I'm only here to supply the muscle."

"Man, I wish Dr. Forsythe was back from his trip." Tyler scratched his head while trying to make sense of the writing. "Okay. What I do know is that this was indeed done by Aleister Crowley."

"Great. Now we're getting somewhere. Now, what the hell is it?"

"Well, see, that's the hard part. From what I can gather, it says the six records are some sort of instructions."

"Instructions?"

"Yeah, like you're supposed to play these in some sort of order and it will unlock a…"

"Unlock a what?"

"See…that's what I don't know. It doesn't make any sense. It's all garbled up. It says something like '*The wise man will unlock the door to…to…*' "

"To what? C'mon man!"

"Don't rush me! I'm doing the best I can here. '*Unlock the door to King Solomon's go…goesh?*' "

"Goesh? What the hell is a goesh? Wait! Do you mean gold? *King Solomon's gold?* Oh damn!"

Tyler frowned, as Logan danced around in frenzied excitement at the prospect that they were about to hit it rich.

"Dude! King Solomon's gold. All we have to do is figure out what order to listen to these records," Logan said, while fist bumping a reluctant Tyler.

"I…I don't know if that's right. I'm not sure if I'm reading this right."

"What else could it be? Gold from King Solomon's lost mine. We heard about this in Sunday School while growing up. You saw all of the stuff here. This Langston guy has been everywhere. He has maps and things from all over the world. I bet he figured out in what order to play these records in and found the gold."

Logan's eyes sparkled like the riches he hoped to find. It would be hard for Tyler to bring him back down to earth. These entries in the journal could mean anything. They could also mean nothing. It could all be nothing more than the demented ramblings from a famous historical nut job that was into some weird shit.

They decided Tyler would take the book home and try to crack more of Crowley's code. Tomorrow was Saturday. They normally didn't work weekends, but something told Tyler he and Logan would be back over to Nottawa Lake before Monday.

He went home and couldn't get to sleep. All he could think about was the strange writing in Crowley's journal. Tired of fighting the insomnia, he decided to do some more research now that he could use his computer. After a couple of hours of digging into the foreign language and symbols, Tyler had more questions than answers. It was after 3 a.m. Maybe he'd head over to the college tomorrow and see if he could find any answers there.

After a fitful night of sleep, Tyler was pulled from his slumber by the sound of the neighbor's lawn mower. Bleary eyed, he rolled over and looked at his phone. Shit. It was almost noon.

He hopped out of bed, threw some clothes on, and grabbed a hat, the ultimate bed head fighter for a college student. Throwing the journal and all his notes in his backpack, he grabbed a couple pieces of cold bacon leftover from his mom, who had made breakfast, and headed out the door.

Covington University had a renowned history and ancient language department, for which Dr. Forsythe was the chair. Tyler's befriending of the professor a couple of years ago afforded him leeway in the department. He was given door codes to get into their offices and passwords for their research systems, usually only accessible to grad students, not underclassmen.

After punching in the door code to get into the department, Fran waved hello as he walked by. All of a sudden, he stopped in his tracks when an idea struck him.

Going back to the front desk, he pulled out Crowley's journal. "Hey, Frannie. Do you have any idea what language this is or have you seen these symbols before?"

Fran was not only Dr. Forsythe's grad assistant, but was also considered his right-hand woman. She had helped Tyler on numerous assignments. If there was anyone other than the professor who could figure out this language, Tyler bet it would be her.

She peered through the lenses of her glasses to study the journal. "Let's see. What do we have here?" Her forehead wrinkled as she used her index finger to guide her line of sight across the Crowley's scribbling. "Where did you get this?" she asked cautiously.

"It was in a house we've been cleaning out on Nottawa Lake that was owned by the late Carter Langston."

Fran looked up and studied Tyler's face for any sign of a practical joke. "Carter Langston? Are you sure about that?"

"I'm positive. You should see all the stuff we've found. This journal was locked away with some old records that had some weird chanting on them."

Fran's eyes went wide. "Records? Were there six of them?"

Tyler recoiled in surprise. "Yeah. How'd you know?"

Her hand went to her mouth. "Oh my god."

"What? What are they?"

Instead of responding, she quickly flipped through more pages of the journal, biting her fist as she read. When she got to the part that she was looking for, she turned to Tyler. "You played these records?"

Tyler nodded.

"In what order?"

"Huh? Why?"

"In what fucking order?" she demanded.

Tyler was stunned. He'd known Fran for three years and she'd never said anything stronger than *darn* for as long as he'd known her. "I don't know." He tried to remember. "I think we played the first two or three before we quit. We couldn't understand what they were saying."

"That's not the point. We have to get these records back before anyone else listens to them."

Tyler couldn't make heads or tails of what she was getting at. Suddenly, he became suspicious. "Why? Does this have something to do with King Solomon's gold?"

"Gold? Where did you get the idea that these have anything to do with gold?"

"Because right here," he said, flipping through the journal to the entry he was looking for. "It says, '*The wise man will unlock the door to King Solomon's gold.*' "

She shook her head.

"No, you read it wrong. That doesn't say gold. It says goetia. It's referring to the Lesser Key of Solomon. A grimoire that Crowley believed, if read in the right order, would unlock the door to Hell."

Tyler placed both his palms on the top of his head and shook it back and forth in disbelief. What the hell was she saying? "C'mon. You expect me to believe that playing some records will…"

He couldn't finish the question.

"Look. You have no idea what you're messing with here. Crowley was rumored to be into some very dangerous stuff. That was one version of the story. Another one says he was experimenting with mind control triggers, very crazy psychological manipulations. And very dangerous. It may not be a literal door to Hell, but the rumor has it that, after listening to these chantings in the right order, it drove the person insane and they clawed out their eyeballs screaming about not wanting to see 'it' anymore."

This last part was a gut punch to Tyler. "Oh Jesus! Logan! He's got the records" He reached into his pocket, pulled out his phone and called his friend. It went to voice mail. "I've got to find him."

Fran grabbed her jacket off the back of her chair and said, "I'm coming with you."

He tried half a dozen times to reach Logan as he sped toward his house. Each time it went to voice mail. Tyler whipped into Logan's driveway and only saw his parent's car. After a quick conversation with his parents, they confirmed what he was afraid of—he wasn't there.

Tyler got back in the car and made a beeline for Aunt Irene's. He broke numerous traffic laws on the way there. The whole time Fran kept trying to call him. Each call ended with the same result.

Finally, he skidded around the corner onto Buchanan Street and screeched to a stop in front of Aunt Irene's Craftsman. Logan's car was in her driveway. All of the lights were off in the house and an eerie silence hung like a thick fog in the air.

The two carefully made their way up the driveway toward the steps going up to the side entrance. Tyler had a peculiar feeling of dread gnawing at the base of his stomach. Something wasn't right.

He opened the screen door and knocked on the inner wooden door. Tyler went to knock again, but it swung open slowly, emitting a long creak, making gooseflesh come out on his arms.

Fran rubbed herself, as if trying to warm up.
Tyler gulped and broke the silence. They treaded lightly through the kitchen. "Hello?"

No answer.

"Is anyone home?"

Still nothing.

"Irene? Logan?"

A smell assaulted their nostrils as they approached the dining room. When Tyler was ten-years old, his parents took him and his sisters on a trip to Yellowstone National Park. There was a spot in the park that had a hot spring called Sulphur Caldron. The acidic odor was so strong it burned young Tyler's nose and made him sick to his stomach. He had never smelled anything like that before or after that day, until now.

As they crossed the threshold into the dining room, they could hear a scratching noise rhythmically repeating over and over. They looked over to the Victrola and found the needle at the end of the record, Crowley's record. Tyler reached over and returned the arm to its resting place and clicked the knob, shutting the turntable off.

A weak moan caused the two to whip around in the direction from which it came. From the back room, Tyler imagined was Aunt Irene's bedroom, there came a scraping noise that sounded like someone dragging something across the hardwood floor followed by a thump.

"Hello? Logan?" Tyler's throat felt as dry as desert sand.

Fran latched onto Tyler's arm as they tip-toed across the room to the hallway, leading to Irene's bedroom. As the two turned the corner into the gloomy hall, a gasp emitted from the shadow of the floor.

Tyler reached over, flipped on the light switch. The light instantly cut through the gloom and illuminated Logan, stretched out and face down on the floor. There was a thick streak of blood trailing on the floor from the bedroom to where Logan's legs were once attached to his torso. Now there was nothing from the waist down but shredded flesh and twisted ropes of intestines resting in a pool of blackened blood.

Logan attempted to lift his head to look at Tyler and Fran through milky eyes. With the last bit of his strength, he stretched out a bloody hand, reaching for his friends. "Heeelllp…"

Fran let out a blood-curdling scream, and something heavy thrashed from inside the bedroom.

Oh God! Aunt Irene!

Tyler leaped over Logan's destroyed body, his mind only reacting to some instinct in his primal brain, intent on saving Aunt Irene from the same fate as his friend. He smelled it before he saw, prior to hearing it, and stopped in his tracks at the bedroom door.

An unearthly roar blistered the air. The odor of hell whipping Tyler's hair back, like hurricane winds. Before him, crouched down with Logan's mangled femur in its talon-like claws, was the thing of nightmares. It stood up and stretched to its full height, causing its reptilian-shaped head to smack the ceiling, plaster dust raining down around it. The demon's black, wart-encrusted tongue lapped over its prize, while its evil yellow stare studied Tyler.

He didn't remember turning to run. He didn't remember grabbing Fran's shaking arm and launching her out of her terrified paralysis toward the door. He didn't remember saturating the house with the can of lawnmower gas he'd found in the garage. Nor did he recall throwing the lit paper to ignite the house, hoping to send that monstrosity back to Hell. But in time, Tyler would remember everything.

The Other

by Laurel Hightower

Mark Beckham couldn't have said when he started noticing the presence of the Other. Things had been so shitty lately, it was as though time was a muddy, sluggish river, and the landmarks he used to rely on were slipping away. He supposed it didn't matter—it was here now, and had been for so long, he wondered if there'd ever been a time before, a time when things made sense, when he felt like himself. It was hazy, trying to look back. When he tried too hard, he got queasy, his head aching, so he stopped. There was only now. There was only the two of them: the Other, and Mark.

For a while it was only that; a feeling. The first time he realized it was something more dangerous, he had woken in the deepest hours of the night, feeling wrong, as though he'd just fallen back in his body. His chest heaving, trying to catch his breath, his gaze had strayed to the ceiling. There it was, clinging up there, a black so dark that the moonlight filtering through the blinds couldn't reach it. He waited for his eyes to adjust, for the shape to resolve itself into something harmless. Then it moved. No, that wasn't right. It didn't just move, it *loomed*.

It wasn't a dream. Mark knew the difference—was no stranger to haunted sleep. As a child, he'd woken screaming from night terrors that, while they were lucid and intense, faded as all dreams do as soon as he woke. Even the sleep paralysis he'd suffered back then couldn't compare. The horror of being frozen in place while every crawling thing he'd ever seen in a scary movie came creeping up to him still dissipated as soon as movement returned.

The Other was something different.

When he first saw that looming shadow, he thought that was it, that he was paralyzed again. But when he tried to move, he found he could squeeze his hands and wiggle his toes. He didn't try for long—any movement seemed to make the creature move faster, caused it to ooze closer. Almost whimpering, Mark lay still, hands scrunched in the blanket pulled up to his chest, breathing shallowly, eyes wide and focused on the living darkness that crept ever closer. He didn't sleep again that night, and the Other never left.

He tried to tell Teresa. He didn't know if she'd believe him, but he didn't want to be alone with the knowledge, with the presence. They'd been married for twelve years, for Christ's sake. That had to count for something.

"It was like someone leaning over me," he told his wife the next morning, red eyed, over strong coffee at the kitchen table. "Something big, and wrong. And it just kept coming closer, a millimeter at a time, watching me, its dead eyes not blinking. By the time you woke up, its nose was nearly touching mine."

He shuddered, choked back a sob, the terror still that real even in the light of day, no longer alone.

He wasn't sure what he expected Teresa to do. Comfort him, at the very least. She was open minded, believed in ghosts and ghouls far more than Mark ever had, but the way she stared at him, with such incredulity, he knew there would be no acceptance, no relief. Nor was it a loving gaze—searching her face in the harsh morning light, he could have sworn she hated him. The anger and disgust in her eyes was unmistakable.

"You—" she bit out, then stopped, bottom lip gripped between her teeth.

He sat back, eyes wide. "What have I done to make you so angry?"

The laugh she gave was almost a sob. She shook her head, pushed away from the table, and went back to lie down in their bedroom. When Mark peeked in on her later, she was lying on his side of the bed, staring up at the corner, tears running down either side of her face.

So he was alone with it. There was no one else he could think to tell, and after a reaction like that from his own wife, he doubted he'd have the courage to try.

Instead, he began to study the Other. He watched it from the corner of his eye so he didn't have to meet its gaze, could pretend it didn't see him doing it. He soon found the Other was with him a large part of the time. Not just at night, watching and looming; it rode behind him on his way to work. It perched in the darkest corner of the fluorescent-lit office where he spent most of his days. Days that bled into each other, where Mark was a drone among other drones, exchanging little more than hellos with his co-workers. He realized, after a time, that they were treating him differently, too. There'd be odd looks exchanged whenever he entered a room, or often after he finished a phone call. He'd try frantically to remember what he'd said, whether it had been over the top or embarrassing, but the details always escaped him. His memories were like smoke dissipating as soon as he tried to touch them, and he was left with nothing he could trust.

Shuffling into the break room for coffee one morning, he interrupted a low-voiced conversation between two of the women in accounts receivable. He searched his mind for their names, Tina, and maybe Sarah? He wasn't confident enough with either to address them individually, so he settled for a polite smile. The silence stretched as he poured himself a cup, and he looked up, planning to make some genial observation to alleviate the awkwardness. The wide-eyed stares and pursed lips on the faces of both women stopped him, and instead he ducked his head and hurried away. *What the fuck did I do?*

It went on that way, with conversations ending abruptly when he came into sight, his co-workers avoiding him, whispers and stares behind his back. It was obvious to Mark, as dazed as he was, that even if they couldn't see it, other people knew the Other was there. He wanted to tell them, to scream that it wasn't him, he wasn't the problem, but he knew it wouldn't help. They thought Mark himself was oozing the sense of wrongness into the atmosphere, and his isolation and fear increased every day.

He tried once more to speak to Teresa, to tell her how it was affecting his work, his wellbeing, but she just uttered a shattered laugh.

"Your mental fucking wellbeing, huh? Well, boo fucking hoo." She stomped out of the kitchen and a minute later, he heard her thumping and slamming in their shared bedroom. He was too afraid to follow her, slunk to the back porch instead, where he didn't have to listen. By the time he crept back in the house after nightfall, her things had been moved to the seldom used guest bedroom.

He sat at the kitchen table and tried not to cry. Teresa never treated him like this. She was the most empathetic, loving woman he'd ever met. She didn't care that he was a grown man in his forties. She encouraged him to feel his emotions, to be honest with her, to take care of himself. She'd done much to reverse the damage his own father had caused him, one of those toxic He-man types who browbeat any sign of weakness or humanity out of his young son. It didn't make sense for her to dismiss him like this, to make fun of his attempt to communicate with her. Why was she so angry? What had he done? He couldn't remember.

It was that black hole in his memory that kept him off balance, prevented him from calling her on her cruel behavior. It was all out of proportion to what was going on, so her outbursts weren't about the here and now. He must have done something in one of those fugues, bad enough for her to still be this angry, and it was worse that he couldn't remember what it was. Had he cheated on her? Surely not—he'd never been tempted to do so in all their time together. He wasn't that kind of a man.

But was she that kind of woman? Mark noticed his wife's increasing distance, the way she barely acknowledged him. Sometimes he'd turn and catch her watching him, a look of open disgust or fury on her heart-shaped face. She spent most of her time in the house away from him, doors locked between them. Heading to bed alone one night he'd passed the guest room and stopped when he heard her voice. Thinking maybe she was calling good night to him, he waited, but it soon became clear she was on the phone. Hating himself, he crept closer, pressing his ear to the door. He couldn't make out her words, but her tone was passionate, upset, and he crept away. Was she speaking to a lover? The thought of it twisted a knife deep in his gut. He wanted to confront her, but whenever he thought of her doing such a thing to him, he wanted to vomit. He didn't know what he'd do if he lost her to another man.

So he kept his silence. Not asking her, not pausing at her door to listen, instead covering his ears when the sounds of her secret conversations reached him. He cultivated a deep, suffocating silence that permeated the entire house. It was dark in there, so dark. Why didn't the sunlight make it inside?

He thought, too, that someone might be sneaking into the house. He always tucked his running shoes under the tall wooden secretary that stood by the back door, but whenever he looked for them, he found them on a drying mat in the kitchen. He left his keys in his jacket pocket, only to find them hanging from a ring. The worst part was that these visitations seemed to take place while he was home, and he never saw who did it. It could have been Teresa, he supposed, but she never voluntarily came within ten feet of him, so why would she mess with his things? It was only later he started to think he might be the one doing it, which was somehow so much worse.

One morning he woke to agony in his legs and feet. He bit off a scream as he sat up, then looked down at the sheets, mouth agape. What he saw made no sense. His feet were bare, dirty, and abraded. Dried mud clung to his skin, from his feet halfway up his calves. Blood oozed from a dozen open cuts, smearing the sheets with dark brown stains. Two of his toes felt broken, and muddy footprints led from the back door all the way to the side of his bed. Had he been sleepwalking? He must have been, but it had never happened before. What the hell was wrong with him? What was he doing all these nights when he wasn't himself? Could he be hurting people in his sleep, as he was hurting himself? Was that why so many people viewed him with distrust? Had he earned it, somewhere in the darkness of a mind that was no longer completely his?

Once he came home from the grocery, and as he stood putting food away, he was frozen by the box of cereal he held in his hand. Peanut Butter Captain Crunch? He was a Raisin Bran man, and had no memory of picking it up. He was staring at it, bemused, when Teresa came in the kitchen. She stopped, her eyes on the cereal, and tears started to her eyes. Before he could go to her, she was gone again. He couldn't explain her reaction, why a box of kid's cereal would upset her so much, but there was so much he didn't understand these days.

Was it dementia? Was that why he was so confused, felt so disconnected? Or was he suffering from some other mental illness? The swathes of unaccounted for time, the inescapable reality that he was going walkabout in the middle of the night. Personality changes could explain the way Teresa acted around him, the strange way his co-workers treated him. Maybe he was having a breakdown, or had done something awful in a fugue state. That would explain his feelings of being out of place and just plain *wrong*. Crazy people never think they're crazy; at least he thought he'd heard that before. Yet another argument in favor of an organic cause.

It was the claw marks that convinced him. He woke up in worse pain than usual, a stinging bite across his back, chest, and genitals. His hands flew to his crotch in a protective gesture—what the hell was wrong with his dick? He limped to the bathroom naked, seeing his pajamas crumpled on the bedroom floor, torn in jagged strips. Standing in front of the mirror, he saw deep, bloody scratches in long sets of four, repeated over and over across his body. The tender flesh of his penis and scrotum clawed and bloody, the sight enough to make him gag. How the fuck had this happened? Had Teresa done this? Filled with rage, had she snuck in here and done it while he was sleeping? Feeling the sharp, nauseating throb of pain, he didn't understand how he could have slept through such an attack. Nothing made sense, until he noticed the thick chunks of dried skin and blood stuck beneath his nails.

He broke down, hunched over naked on the cold bathroom tiles, head in his hands, his filthy fingertips held away from his face. How could he have done this to himself and not noticed? Not woken even when he'd clawed his own penis, drawn blood from his scrotum? No, something inside him was *making* him do these things to himself.

Possession. The thought, once it struck, was blinding in its clarity. It sounded nuts, but it felt right. Nothing else explained his behavior, the things he'd done to himself, the way his memories weren't his own. That had to be it, didn't it? And even if it wasn't, even if the very conclusion was a defense mechanism of an altered mind, it was something. A direction, a course of action, even if it was the wrong one. It would be better than standing still.

He gulped back tears, stood, and met his own bloodshot eyes in the mirror. He needed to get help. It didn't matter whether Teresa believed him or not—she was at risk here, too. If he could cause this much damage to himself and not even feel it, what might he do to her in the same state? Even as much as her behavior hurt him, he loved her and couldn't bear the thought of causing her pain.

Mark knew little about exorcisms. He was a lapsed Presbyterian, and things like that weren't covered in his confirmation classes. Teresa was the horror buff, but he'd watched *The Exorcist* with her, and a few other movies along the same lines. It seemed pretty clear that a first step was to enlist the help of an exorcist, a priest of some kind.

Though they'd never once attended church as a couple, both of them in agreement that their time could be better spent, Teresa came from a Catholic family. He'd met the priest from the church she'd grown up in several times—Father Xavier was a favorite guest at all holiday celebrations at his in-laws'. Mark would have preferred someone from his own faith, if only so he didn't feel like he was poaching, but he didn't even know if there were Presbyterian exorcists. So, Father Xavier it would be.

When Mark called him, the priest sounded surprised, then wary. After some hesitation, Father Xavier agreed to a meet at his church, which created another worry for Mark. If he was possessed, could he enter sacred ground? Or would the demon who might even now be clutching tight to his mind and soul prevent him from crossing the threshold?

When he arrived, the priest stood just inside the church doors and beckoned him forward. Mark took a deep breath and crossed, but nothing happened. No lightning, no fire and brimstone. No melting away like the Wicked Witch of the West. He felt a little uncomfortable in the face of all that opulence and history, but that would be true of any church.

Xavier watched him, his mouth grim, then chose one of the crimson cushioned pews. "Sit, please," he said, indicating the row behind his own, twisted so that he was in profile. An unconscious reminder of the confessional? Mark wondered as he sat where he was told.

"Tell me why you're here," Xavier said, his tone on the unwelcoming side of stern.

It was daunting, but Mark reminded himself this was Teresa's priest. She might have been confiding in him all along, and who knew what she might have said? Perhaps the man had reason to distrust him.

In a disjointed fashion, he told Xavier everything, all that he could remember. The feeling of haze and unease in his own home, the way it seemed like the Other had control of his body at times. Its looming presence in his home and car.

"I think it's affecting my wife, Father Xavier," he said, his voice breaking. "She looks at me like she doesn't know me, and it hurts so much. I'm so afraid of what I might have done to make her feel that way. I'm afraid of what I might do."

When Mark finished, Xavier continued to watch him, his mouth pursed, dark eyes unreadable. He tapped one finger against his lips. Mark was having trouble holding the priest's gaze, lifting his eyes instead to the soaring, ornate ceiling of the cathedral, his heart at first lightened by the beauty of the structure, before he found it again. The darkness. The Other.

He could have cried. It was here, even in a church, it had followed him. It had no respect for boundaries, spiritual or otherwise, and Mark felt defeated. As he watched, eyes wide, mouth open, the thing skittered at impossible speeds across the ceiling and down the huge pipe organ that took up the entire back of the church. It moved in an almost stop-motion fashion, jerky in the flickering light of the prayer candles, but it didn't stop when it reached the floor. Instead, it came for him.

"What the hell?" Mark cowered, scooted along the pew until he reached the end. He was certain it was here for him, that this time, in broad daylight—and in the presence of a priest, no less—it would stake its claim.

Then it stopped, just behind the priest, who looked as though he hadn't noticed Mark's irrational behavior, or the movements of the Other. It stood behind Xavier and pressed close, a whisper in his ear.

The man's eyes narrowed. "What exactly is it you wish me to do, Mr. Beckham?"

Mark frowned, sat up, his eyes still on the Other. "Isn't it obvious? I want you to get rid of it. I want to be the only one in this body. Don't you understand that? How can I live like this, with someone else trying to control me half the time?"

The priest's lips curled in derision. "That's what I thought you'd say."

He stood, stepped away from Mark. "You need to leave, Mr. Beckham. I can't help you. I *won't* help you."

Mark scrambled to his feet, staring at the priest. "How can you say that? How can you turn me away? I came to you for help."

"Because you are unclean. You are unholy, and I will not help you achieve your aim. I answer to a higher power than you, sir."

Mark sputtered, stung. Was this real life? Were priests allowed to do this? He could have understood disbelief, but not condemnation. "You're supposed to be about forgiveness—whatever I've done, whatever Teresa's told you, you have to believe I didn't know what I was doing. I would never —"

Xavier stepped closer, loomed over Mark, fury on his quivering face. "You dare to speak her name. Get out of my church! Out, out, out!"

Mark turned and ran. He had no choice—he believed, in that moment, the priest would strike him, would drive him from the church if he didn't leave himself.

For hours after he left, Mark wandered the streets of downtown, feeling lost. His confusion didn't last though, as the answer to the priest's behavior struck him like a lightning bolt.

The affair—Teresa's affair. The man Mark's wife had been having hushed conversations with, the man who may or may not have been creeping through Mark's house, moving things around. Making him doubt himself, making him think he was crazy. It was so obvious he could have kicked himself. The priest was older, but not by much, and his dark good looks had caught the attention of many a female parishioner. Of course it was Xavier, and of course the man didn't want to help Mark—he was only waiting for his chance, for Mark to be out of the way.

He wanted to believe they were the source of the whole infestation, that Xavier and Teresa had orchestrated his descent, his insanity. But the presence of the Other could not be denied. It stuck close to him as he wandered the dusky streets, the sky gray and heavy. Rain had threatened for weeks now, but he couldn't remember a time when the world hadn't been gray. And still the thing haunted his footsteps. It even showed up in his reflection as he stopped at storefronts to peer inside. A looming, dark shape, coming ever closer. He shuddered, refusing to look over his shoulder.

Mark was so intent on avoiding his reflection that he almost missed the sign for the healer. He would have if it hadn't been hanging so low, the iron post it was attached to leaning just enough that it grazed his hair as he passed.

He half screamed, jerked to the side, and almost stepped into the street, certain it was the Other, finally strong enough to manifest. A hand reached out to steady him—warm, real, feminine, a thick sweater bunched to the elbow. A kind face looked up at him. Round behind glasses, hair frizzed up in the damp. She could have been almost any age.

"Sorry about that," she said. "Been meaning to get it fixed. Scares the daylights out of people when they're in their own heads."

"It's…it's okay," choked Mark. "I'm all right."

Her smile faded as she looked at him, still not breaking contact. "That's not quite true, is it? You're not all right at all. Why don't you come inside? I was just making coffee."

He felt like he should say no. It was likely a come on, a hoaxing sales pitch. But the shop behind her was as warm as her interest, and Mark so wanted to be warm. He felt like he'd been encased in a cold, damp fog for ages.

Mark settled in a comfortable chair by a fire, a hot cup of excellent coffee she'd made in his hand. She sat across from him and smiled.

"No one ever comes here by accident, you understand."

"No?" he asked, casting a glance around the shop. There were shelves of books and cases of esoteric items, the sort of thing Teresa would call *woo woo*. "What exactly do you do here?"

The woman smiled again. "I'm a healer. My name is Angela."

He shook her outstretched hand, and she lost her smile again. He let her go, hunched back away from her. "What's the matter?"

She shook her head. "Sorry, it's just so…obvious. You need help, don't you? You need healing."

He glanced at her herbs and bowls and incense burners again before dropping his gaze to his lap. "I don't think you can heal what's wrong with me,"

She sat up, one eyebrow arched. "No? Is that because the Catholics failed? You think they're the only ones who can get rid of an unwanted spirit?"

He stared at her. "What the hell? Have you been following me?"

One corner of her mouth lifted. "Well, no. You absolutely reek of the incense they use at Saint Francis's."

Mark laughed, relaxing again. "Neat trick."

She grinned back at him. "It is, isn't it? Of course, that doesn't explain how I know about the spirit sharing space inside of you." She put a hand up when he would have spoken. "Don't bother to deny it. I can see it plain as day. You want things to be put right, don't you? Everything back in its proper place?"

He still felt as though he should deny it, but that was stupid. He needed help, and maybe this odd woman could give it to him. He nodded. "More than anything."

She leaned closer, her blue eyes hard, scanning him. "You're sure about that? This kind of healing has everything to do with intent, so if you're not committed to making things right, we might as well not even start."

He set the coffee cup down with a bang. "I want it right. It's all I want, and there's nothing I wouldn't do to get it that way. That clear enough for you?"

She kept up that hard, searching stare another long minute before smiling again. The strange woman stood. "Then what are we waiting for? Let's get you home."

He couldn't quite believe how quickly things were happening, but since Angela seemed intent on accompanying him home, to start the healing as soon as possible, he went along with it. The thought that he could end this living hell gave him a buoyancy he wouldn't have expected. He didn't even think about how it would look, bringing a strange woman home with him, without any warning.

As he unlocked the front door, he apologized for the mess, the smell, the damp and gloomy atmosphere. His excuses dried up as he realized he wasn't the only one who'd brought company. When they stepped into the living room, two figures rose from the couch. Mark peered into the worsening gloom and recognized Father Xavier with a jolt of anger.

"Who the hell is that?" said Teresa, and he could barely believe her audacity.

Xavier laid a hand on her shoulder, stepped in front of her. Blocking him from his own wife. "Don't engage, Teresa. We've talked about this."

"Don't *engage*? With her own husband? Is that what you've been coaching her to do? You sick bastard," Mark snarled, hands curled into fists at his side.

There was a flutter of movement in his peripheral vision, and the room darkened further, the damp almost a rolling mist advancing through the house. It shouldn't have been possible, but then he saw it. The Other, slinking in to loom behind the priest's shoulder, as it had at the church.

Mark gave a choked laugh. "It's with you, isn't it? Or you're with it. However you want to look at it."

That warm hand fell on his arm again, and Mark stepped back. He looked down at Angela. "Do you see it?" he asked, his tone begging her.

She smiled, nodded, patted his arm. "Plain as day. It's right there behind the priest."

Xavier looked behind him, but saw nothing.

Teresa shrunk away but glared at Angela. "Who *are* you? And what do you think you're doing in my home?"

Angela stepped in front of Mark, her smile brighter than ever. "I'm here to help, Mrs. Beckham. This man has told me he needs an exorcism. I'm going to give it to him."

Mark waited for what they would say, ready to defend his request, but Teresa only cried, big tears welling in her eyes.

The priest shook his head. "Don't you think we've already tried that?"

His words were like cold water down Mark's spine. It was true. He was possessed. There was something else in his body *right now*. They knew it too, but had kept him in the dark. He wanted to break down all over again, his eyes on his wife.

"You knew, and you still treated me this way?" he asked, desperate for some sign of remorse, of love, of humanity from her, but she wouldn't look at him.

Angela turned and took his hands, and again it was the warmest part of his body. Only around her did he finally feel free of the damp and hazy darkness.

"It's all right. I thought that might have been the case. It explains your disorientation, the way you're only half seated in there. The way some of your memories are his, and some are yours. A failed exorcism leaves its own marks."

The priest stiffened at her words. Mark smiled, glad she'd gotten a barb in under his smug armor. Failed, yeah. Just like he'd failed in his Christian duty to help Mark when he'd begged him.

Angela turned to face the other two again but kept one of Mark's hands in her own. "I have different methods than yours, Father. Call it a holistic approach. I might be able to fix this, but I could use your help." She smiled at Teresa. "Both of you, if you're up to it."

Mark wasn't sure how he got there, but before long he was lying in his bedroom, his cold, empty gray bedroom, staring up at the ceiling. The Other loomed there, that endless, soul-sucking darkness staring him right in the eyes.

Xavier stood out of the way, at the head of the bed. Teresa knelt next to him while Angela finished her preparations. They weren't extensive—candles, sage, some bustling little activities just out of sight. She hummed as she worked, and Mark found himself soothed by it, almost hypnotized. Until he looked up again and found himself eye to eye with the Other. It was lying on top of him, its cold, cold body covering his own. He was shaking, waiting for the fight for his body, for his soul. He felt its creeping presence press against him, this time worming its way into his ears, his nose, his eye sockets. It surged into his mouth when he opened it to scream, and he struggled, choking on the darkness that was filling his body. Trying to bat it away, to claw it away from him, but he couldn't gain purchase on its slippery surface. He turned his wild eyes upon the healer, who smiled again and patted his hand.

"It's all right. This is supposed to happen. It's part of the healing. Part of making everything right." She turned her gaze to his wife. "Teresa, this is the scary part. Can you hold his hand, please? Think about your husband. Hold him in your heart and mind, and keep that image there."

He felt her cold hand take his, and the fear abated, just a bit. He turned his head to see her, his vision almost obscured by the blackness that was seeping into every pore. She smiled back at him, tears in her eyes, and he felt, for the first time in a long while like this might be okay. Like he might make it out the other side as the man he'd once been.

Something blinded him, his body engulfed in freezing darkness, surrounded by rolling fog on all sides. The healer was speaking, but he couldn't make out the words. He only knew they were making the fog thicker, the damp colder. He no longer felt Teresa's hand, and he started to panic. He didn't know how much more of this he could take.

A wrenching pain shook him out of the thought, feeling as though his body had exploded at the molecular level. He screamed in silence, untethered, scattering through the heavens. It felt like he was flying, upside down and rolling over and over on an endless descent. Then he was falling, finally hitting the ground with a soul shaking thud.

"Mark?" It was Teresa's voice, thick with tears, but she seemed far away. "Mark honey, is that you? Did you come back to me?"

He tried to answer, but he had no voice.

"Squeeze my hand if you can hear me."

He tried, but he couldn't feel her hand at all. He opened his eyes, and couldn't understand what he was seeing.

It was himself, lying down on the bed, Teresa at his side, the priest and healer leaning over him. Had he died? Was this an out-of-body experience?

His body's eyes opened, then sat up, coughing. "Oh Jesus," said the mouth that had so recently been his. "Oh Christ, I thought he'd never leave. I thought I'd be stuck with him forever."

"Mark!" Teresa cried, and threw herself on his chest.

Mark—the other Mark—wrapped his arms around her, tucked his chin in those soft curls. "I never left. Even when I wasn't...inside, I stayed. I was here."

He watched as long as he could, bereft in a barren landscape. One he was starting to remember, to recognize. The place he called home until just a few weeks ago, when he'd found an open door, seeking in the night and the dark. He'd only wanted to be warm, he thought, as the fog pulled him in. The last thing he saw before he melted back into the damp, gray nothing, was the healer looking up at him, her smile sad, her tone apologetic.

"I *am* sorry, my dear," she said, her voice fading. "We had to set it right, and you weren't meant to be here."

And then he was alone again. In the dark, the damp, the mist. Alone and searching, for light, for warmth. For an open door.

Legion Cast Forth

by Robert Ford

Cletus Estep cracked the pull-tab on his first Budweiser of the day and took a long drink. The morning sun had barely risen over the horizon, and steam rose from the rippled tin roof of the hog barn.

He spit over the railing of his porch and then hitched up the rear of his torn jeans. Behind him, through the screen door, Cletus heard the sound of his wife Janice frying eggs and bacon, though he had to attend to some business first before breakfast.

A plain white van turned into his long dirt driveway, and Cletus watched it approach. He took another slurp of beer, set the can down on the railing, and then walked down the porch steps as the van slowed to a stop in the patch of mud. He hocked up and spit again before the van doors opened. The driver was tall and bald, and thick as an oak tree—the kind of man who had a second job as a weekend bouncer at the roughest bar in town.

The man who got out of the passenger side was a familiar face to Cletus—Father Thomas Monahan.

"Mornin' Mr. Estep." The priest approached and put his hand out to shake.

Cletus took it, though he hated doing it. The skin of the man's hand felt too smooth—almost silky—and it was all too evident to Cletus the man had never seen a day of hard work in his life. "Mornin' Father Monahan. Whatcha got for me today?"

Mr. Oak Tree opened the rear doors of the van and Cletus saw an ambulance gurney with a man lying on it, wrists and ankles bound to the aluminum frame with leather straps. The man lifted his head, leveled his gaze on Cletus, and then began making a mix of growls speckled with foul language.

Father Monahan grimaced and turned away. "Only one for me today, though I hear Donovan will be along shortly as well. He's got the paperwork for both of us."

"Father Donovan works up in the city, yeah?" Cletus kept watching the man on the hospital gurney, the way the man's eyes rolled in their sockets like miniature Magic 8-Balls. Dark circles rested below those wild eyes. The man snapped his mouth and bit at the air, his growls low and rumbling in his throat.

The priest cleared his throat. "He does, yes. It's been…very active there lately."

"Active, yeah. About that." Cletus turned to Father Monahan. "It's about time we talked about rates again. I mean, as many as has been coming in lately, it's only—"

"You'll have to talk to the main office about that, Mr. Estep." Father Monahan put up his hand in protest. "I'm only a man of God. I don't control the—"

"*Purse strings*. Yeah, you've said that before. It's just, I'm a simple farmer, and every single hog the church—"

"Mr. Estep, I apologize, I do. But I have no say in the matter." The priest turned away from Cletus as Mr. Oak Tree stood waiting as the van's electric lift descended with a loud whine. As the base of the lift touched ground, the man on the gurney thrashed in place. Mr. Oak Tree's thick hands gripped the aluminum frame behind the man's head and he wheeled the gurney across the muddy driveway.

Father Monahan walked away backwards, still speaking to Cletus. "Call the head office. That's a business matter."

"Yeah, all right…just that—"

The man on the gurney growled loudly into the morning air and then made lewd licking motions with his tongue, pale as a hunk of fatback. His voice was low and gruff, sounds like scuffing a boot over road grit. "Bring me Mother Mary! Let me lick that bitch—"

"Do you have a vessel chosen?" Father Monahan interrupted, speaking over the foul things the man on the gurney continued to spew.

Cletus chewed on his lower lip and stared at the priest. "There's a big sow in the second stall, spotted with big black and white splotches. You'll see her."

Father Monahan gave a curt nod and walked toward the hog barn, Mr. Oak Tree pushing the gurney behind him.

Cletus watched for a moment and stepped back onto his porch, grabbing the Budweiser for another drink. The cold can felt good in his hands, almost like it could erase the smooth, waxy feeling of the priest's handshake. Cletus's palm was slick, as if someone had rubbed bacon fat over his skin.

Another van—this one a pale shade of blue—turned into the drive and came to a stop beside the first vehicle. Cletus took a seat and waited until Father Donovan got out of the van and approached, holding a yellow slip of paper in front of him, like an Easter flower. "Good morning, Mr. Estep. Here's the delivery receipts for today, me and Father—"

"Monahan, too. Yeah, he mentioned." Cletus cleared his throat. "Wouldn't happen to know who I could talk to at the head office about a raise in price, do ya?"

Father Donovan shook his head. "Ain't a single one of 'em whose ass wouldn't pucker up tight as an altar boy's if you asked 'em for a few dollars more. Best bet is to call Karen in the accounting department. That nun's older than the Dead Sea Scrolls, but see how far you can get with her."

Cletus nodded. "Thank ya, Father. Appreciate it."

Behind him, a man the size of a pro-wrestler wrenched a gurney from inside the van onto an electric lift. Midway through the lift's descent, it jolted in place and then hit the gravel driveway hard. The thin teenage girl strapped to the mattress pad released a wildcat shriek. Cletus turned away as the girl threw up on her chest in an incredibly impressive spew of brown.

"Got a vessel in mind? Something without tusks, preferably. This one is a bit…" Father Donovan glanced at the girl, writhing on the gurney and jerking at the leather straps that held her in place. "Unruly."

Cletus stood from his chair to get a better look at the girl, and the smell of piss and shit made him wince. Her long hair was greasy and twisted out from her head in clusters. She lifted her head from the thin gurney pad and glared at him. Snot ran in rivulets from the girl's nose, and she flicked her tongue out to lick it off her upper lip and pulled the slimy string back into her mouth.

"Yeah, there's uh… stall four. All white sow with one black spot on her back." Cletus felt a chill rush through him as the girl's focus remained fixed on him. Those eyes were anything but the eyes of a teenage girl. They looked ancient.

"Tathan Ba liiiiiivvvvessss!" The girl screamed, and the pro-wrestler swatted her on the side of her head.

"Steven!" Father Donovan's tone was harsh, and the big man gave a light shrug before he began pushing the gurney toward the barn. The priest stood in place, watching, and then sighed as he lowered his head. "Now there was a herd of many swine feeding there on the mountain, and the demons implored Him to permit them to enter the swine."

"And He gave them permission." Cletus uttered the response in a monotone, wondering how many times he had said those words over the past five years.

Father Donovan nodded and headed toward the barn.

Cletus listened to the crunch of gravel beneath the man's shoes. How often had he heard the sound of a priest's footsteps heading toward one of his barns? How many priests had come here in the past five years, delivering vans full of evil?

He raised the can of Budweiser and took a three-count swallow. It was quiet inside the house, which meant Janice was done making breakfast. Cletus sat a moment longer, listening to the litany of screams coming from his hog barn, and then he finished off the can of beer and crumpled it in his fist. Tossing it toward the others in the corner of his porch, Cletus went inside, anger beginning to burn him up inside.

The living room of the farmhouse was simple but as weathered as the peeling gray clapboard on the outside. The coffee table had dog-eared stacks of *Field & Stream* and *National Hog Farmer* magazines, along with a few empty cans of Budweiser and a crumpled bag of Middleswarth barbecue chips. Faded wallpaper as old as President Truman decorated the walls, along with a few photos and a watercolor painting of a covered bridge in a frame too ornate for the subject matter.

Cletus walked past the living room, into the small kitchen, and took a seat at the table. The fried eggs were speckled with pepper and the strips of bacon perfectly crisped, just as he liked it. *Janice might be as smart as a box of frozen broccoli,* Cletus thought, *but she's a damned fine cook.*

Janice was at the kitchen sink, pouring the grease from a cast-iron skillet into an empty pickle jar. "Breakfast is better when it's hot. Wasn't sure you was gonna make it in time."

"Damned leeches in white collars. No one knows anything 'bout how to give us more money, but they damned sure know how to deliver demo—"

"Honey, you know I don't like hearin' about it."

"Just that these holy fuckers come here half a dozen times a week and expect—"

"Cletus." The tone of her voice wasn't harsh. Instead, it was calm and cool, the patient, Zen-tone of a librarian speaking to students whispering too loud.

"Yeah, all right, Punkin. All right." Cletus stabbed into the hard yolk of an egg and sliced it with his fork, shoveling a bite into his mouth. The pepper stung but it felt good. It mingled with his anger just fine.

He ate in silence as Janice puttered around the kitchen counter, cleaning and tidying as she went. Wasn't long before Cletus heard the engines of the vans start up again, and the sound faded as they drove away.

Crunching on his last strip of bacon, Cletus stared at the patterns of grease and egg on his plate.

I'm gonna call the head office. I'm barely scraping by while these bastards pay me a hundred dollars a head to come out to my farm and stuff demons into my hogs. Hell no, enough is enough. They're out there fartin' in silk sheets, livin' large off them church donations. Here I am, with a ten-year-old rusty heap of a pick-up and back taxes.

Cletus savored the last bits of bacon in his mouth, wiped a flannel-covered forearm across his face, and pushed away from the table.

"Enough for you?"

"Plenty, Punkin, plenty. Delicious as always." Cletus left his plate on the table and headed toward the living room, taking a seat on the flower-patterned sofa. He reached for the black rotary phone on the end table, picked it up, and held it for a moment. Cletus took a deep breath and released it, trying to calm himself before he made the call. He pushed a fat fingertip against the plastic holes of the rotary, and dialed the number from memory.

"Vatican Services, how may I direct your call?"

"Accounting department, Karen, ple—"

The tone went silent before Cletus finished his sentence, and he heard the sound of a ringing phone on the other end.

Seven, eight, nine.

"Accounting, how may I help you?"

"Hello, I'm trying to reach Karen. I was told—"

"This is Karen."

Cletus leaned back against the couch cushions. "Yeah, Karen, this is Cletus Estep. I run the Relocation Farm out in Glen Rock, Pennsylvania and—"

"How may I help you, Mr. Estep?"

Karen's tone was sharp and impatient. It made heat course through Cletus' veins.

He exhaled slowly, his grip tightening on the phone receiver. "I'm calling to discuss a rise in billing rates."

"Current contracts for existing Relocation Farms aren't up for renegotiations until the end of term, Mr. Estep, and your contract is..." There were clicking sounds on a computer keyboard. "In effect for another eighteen months."

"Yes, I..." Cletus gritted his teeth. "I understand that, but I hadn't realized how many hogs the church would be—"

"I'm sorry, Mr. Estep. That is a consideration of business you should have undertaken at the start of placing your contract bid with the head office. We do appreciate working with you as a vendor, and look forward to discussing new terms as we near the close of your existing contract."

Her nasally voice made pains shoot between his eyes. "Yes, but if you could just take a look at the contract, you'll see there was an expectation of—" Cletus heard a click on the end of the line. "Hello?"

Dead air.

"Hello? Karen?"

Nothing but a long quiet on the other end.

"Motherfuckers!" Cletus slammed the phone back down in its cradle, and Janice came running into the living room.

"Honey! What's wrong?" She held a kitchen towel in her hands, a wide-eyed expression on her face.

"Those sons o' bitches at the Vatican, vaults of gold bars and valuables in the basement, and I'm drivin' around in an old rust-bucket Ford because I can't afford to get a new one. That's what." He rose from the couch and clenched his fists at his sides. "Should've known not to trust 'em. Not a damned one of 'em."

Janice opened her mouth like a goldfish trying to breathe, and then closed it again without saying a word.

Movement from beyond the living room window caught the attention of Cletus. A rig was making its way down the driveway. Boden Meats was emblazoned on the side of the metal-slatted trailer in large yellow letters with thick black outlines.

The company had been around close to a hundred years and prided themselves on having the freshest meat products in the region. And more importantly, the company distributed everything from rump roasts and chops, to sausages, bacon, and pork rinds to the surrounding five counties.

A slight smile appeared on his face, and as Cletus watched the rig back its trailer up toward the barn, he unclenched his fists and his smile widened into a grin.

Janice took a step away from him, and then another.

Cletus turned to his wife, that lopsided grin still smeared on his face, and Janice hurried away into the kitchen. He glanced at the rotary phone. "Negotiate this, assholes."

It took over an hour, but Cletus and the driver loaded over a hundred hogs into the truck, and Cletus watched the plump sow with black and white splotches waddle up the ramp into the trailer. He caught a glimpse of the pig's eyes—deep and dark with blown-out pupils. The wisdom there, the...*experience*.

After the priests began to come to the farm, seeing the change in the eyes of the pigs had always unnerved Cletus. Changing from the eyes of an animal to something else, something *otherworldly*.

"Whew! Goddamn, these pigs're a bit feisty today!" The driver locked up the rear gate of the trailer, and then took his hat off and wiped his arm over his sweaty forehead.

"Got a little fire in 'em today, don't they?" Cletus smiled.

As the driver walked back to the rig and got in, Cletus stepped to the side and stared through the slats of the trailer. The grunts and snorts inside as the hogs jostled against one another stopped in unison, until even the sound of their cloven feet against the metal planks went quiet. All along the gap in the side of the trailer, Cletus saw them glaring at him—a long, silent row of beady black eyes.

Cletus whispered to them. "You all have fun out there."

They erupted at his words, clamoring against each other, the calm shattered to pieces. Cletus listened to the noises they made. Over time, you began to understand the different sounds they made. Sometimes it was aggression. Other times, plain hunger. Hell, they even made certain noises when they were playing with each other. But now, the squeals coming from inside the trailer were very specific. The low snorts and grunts, high-pitched shrieks—these were different.

The hogs were *excited*.

For three days, Cletus went through his daily routine on the farm—distributing feed and clearing manure from the hog barn. The grunts and squeals from the *clean* hogs that remained, were content and happy. The glint in their eyes was born of simple animal desires and held none of the deeper intelligence of the hogs hauled away in the back of the trailer.

Father Monahan came back on the second day with two gurneys in the back of his van, holding two men screaming obscenities at the top of their lungs like dueling lunatics. Cletus smiled and nodded. "Stalls four and seven on the right."

The priest and his driver pushed the gurneys toward the barn, and when they came out an hour later, the men strapped down were as calm and placid as could be. They wore bewildered expressions on their faces, confused and disoriented, as they were loaded back into the van.

From the barn, the two demon-filled pigs squealed with rage. Cletus stood from his chair on the porch, crumpled his Budweiser can and tossed it with the others, and then walked inside the house for dinner.

Janice had made meatloaf and set plates of it on tray stands in the living room. Cletus grabbed a fresh beer from the fridge, popped the tab, and took a seat on the battered couch. The TV was on and Cletus made a face at the image. The flat screen was only a few years old and was a cheap model to begin with. The upper left of the screen was splotched with darkened areas so the evening news anchor appeared to have patches of sunburn across his face and stains on his gray suit. Cletus glanced through the living room window at his old rusted truck and then gritted his teeth. He was tired of the *we'll-make-do-with-what-we've-got* attitude.

The newscaster began speaking about the spike in violent crimes taking place in the area. A murder-suicide with a husband and wife in a high-end neighborhood community. A murder at a gas station—an argument over something trivial that ended with a man shoving a gas nozzle into another man's eye socket.

Janice almost choked on a bite of her meatloaf over that one.

Cletus held his beer mid-way toward his mouth and smiled.

A spike in bar fights. Arguments ending in bloody hospital visits at schools, churches, even a hospital over in Waylon County.

Each and every county Boden Meats distributed their products to.

He drained the last of his beer can and set it aside. Cletus didn't even want another one tonight. He turned to Janice, who had switched to her knitting needles as the news continued. "C'mon woman, put that shit down. Let's go upstairs and get a little spunky."

She giggled, stared at him and gauged how serious he was, and then tossed her knitting needles aside, racing upstairs ahead of him.

That night, Cletus had the best night's sleep he'd had in months.

Over the next few days, the news got worse. Even the governor was concerned, throwing out a theory about underground gases leaking in the region, and requesting the EPA be called in to do some testing.

Robberies. Assaults. Arson. Rapes. A man stabbed his wife and mother-in-law with a grilling fork during an after-church barbeque, then pushed his father-in-law's head into the grill itself and slammed the lid in place.

Each report of chaos made Cletus smile more. In fact, he'd even gone to whistling happy little tunes around the house, leading Janice to avoid him during these unusual moments of joy, an emotion he was certain she'd never seen Cletus have once in their nineteen years of marriage.

The vans kept coming in—sometimes twice a day now—and Cletus kept watching his bank account as the direct deposits flowed in.

Father Donovan and Monahan looked haggard when they arrived. Two other priests—young, fresh recruits—began arriving. Cletus never even bothered to introduce himself, only sat on his porch and watched them wheel thrashing, wailing bodies into the barn. Sometimes Cletus would listen to their prayers of exorcism as they cast the demons out into his hogs. Other times, he'd smile to himself and head on inside to watch an episode of *Days of Our Lives* with Janice.

No negotiations on price? Well then, I'll make it up in volume, you holy bastards, he thought.

Cletus had to spend some of it to buy new hogs to bring in, but it would be spring soon and he expected to have a banner year of piglets, more than enough to replenish his farm. There was more though, more *opportunity*, and Cletus knew it.

He rose one sunny morning and headed to the barn, walking the rows between the stalls until he picked one sow in her prime. He stood in front of the wooden slats and eyed her up. She stared back at Cletus and grunted, opening her wide mouth and baring her teeth. The sow chomped, making a thick popping sound.

Those eyes, those goddamned eyes. How many hells have they seen?

"Ready to look through a new set of eyes, ol' girl?"

The sow grunted and let out a squeal, her hooves clicking in place.

Cletus raised a pair of electric pliers in his hand, reached over the rails and jolted the old sow with current. Her thick body fell to the cement, her legs twitching, and Cletus stepped into the stall, withdrew the butcher knife from the sheath on his side, and slit the sow's throat as she lay there, those black, knowing eyes, watching him the entire time.

It took Cletus the better part of the day to slaughter the hog by himself, but in the end, he had a table stacked with pork shoulders and ribs, ham hocks and pork belly, cuts of loin, legs, and a stack of pork chops. He took great care as he worked and wrapped them in white paper packaging, put them all in the cold storage locker at the rear of the barn. When he was finished, he headed to the house to wash off and sit on the porch for a while, sipping cold beer tasting of the satisfaction of a long day's work.

On the eleven o'clock news, Cletus sat by himself in the living room and watched. The governor was calling in the National Guard to help control a riot at a boarding school up north. Half a dozen teachers had been murdered at the school, and though details were unclear, it sounded like students were holding the headmaster hostage, though they hadn't made any demands.

To the south, in Coster County, a minor fender bender on Route 81 resulted in absolute chaos on the highway. A pregnant woman with a tire iron murdered a truck driver on a long haul from New Jersey. A police officer on the scene had been shot and then stuffed into the rear of a garbage truck and compacted.

In Harrington County, a dog catcher's wife went crazy at a hair salon appointment, stabbing a hairdresser in the throat with her cutting shears and then biting the face of a FedEx man as he delivered a package. Drugs were believed to have been involved.

Cletus grinned and pushed the off button on the TV remote.

Tomorrow, he'd deliver all of his freshly cut pork to the local market. It was time to deliver the goods right here in town.

He turned off the living room lights and stood at the screen door for a moment. Cletus could hear the hogs squealing and bellowing out in the darkness.

Janice poured Cletus a thermos of hot coffee and handed it over to him as he came into the house. "Long day ahead, and maybe this'll help."

"Thank ya, darlin'. And oh… I think I'll be done early today." He grinned and noticed Janice stepped away from him. He paid no mind to her reaction and headed out the door to his truck, whistling as he walked.

The price on the meat Cletus brought to market had always been fair—low enough to compete with the local grocers, but priced slightly higher because of the freshness. But that day, Cletus ran a sale on everything he had brought. Two and a half hours later, he found himself wiping down his empty vendor booth at market, a wad of cash in his pocket, and a gratified smile on his face.

He recognized the faces of some people that bought from him. Faces of some who had once stood outside the municipal building and protested about a pig farm in the area. How much it stunk. How it lowered property values. This, that, and the other.

Cletus only smiled at them as he handed over bundled packages of rump roast and pork chops. Reputation had gotten around about his meats—how fresh and tender they were, almost sweet—and people had lined up at his booth. He pulled the canvas cloth over his empty meat counter and draped it over the glass, taking a moment to smooth out wrinkles, and then Cletus whistled as he walked from the market and headed to his rusty old Ford.

The phone rang as Cletus walked inside the farmhouse and he glanced at it as he paused in the hallway. It rang twice more and went quiet.

Callin' to negotiate prices now? He smiled. *I'll let you stew on it a while. I'm sure you'll be calling back.*

Cletus continued on and met Janice in the kitchen. "Toldja I'd be back early." He kissed her on the cheek and she smiled at him as she continued marinating pork chops in her large blue ceramic bowl. "Deliveries today?"

"Five of 'em." Janice nodded. "Well, five *vans*. Don't know how many they…you know I don't like seeing 'em like that." She put the bowl of chops into the fridge and turned to him, wiping her hands on a kitchen towel. "They left the paperwork out on the front porch."

"Good, good." Cletus pulled a can of beer from the fridge. "Think maybe I'll sit on the porch a while and rest my eyes. Been a busy couple o' days."

"Go on then. If y'sleep too long, I'll come wake ya."

Cletus sat outside and breathed in the scent of hay and pig shit. *Smells like money,* he thought, and took a heavy swallow from the can. He propped his feet up on the porch railing, and it wasn't very long before he drifted off.

Three more delivery sheets were on the porch, sitting beneath a rock, when Cletus woke up. He hadn't even heard them pull into the drive, let alone approach the porch.

Three more direct deposits. Maybe I can start considering a new truck and a TV that don't look like I'm watching people with the black plague.

The smell of frying pork chops caught his attention, and Cletus stood and stretched. He grabbed his unfinished beer and went inside to sit at the kitchen table. Janice set a plate down in front of him as he scooted his chair closer. Two chops, some green beans, a small mound of mashed potatoes, and a thick slice of fresh buttered cornbread. His stomach growled, and he grabbed his fork and serrated knife by his plate to slice into the browned chop. Cletus bit into the cornbread and steered a hunk of pork chop into his mouth. The tender and buttery mixture made his stomach growl more, but damned if it didn't taste amazing.

Janice brought her own plate to the table and sat. "I know it's been busy, Cletus, and I know you work so, so hard. But I need you to restock the freezer."

Cletus swallowed his food and went back for a second bite. He nodded and spoke with food in his mouth, even though he knew Janice hated when he did that. "What're we down to?"

"We're plumb out of meat. I tried talking to you about it the other day, but you was busy loading up the truck for Boden Meats." Janice frowned at his full mouth, sliced her pork chop into bite sized pieces, and forked one into her mouth.

"Tonight's dinner's the last of what we had?" Cletus chewed and washed it down with a drink of Budweiser.

"No, baby. Been out since last night. Got some hamburger meat and a pack of chicken breasts, but that was it for pork."

Cletus chewed another bite of the chop and then slowed. He cleared his throat and swallowed the tender lump.

Janice took a sip of her iced tea and grimaced. "Needs more sugar." She stood from the table and took her glass with her to the kitchen counter.

"If we've been out since yesterday…" Cletus looked down at his plate. "Then where did these chops come from?"

She glanced at him as she pulled the container of sugar from a kitchen cabinet. "Well, I…like I said, I know you've been workin' so hard. I took a little package of chops from your truck before you left for market. You was busy and I figured one little package for us wouldn't be—"

"From my truck? You…" Cletus felt his chest tighten. "You took a…a package of that sow I just slaughtered?"

"I'm sorry, honey, but yeah. We gotta eat."

Shadows swirled inside Cletus, something dark and mercurial. An icy heat began to form behind his eyes. It curled and boiled like thunder clouds, gray and purple and engorged. He felt it then—truly and purely—that ancient filthy wisdom inside him. Cletus blinked as his vision doubled. He shook his head and watched his wife add sugar to her glass of tea.

"That's fine, Janice." The voice wasn't his, the sound of heavy rainwater over gravel.

Cletus felt his grip tighten on the serrated knife in his hand and stood from the table. With his own eyes, and through the eyes of the old one inside him, Cletus watched as his wife slid a carving knife from the wooden block.

Angel Dust

by Shannon Felton

It was in sixth grade that you came home and found the drugs scattered across the coffee table. The house was dark—curtains drawn—so you almost didn't notice the body on the couch. That's all it was by then. Just a body.

You wonder if walking in on your dead mom has screwed you up for good.

Congratulations, of course it has.

That's why you're going to sleep with this guy. He's an accountant, in town on business, the sleeves of his white shirt rolled up to his elbows. You stopped him outside the gas station to bum some change and he offered you fifty bucks to go back to his room instead.

The sky is smoggy, the street silver, and the litter tumbling across the parking lot is going more places than you are. So of course you say yes. You just watched a homeless guy pull a half-eaten hamburger out of the trash can for chrissake.

And it's not like doing it this one time means you're a prostitute. It doesn't mean anything at all. Because none of this is real. It's not the life you were meant to have. It's a do over. A freebie.

In his car you wonder what it's going to feel like, if this is as low as you can go. There's a thrill in disgusting yourself.

The businessman fucks you doggy-style in the shower. You stare at the tile wall, water runs into your eyes, you wish it were tears. So that's what you pretend. You tell yourself you're crying. That you're upset. In your imagination you can be somebody who doesn't want this. He slaps your ass a few times. Hard. Harder than he should have. Then it's over. He gets dressed in the bathroom while you go through his briefcase. Then he comes out, gives you the money, and you leave. That's it. "Nothing major," you'll say. He's getting married in a month. At least you aren't her.

But it's not nothing, and as you wander down the street, you stop outside a Subway and look at the "Help Wanted" sign. You go inside and ask for an application. You don't know why. Maybe you're just tired. Maybe it's all too much. Maybe you want to see for yourself.

The cheerleader-types at the front counter laugh you out the door. In your anger, you threaten to slit their throats. That shuts them up. You don't bother waiting around for the cops.

You spend your nights downtown, hanging out with the hookers and the drunks, waiting for something—anything.

A red baggie floats by in the gutter water and stops against a dam of used condoms and Styrofoam cups. You pluck it out and hold it up to the blue light of the "Check Cashing" sign.

"They call that angel dust," a homeless man says. "But it's really the Devil's dust."

You pocket it, anyway.

"*He's* the one leaving those around, you know." The wheels of the shopping cart squeak as he pushes it over to you. "Have you opened it yet? You'll see."

"The baggie?"

"Your third eye."

"What?"

"I have a place," he says. He jerks his head to the left. "I can show you."

Raindrops are beginning to fall, leaving fat rippling circles in the puddles, and cops are cruising the street. So you figure, what the hell. You push yourself off the curb, grab your bag, and follow him down to an overpass.

He stops his cart on the sidewalk beneath the bridge and grabs his belongings. You help and then follow as he climbs the dirt hill up to his camp. It's littered with empty beer cans.

He drops his bags next to a stained mattress and digs through one. "I'll teach you an exercise," he says. "It'll help you focus your mind."

He pulls out an apple from the bag and from his coat, he pulls a needle. He sticks it through the red skin—sharp end up—and then rips a small square from the corner of an old newspaper. Folding the corner in fours, he flattens it, then centers the crease on the needle. The paper wobbles on its axis like a carousel canopy. He hands the fruit to you.

"Now, with your third eye," he says, tapping the space just above and between your eyes. His fingers are ashy and his nails yellow. "Imagine there's a string dangling from the edge of the paper. Go ahead and visualize grabbing it, then use it to spin the paper."

You sit down on a pile of clothes and lean back against the concrete wall. Pinching the air, you tug but the paper doesn't move. Again, you visualize the string, can almost see it this time, and tug.

Nothing.

"Keep trying," the old man says. He sits down on the mattress and hits the bags into the shape of a pillow.

"What's this supposed to do?" you ask.

He lays down and snuggles in, wrapping his old army coat tighter around him. "Just practice," he tells you. "You'll see."

Within minutes he starts to doze off and his mouth falls open. It's getting dark, and in the orange of the city lights you can see his rotten teeth peeking out between his beard and moustache. You look back at the paper and try again. Still nothing.

You stare at the apple, thinking if magic were real, what you'd really like to do is curse those stupid bitches at the Subway.

And you know all about curses.

The homeless man snores. You reach into your pocket and pull out the baggie.

Soon, you've never felt better. In fact, you've never felt this good before. Colors and shapes kaleidoscope in your mind. A door opens and finally, you *can* see.

You look down at the apple and don't even have to imagine the string. The paper is rotating all on its own. Just like magic.

Imagine that.

You open your eyes.

The homeless man is gone. Sirens wail, piercing your eardrums. A burning smell cuts through the air and a firetruck flies by, red lights searing your vision. You know even before you go and see. You know, but you don't believe.

"It happened so quick," someone in the crowd says. "Freak accident."

Paramedics roll the Subway girls out on stretchers.

Did I do that? you wonder. It makes you think of Urkel and you start laughing. Faces swim around you—angry, scowling faces—and you laugh even harder.

You smell chicken and it reminds you of how you used to sit on the floor in front of the TV while your mom made dinner in the kitchen. She always cooked chicken, said it was cheapest. Then you realize that's the smell of burning flesh and you throw up.

"Let's get you out of here," a voice says. Hands dig into your armpits and lift you up. He's ugly but you don't care. You're ugly, too.

You look up and spot two guys oompa-loomping down the sidewalk. Not guys—fat-bellied demons disguised in flannel and denim, their squat legs carrying them in the direction of a gas station.

You grin.

"Are you ok?" The ugly man asks.

Of course you are. You can see.

Headlights shine over you. You lift your eyes and squint. You've been huddled by the trash can all night, a pile of cigarette butts at your feet.

One of the demons comes out of a dingy four-square house across the street and kicks a ball into the weeds.

You stand up and head over to him.

"Who the fuck are you?" he snaps.

You don't answer.

He looks you over. "You're high as a kite, aren't you?"

You shake your head. "I'm not high, my mind is open."

He grins. "Yeah, well, it's not really fair only one of us is having a good time, is it?"

You let him drag you by the elbow to the back of a shed. He unzips his pants and bounces his half-erect penis in the palm of his left hand. He isn't wearing underwear and the denim has chafed his shaft.

You hope it's from the denim.

"Come on, now," he says. "You do this right, maybe I'll get you a little more dust."

You don't move. He lets his dick dangle so he can pull a switchblade from his back pocket. "But if you're gonna fuck around with me…" He steps closer towards you and you visualize—

"Knock it off, dickweed," a woman says. She's standing at the side door of the house with a bag of trash. "Come over here," she tells you. She tosses the trash in his direction. "Throw that away and then get the fuck to work, Timmy."

The demon tucks his dick away and zips his pants back up. "Stupid ass bitch," he sneers at you.

The house has been converted into apartments and the private entry smells like cat piss. It gives you a headache. You follow the woman up a narrow, hollow staircase and through a beaded doorway to the living area.

Skulls and salt and stones sit on the coffee table in front of a ratty couch. Candles and incense burn, barely covering the musky scent. The windows are covered by thick tapestries, woven with symbols and charts.

"Don't let ol' Timmy get to you," the woman says. Outside, you hear a train whistle and a man scream.

"Don't worry," you say. "I won't."

She hikes up her flowing skirt and sits cross-legged on the ground, picking up a joint left smoldering in an ashtray. "Where you been staying?" she asks.

"Nowhere," you tell her.

She inhales. "Maybe I can help you out with that." Exhales. "Streets are crazy out there right now."

"Because of the Devil's dust?"

She reaches under the coffee table, opens a box, and pulls out a deck of tarot cards. "My friend went totally bonkers on that stuff." She shuffles. "Said there was a voice in his head that kept talking to him, telling him to do awful stuff. Hypnotizing him or something—Cut."

You reach out and cut the deck.

"One day he strangled his grandmother, and then raped his thirteen-year-old sister and set her on fire." She laughs as the cards slap the table face down. "Chopped off his own genitals afterward. But before he bled out, he claimed it was Satan himself talking to him."

"Do you think it was?"

"Well, the Master works in mysterious ways, doesn't he? Isn't that why you're here?"

You pick up a skull. "So, you're into that stuff?"

"I dabble."

"Me too."

She smiles at you and turns over the first card.

It's Death.

They are all Death.

Her hand shakes as she looks at the last card and then back up at you. "Who are you?" she asks.

Her nose cracks when the skull hits it. Blood pours down the front of her peasant blouse.

"*Mitch*!" she screams.

A door opens and the other demon steps out. The woman backs away from you, pushing on her palms and heels.

"*Devil's dust,*" she hisses to him.

He nods in understanding and moves for a baseball bat leaning against the wall. It's spiked with nails.

He stops as a drop of blood escapes from his right nostril.

"What the hell—" He lifts his fingers to his upper lip, staggers, and pulls them away. His right frontal lobe collapses, pushing his eyeball out from the socket with a pop. The other side pops and he falls to his knees as piss wets the front of his jeans. The back of his skull crumples and then his jawbones crunch down and with a wet gargle, his nose and mouth cave into his throat.

The woman lets out a scream that scratches out of her throat like glass.

"Be quiet," you say to her.

Her screams turn into a high-pitched wail, like air whistling from a balloon. You sit down on the couch and wait.

Her wails become whimpers. "This isn't you," she sniffles. "Whoever you are in there, something has got control of you."

You ignore her. She wouldn't know, wouldn't understand what you've been through, how you've felt, the pain you've suffered. The ache in your heart, the corpse of your soul.

The woman tries again. "What's your name, sweetie?"

Your name is Garbage. You are the fly that lands on shit, the dog chained outside and left in the rain. No one. And you feel Nothing. That's who you are to do something like this.

The woman sniffles, leans towards you, and clasps her hands between her breasts.

"You're just on something, honey," she says. "It's okay. This is all okay. We can fix it."

You pull the red baggie out of your pocket, still sealed. You never needed it. You've got enough of what it offers all on your own.

You toss the baggie at her and her eyes narrow. "So you're just crazy then or what?"

You can't argue with that.

"Snort that," you say.

Her eyes widen. "No."

You lean forward and pick up the bat. "Fucking. Snort. It."

She whimpers, but her shaking hands rip the seal, anyway. She dips her pinky nail in and then brings the underside up to her bloody nostril and sniffs.

You grab the container of salt off the table and walk in a clockwise circle while pouring, then criss-cross through it, drawing symbols on the carpet.

"Get in," you tell her, pointing at the circle with the bat.

She sniffles up blood and snot and steps in. You draw another circle, criss-cross through it, and then sit down within the pentagram.

You reach into your bag and pull out the apple and the folded white paper.

"I know all about you," you say.

The woman closes her blackened eyes and her head rolls on her shoulders. "What about me?" she asks. She's on the edge of flying high.

"You manufacture and distribute dirty drugs to desperate people."

The woman giggles and swishes her hair in front of her face. She lifts a hand and runs it across her chest and down her arm.

"So what?" she says, dreamily. "Who cares about some stupid ass junkies when we're talking about the King of the Underworld."

"How about we summon him now?" you say.

The woman giggles again and sways back and forth. The blood has cracked and dried around her nostrils, lips and chin. "Why would we do that?"

"So you can meet your maker." You set the apple down in front of you and wait.

The night has grown quiet by the time she starts shivering. The wall clock clicks its way to twelve. "Hey," she says, her eyes growing wide. "Who's there?"

You don't answer. She's looking past you at something else. The paper on the needle slowly rotates.

"No," she says, shaking her head. "No, stop it!"

Her hands fly up and start slapping and clawing at her head. "Get out," she whines. "*Get out*." She pulls at her hair, great chunks coming out from between her fingers. Her scalp bleeds.

"Oh God, someone—please someone—get it out!" She seizes in the circle, her back arching and her bones cracking. A scream rips through her and fingers fly up to her face in a frenzy. Within seconds she's clawed out her own eyes. They roll towards you, coating themselves in salt, and stop right at the edge of the circle.

She lays there panting and you think of how your mom had laid there, head hanging back, all the blood collected behind her swollen bulging eyes, her white tongue lolling out of her mouth like a dead stupid cow's. You think of how she shit herself, how the brown, stinky mess of it had soaked through her nightgown and all you could say was that at least her back wouldn't give her anymore problems—

Slowly, creaking, the woman's body rises into a seated position and the bleeding holes of her gouged eye sockets lock onto you. Her voice deepens. **"You fucking dumb whore. "**

She stands up on wobbling legs and lunges for you, but the circle of salt holds her back. The paper spins around on the needle in a blur.

"You goddamn little bitch. Who do you think you are?"

You stand up, reach into your bag, and pull out a bottle of gas. You shove the paper into the spout and light it.

"Go to Hell," you say. You set the bottle on the table and within seconds, the wood catches. You head downstairs, the caged woman roaring behind you, and stop at the spot where the cat piss smell lingers. Hopefully, the space behind the wall is the only lab. If not, you'll find the rest.

Then you run.

It's seven o'clock in the morning when a squeaking noise wakes you from your spot on the bench. You open your eyes and shield them against the glare of the rising sun.

The homeless man stares down at you. He clicks his tongue and shakes his head as you sit up.

"I done told you," he says. He lifts a finger over each ear and wiggles them. Horns.

You sit up and rub your head. "Who are you?" you ask.

He laughs and taps the center of his forehead. "Keep that eye open, girlie." Then he's gone, disappeared around the corner.

Limping, dirty, and tired you head to the payphone at the corner gas station. You see more of them on your way—fat-bellied demons hiding behind masks—but you'll get to them another time. You have something more important to do.

"I'd like to report someone," you say. You look down at the papers from the hotel and read off the information, telling them everything you know about the accountant.

You hang up and head into the bathroom, washing your face free of the caked-on mascara and lipstick. Then you look up into the mirror at the girl we used to be.

"I did this," you say to me. "Not you."

I smile back at you through the glass.

And then you're gone.

What I Wouldn't Give

by Chad Lutzke

The demon sat across from me in my living room. He stunk. Like old chicken. This was no sulfur and brimstone shit but a different funk altogether. And I wondered if a shower couldn't fix that, or if it was just a demon thing, stinking like old chicken.

He was green, not red. No horns, no tail. No booming voice or hissing gurgle. Matter of fact, his voice was high-pitched and cracked like a teen whose balls hadn't dropped. I had to stifle a laugh when I first heard it. So far, every expectation I had regarding the dark side and its minions wasn't met at all. Including the fear you might expect would accompany such a meeting. But, this guy? He wasn't exactly intimidating. And that made the whole ordeal hard to take seriously.

"So, I sign this paper here and the guitarist gig is mine?" I asked him as I pointed to the old parchment that sat on the coffee table between us. Parchment. Cliché, right?

"Yep," he said while he chewed gum. Big Red. I don't know if he was trying to hide his smell or if smacking gum was a demon thing.

"And by signing this, that means you get my soul, right?"

"Uh-huh."

"What are you going to do with it?"

"Keep it away from you."

"Why? I mean...what's in it for you? What could you possibly get out of having it?"

"It means you won't have it." The demon was getting irritated.

"So, it does nothing for you other than me not having it."

"Right...now, do you want to shred or what?"

"So, you collect the souls, but you can't even use them? That's like hating baseball but collecting all the cards just so someone else can't have them."

"Yep."

"You know what we call that here? We call that a dick move. You're a dick."

The demon frowned and his eyes burned orange, casting images on my living room wall of famous guitarists, like he was teasing me: Angus Young, Zakk Wylde, Slash, Yngwie Malmsteen, George Lynch, Randy Rhoads, Eddie Van Halen, and Jimi Hendrix. All in various poses, performing face-deforming solos. Curled lips, gritted teeth, and scrunched eyes.

"This could be you."

The images began to move, each its own animated film. And I could hear a cacophony of strings, all in varying tones of distortion and sustained feedback that seemed to massage my ears and tickle my spine. It was euphoric, and I watched with wide eyes as the animations entranced me, pulling me to slice my skin and hurriedly mark my name upon the waiting parchment.

I looked at the guitar that sat in the corner of the room. A Fender Stratocaster. I'd picked it up less than a dozen times in the two years I'd owned it, its pickguard still shiny, its frets unscathed. I'd played it no more than four hours total, bending the strings, strumming each one with a pick held insecurely in my hand. Each short session with it felt like kissing a girl for the first time, one well out of my league, my hands apprehensive and clumsy.

"Think of the chicks you'll get," the demon said. "When you're up on stage in your bulging Spandex."

"Yeah, Spandex isn't a thing anymore, man. Try again."

"When you're up on stage with your sequins and your scarves."

"Again, not a thing."

"Bullshit! Steven Tyler still does it."

"Yeah, but Joe Perry doesn't. Remember. We're talking guitarists here."

The demon sighed, clearly frustrated. He spit his gum onto the table, and it stuck to the parchment near the line that said, "sign here."

"When you're up on stage with your leather and your spikes."

"Closer."

"Denim and T-shirts?"

"There we go."

"Chicks dig denim and T-shirts," he said uncertainly. I got the impression he didn't know shit about music.

"Dude, I'm married. Happily married. I just want to be able to shred. That's it. Can you do that or not?"

"Grab your guitar." A wide grin split his goblin-like face as he pointed toward my Stratocaster.

I picked up the Strat and rested it on my leg, pulled the pick from between the strings.

"Plug in," the demon said.

My amp was small and came as a package deal with the Fender. I couldn't tell if it was a shitty amp or that was just my playing, that maybe someone who knew what they were doing could make the thing sing. As for my playing? The amp was there to sustain every bad note I hit, an insulting scream that polluted the ears of any nearby.

The demon crouched down and messed with the few knobs there were, cranking the one marked "reverb" to 10. "Too bad this can't go to 11...am I right?" Even his jokes were bad.

He flicked the on switch and the living room filled with an electric hum, waiting for me to interrupt its voltaic purr.

"Play."

"Trust me," I said. "You don't want to hear me play. Hell, I can't even pull off 'Smoke on the Water' without tripping over myself."

"Just play."

I caressed the strings, making screeching noises as I stalled, searching the fretboard on exactly where to start, when suddenly my fingers took over with a mind of their own. Muscle memory that came out of nowhere. And before I knew it, I was playing some kind of Dick Dale surf music straight out of the '60s. Not really my thing, but that shit felt great.

And then the flow stopped. Whatever worked my fingers before with such speed, accuracy, and tenacity, just disappeared. And my fingers failed to create anything else worthy, shaking with adrenaline. Virgin digits on a prom-night bra clasp. The magic was gone. But for one beautiful moment, my fingers made the amp belch a succession of notes that no doubt was the demon's doing.

"Do it again," I said.

"Sign that and you can play all the surf rock you want." The demon handed me a red felt-tip pen. "It's not blood, but it'll do."

"That was nice and all, but I don't want to play surf rock."

"Ahh. You want to make that thing your bitch, with arpeggios and what not...some real virtuoso stuff."

"Not really."

"Classical? Flamenco?"

I shook my head. He picked up his gum and put it back in his mouth, chewed it.

"You're a bluesman. You want some Stevie Ray Vaughan stank on that thing. I won't do Jimmy Page, though. That was a one-time deal only. I still get shit back home for that. And if I hear one more joke about stairways and Heaven and glitter and gold, I'm gonna lose it.

"Kirk Hammett," I said.

"The Metallica guy?"

"That's the one."

The demon looked at me with a cocked brow and tilted head, scratching his chin. "You realize that's all wah-wah, right?"

"What do you mean?"

"I mean, he's got a boner for that wah pedal of his, never shreds without it. You can polish any turd with a wah and it'll shine like a diamond. Doesn't take much."

"I don't care. That's my favorite guitarist, and that's who I want to sound like."

"I suppose you could have picked somebody worse, like that fella from U2 with his pitch shifters and delay pedals. I'd like to see that cat in a room with Yngwie."

"You know Yngwie's a horrible songwriter, right?" I said. "There's a big difference between musical masturbation and writing a good song."

"Ha! You ever seen that boy play?"

"Yngwie? Yeah, plenty. He's all speed and no soul. It gets old, real quick."

The demon chuckled and a wisp of smoke spilled from his mouth. "No soul is correct."

"Is that your doing?" I asked.

"Maybe."

"Well, if it is, I certainly hope you throw in some songwriting talent with our deal, because I don't wanna just want sit around playing scales. I want to write songs."

"I got you. Now, sign the thing."

I took the pen and uncapped it. There was no fine print that I could see. Only a straight forward contract I'd already read half a dozen times, spelled out in plain English.

"Kirk Hammett and songwriting ability. No surf shit, just metal," I said.

"Horns up! Hope to die."

I eyed the demon's face, looking for a tell. Some sign of mischief, anything that reeked of deceit. Then headlights painted the living room curtains with a brilliant light.

"Dammit! Lisa's home early. You gotta go!"

"Sign it and I'm gone."

"I will. Just come back later, after she's in bed."

"Do it now and I'll toss in some hair."

"Hair?"

"Yeah, we'll grow that shit right down your back. Your wife'll love it."

"What's wrong with my hair?"

"It's too short. Won't match your new skills."

A car door slammed outside, footsteps up the walk.

"I don't want long hair. Dude, you've gotta leave, now!"

"I'll hide."

"Hide? Can't you just disappear, like poof and you're gone?"

"Yeah, but it leaves behind this sulfuric gassy thing…you don't want that. The wife will start asking questions. The next thing you know, you're in the doghouse and your wife thinks you're cheating on her because you can't lie for shit. I've seen it before."

"You stink, anyway. What difference does it make?"

"I do not!" The demon stuck his nose to his armpit.

"Get behind the couch." I shoved the demon toward the other side of the room. His skin was cold and clay-like. He got on all fours and squeezed in behind the couch.

"Hey, man. There's a cat back here… I hate cats!"

"Deal with it."

"I think I might be allergic."

"Shut up!"

I sat in my chair and grabbed the nearest magazine—A Fingerhut catalogue—and pretended to read as my wife walked in.

"Hey, honey. Did Jennifer call?"

"Nope, nobody's called."

"She's supposed to let me know about Saturday." Lisa took her coat off, set her keys on the counter, and came to the living room. "We're still on for this weekend, right?" She kissed my forehead. "Vacuum cleaners, huh?"

I looked down at the catalogue, at the display of vacuums with various monthly payments announced in bold, red font.

"Just flipping through. You know it wouldn't hurt to get a new one. Maybe one of these bagless ones. Could save us some money in the long run."

"Yeah, I don't think so. Those don't work nearly as well as ours." She sat on the couch, kicked off her shoes. "What's that god-awful smell? You smell that?"

"It might be the garbage. I cleaned out the fridge."

"Ugh, it smells so bad. Did you toss the chicken?"

"Yes, I'm sorry. It's been sitting there all day. I'll take care of it."

I glanced at the couch. I could see the demon's foot sticking out, pale green and callused, his toes wiggling.

Lisa grabbed a book of matches and lit a candle on the end table. "We need incense. Jennifer's house always smells so good, like Nag Champa. Every time I'm over there it smells like that…Oh! You've been playing?" She pointed at the Strat.

"Figured I'd dust her off."

"Good. I think you should stick with it, practice every day. Then write me a beautiful song, like 'Stairway to Heaven.' "

An ungodly sound came from behind the couch. It wasn't anything that would go unnoticed. It was loud and obvious. And demonic.

I was busted.

Lisa jumped from the couch and followed my gaze. Then she saw the foot, toes scrunched as though trying to hide.

"Mike? What the hell is that?"

"What's what?"

"That!" She pointed.

I couldn't play stupid anymore. The dumbass had his foot right out in the open. And then he made that noise again. We both had some explaining to do.

"Dude…she can see you." The demon didn't move, like he wasn't convinced the jig was up. "We're both staring right at you, man. Come out."

The demon wiggled his way backward from behind the couch, and my wife's jaw dropped. She didn't say a word, only stared.

"Sorry, man," the demon said. "I tried."

"Uhh…Lisa, this is…" Then the demon gave a name I couldn't pronounce if I tried. "He's…a demon."

"Pleased to meet you."

"What the hell is this, Mike? I'm really confused."

"He's here to teach me how to play guitar."

"Guitar lessons. In our house. With a demon…who smells like shit by the way!"

"That's the fridge. Mike cleaned it out."

"Actually, man. You really do reek. Now, will you shut up and let me talk to my wife?"

He sat in the chair, slouched and pouting, while I tried to explain to Lisa my plan and what it could mean for our future.

"So, by signing that paper, you get to play like Kirk Hetfield, and I get no husband in the afterlife?"

"Hammett. Kirk Hammett. And we don't know if there is an afterlife, or any spirit world or any of that."

"Mike, there's a freaking demon in our living room asking for your soul. I'd say we have a pretty good idea."

"She's got a point, Mike…but don't let that stop you from giving me your autograph. The first of many you'll be giving, no doubt."

"I can't believe you're even considering this, Michael. This is ridiculous."

"How else am I gonna be able to play like that?"

"Oh, I don't know…maybe put ass to chair and actually practice!"

I knew she was right. Maybe I wouldn't ever play like Kirk Hammett, but at least practicing would get me somewhere, and with a feeling of accomplishment. Plus, there was the matter of the soul I'd get to keep. "Sorry, demon. She's right. I don't know what I was thinking. Thanks anyway."

"Thanks anyway?" The demon spit his gum out again. It bounced on the carpet and sat there in a ball, and I wondered if wintergreen flavor may be more helpful in hiding the chicken rot. "Dude…you sign that paper or I'm taking your finger's like I did Iommi's."

"Dick move, man."

"You'll do no such thing, you stinky piece of shit," Lisa said. "Now get the hell out of my house."

And just like that, the demon disappeared. And a gassy cloud appeared just like he said it would, reeking of burnt matches and flatulence. I turned to Lisa. She wore a pretty serious frown. I'd never seen her that pissed. I felt bad and hugged her, contemplating what I'd nearly done—given my soul to a hideous, gum-chewing thing that smelled like ass.

I broke the hug and looked in her eyes, told her I was sorry and promised I'd practice and one day write her a song. Then the demon appeared again in another gaseous cloud.

"Sorry…forgot my gum." He picked the wad of gum off the floor and popped it in his mouth, then poofed away again. Another cloud left behind. I buried my nose in Lisa's hair and breathed deep the scent of her shampoo.

"Hey," I whispered. "You ever hear of a wah-wah pedal?"

Hellseed

by Tim Curran

In the black, star-blown night, Maria shivered in the cabin. Bathed in cool/hot sweat, flooded with it, drowning in it, she remembered some vague febrile nightmare about a juicy plum hanging from a stem and the mouth that bit into it, sucking the moist pulp and scarlet juice.

For one frantic moment in which her body tensed with paroxysms of utter terror, she could not remember where she was or even who she was…but that passed quickly enough and she then wished her memory had not returned at all because she knew what had brought her to this place in her life and she dearly wanted to scream.

No, no, no—

Breath in, breath out, relax.

The baby. Think of the baby.

But she could not relax because she was gripped by the certainty that she was not alone in the room. She heard a low, wet breathing, sensing motion and heard a strange crackling between her ears. Whatever had come into the room with her brought an awful fetid smell she likened to cauldrons of warm vomit and steaming cesspools, narrow boxes filled with rattling yellow bones. She could hear it moving with fleshy, viscous sounds like a monstrous slug inching its way over the floor.

She was paralyzed.

By fear. By the thing that had come in the dead of night. She tried to cry out for Luis. *It's happening. The prophecy is being fulfilled.* But the words echoed only in her mind, autumn leaves tossed by storm winds.

Oh, Luis, it has come for me just as they said.

It was on the bed now.

It was crawling up her bare leg with a warm flabbiness, leaving a burning trail of slime as it climbed her. She could feel its poison seeping into her, atrophying her muscles and making her blood boil with fevers. Its nubby fingernails dug into her hips, its hot rancid breath at her thighs, its looping sandpaper-rough tongue licking between her legs like a cat with a bowl of milk. In the pale moonlight filtering in through the window, she saw a vague bulbous shape, dark eyes glittering like blood-seeped pearls.

Inside her, the baby rolled over.

Her mind fractured, nerves exposed like bare wires. She felt the slimy puckering mouth at her belly and then teeth like hot rivets as it bit into her.

She screamed as it sucked her body heat into its maw, leaving her cold and violated. The baby kicked and shuddered.

But it was only the beginning and she knew it. The prophecy of the hags was made real.

She felt the fingers first.

As they slid up her legs, they were cold like thawing meat, impossibly long and surgically-delicate, the blue-gray of a corpse a week in the grave. Maria trembled, her teeth chattering, her mind imploding into itself like a distant dying star. She was unclean and would now be made pure. The fingers slid up her thighs and her flickering eyes looked into a distorted face that was the split maidenhead of insanity, something sutured from a dozen faces, a fractured death mask sewn by worms in fine grave threads. Maggoty lips pulled back from graying, gnarled teeth which sprouted like twisted roots from barren soil.

Her voice was broken and sobbing: "Please…please no, not the baby…*oh dear God, not the baby…*"

Then the fingers were at her belly, growing longer by the moment like knife-edged shadows, their nails tapering and sharp like beavertail daggers. They pierced the flesh of her abdomen and she screamed at the violation with the manic, hysterical shrilling of a mind completely unhinged. The grave-cold fingers slid into her, impaling her as the demon entered her inch by terrible inch, a thing of filth and mud and dirty straw that now crawled beneath her skin to make communion with the child she carried.

She would not eat. Luis could not compel her to do so. Something awful and beyond belief had ripped her soul open and when she spoke, it was with the threadbare fragments of a working mind. He brought her sowbelly and beans, stew and mutton, fried apples and johnnycakes, all to no avail. She mumbled nonsensically, drifting uneasily between dream and reality, often occupying some misty netherworld in-between.

A thin and ragged man whose fortune had now fallen to dust, Luis would stand before the grimy window and stare out at the yellow fields and dark clustering woods, worrying, thinking, an indefinable terror taking shape inside him.

"I cannot stop this," he whispered again and again. "Not with guns or knives or my bare hands. It's beyond what I know."

As he watched his wife writhing with nightmares, sweat shining on her pale face, his hatred was a burning brand singeing his insides. But there was nothing to direct it upon. He could only watch, day by day, as she grew thinner and weaker, gravity pulling her features in cadaveric directions from which, he feared, there could be no return. The incubus in her belly owned her, and it would take her life as atonement for promises broken that no man could dare keep.

"*You ask...too much.*"

"*But you were given all.*"

"*But...*"

"*Deliver the child unto us or we shall exact payment.*"

Shivering, he pulled from a bottle of whiskey, thinking of horror and damnation.

The darkness was the worst, and he would keep watch with his rifle far into the ebon watches of night. His eyes would be heavy-lidded, bloodshot, burning like they were full of sand, but he would not close them. He did not dare. He had enemies. Enemies of his physical being and his soul. Now and again, just past the witching hour, he would hear a curious flesh-creeping rattle from the woods outside as of gathering snakes and smell odors of carrion on the night-breeze, and see dozens of glistening ophidian eyes watched the cabin. It was there and then it was not. Sometimes he saw the hags. Or thought he did. They were crow-black phantoms haunting the edges of black thickets. They would dance in the moonlight, faces greased with bear fat, wearing bloody animal skins, clattering bones and skulls, screeching and yammering to impure, malefic gods. But like morning fog, they were there and then gone just as quick.

Though he once had commerce with them, he now feared them. They could give you things, make things happen for you, but only at a terrible price. And sooner or later, they always came to collect. He had heard stories about what they did with those who did not honor their bargains—horrible things about the hags dismembering their victims alive, burning them piece by piece in sacrificial fires.

These thoughts were a cancer in his brain, a disease that ate into his mind, so he went outside and chopped wood, listening to the sounds from the woods and wondering what was out there. If they came now in the daylight, he would fight them with his rifle and his axe...and he would lose.

But he would draw blood and exact pain and that was the best he could hope for in these dark, desperate times.

When he came back in later, muscles aching, his wool shirt glued to him with perspiration, Maria was awake. Her eyes were wide and glistening as if they had been oiled.

"The baby," she said.

"What about it?"

"It will come soon," she told him, offering him the wooden grin of a puppet. "I feel it will come soon. We need to be ready for it to come into the world. It has waited a long time."

His hands trembled as he poured water into the speckled blue basin to wash her with. She no longer referred to the child as *he* or *she,* but as *it.* She was a vessel now for something grotesque and aberrant and she knew it. The Maria he knew was gone, replaced by this glass-eyed doll with its painted-on carnival grin, an incubator and nothing more. Through her, the hags would bring hell into this world.

"We'll be ready," he said in a dry voice. "When the time comes. Midwife Nash will—"

"Not come," said Maria. "She is unclean and she will not witness what comes to pass. Make ready. The child will be hungry. It will not want milk. It will want blood and well-aged, well-marbled meat."

He turned away, physically ill, spiritually defiled. He could barely stay on his feet. They had her. The hags owned her. She was a ragdoll with blank shoe button eyes that they played with. He stood there, stirring the coals in the hearth, feeling that his world had been destroyed by an infectious insanity now. It had been turned inside out, disemboweled, its fly-specked entrails cast at his feet. Yes, it still spun but in distorted lunatic orbit.

"Oh, Maria," he said, tears in his eyes.

She looked through him and beyond with leering, jaundice-yellow eyes that were funhouse mirrors reflecting the light of dead moons.

"You will make ready," she said in a hissing, reptilian voice, "for the time of the birthing is at hand."

Then her eyes closed and a gray pallor of death set into her face. She still lived. She still breathed. But inside she was dead.

Three days later, the darkness was broken by a thin wailing voice, the sound of a woman whose nerves had been scraped raw and whose mind was emptying itself with a scream.

Luis waited across the room. The cherry of his cheroot glowed orange, illuminating a face that was craggy and pocked, weathered by wind and baked by the sun.

"Is it time?" he asked.

Maria trembled with rolling convulsive waves that seemed to start at her rounded belly and moved up into her throat, strangling off all words. She made a gagging sound as if hands were squeezing her windpipe shut.

Trembling, Luis watched her, thinking of the old hags beneath a black moon and nameless things growing, waiting to be born.

He walked over to the bed, saying, "Sshhh, sshhh, my darling. Sooner started, sooner done."

It was one of those things his mother used to say many years ago, and it came to him now in this hour of nightmares.

Maria breathed in and out with great effort. "Have they come, Luis? Are they here?" she managed.

"No, no, they won't come."

He stepped over to the window. All was silent out there across the empty fields. Their neighbors were either too frightened to approach the farm or they had not yet heard about what was happening. He looked up at the moon and horrors unseen filled his mind until he made a low moaning in his throat.

Wait.

What was that?

Oh, dear God, they *had* come. He could see the old women standing out there. They were waiting. They still laid claim to the birth. There were three of them, withered shadows like ancient dead trees, black shawls pulled over their heads, faces like dry cane straw. Hags and shrews, wormseed and blight. They had come for what was theirs. An arrangement had been made. They kept their part of the bargain and they expected him to do the same.

He knew what it meant to deny them.

He knew their terrible wrath.

He knew what they could visit upon him and those he loved. He cursed them under his breath and thought about the rifle in the other room. Wicked things, those terrible wicked things just waiting for the birth of the child. He would kill them if only he could be sure they would stay dead.

They had not moved out there.

They waited still as graveyard statues rooted to the soil.

"You will not have the child," he said under his breath. "I defy you. I will not hand the baby into your skeleton hands."

You will keep it? You will make the hell-spawn your own? their voices said in his mind. *You will tend to the horror of the birth? You are cursed all the days of your life, little man.*

The labor pains began to spike now. Maria trembled and sweated, thrashing and jerking with contractions. Oh! And the old hags knew it. They began to mutter and make sign in the air with their gnarled fingers. It grew dark out there now as a caul formed over the face of the moon. They expected his treachery, and they brought darkness to his house.

The child was coming now.

The hags were shrieking with delight.

He would deliver the child when they stood at the threshold like wraiths with outstretched fingers. He would kill them and be done with this awful business.

You are cursed all the days of your life, little man.

"Push," he told his wife. "Push, Maria."

He felt the child now and outside, the hags grew excited. Their curse was realized and the abomination incubating in his wife had come to term.

Maria writhed and shook with terrible spasms. The head of the devil-spawn came out with an eruption of blood and tissue. The room filled with a repulsive, singed porcine stink. Though his belly convulsed in greasy waves, Luis took hold of the child and helped it into the world, bringing it out into the guttering candlelight. It squirmed in his hands, exuding a gushing slime. It was bloated and larval, wiggling with a profusion of limbs. It did not cry out like a babe—it buzzed like a fly.

Its puckering mouth fastened to his thumb like a hungry suckling. With a cry, he set it in the black lacquered trunk and quickly shut the lid. It slithered and scratched in there, but he could look upon it no more.

Gore dripped from his hands. He was stained red right up to the elbows.

Maria, stricken mad, looked up at him. "Is it…is it a healthy child, my husband?"

But he could not answer that. He could not fabricate a lie as he heard the buzzing from inside the box as if it was filled with trapped meat flies. And out in the dark thickets, the hags shrieked to the nacreous globe of the moon high above.

The sound of the baby set his flesh to crawling so Luis spent a lot of time outside, scanning the woods for trouble and sighing when he did not find any. Even the priest would not come now. Not after what he saw in the box. No one would come. In the dreadful days following the birth, Luis spent a lot of time chopping wood to work out his fear and frustration, the sense that evil was spreading around the farmhouse in black, drooping webs.

It had been two weeks. He had slept very little. The child was of great concern, of course, but what worried him even more was Maria. The birth had traumatized her and most days she would barely even speak. The scars laid across her soul were deep and hurting. She rarely got out of bed or had any appetite. What food she took he had to force upon her.

As he sectioned pine logs, he wished he could get a doctor to look at her, but even the doctor stayed away. He continued chopping and was surprised when a wagon pulled up. It was Marcel whose spread lay on the far side of the big thicket. He was a cousin twice removed, a small, almost elfin man with a shaggy beard and laughing eyes.

Today they were not laughing.

"How is Maria?" he asked.

"She is not well."

Marcel sat by the fire pit, adding a slat of pine and stirring up the coals until the fire began to burn again. "I hear things, Luis. I hear terrible things."

"Do you?"

"Yes. But I do not listen to them. No. Instead, I ride three hours to come here and hear what you have to say."

Luis packed his shale pipe with rough-cut tobacco. "And if I have nothing to say?"

"Your eyes have already spoken volumes. The child…is it true?"

Staring into the fire, smoke drifting from his nostrils, Luis could only nod. "Something that might happen in a million births, I suppose." He shrugged. "Maybe we are cursed of God."

Marcel, arms folded over his round belly, shook his head. "Do you really think it is God who curses you? Maybe it is another."

"I don't believe in curses."

"Maybe you should."

Luis smoked in silence. He looked out across his fields. It amused him to think that in this country where there was very little rainfall and the crops had to be irrigated, water had always been plentifully abundant. The rains always fell when they were needed, filling the irrigation ditches. The wells he dug always found pure spring water. Blessed. Yes, he had been blessed. But since the birth of the child, the hay fields had withered, crops dying in the fields. Even his prized yellow chilis had been affected by some unknown blight, their bright waxy fruit darkening with stem rot.

"Where are your chickens?" Marcel asked.

"They are no more. Diseased. I destroyed them."

"Tell me."

Luis shrugged. "Day by day, they acted oddly. They pecked themselves and each other, shedding their feathers in bunches. Their flesh turned gray. When I cut into one, the meat was dry and black. Horrible smelling. I burned them."

"And your cows?"

"The same. They went blind. The milk they gave was sour and filled with…with parasites." He shrugged again. "I am near ruin."

Marcel considered this for a good long while, then he said, "I once knew a man. A good man. A kind man and, yes, a righteous man. His downfall was vanity and ambition. He did not wish to start humbly as most farmers do. A small plot of land was not enough for him. He worried others would look down on him and his pride would not allow it, so—"

"I don't want to hear this," Luis told him.

"So…he asked favors from the old hags that some called witches. He wanted a great farm and a lovely house, barns and coops and abundant orchards, fields and pastures which were green and growing. That which takes a man a lifetime to accrue, he wanted now. These old hags, these *brujas,* these forbidden necromancers and resurrectionists, had been the ruin of many who reached beyond their station for those things that were not theirs to have. Yes, these hags were known for their power of enchantment, their devil's brews and love potions, their ability to call the demons of Hell to their fireside, to summon things from the black holes between the stars and to commune with those long dead and turned to dust.

"Now, this vain, ambitious man asked for these material favors and riches. Even the terrible price did not deter him. The hags kept their promise. The man soon had the largest, most successful farm in the county. For many years, he lived full, fat, and proud. Then his wife was taken with child and the hags came to visit. On a terrible windy night, they flew down from the mountaintops and high caves and up from the low hollows and flooded, secret crypts, riding on their broomsticks, spreading moondust in their wake. They were ugly creatures, thin, fat, hideous. They stank of rancid bones and cauldrons of human grease. They wore graying shawls sewn from the shrouds of stillborn children and those babes they had strangled in their cribs, sucking away their breath and drinking their blood. They came to have an audience with the vain, ambitious man, human crows and graveyard ravens. They arrived with a glow of hellfire, a blizzard of ashes blown from cremated corpses, and brought a stench as of a thousand defiled graves. Now that the womb of your beloved bears fruit, they said, in nine months' time we shall exact our payment for services duly rendered. You will make an offering of the swaddling babe and place it plump, pink, and soft at our feet for we have need of its skin and bones and the juice we can squeeze from its soft underbelly—"

"Shut up! Shut up!" Luis cried, dropping his pipe into the fire.

But Marcel would not shut up because there was a terrible truth behind his words and a lesson that needed learning and he was the teacher, a hard master but a fair one. "Yes, well, the vain, ambitious man refused payment. He had what he wanted, gained through dark sorceries, and now he refused to make good his end of the bargain. That night, the hags cursed him. They cursed his child. They cursed his farm, his wife, his livelihood. They brought down hell from dark spaces and cold places and exhaled a burning dry wind of pestilence over all and everything the man held dear and—"

"Stop," Luis said.

"—and they planted a demon seed in the child because it was the most horrific punishment their twisted minds could conceive of."

Luis was standing now, fists bunched, his heart burned black with the need for violence. "I will not listen to any more of this and you, family or no, will not speak of blasphemies here."

Marcel shook his head, laughing without humor. "Oh, Luis…why did you not listen? No good ever comes of the hags. It was a truth we learned as boys at Grandmammy's knee. No good ever comes of witchcraft."

"I do not believe in witchcraft or those who practice it. They are fluff, stories, yarns told by old women."

"But do you believe in good luck?"

"Yes…I…yes, I do."

"Then look around you, cousin of mine, and see that yours has evaporated! That good has been replaced by bad and that your fine, much-admired farm and its many holdings is decaying like a rotten tooth, blackening and crumbling. Soon, your precious lands will be one awful, filthy pig wallow!"

"I tried to make it right!" Luis cried. "I begged! I pleaded! I offered them anything, even my own life, my own soul!"

"And the child?"

"They didn't want it! It was too late! It had been born! It was accursed!" He was sobbing now, ashamed of what he had wrought and brought into being. "I had turned against them in my heart."

He admitted to his cousin that he had gone to them, threatening to kill them, and they had laughed and stolen his sight. For three days, he could see nothing.

"I did not…I could not imagine the price would be so high!"

Marcel said nothing more for some time. He thought of the men of the valley and how, when in their cups and the tequila had inflated their chests, they talked of going up through the dead forest to the blasted hilltop which was the lair of the hags known as the *Hermanas de los Muertos*, the Sisters of the Dead, and burning them out once and for all. But it never happened because they were afraid. And those few brave and foolish souls who did venture up there, never did return.

"The child is inside?"

"It's not a child."

"Is it inside?"

Luis nodded. "Yes. In the box."

Marcel stood, not a large man, but a round one, a wise and mighty man in many ways who accepted what was given him in this life, what he earned, sweated and bled for, and never dared ask for more. "I shall go see this child."

"No! Please do not look at it! Do not!"

But Marcel brushed him aside. He went inside, standing tall, belly filled with iron, arms corded with muscle, a steely glare in his eyes. Luis sat down on a stump and whimpered, waiting for the screams of his cousin Marcel that would come when he looked upon the child. He did not wait long.

Marcel stumbled from the cabin. It looked as if the blood had been sucked from him. He shook his head from side to side. "Dear God," he mumbled. "Dear God."

"I told you."

"Yes, you did."

Marcel sat down. He smoked, but said nothing. His voice would not come. He stared off across the blighted fields which were a reflection of his soul now.

"Listen," he finally said, "this must be made right. This cannot be allowed to go on. You know that, don't you? You cannot keep that monstrosity in the box, feeding it meat scraps forever. Something must be done."

"Yes."

"I will return in two days. Then, together, we will do the awful thing. We will cleanse the world of this horror."

It was dark and the child had gotten out. It would make a terrible mischief and Luis knew it. He sat by a fire near the barn, waiting for it with his rifle. He would kill it. When it returned, he would kill it. There was no other thought in his mind as he stared into the fire and watched the flames jump and dance. If he did not kill it, people would come for him. They would burn him out.

He sat there for many, many hours, waiting for the varmint to return, because it had to come back. The box was the only home it had ever known.

The night was blacker than sin. He could not see into it. The light of the fire could not penetrate it. He listened for the demon child to return. He listened so hard that his ears started to hurt after a time. Now and again he heard a strange rustling in the thickets. Each time, he set aside his bottle and stood drunkenly with his rifle in his hands.

"Come out!" he cried into the night. "Show yourself!"

But there was never anything. Once he heard the madwoman cackling in the house, but that was it. A screech owl wailed in the woods. Insects chirped and whistled. He was alone, yet he was certain it was near. Watching. Waiting. He thought more than once in his alcoholic delirium that a dozen rawboned arms reached out of the shadows at him, that some freakish teratoid human matrix was creeping up on him to shove its wriggling afterbirth down his throat. But there was nothing.

Nothing at all.

Around four, the clouds parted and the stars came out. The bottle empty, he drifted off. When he woke in the streaming, hot daylight, he stumbled into the cabin.

The box was gone.

"Sooner or later, it had to happen," Marcel said later that day when he returned. "Something like that…a devil birth…it would not be content with scraps. It would need flesh and blood. It would need to take lives. Such is its nature. Let us stop it before it kills again."

Marcel brought stories with him, twice-told tales he had picked up from terrified peasants. Something that had been seen crossing a road by moonlight. A farm less than a mile away whose livestock had been slaughtered in the night. People vanishing in the fields after dark. There was a single source to all of it and they both knew what it was.

Luis made sure there was plenty of food for Maria. He explained to her that he might be gone several days. She did not seem to understand, she spoke endlessly of the baby and that once it was born, how wonderful things would be.

They saddled their horses, packed biscuit and jerky and water. Armed themselves with knives, Colt pistols, and two fine Spencer repeating rifles Marcel had also brought.

"I have put all my affairs in order, Luis," he said. "So now, let us do this thing and may God help us. You know, as I do, where we must go. There is only one place the demon child would hide. We must meet it there."

It was late that day when they reached the shunned place. The awful place. The closer they got on that warm, dry afternoon, the more people they saw. Farmers, all. They carried simple agrarian weapons in their sunbaked hands—scythes, billhooks, hayforks—and stood silently about in the sunshine, wanting to fight but afraid to bring hell down upon themselves. They knew where Luis and Marcel were going. Some told them to turn back before it was too late. Others encouraged them in their campaign. And still others told them they were being lured into a trap. No matter, they went on, taking the crooked road to the hilltop, the squatting ground of the hags.

As they rode higher, they began to come upon the dead in all forms. Animals and humans alike had been slaughtered, the dusty earth drenched with their blood and foul secretions. Men, women, and even children hung from the dark twisting trees that lined the road. They were dismembered, eviscerated, shattered and cast about, staring with hollow eye sockets, pale and leeched things, skeletons cloaked in white, rubbery skins. Whether they were the result of vengeance by the hags or sacrifices to them, neither man knew.

"Do not look," Marcel said.

Eventually, they came to the hilltop which was an ossuary. Bones were scattered in all directions—in the grass, dangling from trees, sculptures of vertebrae and femurs and jawless skulls hanging from poles driven into the ground. It all led to the house of the hags, a black, grim, and uninviting pile of sharp-peaked roofs, shuttered windows, and crooked doorways. Flies filled the air and buzzards pecked away at blackening offal.

Inside, there was no one. The hags had fled. They had known death was coming, so they decided they would meet it another day. The floor was dirt, a small fire blazing in a pit. The walls were crowded with shelves that held jars and bottles, curious glassware and earthen pots, nameless things neither man was interested in exploring. The air was warm. It stank like the den of an animal, a fusty sickening odor of old blood and older death.

Both men lit kerosene lanterns and studied the horrors around them.

Yes, the hags were gone, but the black lacquered trunk was there.

The box was waiting for them.

"Open it," Marcel said, raising his rifle.

Beads of sweat ran down Luis' face. He shook and shuddered. "But I—"

"Open it."

As he approached it, thinking it was but a trick, that the box was surely empty and they had been deceived by it, it moved. Something inside it thumped. Thumped again. The box slid three inches through the dirt.

Luis opened it and stepped far back.

At first there was only a hot stench that blew into their faces with a cremating heat—the acrid, sickening odor of burnt feathers and corpses bundled in gray sacks—then a hand came out, its scabrous fingers tapping away on the outside of the box. It was followed by another and yet another. A leg emerged, then two more. Then the demon showed itself: a creeping human emulsion, a catastrophic anatomical meltdown, a perpetual motion machine of multiple corpse-white torsos welded together at right angles to one another spurred on by dozens and dozens of bicycling limbs. It was a great rolling ball of anatomy.

Luis and Marcel emptied their rifles and pistols into it. The demon birth squealed and shrieked, but did not stop. Not until they tossed their lanterns at it. The hissing flames engulfed it, the straw-dry walls of that ancient hovel catching. Soon enough, the entire place was burning and the demon was trapped within, consumed by the flames that gave it birth.

Outside, smoke blowing all around them in black tendrils, Luis and Marcel watched the house become the pyre of the hell-spawn. It roared like an angry beast. It screamed like a woman. And, finally, when none of that worked, it sobbed like a child. Then the roof fell in on top of it and buried it alive in flaming lumber and hot coals.

Soon enough, there was no more sounds, save the popping and sputtering of the great fire that burned on the hilltop.

When Luis returned to the cabin, exhausted and aching, his face and clothing smudged with soot, it was late. The stars had come out. He drank whiskey straight from the bottle and smoked a cheroot, thinking, wondering, and, yes, daring to hope.

After a time, he went inside. He went to the room of the madwoman whom he no longer referred to by her Christian name. He still loved her, of course, but that love was tainted now, discolored, poisoned like a well that had once offered only cool water and now brought sickness to all that drank from it.

"Luis," Maria said. "I waited for you."

He was brightened by the fact that her voice sounded clear and rational, no hint of the madness that had muddied the waters of her mind for so long. He lit the oil lantern. She lay on the bed, her eyes bright and her smile genuine.

"While you were gone, the old women came," she said.

He felt a stab of fear in his stomach. "What...what old women?"

"The old women in black," Maria explained. "They took care of me. They told me how things will be."

Luis could barely stand as Maria exposed her round belly, lightly rubbing her hands over it.

"The first child did not work, Luis. But this one will. And if not this one...then the one after or the one after that..."

He sank to the floor. Yes, the prophecy of the hags had come to pass. He was most certainly cursed all the days of his life.

Devil's Ink

by Mark Towse

It's been nearly four weeks since I last put pen to paper. Each day that passes, the disconnect seems to grow, and I'm worried I might not find a way back. Elly says it's because I'm locking myself away from life. She challenges me. "How can the promising new find, Tristan Kowalski, conjure new worlds if he doesn't even acknowledge his own?" Last time Elly visited, I told her not to come back—that I needed space. She may be happy enough swimming in mediocrity with only minor flashes of anything credible, but I'm not. Sacrifices must be made.

The view is usually enough to inspire: rolling hills, decrepit farm buildings, skies that carry a bounty of orange and gold endlessly stretching into the distance. Yet here I am, pen in hand, and a headful of second-rate ideas to embarrass me. Of late, I don't feel worthy of the pen, as though its beauty undermines me; solid gold, ornately decorated with all sorts of other-worldly scenes, and the words "For Tristan" etched down one side. We've done great work together, but now I find myself clasping it tightly like a weapon rather than a tool, full of rage and impatience.

I have nothing. Nothing!

Slamming my fist into the desk, I let out a scream—a wild maniacal cry of hopeless desperation that echoes through the house. Even the crows outside take flight, cawing their noisy disapproval.

And it happens—just like that—a moment of unequivocal clarity.

It's as though the crows have lifted the veil of bile and fogginess that has been shrouding my brain in recent weeks. The idea is forming. I can feel the adrenaline kicking in—heart rate increasing, goosebumps randomly prickling across my skin, and the pen shaking in my grasp.

As if on cue, a haunting wind whistles across the front of the house. The rotting sash windows gently rattle in their frames and through the glass, I watch the dark clouds roll in impossibly quickly, swallowing sunlight and the innocence of day. Suddenly, it's a much more sinister scene, and it sends a shudder down my spine. I've felt this before, a sudden shift of energy. But not like this; never this powerful. It's as though something is here with me.

Nestled between the bandages, painkillers, anticoagulants, and medical tape is the confronting but exhilarating sight of the fresh steel blade. Hand still shaking, I purse my fingers around it and delicately roll up my left sleeve. Partially healed wounds from my last success still appear sore, and the entire arm is still tender to touch, nerve endings screaming in protest as I tentatively search for unblemished areas. I try the other arm, but hard scar tissue weaves its way from the wrist to bicep—needlework isn't a strong point of mine. Unbuckling my belt, I slide it from around my waist and undo the button of my pants. They fall to the ground, revealing more of my handy work. Finally, I find some untouched flesh on the underside of my thigh and ready myself, doubling up the belt and placing it between my teeth.

"Why do you insist on using red ink?" my publisher once asked.

I was taken to the edge with the last story—couldn't tell you how much blood I poured into that one, but it was worth it. I know how far I can go, which veins to avoid.

The familiar bitter earthiness of the belt gathers at the back of my throat as I try to steady my hand. Three—two—one. I run the blade across my thigh and wince at the slightly delayed pain, watching as the crimson begins to trickle down my pale skin. Pushing it further in, I twist the blade, biting down hard as pulses of pain vibrate down my leg.

Christ!

Deep breaths, Tristan; look beyond the pain and think of what you are achieving.

I dip the pen into the beautiful redness and quickly begin to scribe the first few words across the paper. Relief is immediate as the taunting blankness gives way to lines of prose that make me want to laugh and cry. I'm in the zone; on a roll, unstoppable.

I'm not insane. This is no ordinary pen, you see. It was a gift left for me on my bedside table—perhaps by the same entity that is here with me now. I can't recall much about her appearance other than the yellow eyes and black cloak, but it was her words that resonated with me. It must be nearly ten years since she visited me in my sleep to tell me she admired my work; her only critique that my stories could often feel detached, full of redundant words and superficial ramblings rather than accurate depictions of a character's actions or emotional state.

"You are doing yourself an injustice," she had said.

She told me the pen was magic, that it would change my life forever. There were rules, though. It must be human blood, freshly drawn to be effective, and that I could only moderate the pain with household painkillers. Anything beyond this would tarnish the emotional rawness and overall effectiveness. The blood would provide a life source for the pen that would take it beyond simple calligraphy, enchanting it with an intuition that would know what to write even before I could conjure the words. All I needed was the idea, and the pen would do the rest, allowing my characters to bleed onto the paper.

I've already filled four pages, and I want to set a steady pace. I wrap some tape around my wound and relax back into the chair, watching as the clouds begin to roll back. A morsel of light finds its way through the grimy window as I break off some bread and wash four painkillers down with a glass of Chianti. It almost feels as though the presence has left now that I have stopped writing.

I don't need to re-read my work. It is perfection. When I'm finished, everyone will know who Tristan Kowalski is.

My leg pulsates with a satisfying dull throb, but for me, pain means productivity. It means I am working and creating, that I am happy. I knock back the wine and pour another glass.

"Here's to the one they will remember forever," I toast.

Startled, I wake up in the chair, throat dry, my neck stiff. Grabbing my wooden cane, I push myself to my feet and hobble carefully to the bathroom.

My face is cut-free, but tired looking: pale skin with a tinge of yellow, dark circles, and sunken eyes. Carefully, I lift the gauze to inspect the wound—it shouldn't be too painful to reopen. I splash my face with cold water and then return to my desk, easing myself slowly back into the chair. Almost immediately, the morning light fades.

As I work the blade back into my skin, the brighter blood begins to spill over the darkened surface. I can't afford to waste a drop, so I quickly gather the pen and dip it in. And I'm off again.

I have often asked myself if it is cheating, but all the magic pen does is bring out what is already inside of me. I come up with the idea, and the pen only helps in the transition from mind to paper. Besides, something this arduous and painful surely could not be considered cheating. I was gifted this by someone—or something—who believed in me. What am I supposed to do?

Paragraph after paragraph and page after page, I write. I have no idea what time it is. The cloud outside remains consistently grey, and I smashed all of the clocks in the house last week. Also, I have lost count of how many painkillers I have taken. All I know is the emotional charge jumping from the page transcends any pain. Six wounds now gape open from my right leg, but there is a detachment as though I am on a different plain. So much for pacing myself.

I'm at the halfway point in the story, but I'm growing weary. I have started to see things—shadows lurking in the dingy corners of the room— and in the middle of the field, there is a scarecrow that appears to be slowly rotating.

I wake up to see a pool of semi-congealed blood surrounding the chair. Shit, how much blood have I wasted? Why the fuck didn't I wrap my wounds? I have to be on top of this; I won't make it otherwise. The pain is sharp but still manageable, and I wash six painkillers down with some wine. I know any more than that would make my attempts at writing futile. I can only rely on the pen so much.

My body is lethargic—heavy and unresponsive, but if I work all day, perhaps I can finish this dark tale. Groans emerge from my stomach, but any hunger pangs are overridden by the tremendous pain that rips down my leg as I raise myself from the chair. Carefully, I strip off my blood-soaked clothes, grimacing with each move. The devastation I have inflicted on my body over the years is no longer shocking to me, but the scar tissue that works its way across my skin means prostitutes demand a premium. Don't judge me; my love is for my work. Sacrifices must be made.

I grab the blade and urgently survey the uneven landscape of my skin until I find an untouched clearing. With the belt between my teeth once more, I rip through the right side of my abdomen and release a garbled muffled scream. Shit! The blood is coming out too fast; I think I've gone too deep. There is no time to waste, though, so I grab the pen and go to work, paying no heed to the rattles of the windows or the darkness that wraps itself around the house.

A complexity of emotions flows onto the paper. Nothing is lost in translation as the pen dances across the pages, bringing heartache and despair to these real people I have created. I feel it all, and I know the reader will, too. Not one mistake, no edits required—it is a flawless account of darkness.

What was that? Something in the room. More shadows.

The words on the page are beginning to drift in and out of focus. I feel light-headed. *No—not now.* Everywhere I look, I see my blood, fresh, congealed, in-between. There is so much of it. Has my urgency made me careless? I must finish it today. Then I can heal, rest, bask in the inevitable glory.

I carry on—nobody said it would be easy. The scratching on the paper is no longer satisfying. Each stroke feels as though I am drawing the sharp nib across my nerve endings. My body is screaming at me to stop, but the composition continues. I must play this out.

Tears roll down my cheek as I continue to scrawl—a combination of pain and the beauty of the prose that spills. I am so close now. My mind is starting to play tricks on me; the paper has been replaced with human skin, and the scarecrow outside appears to be getting closer each time I look up. *Is it smiling?* There's a cacophony of crows, but I can't see any though the window.

I sink the pen into my chest and grimace at the raw pain that shoots through me. My arm feels weak, and it hurts to hold the pen, but the words carry on. Eyes closing, body throbbing, the final chapter is shaping up nicely. I'm drifting in and out of consciousness, but the ending is coming together in heart-rending scenes of exquisite distress. A couple more pages and I should be—

The crows wake me. I must have passed out again. They scream in my head like some twisted alarm I can't turn off. *Come on!*

My body wants to give up, switch off, but the partnership continues—the pen narrating my inner darkness. These characters are self-destructing, their hate eating them from the inside. And it's magical.

So close—I'm on the last page—this is where it ends.

Is that in my head? The low hum of an engine above the caws. It's getting louder.

Must focus. But fuck, I feel as though I'm losing it.

Words still flow, but each one is becoming more laborious. I am struggling to keep the pace. The sheet of paper seems impossibly far away. Black spots dance in front of my eyes in rhythm to the pulsating pain. Shadows float across my vision, and that mysterious presence feels ever stronger. And the crows—so impossibly loud.

A thundering knock on the door startles me. It couldn't possibly be my imagination. As if in agreement, the crows instantly cease their cries and the shadows leave.

"Tristan," the voice is slow and distorted, but I still recognise it as Elly's.

No. Go away.

Why did the jealous bitch have to come now?

Another knock. "Tristan, I know you are in there."

Please leave.

I am so weak. I'm not sure how long I can keep going.

The sound of crunching gravel brings some relief—she's leaving. I try to regroup for the final push. But she's at the window, her face drawn back in obvious concern and disgust.

"Tristan!" she screams, as she runs down the side of the house

The door. Fuck—I don't think it's locked.

Within seconds, the door swings open. I scowl at her unwelcome presence. Cavernous lines eat into her bloodless face as she cries, "What have you done?"

"It's fine. I'm nearly finished," I say impatiently.

"You need a hospital. You're a mess." She wraps an arm around my shoulder as if to escort me away, but only manages to partially turn the chair.

"Leave me alone!"

"Look at the blood!" she asserts. "You're going to die."

"Fuck off!" My lips curl back around my teeth.

"I'm calling an ambulance," she says.

My tolerance is exhausted.

As she momentarily releases her grip to reach into her handbag, I swing the pen with as much force as I can muster into her neck. Instinctively, she reaches towards her throat with little facial reaction, but as the shock and realization kick in, she drops to her knees, eyes suddenly wide and full of terror. Whimpering follows—no rage, no screams—just a series of pathetic moans. Muted disbelief projects from her eyes, and I can only imagine the internal rush of thoughts in her head that throw her mortality into question.

She wraps her fingers around the pen and rips it out, creating a fountain of blood that sprays to the floor below. I watch her body topple over into the shallow pool of crimson and wince at the thud of her head on the floor.

As she squirms in our combined cocktail of blood, a lengthy and horrific gurgle leaves her lips.

Then, silence.

Without hesitation, I reach for the pen, grimacing at the wave of pain that rushes over me. I have lost too much blood. Elly was right; I'm going to die.

The words start to flow once again as the crows pick up their raucous tune. There is a smell in the room, too—perhaps it is the smell of my imminent death. But I am down to the last paragraph—nothing can stop me now. The shadows that fill my vision are becoming more aggressive, more restless, as though excited about the imminent climax of the tale.

Forcing my eyes to remain open as my entire body vibrates with a raw sensitivity, I write the first few words of the ending. More tears break through as the story approaches its harrowing conclusion.

The smell is getting worse—putrid, like nothing I have experienced before. Sinister darkness fills the room, and I know that cannot be attributed to the clouds alone. Urgently, I dip the pen back into Elly's neck and begin the final sentence.

Shadows peel away from the walls and surround me in a series of black clouds that aggressively splinter into smaller ones and then regroup. An oppressive heaviness in the air can be felt. *Is this what dying feels like?*

I push on with the final few words. It will be finished.

Out of the black mist steps the familiar figure—hooded black cloak draping across her human form—yellow eyes on me, but only darkness surrounds them. "Finish," her low guttural voice prompts.

My life is dwindling away. I feel it. But as I write the last few words, I cannot help but smile. I've done it—my masterpiece.

"The end," I announce.

"It's been a long time, Tristan," the entity says.

"It's perfect," is all I can conjure. "Perfect."

"Do you know who I am?"

"The pen—did you give me the pen?"

"I did. But it isn't magic," she says.

"What? What are you talking about?"

"How else could I induce such passion and intensity without raising the stakes?" she replies.

"It's not magic?"

"No. It's just a pen. You wrote this, felt this, bled this. No words wasted, no redundant branches of prose. I've been here with you, watching your new-found mastery of words. You're ready now."

"But w-why did you lie? And ready for what?"

"I am the devil—and I lie. I had to be sure you were the one."

The crows are back, but this time I can see them. They are in my room, fluttering wildly above our heads.

"You see, I need a writer. Someone to document my work, to portray the fear and torment I create. God has the Bible, but I have nothing. You'll be my writer, and together we will make history."

Piercing caws emerge from the crows as they launch into aggressive swoops—like vultures impatiently awaiting their dying prey. My heart rate is slowing, my life ebbing away. At least I will be remembered for this piece.

She looks almost sympathetic as she clicks her fingers, creating a large orange flame that dances in the palm of her hands.

Not my manuscript. "No, pleeeaassseeee—"

And as the crows drag my soul away from the shell of the body on the floor, I watch the pages of my manuscript burn.

Baby Teeth

by Azzurra Nox

"I had to do it," I say. "I had no choice." I pick at a hangnail, watch the blood pool beneath my thumb and press it against my mouth to suck on it. The taste of copper comforts me as I try to ignore an itch at the center of my palm. I adjust myself on the seat, although the handcuff on my right hand keeps me tethered to the chair.

"I know you've said this before, Melissa. But I'm finding it difficult to understand." The prison psychiatrist stares at me over her black rim glasses. Her dark hair is pulled back in a tight bun at the base of her neck. She sighs, tapping the pencil against her notebook, reading over the arresting officer's scribbled notes about me. "It says here that you killed your daughter."

"You're not listening to me. I had to do it." My voice is cold, unfeeling. Ana wasn't my daughter. At least, not anymore. Something had taken possession of her. Something evil.

The itch on my palm is becoming unbearable to ignore.

"I am listening. I just don't understand why. Why did you kill a little girl who was only six months old? That's monstrous!"

I lean back, a slow smirk forming on my lips. I know how I'm going to sound. There's a reason why they've stuck me here. But I'm tired of not being heard, and this shrink is willing to listen. She probably won't believe me, but I don't care. She wants the truth? I'll give her the truth.

"Ana was possessed," I say. "And if you have the time, I'll tell you how it all began…"

Ana was my first child. I was thrilled when I found out that I was pregnant. My boyfriend Owen shared my same enthusiasm. The moment we found out her gender, we went wild with the preparations. Owen painted the nursery a pale shade of pink whilst I bought onesies decorated with strawberries, bows, and daisies. The first few months of the pregnancy went by without a hitch. Sure, I had morning sickness and odd cravings (suddenly, I loved fried pickles), but overall everything was within the norm.

Everything changed the night we came back from my parents' house and found a dead rat on our doorstep. It wasn't scary—sewer rats were common in an urban city, but there was something off about this. Upon closer inspection we noticed someone had carved an upside triangle with an intersecting V at the bottom of the creature's belly.

"What the fuck is that?" I stepped away, horrified. My hand automatically grazed my own belly, afraid for the innocent life taking shelter in my womb.

Owen kicked the rat off the doorstep and muttered, "Some loser Goths being wise, that's all." He turned the key in the lock and ushered me in. "Don't think about it. There's nothing to worry about." I couldn't stop looking to where Owen had kicked the rat. Was it witchcraft? Was someone trying to place a curse on us? I shook my head; it was a silly thought. This wasn't a Stephen King novel. Whatever kids did that to the rat, they were probably unemployed sad fucks who dressed in black and still lived in their parents' basements.

As if sensing he needed to lighten the mood, Owen said, "By the way, have you decided on a name for our daughter?"

I unglued my eyes from the rat's blank stare and mutilated body. "Yes. I think Ana would be nice."

"That's such a pretty name." He kissed me, then brought his own hand down over my abdomen and whispered against my neck, "She's going to be a very lucky girl having you as her mother."

Owen didn't know then that six months later he would find me in the nursery, clutching a knife. That the blade would be splattered with our daughter's blood.

From the very beginning I knew something was wrong with Ana. I had a prolonged labor that lasted twenty hours, and it wasn't until the last moment it was decided for me that I would have a cesarean section. Afterwards, while I waited for the effects of the drugs to fade, the nurse placed Ana in my arms. I noticed right away that she wasn't crying, being unusually quiet. Her silence perturbed me.

"Is this normal?" I fretted, years of seeing babies come into the world in movies screaming, my only reference for comparison.

"No," the nurse admitted. "But she's breathing fine, and the doctor looked her over and found nothing wrong with her."

I bit my lip as I looked into Ana's deep blue eyes. The infant eyed me with quiet contemplation and instead of being filled with an immense sense of love, I was filled with dread. Something was wrong with my daughter. I just didn't know what at the time.

After several weeks of being back home, I still didn't feel bonded to Ana. I'd read all the baby books and did everything suggested to make me feel closer to my daughter. I nursed her, changed her diapers, gave her a bath, and spent time taking her out to the nearby park so she could get some fresh air. None of it helped me feel like a good mother. I spent nights wide-awake, the only time Ana cried. Owen said it was normal, that all babies cried at night, but hearing her shrill screams only made me bury my head under the comforter, wishing she would stop.

On one endless night when Owen was at work, I cradled Ana's body against my chest, grateful that her eyes were finally shut in a fitful sleep. I stared at her pudgy cheeks and golden curls. She looked so beautiful, so innocent. Why did I remain so convinced something was off? I stood up from the rocking chair and walked over to the window. I knew it was dangerous, but my arms were moving of their own volition. They extended, suspending Ana midair.

Drop her. The thought was horrendous, but it was all I could think. *Drop her. Drop her. Drop her!*

Just when I was about to give into my inner voice, Ana's eyes shot open, glowering at me with a strange shade of crimson. I fell back, and we both landed on the floor. She shrieked the moment she hit the ground, her cries penetrating my head like a sledgehammer.

Why couldn't I make her stop crying? Why did she hate me so?

Ana was onto me. I could feel it.

Strange incidents began to happen to strengthen my notion that something wasn't quite right. One night when I was breastfeeding Ana, I felt a sharp pain shoot through my nipple and yelped in surprise. I dropped her on the ground, and Owen came rushing to the nursery. He looked at me, mouth agape at the image before him. Ana was on her back, red faced and squealing, legs and arms thrust upwards like an overturned beetle. All the while I sat there cradling my injured breast.

"*Melissa, what's wrong with you?*" He seized Ana from the floor and brought her close to his chest, rocking her as a means to comfort her.

"She bit me," I said, dabbing blood from my nipple with a tissue.

"You can't just drop her like that! You could've killed her!" He stormed off with Ana in tow and refused to speak to me for days. A week later, he hired a nanny. He didn't have to explicitly say it, but Owen no longer trusted me with our baby.

At first, having a nanny around was blissful. The late-thirties woman had a warm smile and fat hands. Mary was completely in love with Ana too, cooing over everything the child did, even pointing out to me once that Ana had spelled her own name using the alphabet building blocks.

"That's ridiculous," I said, convinced Mary was playing a trick on me. At twenty-six weeks, Ana was far too young to achieve anything like that. I kicked the blocks away in anger. Even if it was true, it was strange.

But Mary was convinced there was nothing wrong with Ana, that she was nothing but a precocious child. She gushed over every achievement, detailing each to Owen when he came home. By then I was usually hiding in bed, the comforter pulled over my head. I hadn't showered in days, but I didn't care. Maybe Ana had fooled both Owen and Mary, but I knew better. She wasn't a prodigy in the making. No, Ana was something far more sinister.

One night I woke up with a heavy feeling on my chest, like something was pressing down on me. I snapped my eyes open and gasped when I saw Ana sitting upright on my chest, peering down at me. Her eyes were bleeding, and I desperately wanted to wake Owen, but I couldn't move my limbs. Paralyzed, I tried to scream but nothing came. I stared at Owen's sleeping figure and then up at Ana's unearthly face as tears streamed down my cheeks. Someone had to help me! Why couldn't I move? Why couldn't I speak? As though reading my thoughts, Ana whispered, "Don't be scared, Mommy."

Finally, I let loose a scream. Ana fell to the ground, crying so loud.

Owen woke up with a start.

"Oh my God, Ana! *What did you do to her*?" He jumped over me to aid Ana.

"Nothing... She was here, sitting on the bed, just staring at me. And then she spoke!" I shuddered at the recent memory.

Owen glared at me as he held Ana in a protective way. "That's madness, Melissa. I think you need to get some help."

I wanted to retort that I didn't need help, that he was mistaken, but anything I had in mind to say died on my tongue. Ana looked over at me from her place in Owen's arms and I swear she gave me a little smirk. She had won this round.

Bottles of pills littered my bedside table. I stopped trying to get up from bed and allowed Mary to deal with Ana. I wanted nothing to do with the child, haunted by the vision of her sinister red tears and that creepy voice taunting me, *Don't be scared, Mommy.*

The psychiatrist my husband scheduled for me prescribed antidepressants and Xanax. He said it was normal for me to be depressed, that it was something many mothers dealt with after a pregnancy, that my hormones were to blame and I'd be back in tip-top shape in no time. I would've rolled my eyes if Owen wasn't there with me. I needed to at least look like I was making an effort to get well, but in reality I couldn't have given a shit. I only wanted to live in my bed, to never have to leave the security of those sheets and blankets.

"Will you be joining us for lunch today?" Mary said, coming into the bedroom with Ana in her arms.

I peeked out from under the covers and squinted at the clock. It was past noon. Could it really be that late already? I sat up feeling groggy and quickly dug through the bottles of meds I had on the table. I grabbed the one with the antidepressants and took the prescribed amount, swallowing it down with a La Croix I had been drinking the night before. It was lukewarm and flat, but I didn't care.

"I don't know. I'm not feeling well." My hair was tangled beyond belief. I had stopped brushing it three weeks ago. Now, it was a chaotic rat's nest with locks that resembled dreads. Acting like a functioning adult was so difficult. Of course, it didn't help that I became jumpy whenever Ana was in the same room with me.

"Are you sure? We'd love for you to join us," Mary insisted. "Tell her how much we'd love to have Mommy join us, Ana."

Ana waved her hands in response, and Mary laughed at the baby.

I could barely stand the sight of them.

"Please get out," I murmured, keeping my head down. I didn't want to see Ana. I could sense her negative energy pouring into the room by the way the hairs stood on the back of my neck or the goose-flesh riddling my arms. I coughed, catching sight of my breath. When had it gotten so cold?

Mary left without a word. I made a mad dash for the bedroom door, quickly locking it so the two of them couldn't return. Standing there with my back flat against the door, my chest rose in anticipation of a knock that never came. My eyes wandered across the room, surveying the constant state of chaos.

The bed was unmade with wrinkled sheets. Bread crumbs and soda stains were everywhere. If my grandmother was still alive, she would have been disgusted by the scene. And that wasn't all. For many, pregnancy meant being stuck with an extra twenty pounds or more—for me, it was the opposite. My body was emaciated.

I walked over to the vanity and sat down on the cushioned stool. Trying to move my arm to pick up the brush was too much of an effort. Any action was equivalent to trying to walk with a deadweight chained to my ankle. That was when my eyes caught sight of the scissors. Before I had a chance to think it through, I grabbed them and cut off a lock of hair. It fell from my head like a lifeless ballerina, defeated and exhausted. When Owen returned from work, he found me still seated on the stool, my long red curls scattered across the floor. What remained on my head resembled peach fuzz. "What happened?"

I shrugged. "It was too hard for me to brush, so I got rid of it."

I didn't dare look at him for fear he'd be looking at me with pity. I couldn't stomach his empathy. Especially when I was certain he thought I was going off the deep end. He refused to see the truth about Ana, to consider the possibility his daughter might be evil. As far I was concerned, Ana had everyone fooled. Owen. Mary. I knew better. I knew what she was really capable of. It was only a matter of time before Ana struck again.

I woke up to a strange sound.

Crunch, crunch, crunch.

As I slowly sat up, I could tell the noise wasn't coming from the bedroom, but rather from the nursery. I stood up, my feet kissing the cold floor as I made my way towards the sound. My steps were slow and purposeful. I wasn't sure what to expect, but whatever my imagination could have conjured up, it couldn't have been farther from reality.

Ana wasn't in her crib.

She was seated in the middle of the room on the pastel pink rug. Cockroaches crawled around her, and the baby picked one up with careful fingers. Then she gingerly stuck it in her mouth, biting the insect in half.

Crunch, crunch, crunch.

She chewed loudly on the cockroach. Seeing it made me feel sick to my stomach. I gagged, unable to stifle the sound. Ana's head spun to face me, her neck at an irregular angle, the skin taunt from the exertion. "Why are you so scared, Mommy?" Her eyes were as red as the insect leg clinging to the corner of her mouth. A yellow, pus-like substance dribbled down her chin.

Repulsed, I turned away and vomited in the hallway.

From that night on, my suspicion of Ana grew exponentially. I had to find a way to get rid of her, no matter the consequences.

"What do you mean you gave Mary the day off?" I wrung my hands in desperation.

"She had to go visit her mother in the hospital. There's no way I could say no to that, Melissa. Christ, try to be reasonable." Owen was busy cleaning the baby bottles, preparing fresh ones with the baby formula—after Ana bit me, I refused to breastfeed again. "Besides, I think you and Ana could use some time to bond. I know you've been dealing with postpartum depression, but our daughter loves you very much. It's not healthy for her to feel so rejected by her mother."

"I'm not rejecting her! I just don't feel safe around her."

"Safe? Are you listening to yourself?" He scoffed as he filled the bottles and placed them in the fridge. "She's a baby! And all babies need their mothers. Honestly, I've been quite patient with you, but you need to snap out of it and grow up."

"Fine!" I stormed out the door, slamming it behind me.

Owen left for work a few minutes later without so much as a goodbye. Ana was still asleep in the nursery, or so I assumed. I didn't hear her crying, and I knew I needed to check on her, but I couldn't bring myself to leave our bedroom. I was afraid of Ana. All I could think about was her chewing on that cockroach. Owen hadn't believed me when I tried to explain it all to him, how I'd seen her head spin around. He'd stopped listening after I mentioned the cockroaches. He rushed Ana to the hospital, appalled that his child had been eating insects and deathly afraid she could've contracted some illness.

But the doctor assured him Ana was perfectly fine. I, on the other hand, refused to go to the hospital with him. Instead, I locked myself in the bedroom. When he returned home with Ana, I didn't care if she was okay. That night I got out of bed, brought a pillow over to our closet, and fell asleep inside. I didn't need Owen. He obviously thought I was a nutcase, so why try to convince him otherwise? I was just so tired of fighting. All I wanted was to fall into a deep sleep and wake up to find out it was all a nightmare.

I had a dream where I had aborted Ana. It left me feeling a sense of calm I hadn't felt in months. Once I realized it wasn't true, that Ana still existed, the acid burned in my stomach, causing my breath to quicken. I felt ill.

I remained locked in the closet 'til it was almost one in the afternoon. Ana had cried for an hour before giving up, evidently coming to terms with the fact I wasn't going to comfort her. Around noon she shrieked again, probably hungry. Once more, I ignored her.

Then I heard a loud thump.

Had she gotten out of her crib? Under normal circumstances I never would've considered it, but I knew for certain she could get in and out of her crib. After all, Mary insisted she was smarter than the average child, so the fact Ana might be walking before most children wasn't completely unbelievable.

I waited for Ana to cry, but she didn't.

What if she fell and had truly hurt herself? What then? It wasn't concern for her that plagued me, but rather the fear Owen might reprimand me again for my lack of motherly duties. Dread crept into my veins. There was no way I could wait 'til Owen was home to check on Ana. What would Owen say if he found her on the floor, starving and hurt? Guilt gnawed at me, so I decided to venture out of the room.

I tried to be quiet as I approached the nursery. The room was silent except for a musical toy playing the song "It's A Small World."

"Ana, darling?" I tried to fake a caring tone. "Are you okay?"

Silence.

I took two more steps towards the nursery.

"Ana?"

Again, silence. But it was soon followed by a sharp *thump*.

I held my breath before entering. Upon first glance, nothing seemed amiss. Ana's toys were put away in her box, except for a Pierrot clown doll sitting on the toy chest, unwinding the notes to the song. When I heard another *thump*, I quickly turned around and gasped at the gruesome scene before me.

Ana was seated on the floor with a hammer in her hand. She brought it down. *Thump. Thump. Thump!* The hammer was speckled with bits of rat skull, brains, and blood as she brought the hammer down on the dead creature again and again.

"My god!" I couldn't take my eyes off of her or the ghastly sight.

Ana looked up. "I'm going to smash your brains, Mommy!" All I could do was scream. And the more I screamed the more Ana laughed, continuing to slam the hammer down on the obliterated rat.

Doubt clouds the shrink's eyes as she listens to me tell her what happened. When I'm done, she lets out an exasperated sigh.

"What you've just told me is...unbelievable. There's no way your daughter could've threatened you. Your husband said he found you splattered in blood while clutching your daughter's dead body."

"You haven't been listening to me. I told you, Ana was evil."

"Melissa, your daughter was found lifeless with forty-seven stab wounds. How can you justify that?"

"I had no other choice," I state, nervously scratching the inside of my palm. The skin is red, but I keep it hidden under the table. I don't want the psychiatrist to see that it's infected.

"You insist on saying that you're not guilty."

"She wasn't my daughter anymore. She was something...sinister."

The psychiatrist slams her notebook shut and stands up. "Our session is done for now. But I'd prefer if you'd reflect on what you've done. Your only means of getting better is to acknowledge what you've done and come to terms with the fact that you killed your daughter."

I continue to scratch my palm.

"It's too late for me," I tell the shrink with a tiny smirk.

"What do you mean?"

"Whatever was in Ana, it's inside of me now." Without saying another word, I raise my hand and show her my palm. The center of it bears the symbol of an upside-down triangle with an intersecting V. Blood seeps through, dripping down to the table. In a voice that isn't my own, I whisper, "Don't be afraid, Doc. I'm harmless." I break free of the handcuff and leap towards the doctor. She's unable to stop me. I ravage her throat like a beast, relishing the taste of her blood. The taste of copper has always comforted me.

My Body

by Wesley Southard

Meat cleaver in hand and her belly full of blood, Cynthia hid beneath the carving table, trembling in fear. Not only was the ice-cold blood drying on her blouse and face, it rippled uncomfortably inside her. The red across her palms refused to dry, her skin slick with sweat. The heavy, rectangular blade repeatedly slipped from her grip. Eyes blurred with tears, she curled into herself, terrified this day would never come to an end.

Outside, insistent fists continued to beat on the front door.

"You know, Mrs. Owen, I've been at this a long time—a *very* long time—and in all my years of being a restaurant proprietor, I've never been sent such a *beautiful* reporter to cover any of my establishments."

There it is, Cynthia thought, miserably. *Only three minutes in and I'm already being hit on.* At this point in her career, she felt like she should have been used to it, but every time a tasteless compliment or slick one-liner barged in and sat right dead on her lap, it still pissed her off. She was a professional and expected to be treated as such.

Par for the course, she supposed.

The man in the slick, Brioni pinstripe suit, Jermane Welkner, shot her a toothy grin full of affluential confidence. There was no chance he had purchased that seven thousand dollar bragging right here in *this* town. He may have been loaded, but she doubted he came to work on a normal day dressed to the nines. Today, he came to impress. From behind his polished oak desk, the man oozed confidence.

Cynthia shot him a tight-lipped smile. "Let's focus, shall we, Mr. Welkner?"

He presented his hands in surrender. "My apologies, Mrs. Owen. Sometimes I just can't help myself."

"It's *Ms*. Owen."

"*Oh?*"

"So, it says here in my research you own…twenty-one restaurants, with *Mon Corps* being number twenty-two. Your eateries are spread across fifteen states, many of varying fare, though most are in the upper tier of price point. Suit and tie affairs."

"Sounds about right."

Cynthia scanned her notes. "According to Forbes, you're said to have a net worth of nearly six million, and you have a house in nearly every state you have an establishment."

Welkner nodded, adjusting his tie. "Impressive research, *Ms*. Owen."

"What's really impressive, Mr. Welkner, is what you've managed to do with this building. I'm sure you already know, but this particular site has housed nearly ten other restaurants over the last thirty years since the original building was constructed. No matter what the place served—Mexican, Italian, Japanese, Indian—it failed to draw interest and ceased operations. Nothing has ever stayed here for more than six months tops. And somehow you come strolling in with, of all things, a high-end French bistro, and you take the town by storm."

The older man glowed with pride. "Indeed."

"So why here? Why Evansville, Indiana, a city of barely one hundred and twenty thousand people, and not in Indianapolis or Fort Wayne, places where the population is dramatically higher and diversity is better celebrated. This city has always had a deep German heritage, but at the end of the day it barely holds onto its single German restaurant. I'm sure you're aware you're in the middle of chain restaurant heaven, where it's far easier to feed a family on a middle-class budget. So why French cuisine? Why here?"

"These questions seem awfully peculiar, Ms. Owen. Am I under oath here?"

She waved him off. "Not at all. I'm only here to write a short piece about the abrupt success of *Mon Corps* and to have a taste of your fine food as part of my article."

"A food blogger?"

"Not quite. I'm employed by the Courier Press, not as an independent."

"And how does one become the local paper's food tester?"

Cynthia bit the inside of her cheek to keep herself from throwing her notebook at Welkner's waxy, product-heavy face. "Well, long story short, I failed out of culinary school and moved back home from New York and needed a job. Not having the heart to rejoin a kitchen staff, I saw the paper was willing to pay someone to test and grade new restaurants and do write ups on whether or not I would recommend the new kids in town."

Welkner cocked a teasing eyebrow. "And do we pass, Ms. Owen? Are we *cool* enough for this school?"

"That remains to be seen. How's the food?"

Laughing, Welkner smiled and pointed at her. "I like you, Cynthia—may I call you Cynthia? You can call me Jermane. In fact, I prefer it."

"Ms. Owen is fine. And you still haven't answered my question."

"Which was?"

Cynthia inwardly rolled her eyes. "Why are you the only one that stuck?"

Welkner leaned back in his chair, hands linked behind his head. "It's quite simple, actually: I have an eye for what works and what doesn't. Much like all of my other establishments, I saw an opportunity, so I pounced on it. It's like this. McDonald's doesn't just sell two billion burgers a year by accident. They're not so much of a burger joint as they are a brilliant real estate company. They always know the *exact* right place in every single town they lay brick down on to open up their grease traps. Turn that way, a McDonald's—turn back behind you, another damn McDonald's. I noticed that early on in my career, and I took that strategy to heart. Each one of my twenty-two restaurants, including this fine building we are sitting in, are located in the very best area of that chosen city, and if they aren't already standing, like this one, I buy the land and build it. Not only do I serve the finest food at my restaurants, I have the eyes of everyone in town, whether they can afford it or not. Middle class or lower, they'll find the means to dine with me."

Cynthia hated to admit it, but this was going to make for an interesting article.

"As far as it being French," he continued, "this is a new venture for me. I blame that on Alex."

"That's Alexandre Boucher, correct?"

"Correct. He searched me out, and we found this town and this building. His food is quite delectable, and it's caught the appetite of all the local…what are Indiana residents called again?"

"Hoosiers."

"That's it. It's just that straightforward. This town was dying for a taste of Europe they've never experienced, and we're giving them what they want."

"You certainly are, Mr. Welkner. From what I gather, your sales have doubled, sometimes tripled, nearly every week since you opened two months ago."

He grinned smugly. "If you try the *Bouillabaisse*, you'll understand why."

"I plan on it." Cynthia closed her notebook and stood. "In fact, I plan on sampling most of the dishes here tonight. Can't give a proper evaluation if I don't."

Welkner rose with a grunt. "And I will make sure you receive the best service possible. You'll be sitting at my personal dining room table."

As they exited the office, the heat of the kitchen hit her like two hands to the chest. Kitchen staff hustled and bustled in their crisp white uniforms and hats, cutting, slicing, mixing, and mashing. The inviting aroma of frying duck and spiced sausages permeated the air, mingling with the rich scents of sage and tarragon, instantly making her mouth water. The feeling didn't come often, but when it did she missed the rush of a bustling kitchen on a hectic Friday night.

She turned back to Welkner. "Would you mind if I spoke to Mr. Boucher for a moment? I'd like to get a few quotes for the article."

Welkner shrugged. "That's not up to me. I'll take you to him, but he's not much of a talker, especially when he's in the zone. Let's go see if he's up to it."

A quick walk up the far side of the kitchen, and they faced the frenzy of the front line. A half a dozen men and women worked the grills and ovens, each one sweating in silence. A young woman, who Cynthia assumed was the sous-chef, worked shoulder to shoulder with a much older man in an almost comically tall chef's hat. His thick black mustache and eyebrows gleamed with perspiration as he intently worked on plating an order of *Salmon en papillote.*

Dodging the busy waiters, she stepped around to the other side of the heated pass window. "Mr. Boucher? Mr. Boucher, my name is Cynthia Owen. I'm a reporter and food critic for the Courier Press. I'm doing an article about your restaurant and would like to speak to you for a moment, if I could."

Without moving his head, Boucher lifted his eyes slightly and glanced at her, then returned to his work just as quickly.

"You've got quite the setup here, Mr. Boucher. I'm rather impressed."

"*Merci.*"

"Is it always this busy on Fridays?"

He remained focused on his work, handing the plate to his sous-chef before grabbing another from the grill chef behind him. "*Oui.*"

She could already tell this was going nowhere. "I, um, I learned a bit about the start of the restaurant from Mr. Welkner, but I still have a few more questions. The name of the place, *Mon Corps.* Why exactly did you choose to name it 'My Body'? Seems like an odd name, wouldn't you say?"

He remained silent, carefully placing diced tomatoes onto a plate of chicken confit. Then he muttered, "French food is good for body. For soul. Hearty. Delicious. Makes people happy."

Cynthia nodded. "Okay, that makes sense. And I have to agree. I'm a big fan of French cuisine. I just have one more question. I did a bit of research before I came here tonight, and I cannot seem to find any information about you out there at all. I asked around and made some phone calls, but no one has ever heard of you, Mr. Boucher. Where exactly did you come from before partnering with Mr. Welkner?"

The kitchen line stopped moving. The grill cooks all turned to look at her with blank expressions. The young sous-chef side-eyed her boss. With a frown, Alexandre Boucher lifted his head and glared at her. The sudden silence made her shiver.

Without a word, Boucher grabbed two empty meat containers from the chiller in front of him and a large carving blade and exited the line. With several long strides, he skulked to the back of the kitchen. He then unlocked a thick, metal door with a key attached to his belt and stepped inside a dark room, slamming the door shut behind him.

Welkner placed a hand on her shoulder. "See? Not much of a talker, but a whiz of a cook."

Cynthia swallowed as she stared at the back door. "That's okay." She turned to face him. "Might I ask, where does that door lead to?"

"To a sub-basement. It wasn't here before we moved in. Boucher insisted we have it built. It's where he stores a lot of the food, mostly the meats. Something about the natural coolness of the earth or whatnot. All I know is it cost me a damn fortune, and he won't even let me down there to see what I paid for. Anyway, enough chatting. Let's get you seated."

"That sounds good, but I'll find it on my own. My boyfriend is probably already at the table waiting for me."

Welkner seemed to shrivel. "A boyfriend? You're breaking my heart, Ms. Owen."

"If the food isn't good, I'll really break your heart on page five tomorrow."

The front doors to the restaurant crashed open. From underneath the carving table, Cynthia stifled a scream and gripped the meat cleaver tighter. Footsteps scattered throughout the dining room. A moment later, the kitchen doors swung inward.

Grunting, Cynthia fell back onto her pillow. Above her, Greg followed suit, collapsing onto his side of the bed with an exhausted sigh. Both were drenched in sweat, both waiting for their breaths to find them again.

"Holy shit," her boyfriend stuttered.

"Yeah."

"Like, *holy shit!*"

"I know."

Greg wiped his face. "What the hell got into us?" He began to laugh. "I'm so damn full I could burst, and all I could think of on the way back was how bad I wanted to get home and jump into bed with you. Is that crazy?"

Cynthia grinned and laughed, as well. "Hand me that towel." After tossing her the wash rag, she began to wipe off her bare stomach—a stomach full of quite possibly the best food she had ever eaten. Dozens of delectable samples of *Coq au Vin*, *Cassoulet*, and *potatoes Dauphinoise*. A steaming bowl of *Boeuf Bourguignon*. A hearty slice of *Quiche Lorraine*. The lamb chops—*my God, those lamb chops!* They ended the meal with chocolate drizzled *Profiteroles* and a *mousse* so rich it hurt her teeth. For all the doubt she had going in, Welkner definitely put his money where his mouth was. Part of her wanted to shred the arrogant prick in her review, but the immense satisfaction buzzing through her body—not to mention the great, spontaneous sex she and Greg had the moment they came back home—the place would receive probably the best score she'd given out in her eight years on the job.

Never in all that time had she continued to think about the food long after she ate it. Hours after Greg finally fell asleep, Cynthia sat awake, staring at the ceiling…wishing she could get another taste. It was absolutely incredible. Every dish, every single bite was like a little slice of perfectly-cooked heaven. She could only dream of being able to prepare food like that, which was the exact reason she couldn't cut it in Hyde Park and had to move back to the Midwest with her tail between her legs. No matter how well she was doing now, it was always her biggest regret, and seeing firsthand what she could have been brought back the same feeling of shame she felt all those years ago. If she wasn't worth a damn in the kitchen, she could damn well help others be.

In the dark, she pulled out her laptop and did a little more digging on Alexandre Boucher. Once again, she came up empty. Not a single article, not a solitary shred of back story. She knew most chefs to be eccentric and outgoing, always searching for the limelight, but to have one as talented as Boucher presumably appear from thin air was disorienting. This was a first for her, and for some reason she couldn't let it go.

She closed the laptop, then her eyes, and dreamt of warm meat.

They scrambled into the kitchen by the dozens, their footsteps erratic and purposeful. All around her various metal instruments hit the concrete floor as the crazies tore the room apart, tossing aside anything not already anchored down. Underneath the carving table, she curled in tighter, carefully shifting two large, plastic mixing tubs so they would better hide her.

Sitting at her desk, Cynthia couldn't concentrate. Her head throbbed, and her stomach ached deeply. It was only 10:00 a.m., and everyone around her was grating on her nerves. Questions and answers, sign this, approve that, look at these—*shut the fuck up!* She liked to think of herself as a fairly easy-going, happy person, but she couldn't shake this enduring annoyance of everyone around her. People she'd known for years, who she considered her closest friends, were now like flies constantly landing on her face.

What the hell is wrong with me?

She knew what was wrong, and she didn't care to admit it. It was embarrassing that she couldn't stop thinking about *Mon Corps*. She was a professional, and the fact she continued to obsess about food she had eaten over a week ago made Cynthia want to bang her head against a wall. She should have been preparing for tonight's assignment, a new Mexican restaurant opening over in Newburgh. Instead, she found herself daydreaming about *cordon bleu* and *Magret de canard*. She typically didn't double dip into past eateries, specifically those she reviewed for work, but the thought of not tasting Boucher's *Tête de veau* again drove her absolutely crazy. She had to know more about the man and his food. Perhaps...she would go again.

Cynthia's cell rang. "Greg? Everything okay?"

"It most certainly *isn't* fucking okay. I just got fired!"

"What do you mean *fired*?"

Greg laughed sarcastically. "Fired, Goddamn it! I finally had enough of Morrison's shit, so I punched him right in the nose! You should have seen it. Blood went everywhere!"

Cynthia sat up straight. "Wait—you *hit* your boss?"

"I don't know what came over me, Cyn. He started mouthing off again this morning, and I just...*snapped*. I hit him in front of everyone at the plant."

"Christ Almighty, Greg!"

"And that's not even the best part."

She pulled a face. "*The best part?*"

"The moment he hit the ground, I straddled him and just started *wailing* on him. It took, like, three co-workers to pull me off of him. Well, I guess they're not co-workers anymore. I assume I'm shitcanned."

"Greg, that's terrible!"

"Screw it. I'm heading home. I don't feel like meeting you in Newburgh for dinner. Just go on your own, okay?"

Before she could answer, he hung up. She sat there for a little while longer, staring at her computer and the lack of answers Google provided about Boucher.

Yes...perhaps she *would* go again.

Hours later, while she gorged herself in a corner booth at *Mon Corps*, in a dining room packed to the gills with enthusiastic, hungry patrons, Cynthia saw Greg sneak in and pick up a take-out order at the front desk.

A woman screamed and darted across the kitchen. Cynthia assumed she was part of the janitorial staff, hiding just like her, and had stayed there while Cynthia raided the kitchen. The terrified woman ran for the back door in a panic.

In a flash, the crazies tackled the woman to the ground. While she kicked and screamed, they grasped her by the quarters and lifted. The woman screamed and cried in horror. The crazies laughed and laughed. Once they had a solid grip, they walked her across the room toward Cynthia's table and slammed her down on the polished steel surface. Hiding beneath, Cynthia gripped the cleaver tight.

Dozens of legs surrounded her. The woman's feet stomped on the table top above Cynthia. Butcher's knives in hand, the crazies continued their hysterical laughter as they rained their sharpened blows down on the woman. Like her screams, her struggles eventually diminished. Bright red blood spilled over the sides of the surface and raced down the table legs, splashing the floor.

Heart pounding, Cynthia carefully reached out amidst the chaos and smeared some on her hand. She popped a wet finger into her mouth.

The thing growing inside of her thanked her.

It had been three days since she'd heard from Greg and nearly a week since she'd even seen him...and for some reason it was the last thing she cared about. She had confronted him that night after seeing him at *Mon Corps*. He denied it to her face. They shouted back and forth, calling each other liars. When the subject of being out of work came up, he snapped and hit her. She hadn't expected it, his strike swift as a snake bite. And he laughed.

He fucking laughed.

While he was cackling like a maniac, Cynthia snatched the letter opener from her home office desk and shoved the dull blade into his thigh.

Then she, too, started laughing.

Shocked, Greg screamed and hobbled out of the house, and she hadn't heard a peep from him since. The pain she caused him, the sudden act of violence toward her partner, made her feel sick…but something deep down in her guts told her it was the right thing to do. It spoke to her in whispered words. It *thanked* her.

Pushing the voice away, she sat behind her desk at work and continued her online search for information on Boucher. Every corner she could scour, every site dedicated to international chefs, continued to come up empty. Frustration was beginning to build, and everyone around her purposely stayed clear. A small part of her wanted them to get close, to annoy the shit out of her so she would have an excuse to strike. She was beginning to think Greg had the right idea. Instead, she listened to their background chatter as they gabbed about their weekends and family gatherings. More than a few times she heard mention of *Mon Corps*.

Instead of searching for Boucher's background, she instead did some digging on the actual building the restaurant occupied. Built in 1991, it was originally designed for a national Tex-Mex chain, but after several dozen people got sick from undercooked food, the restaurant shamefully closed its doors. Not even six months later, a local couple bought it and opened their dream pizza joint, only to see it fail due to lack of interest. The building remained closed for nearly a year that after before being sold to another company, an upscale East Coast seafood micro chain, wanting to test the waters in the Midwest. When the waters proved too cold, they packed up and left, allowing for six more eateries to give it the old college try. All failures.

So damn strange. How is it possible nothing caught on?

Her research only got weirder. When she went to find any info on the previous owners, what she discovered was shocking. Despite their age and health, every single one of them was now dead, having passed away not long after their restaurants closed. Cynthia sat back and stared at her computer screen in bewilderment. That couldn't be right. And yet, every obituary she dug up only added to her confusion.

Like it was destined to be Mon Corps...

A hand on her shoulder startled her back to reality. Her line-editor, Mary Sestero, was glaring over her with a sneer. "Cynthia, what the hell is wrong with you? You were supposed to go to Newburgh last week, and instead you hand me another fluff article about that damn French place? Care to explain yourself?"

Bleed. Make her bleed.

Cynthia had no idea where the voice came from, but she obliged it. She quickly stood and backhanded the woman across the face. Mary stumbled back, holding her wide-eyed, shocked face. Blood trickled out of her nose. Cynthia, just as shocked as Mary, stared her down.

Something thick and heavy coiled around in her stomach. This time it said, *Again. More blood.*

Mary staggered away. The rest of her co-workers were frozen in stunned surprise.

Now. More blood. Now.

"No..."

Feed me.

"*No!*" she screamed.

The large plate glass window overlooking the upstairs lobby exploded. A man Cynthia didn't recognize leapt through the opening. Pistol in hand, he howled with laughter as he opened fire on the office. Blood bloomed across the white walls as her co-workers screamed and collapsed, each of them now full of dime-sized holes. Since her desk was so close to the back stairwell, Cynthia quickly ducked out the room and down the steps. Heart racing, she ran through the car park, hopping over several other dead bodies on the way, and found her car. She winced as dozens of random gunshots popped outside of the building. Some were far away. Others were much closer. Screams and maniacal laughter filled the air.

Hoping to find Greg, Cynthia raced home, all while the lump in her stomach begged for more blood.

The poor woman above her had completely stopped moving, and it was easy to see why. The crazies surrounding the table danced joyously in the pool of fluid they had created on the kitchen floor. Cynthia knew she should be revolted, but the copper taste on her tongue reminded her she was no saint.

Then the crazies stopped. All in unison, they turned. The back storage door slowly creaked open, revealing an empty black maw beyond. As if by instinct, they shuffled through the open door, disappearing beyond.

As they exited the room, one of the crazies slipped in the blood in front of her table and collapsed to the floor. The man sat up on his elbows and turned toward Cynthia.

Greg grinned at her with blood-stained teeth.

Traffic was a literal nightmare. Cynthia weaved between dozens of stalled cars, manned and unmanned. Pileup after pileup. Smoke and gunshots. People being pulled out of their houses and stabbed repeatedly in the streets. Faces shredded by fingers. Men, women, and children—no one was spared. It seemed as though the whole town had gone crazy, and if the voice coming from her gut held any sort of sway, she'd be right there with them.

Hands shaking with adrenaline, she pulled to a screeching stop in front of her house.

Cynthia stared in horror.

Greg, the man she once considered the love of her life, was repeatedly beating their neighbor and his twelve-year-old daughter on their lawn with an aluminum bat. The girl's head was almost gone, bones and brains mashed into a sloppy, pink soup. Sweat dripping down his blood-speckled face, Greg looked up to Cynthia and laughed.

"What do you think, baby? French sound good tonight?"

Greg hobbled toward the car.

Cynthia hit the gas.

"How about it, Cyn?" Greg rasped, sitting up on his knees. "Have we done enough sinning yet?"

"Stay away!" Cynthia kicked the mixing bucket at Greg, who quickly batted it away. She swung the cleaver at him, warding him off. "Don't you fucking touch me!"

"Don't be like that, baby… It's all over now. We did exactly what it asked."

"W-what are you talking about?" she asked, still swinging the blade.

Greg smiled wide, unbuttoning the polo collar around his throat. "Let it take you over, Cyn. Feed it and add to its body." He winked. "Help him live again."

His body activated into an uncontrollable shake. Greg pitched forward on his hands, groaning in pain. Blood spurted from his lips. Eyes wide, he threw his head back and, giving one last hoarse scream, his throat bulged and exploded. Cynthia cried out as something long and dark red hit the floor with a wet, mushy slap. Greg's lifeless body collapsed on its side.

Cynthia gazed in horror as the long piece of meat reared up like a snake and slithered off toward the back storage door.

With nowhere to go, Cynthia drove to the only place that made any sense to her. The answers she sought were at *Mon Corps*, and at this point she would kill to get those answers.

Kill. Kill. Kill.

"*Shut up!*"

Though it was closed on Mondays, she wouldn't let that stop her from getting inside. Adding to the chaos among her, she used the lug wrench she kept in her trunk to pop open the front door. She stepped inside, then relocked and barricaded the door behind her with the couch from the front lobby. No alarm sounded at her intrusion.

"Alexandre Boucher!" she yelled to the empty, black dining room. "Where are you, you son of a bitch?" When no one answered, she sprinted into the kitchen. "What the hell have you done to us? What's in your food?" She flicked on the lights and found the kitchen similarly deserted.

Then the smell hit her. All the food. All the scents. All the spices. All the *meat.*

Feed me.

Cynthia's eyes blurred, head cocked.

Feed. Me.

Her senses overpowered her. Before she knew what she was doing, she dashed for the freezer locker near the salad station and threw open the door. She inhaled deeply, letting her nose drive her legs.

In the back corner of the freezer, a few buckets of chilled meat sat on a metal rack. Without thinking, she dove for the nearest bucket and dug her fists into the raw meat, smashing as much of it as she could into her mouth. The voice inside her stomach moaned with excitement as Cynthia lifted the bucket and drank the icy blood within. Being a longtime cook, she was confident in her ability to identify just about any type of protein offered to her—not to mention the fact it was part of her culinary school curriculum—but she had never tasted anything like this. And now that she had it dripping in her mouth, she could tell this was the very meat used in nearly every dish at the restaurant. Maybe it was prepared in different ways, mixed with different spices and ingredients, but the tang—the *potency*—was so utterly indistinguishable.

What are you, you delectable monster?

The bucket now empty, the lump inside her guts sang with glee. Cynthia dropped the bucket and stumbled backwards toward the door, now feeling the weight of what she'd just done. Disgusted, she re-entered the warmth of the kitchen and ran for the sink, jabbing two fingers down her throat.

More blood. More.

Before she could expel the contents of her stomach, countless angry fists erupted against the front door of the restaurant.

After the raw, red thing had burst from Greg's body and slithered out of the room, Cynthia slowly crawled out from under the carving table. Keeping the blade tight in her grip, she carefully stepped over Greg's nearly-decapitated head and followed the trail of slimy blood toward the open back door. She turned back, quickly checking the rest of the kitchen for crazies, and then stepped through the doorway.

The door slammed shut behind her.

Smothered in black, Cynthia quickly remembered her cell phone. She pulled it out and shook it, activating the flash light. She expected some sort of walk-in freezer, one big enough for hundreds of pounds of Boucher's meat, but the sudden brightness simply revealed a long, dark hallway that didn't appear to end. Beneath her feet, bloody footprints and a wide, slimy trail led down the path.

Carefully, she tottered down the narrow walkway. The further she traversed, the more the floor sloped downward. Soon, the warm summer air disappeared, replaced by the crisp, natural bite of deep earth. She imagined she was now somewhere underneath the expressway, across the restaurant's parking lot. Welkner really had no idea what he paid for.

Eventually the hallway came to an end. A carved, dirt doorway opened up before her. Cold, inky black rested beyond.

Trembling, Cynthia stepped through.

The room was cavernous and hollow like a carved-out gourd. Lifting her arm, she swept her flashlight back and forth. Beneath her feet, hundreds upon hundreds of fresh, dead bodies lay face-down on the dirt-packed floor. Similar to Greg, their throats had been the means of escape for the sludgy red creature gestating in their stomachs…presumably the same thing egging her on. Just looking at them made the thing inside her wriggle with excitement.

The hushed sound of their slithering filled the room.

Gingerly, she stepped around the bodies and continued to arch her light. Her beam caught something in the far corner.

Cynthia gasped.

In the wide circle of light, a massive body sat slumped against the wall. At least fifteen feet high, there wasn't much left to the being—*whatever* it was. Its bones were yellowed with age and mildew. Its skull was the size of a buffalo's, with a wide-set, razor toothed mouth that reached well to the back of its neck. Two sizable horns curled up from its temples. Cynthia knew she should be terrified, knowing damn well what she was looking at, but she felt…fascination. Wonder. Sadness.

A large hand fell onto her wrist. Cynthia shrieked, nearly dropping her phone. Boucher stood next to her in the dark, watching her with a curious eyebrow. He was still dressed in his white chef's smock, complete with his oversized hat. With his other hand, he snatched the blade from her hand and tossed it into the darkness.

"Pitiful, isn't it?"

Cynthia stared at him, wondering where his French accent had gone.

"He was such a beautiful boy." Boucher frowned sadly at the massive corpse.

She whispered, "What is it?"

"My heir."

"I…I don't understand."

"Where we stand, my dear, is old, hallowed ground. You wouldn't fathom the atrocities which occurred in this very place, long before man stepped foot in this world. To do so would drive you mad. I owned this land, every nook and cranny. Then your beloved God created you wriggling fissures, and you set your hooks in and destroyed everything I created. You people slayed my baby boy and buried his corpse as if he were nothing more than a mutt's fecal matter."

Boucher's grip tightened on her wrist. What little light from her phone that reached his hand showed his fingers had lengthened by several inches and flushed to a deep ruby red. Cynthia sensed him growing taller beside her. She kept her eyes locked onto the rotted skeleton ahead. They lingered on the small strips of petrified meat still clinging to the bones. Her mouth began to water.

The thing beside her leaned into her ear. "Tasty, wasn't he?"

Feed me. Feed me.

Cynthia wretched.

Boucher cackled. "No part of him went to waste, and no one could deny his power. You're all so predictable. Like little piggies, you'll fill your greedy mouths with anything, not even thinking twice about it. And for that I am eternally grateful."

Boucher continued to grow taller, wider. The slithering grew louder.

"A millennia of searching led me here, back to my missing child. But no tears. This is not a sad occasion—quite the opposite. You see, like all other creations, everything's perennial. A prince can never really die. He sleeps..." Still gripping her hand, he gradually moved the flashlight's beam until it faced the opposite wall. "...waiting to be remade."

Cynthia screamed.

A massive red figure filled the dull light of her phone. It sat with its legs straight out, filling up the entire corner of the room. Sucking in deep, hissing breaths through its nose, the prince's eyes glared down at them. It held its large, paw-like hands out in beckon. Among the corpses, the long, mushy pieces of meat slithered across the floor, then up his arms, legs, and across his trunk. The demon's fresh parts absorbed into his new, hulking body. Each one he soaked in sent pleasurable shivers rippling through his bright, red hide.

"What a handsome boy!" Boucher declared.

When the last of the demon's parts climbed him and became his new flesh, his black, snake-slit eyes turned downward. Numb and shaking, Cynthia gawked up at him, noticing the absence of a mouth on his face.

The voice inside her stomach raged: *Kill! Kill! Blood! Blood!*

"It's all down to you, dear Cynthia." The thing that was once Alexandre Boucher released her wrist and stepped out from behind her.

Much like his son, the demon towered over her with daunting intimidation. Horns raging high over his head, his wide, razor toothed mouth grinned at her. Much like his human form, he appeared far older than she could have ever guessed, but that didn't mean he was any less threatening.

"You know what you must do," Boucher said.

The demon snapped his fingers, and Jermane Welkner came flying out of the darkness. He screamed as he tumbled over the dead bodies near her feet. Before he could jump to his own and run, the elder demon grabbed him by the back of his head and lifted him into the air.

"Let me go! Let me go, Goddamn you!"

The demon scowled, "God damned me eons ago, worm! Defiance and will to conquer Heaven will do that, even to his most loved creation." He turned to Cynthia. "It's all up to you, my dear. Give my son his voice back. Complete him. Let him be whole again and fulfill his birthright. My time is done. It's his turn to rise up and rule. I ask you, let an old dispossessed seraph finally *die*."

Shaking uncontrollably, Cynthia's eyes darted back and forth between the two, unsure what to do. Her brain and heart told her to run, to get as far away from all this death and madness as she could. But her stomach raged like a hurricane over choppy waters.

KILL! KILL! BLOOD! BLOOD!

Cynthia flexed her hands.

She glanced up at the giant, mouthless prince awaiting her answer. His glassy eyes pleaded.

"No!" Welkner cried. "Please, Mrs. Owen! Please don't hurt me!"

Cynthia gritted her teeth, feeling the rage wash over her. "It's...*Ms*...Owen!"

In a flash, she dropped her phone and leapt forward, driving her thumbs directly into Welkner's eyes. The older man screamed. He kicked and lashed out with frantic fists, but Cynthia leaned into him and continued to push as hard as she could. Blood ruptured from his eye sockets and sprayed across her face. Cynthia laughed, relishing the glee that now coursed through her body. The voice inside her stomach squealed with pleasure. When it seemed her thumbs could go no further, she gave them another thrust, and they dug even deeper into the man's head. Welkner wailed the entire time, and Cynthia continued to cackle.

A few minutes later, she released her hands. The elder demon dropped Welkner's corpse, adding to the countless others.

"How did that feel, Cynthia?"

She wiped the joyful tears from her eyes. "Delightful."

Grinning, he stepped back into the darkness, disappearing from the light. "It's now your time, my son."

With a grunt, the massive prince stood. Cynthia dropped to her knees before him. Hands holding her cheeks, manic laugher erupted from her throat, and a few moments later so did the rest of the new king.

The Red Butcher of Wrocław

by Graham Masterton

This year, it was colder in Wrocław than the last winter of World War Two, when the Germans were desperately holding out against the advancing Russian army.

In January, 1945, the temperature dropped to minus 27 degrees and blinding blizzards swept across Lower Silesia from the east. Back then, over 18,000 people in the city froze to death.

I had expected snow. I had *wanted* snow. But what was tumbling out of the sky every morning was overwhelming, like God and the angel Gabriel were having some never-ending pillow-fight. From the weather forecast, I could see our filming schedule would have to be pushed back by a week at the very least, with all of the extra cost and complicated rescheduling that would involve.

I was here in southern Poland to film some critical outdoor scenes for a chilling supernatural movie for Universal, provisionally titled *Chill of the*

Dead, but we had already gone two-and-a-half million dollars over budget. Not only that, our lead talent, Ada St. James, was booked to appear in another movie in only three weeks—a beach comedy set in Hawaii.

So here I was, sitting in the bar of the Art Hotel with the movie's male lead, Olly McBane, as well as our director of photography, Russ Mulroney, and our first cameraman, Jimmy Huong, and the movie's scriptwriter, Cindy Flinders, who also happened to be my current squeeze. We had chosen to sit in the raised area in the bar which overlooks the narrow street outside, and we were all trying to pretend we weren't keeping an eye on the thick fluffy lumps of snow that were endlessly falling past the window, in case they showed the slightest sign of easing off.

"Jesus," grumbled Russ. "We could of built Wrocław in the 007 Stage at Pinewood and called in Snow Business to do the effects, and I bet it would have cost us half of what this is costing. *And* we wouldn't have had to freeze our arses off or eat *pierogi* every morning, noon, and night."

"You don't have to eat *pierogi* morning, noon, and night," Olly told him. "There's plenty of other stuff on the menu."

"Yeah, but I fecking love *pierogi*. It's that *śledź* I can't stand, that pickled fish. That's enough to make a maggot gag."

Russ was short and bald with bulging blue eyes and a bristling ginger beard, and he had the thickest Sligo accent you ever heard. Every "s" sounded like "esh," like "Tings will get wush before dey get bettoh." All the same, he was one of the best DOPs in the business, and two years ago he had been nominated for an Oscar for his cinematography on that horror movie *Blood Season*.

Jimmy Huong was tall and lanky for being Chinese, but then his Mandarin father had married a tall and lanky girl from Sherman Oaks while he was working for MGM in the late 1970s as a sound technician. His father was probably a foot shorter than his mother, but apparently, he used to tell Jimmy that height is irrelevant when you're lying down.

Jimmy had a handsome Tony Curtis kind of a face, but Asian eyes and short black hair that stuck up on top of his head like a scrubbing brush. If he had inherited one Chinese characteristic from his father, it was his total serenity, and his deep-sounding mottoes. Like, "You can make as much cheese as you like from spiders' milk, but do not expect to spin webs."

Ada hadn't joined us. She had wrapped herself up in her fluffy fox-fur coat and gone down to Rynek, the city square, to do some shopping. She had rolled her eyes and admitted that, for her, "shopping is the nearest thing I have to religion."

Cindy noisily sipped the last of her Negroni and looked across the table at me with those hazel eyes of hers and said, "We might as well go back to bed."

Cindy was petite and pretty with a little snub nose and short but messy blonde hair. She was nearly forty but she looked as if she had just celebrated her twenty-first birthday. She was wearing a tight teal T-shirt with "Despair" printed on it in white letters. Despair was some heavy metal band from Fresno she knew, and I suspected she might have had a fling with the lead singer, some messy guy with a nose ring called Frogg.

"I have to call Bob and tell him we're still snowbound," I told her. Bob Kaminsky was president of production at Universal and I wasn't looking forward to telling him that we had filmed only three-and-a-half minutes since we had arrived here, and those were of Ada staring out of the hotel window, and then turning to the camera and saying, "I'm frightened, Jerry. I'm more than frightened—I'm petrified!"

Bob hadn't been too keen on *Chill of the Dead* from the start. He preferred comedies and musicals, and he thought my horror movies were way too extreme. Behind my back he called me "Gruesome Newsome" and a couple of times he had even said it to my face. My movies made a profit, though. *It's Raining Brains* had brought in $64.3 million, even though the critics hated it.

I was just about to get up and call Bob when my daughter, Kathy, came into the bar, wearing her pink duffel coat with the pointed hood and her Elsa from *Frozen* mittens. Her hood and her shoulders were still speckled with snow, although she brushed it off onto the floor and it melted almost at once. Close behind her came Marcin Sokolowski, who worked for the city promoting culture and sport, and who was supposed to be helping us find locations and organise our shoots.

"This is the *best* winter ever," smiled Kathy, perching herself up on one of the chairs. She was eight, skinny and tall for her age, and she had inherited the cheekbones of her Polish grandmother—my mother, Saskia. It was because of her Polish heritage that I had offered to bring her along on this shoot to see the land of her forebears for the very first time. It had given my ex-wife, Melissa, a break, too.

"It's a gas, Kathy. I agree with you," said Olly, lifting his glass up high so the waiter could see that he needed a refill. "In fact, I could happily sit here drinking *piwo* for the rest of my life, so long as I was getting paid for it."

Marcin pulled out a chair and sat down next to me. He was a lean young man with short-cropped hair and a long pointed nose. He was wearing a dark green Puffa jacket and a smart activity tracker on his wrist.

"I have just been to the office," he told me. "I am sorry to say that the weather forecast is not at all happy. The temperature is expected to go down even more in the next two days, and the snow will continue."

"Oh, shit," I said, and Kathy frowned at me and pressed her fingertip to her lips.

"Oh, *shoot*," I corrected myself. "What the two-toned tonkert am I going to tell Bob? If we can't start tomorrow, he's going to pull the plug."

What worried me was that Bob might not only cancel this location shoot, but that he might scrub the whole movie, since we had less than twenty-five minutes in the can so far. *Chill of the Dead* was a zombie movie set around Christmas, with dead people rising from their graves and bursting into the homes of their still-living relatives while they were opening their presents and singing carols and enjoying their turkey dinners. The tagline was *Merry Christmas, Every Body!*

"Kathy—would you like a Coke?" I asked her. "And how about something to eat? You only had that *pączki* for breakfast."

"No thanks, Dad. I'm not hungry," said Kathy. She was standing up again now because she could see four or five children out in the street having a snowball fight. On the sidewalk outside St. Elizabeth's Church, another two of them were building a huge snowman. "Can I go outside and play with them?"

"You don't speak Polish."

"I know, but you don't need to speak Polish to throw a snowball."

"Okay, but stay where I can see you."

"I will."

She pulled on her mittens again, jumped off her chair, and went down the hotel steps into the street. I could see her scooping up a handful of snow, packing it together, and throwing it at the nearest boy, hitting him smack on the side of the head. Before I knew it, she was right in the middle of a fierce barrage of snowballs, and obviously having the time of her life.

"How about that," said Russ, shaking his head. "I haven't had a snowball fight since I was at school in Cleveragh and I had to walk all the way home with my pants and my socks all wringing wet. But I'd give anything to be seven years old again and go out there and chuck a few snocks around."

"If you were seven years old again, you would have to be very careful here, in this street, with the temperature so low," said Marcin. "So the legend says, anyway."

"Oh, I was a *fianán diana* in them days. A tough little cookie, and no mistake, even though my ma said I had the brains of a bag of Legos."

"No matter how tough you were, that would not have saved you from *Czerwony Rzeźnik*," Marcin smiled.

"And what's that when it's at home?"

"*Czerwony Rzeźnik* means the Red Butcher. His name is famous in Wrocław...especially among the older generation. Near the end of the war, when Wrocław was under siege by the Russians, and it was colder than it had ever been in Lower Silesia in all of recorded history, everybody of course was starving as well as dying of hypothermia.

"But here...right here on this corner outside St. Elizabeth's Church, a kind of a temporary stall was set up, with a coke brazier, and this is where the Red Butcher was selling sausages. They called him the Red Butcher because he was dressed all in long scarlet robes, with a hood. And that is why this street is still called Kiełbaśnicza, which means "Sausage Makers' Street."

"It was a few days before parents began to come looking around here, saying that their children were missing. Of course it was different then...the city was under constant bombing and shelling and sometimes children wouldn't come home because they were sheltering somewhere, with their friends maybe.

"But more and more children were going out and then never returning home. Their parents searched all around the old town for them, and at last they discovered heaps and heaps of their bones and all their discarded clothes—and guess where?"

Marcin pointed out of the window across the street. "*There*—there is where they found them, hidden in the crypt of Elźbiety Węgierskiej. After that, they knocked over the sausage stall and chased after the Red Butcher, but he escaped into the church and they could not find him. He was never seen again."

"Oh my God, is that true?" asked Cindy. "He was really making sausages out of children?"

"You wouldn't believe what people will eat when they're starving," put in Olly, as the waiter handed him another beer. "I was in that movie, *Forlorn Hope*, about the Donner Party. You know, those pioneers who got stuck in the Nevada mountains in the middle of winter and ended up eating each other."

"It sounds like the kind of food they serve up in Chinese markets," said Jimmy. "Bat soup, pangolin pie, children sausage."

"You're one sick chink, Jimmy," grinned Olly.

I stood up. "I must go call Bob. If I stretch the truth a little, and tell him we've shot some great snow scenes, maybe he'll go easy on us. Order me another *Żywiec*, would you, Cindy, and maybe some *Kalisz wafers*. And a plate of those pickled mushrooms."

I went upstairs to our room on the first floor and sat on the bed and phoned Bob. He was in a surprisingly amenable mood, which made me suspect his new discovery, Jillie Burnside, had been nice to him last night, in spite of being half his age. I made up some story about all the fantastic snow scenes we'd been able to shoot, and how they were going to give *Chill of the Dead* some real class that would lift it way above your run-of-the-mill horror movie. In fact, we might even have a chance of winning a Golden Globe.

Actually, I don't think Bob was even listening to me, and I could hear girlish giggling in the background. After a while, he interrupted me and said, "Fine, Dave, whatever. You carry on. I know I can trust you to come up with something truly ghoulish. When do you think you'll be coming back?"

"Let's say a week to be on the safe side, Bob. I don't want to rush a production this good. You know what they say about ships and ha'porths of tar."

"Ships and what? No. No idea what you're talking about. Jillie— behave yourself, Poppa's on the phone!"

"Not a problem, Bob. I'll call you again tomorrow."

I stood up and went to the window which overlooked the street. Three boys were still throwing snowballs, but the kids who had been building the snowman appeared to have abandoned it, and it didn't even have a head yet. What disturbed me, though, was that there was no sign of Kathy.

I opened the window as far as I could and called out, "Kathy! Kath! Are you down there?"

The boys looked up at me, but clearly they didn't understand what I was shouting about, so they went back to throwing their snowballs.

I pressed the elevator button, but when it didn't open immediately, I ran down the stairs. As I passed the bar, I could see Russ and Olly and Jimmy and Cindy and Marcin all still sitting at the table, laughing. I yanked open the heavy hotel door and went down the steps into the street. It was bitterly cold out there, a dry cold that dropped into my lungs like somebody dropping an icebox onto my chest, and the snowflakes were tumbling around me so thick that I could see no further than the end of the high church wall.

I went up to the boys and said, "A girl. *Dziewczyna*. Have you seen her? She was out here tossing snowballs with the rest of you. A young girl. *Młoda dziewczyna*. She was wearing a pink coat. *Różowy*."

The boys looked at me blankly. Jesus, I wish I'd listened when my mother was trying to teach me to speak Polish. Even the few words I did know I was probably mispronouncing so badly that they couldn't understand me. *Jiff-chin-ah*, was that right?

I hurried through the snow up to the next corner. There was no sign of Kathy there, or of the boys who had been building the snowman. One of them had been wearing a fluorescent yellow anorak, so he would have been hard to miss. I went all the way around the church and then down to the next street, shouting out, "Kathy! Kathy!" so that passers-by turned and stared at me, all huddled up in their snow-covered coats, while I was wearing nothing but a blue rib knit sweater.

I stood by the headless snowman, listening. The snow had built up into such a thick carpet in the streets of the old town that I couldn't hear any traffic, only the flat clanging of trams along Nowy Świat at the end of the street.

"*Kathy*," I said, and then realised I had said that almost soundlessly, too.

I walked back quickly to the hotel. As I came into the bar, Marcin looked up at me and said, "David? What is wrong? Have you been outside?"

"My *God*, Dave," said Cindy. "You look like Frosty."

"Kathy's disappeared. Didn't you see her go? I thought I asked you to keep an eye on her."

Cindy turned around and stared out of the window. "Oh, no! She was there only a minute ago. I saw her!"

"Children can vanish in a minute, Cind, and Kathy's vanished. I've looked all around the church and up and down the street, and I can't find her anywhere."

"We will help you look for her," said Marcin. "She cannot have gone very far."

"I tell you, boy, it was literally only a minute ago that I saw her," said Russ. "She was right over there with them lads packing snow onto that snowman."

Olly swallowed the last of his beer and stood up. "Come on, guys. We'll all go and look. Grab your coats."

We all put on our coats and jackets and went outside. Olly and Russ and Jimmy split up, with Olly going down to the market square and Russ heading up to Nowy Świat and the Oder River, while Jimmy went to look along the narrow streets behind St. Elizabeth's Church. Cindy stayed with me, and Marcin acted as our guide and our interpreter. I knew "young girl" and "pink" and I even knew *zaginiony*, meaning missing, but that was hardly enough.

First of all, Marcin went over to the boys who had been throwing snowballs. They had given that up and now they were demolishing what was left of the snowman by drop-kicking it.

He spoke to them for a few minutes and then came up to Cindy and me and said, "They said your Kathy was helping the other boys to make the snowman when a priest came out and said something to them, and they followed him back into the church."

"But Kathy doesn't speak Polish, and she knows she's not supposed to go off with strange men."

"Well, he was a priest, so perhaps she trusted him. It seems as if the boys did."

"They must still be in the church, then. But what have they been doing in there? They've been there for what— at least fifteen minutes?"

I ran up the steps to the church door, nearly slipping over, and Cindy and Marcin followed me. The door creaked when I pushed it open, like the door in a haunted castle. Inside, behind the inner doors, it was gloomy and musty and smelled of stale incense.

St. Elizabeth's had been built in the fourteenth century in the Gothic style. It had soaringly high vaulted ceilings and narrow stained-glass windows decorated with angels and a benign-looking Virgin Mary. This afternoon it was almost empty except for a priest lighting candles behind the altar and one elderly woman praying in front of one of the side-chapels. Every footstep and every word echoed.

"It does not appear as if they are in here," said Marcin. "They could have come in through these doors and then out through the doors on the other side."

My heart was beating hard and I was beginning to panic. What would some priest want with Kathy and a couple of snowballing boys? Unless he wasn't a priest at all, but only dressed up to look like one, so that he could gain the children's confidence. Even then, though, surely the boys would protest if he tried anything sexual.

I circled around the church, looking in all of the side chapels and even opening up the confessional. Cindy and Marcin came after me, and our footsteps clattered like horses cantering. When I approached the altar, the priest who had been lighting the candles blew out his taper and came up to me. He was short and bald with a cast in his left eye, so he looked as if he were watching somebody behind my right shoulder, too. He said something but even though it sounded kindly, I didn't know what he meant. Marcin came up and translated for me.

"He asks if you have are looking for something, and perhaps he can help."

I nodded to the priest, trying to work out which of his eyes to look at. "You bet I'm looking for something. My eight-year-old daughter. She was brought in here by another priest—her and two young boys. She was wearing a pink duffel coat, with a hood. And red rubber boots."

Marcin spoke quickly to the priest, who listened, but then shook his head.

"He says he has only just come out of the sacristy to prepare for the next service, so unfortunately he did not see anyone of that description come into the church. But he wishes you the best of luck in finding your daughter and prays you will find her safe and well."

Cindy said, "What are we going to do now? I mean, where do you think he could have taken her? And for why?"

"We'll have to call the police, Marcin," I told him. "The sooner they start looking for her the better."

"Okay, yes, of course," said Marcin. He took out his phone and prodded it, but when he lifted it to his ear he said, "There's no signal in here. We'll have to go outside."

We headed quickly back towards the main entrance, but before we reached it, Cindy suddenly stopped and tugged at my sleeve and said, "Dave—*there*—what's that?"

"What's what?"

She pointed through the brick arch next to us, towards a dark oak door.

"There," she said. "There's something stuck underneath it."

I took a closer look. She was right. There was something pink trapped under the bottom sill of the door, and almost at once I realised what it was. With my heart palpitating even harder, I dropped to my knees in front of the door and tugged it out. It was one of Kathy's *Frozen* gloves.

"*Marcin!*" I almost screamed at him. "*Marcin!*"

As Marcin came running up, I tugged hard at the door-handle, but the door was firmly locked.

"This is Kathy's glove. He must have taken them in here! Quick—get that priest to open this door!"

Marcin stared at the glove in horror. "You are right—I saw her wearing these same gloves."

With that, he went back across the church, dodging his way around the altar, and just managed to catch the priest before he went back into the sacristy. The priest came hurrying up with a large bunch of jangling keys.

"He prays they have not left the key in the lock on the other side," Marcin interpreted, as the priest fumbled through the keys to find the right one. At last, though, he picked out a large key with a bit that was shaped like a demon's sigil, pushed it into the keyhole, and turned it. With a complicated clicking, the door opened up, and he pushed it inward. It shuddered on its hinges as if it were warning us not to come in.

On the other side of the door there was a short landing with an iron railing, and then a curving stone staircase. I was tempted to shout out, to find out for sure if Kathy was down there, but I thought it would be safer if I kept as quiet as I could. If that priest was unhinged enough to bring children down here, I didn't want to startle him into doing something crazy that might hurt them.

The brick walls of the staircase were illuminated by a dim, wavering light from below, so presumably there was somebody down there. Cautiously, I started to make my way down the steps. It was chilly down there. Not the bone-dry cold of the street outside, but a damp, breathy kind of a chill. The chill of the dead.

I heard a young boy's voice, and then somebody harshly saying "*sshhh*!" I turned and looked around. Marcin was coming down the staircase right behind me and Cindy was close behind him.

I crept down the last few steps of the staircase and found myself in a low-ceilinged crypt. Two paraffin lamps had been set up on either side of the crypt, and they threw dancing silhouettes on the walls. It looked as if the shadows in the dark recesses all around had mischievous lives of their own, and kept leaping out to frighten anybody who dared to come down here.

Sitting back-to-back on two upright chairs on the left-hand side of the crypt were Kathy and the boy in the fluorescent yellow anorak. They were lashed tightly together with blue-and-white washing-line cord. Kathy turned around and shook her head, her eyes wide, as if she were imploring me not to shout out loud.

She didn't need to tell me. What I saw in the middle of the crypt stunned me into silence, and I heard Cindy let out a squeal of disgust. On a long wooden table lay a partially dissected body, its head removed, its ribcage and its pelvis stripped of flesh, and strips of raw meat heaped up beside it. Where its head had been there was a beige woollen beanie, soaked in blood, and where its feet had been, there was still a single lace-up boot. The other had dropped onto the floor.

I said, "Right, Kath, let's get you out of here, right now. You and your friend. Marcin—call the cops."

I made my way around the table to untie Kathy and the boy in the yellow anorak, but as I did so I was stopped in my tracks by a hoarse, high, hair-raising screech. Out of the darkness at the far end of the crypt, a figure appeared—a figure robed in red, with a high pointed hood. Its face was masked in black gauze, so it was impossible to see if it was a man or a woman. It was thin and round-shouldered, but so tall its hood touched the ceiling of the crypt, and it came towards us with an odd, uneven gait, as if it were walking on stilts or very high heels.

In one hand it was carrying a huge triangular butcher's knife, stained with blood.

The figure stopped at the far end of the wooden table and brandished the knife at me.

"Marcin—call the cops *now*!" I told him.

Marcin took out his phone, but then the figure hissed and whispered something, so the black gauze was sucked in and out. Marcin held up his hand and said, "Wait, David—" and spoke to the figure in Polish.

The figure hissed and whispered again. Marcin listened, and then he turned back to me.

"He says he is the Red Butcher, and that he has come back because the winter is so cold and there is an epidemic and the people of Wrocław will soon be hungry."

"He's killing *children*? He's insane! Call the police!"

"He says he is a man of God, a cardinal. He is only obeying the word of the Lord. When Jesus fed the five thousand, it was with loaves, yes, but 'fishes' was a mistranslation of 'school.' When the people were starving, Jesus fed them children. The young were rightly sacrificed to keep their elders alive."

"He's crazy! This is like something out of one of my movies!"

"He says you cannot stop him because he has God on his side."

The red-robed figure started to walk in that odd, stilted way towards Kathy and the boy in the yellow anorak, holding up his knife. Kathy screamed, and the boy let out a terrified moan.

I ran forward and grabbed the Red Butcher's wrist. He twisted and struggled and hit me again and again with his free left fist, although he seemed to have very little strength. I wrenched the knife out his hand. When he tried to claw it back from me, I stabbed him as hard as I could, right into the middle of his robes. I dragged the blade upward until I felt it stick against his ribs, and then I pulled it out.

"*No!*" Marcin shouted. "David—*no!*" and Kathy screamed again.

The Red Butcher staggered, and I stepped back, still holding the knife. Marcin rushed up to the Red Butcher and tore open his robes with both hands. Underneath he was wearing a tight white sweater and jeans, but the sweater was slit wide open and already soaked in blood. Out of the slit, his intestines were cascading like a nest of slippery snakes.

"*Karetka pogotowia!*" Marcin shouted. "Call for an ambulance! It's 112!"

He was holding the Red Butcher in his arms as the scarlet-robed figure sank to the floor, his legs quivering with shock.

"Who *is* that?" I shouted at him. "Marcin—what the fuck is going on? Who *is* that?"

I heard Cindy saying, "Oh my God, oh my *God*!" and then I heard the urgent scuffling of footsteps coming down the staircase. Olly and Russ and Jimmy were suddenly in the crypt alongside me. Jimmy started to untie Kathy and the boy in the yellow anorak. Russ knelt down beside the Red Butcher, unfastening the silk cord around his neck.

"I told you this was a fecking stupid idea, didn't I?" said Russ, looking up at Olly. "Oh no, you said, 'it'll be the laugh of the century. Let's scare the shite out of the feller who scares the shite out of everybody else!'"

The boss-eyed priest had come down to the crypt to find out what all the commotion was about. As far as I could understand him, Marcin told him to go outside and wait for the ambulance to arrive.

I set down the knife on the table and knelt down on the cold stone floor next to Russ. He eased off the Red Butcher's hood and carefully peeled the black gauze mask away from his face. To my horror, the Red Butcher wasn't a "he" at all, but Ada St. James. Her eyelids were fluttering and blood was sliding out of the side of her mouth. Marcin was holding his hand pressed against her stomach to stop her intestines from sliding out over the waistband of her jeans.

"Oh Jesus, Ada," I said, under my breath. "Whatever you do, please don't die."

I turned around and saw that Jimmy was ushering Kathy and the boy in the yellow anorak upstairs. Kathy looked back at me, and I had never seen such pain and sadness on a young child's face before.

Ada survived, although it was touch-and-go for a while, and she spent months convalescing. She never acted again, and I never directed another horror movie. I was arrested, but I had a very persuasive attorney, and she was able to persuade the judge that I had acted in self-defence and in defence of my daughter.

I don't think I'll ever get that scene in the crypt out of my mind, not for the rest of my life. I haven't been able to eat pork ribs again, but that's been the least serious effect it's had on me. What it showed me was that death and horror are not entertainments, and the story of human existence has been nothing but an endless succession of appalling tragedies, one cruelty heaped on top of another, from the freezing ruins of Wrocław during World War Two to the misery of refugees in Syria.

I write comedy now, although most of it is bittersweet. If I thank God for one blessing, though, it's that I live in Sherman Oaks. I never have to see it snow.

Dog Eat God

by Kenneth W. Cain

Father Menendez made the sign of the cross. He'd never heard a woman talk like Mrs. Brewer, not outside of a confessional, yet here she was, revealing her most private stories for all close by to hear. What she said made his cheeks flush.

He sometimes wondered what her tits looked like. She always wore such thick sweaters in church, and he was certain she was a D cup, if not bigger. And given the current conversation, he was sure he could have asked her to whip those warlocks out, and she would have obliged. But he wasn't about to do that in front of her son, even if she didn't appear to mind.

What's wrong with her? Is she some sort of—

Mrs. Edith Brown came stomping down the aisle. He noted her instantly, not because of the way she swung her wide hips, but because of the dog.

He held up his forefinger. "Excuse me." Then he was hurrying down the aisle to meet Mrs. Brown. "No, no, no. You can't—"

"Father," she said, "help me. You need to kill my dog."

"What?" The sheer shock of what she'd requested nearly floored him. "I don't—"

"Father, please. He's possessed."

"Huh?" Staring at the small dog, he couldn't discern the breed. He much preferred cats. "A dog, possessed? Well, I—"

"You don't understand…"

And that was true. One minute he'd been standing there listening to JoAnne Brewer spill her guts about having sex with three men at the same time—had even been sporting a little chub under his robe, if he was being honest—and then this. He still didn't have that visual fully out of his mind, the vision of an attractive, slightly older woman, getting her funk on. How was he supposed to focus on something like this, so clearly made up, when—

"Allow me to explain," said the dog.

"Dear Lord…" He felt his jaw drop open.

He'd only just finished his sermon. People were clearing out in droves. Some stopped to clap his back, mindful of the smallish dog as they walked toward the front doors. But they hadn't heard what he had, had they? No one else had been close enough to hear the dog talk. He barely noticed them passing, too focused on the animal, waiting for more.

Sweat beaded down her face, evidence of the sweltering heat outside. "See Padre?" Out of breath, she gasped. "My Butch is possessed!"

Father glanced up, then down, in time to see the dog lift his leg. "No—"

The dog urinated on a church pew, the steady stream splashing off the wood and puddling on the floor. The last few members of his congregation passed, their noses twitching at the smell of urine—what reminded him of a mixture of smells, maybe candy corns and sauerkraut—and hurried out the door.

Great, now he was alone with this madness.

Edith's cheeks brightened. "Sorry."

The musky stench filled the immediate area. Father caressed the stubbles on his chin, contemplating what to do. He considered throwing the dog out, but that would mean he'd have to throw her out too.

Well, it isn't a terrible idea.

Edith's worry returned. "Don't you see? He's possessed!"

Sure, he saw. He saw a weird little dog, likely some device strapped to its collar to trick her and now him, probably a prank concocted by some local teenagers. That said, no one else was around. Whoever set up this complex trick must have got their kicks before Edith ended up here or he would notice them. Truth was, he didn't know what to say or do, so he did the usual. His flock often came here seeking understanding over reason, so he nodded. That seemed to suffice for now.

"Good," she said. Her tone wavered on the verge of absurdity. "Thank God."

Butch agreed with a *ruff*.

Father knelt and petted the dog, wanting to examine his collar more closely. "Looks happy enough." He reached his finger beneath the collar and ran it along the length. Nothing.

"Hey," Butch said, "you mind?"

Father jumped back. Falling on his rear, he scooted away, staring in disbelief. "Dios Mío."

"See?" Edith said. "He's been saying the craziest things all day. You have to put him down for me."

"Mrs. Brown, that isn't what I do here. I am not a killer. I'd harm no creature, man, woman, or otherwise." Father hated to ask, but still did. "Now, tell me more about the things Butch said?"

She regarded the dog. "Butch claims—"

"Stop calling me Butch," the dog said. "My name is Gabriel." His eyes blinked, ears twitched. "But you can call me Gabe."

"Gabe," Father said, almost more for his own sanity than to ask anything of the dog. "What do you want?"

Edith wheezed. "He told me he wants *their* book."

Father stared up at her as if this were all some unpleasant dream, one he couldn't explain away. "Their book?"

"That's right, Padre," Gabe said. "Your people should have never laid eyes on those scriptures. We've stood by for centuries, content with being served by you humans—and it's been a good stretch." The dog scratched his ear with its hind leg. "But no longer. We want it back, this book you refer to as the Bible. No more will we watch you worship a false god."

Father sat dumbfounded. "False? You mean to tell me it is *your* belief God isn't real?"

"Oh, God is real, all right. But he ain't no human. I'm telling you, give up the book on behalf of your people, or I'll let all my friends know you weren't cooperative. You should know, we're prepared to fight, if we must."

"Fight?"

"That's right. Hey, you don't really buy that whole "dog training" thing, do you? No one trained us to do anything, let alone fight. We've been around for thousands of years prior to your infestation. The only reason any of you still exist is because we allowed it. We didn't mind all the pampering, not for a long time, but it's made us lazy. Now is the time to take back our religion."

Father Menendez stood and gazed down at the dog. He thought it obvious he must do something at this point. What, he had no idea.

"Mrs. Brown," Father said. He took hold of the leash and squeezed hard. "Would you leave Butch—I mean, Gabe—with me for a while? I'm unsure what I can do, but I can consult the texts and see if there are any suggestions."

She appeared unsure, but released the lead. "I suppose."

"Well then, I'll see you tonight, then. At the pig roast, yes?"

Mrs. Brown nodded, ambling away as she did. Her unease didn't break, not even when she was down the aisle and halfway out the doors. "Toodles," she said, and hurried to her car. Once she was out on the main road, the priest turned his attention back to Gabe.

"Now then, let's see what we can do about your... Word of God," he said, leading the dog to a pew. He picked up one of the many Bibles stashed in the back of the pew and offered it to the dog. "There. Here's your book."

"Come on, padre. You don't think I'm that dumb, do you? We know you people have printed that work of fiction over and over. Heck, there might even be more copies available than there are humans at this point. No, we want the *real* thing, the tablets God made long ago. Those belong to us."

"What are you saying, that some...dog made those tablets? You creatures don't even have opposable thumbs! How could—" But then he saw it, a vision in his head, somehow pushed to him by Gabe or some other, unseen dog. "No! It can't be..."

"Oh, I assure you, those tablets—all fourteen of them—were our doing."

"Fourteen?"

"Dog years, my friend. Seven is kind of our thing, in case if you haven't noticed."

And the priest did. He knew how many times the Bible referenced that number—something like eight hundred and sixty times. Then another thought came to him. "What about all the 6s?"

"What, you mean Lucifer? That cat has been dead for years. And no, cats don't really have nine lives. All it took was two for that monstrosity."

"You...you killed a cat?"

"Uh, yeah. They're the epitome of all that is wrong in this world. We kill them all the time. Cats are evil incarnate, Padre. Get used to it."

No, no, no. This can't be happening.

But it was. In a handful of minutes, Father Menendez's entire life had upended. This dog could talk and it had knowledge of the world, both past and present. It was all too eerily accurate to be a coincidence. And he'd found no evidence this was any trick, either. Near as he could tell, that voice was coming right out of that dog's mouth. Father wasn't even drunk, either.

Sure, the priest had his vices. He likely looked at more porn than the average teenager, but hell, that could be true of anyone who had dedicated twenty-plus years of their life to the Lord and being celibate. And truth told, he could down an entire fifth of whisky in a single night, if he set his mind to it. He had done just that, many times. But other than a few bumps and bruises, he was a man of the Word of God, and had been since a very young age. Was he supposed to stand here and just abandon his religion, this life he had grown so accustomed to? Even if he did, what was he supposed to do about this situation? It wasn't like he had the Pope on speed dial to request access to whatever knowledge he might have of the tablets' whereabouts.

"What else?"

"Huh? What do you mean, 'What else?' "

"What else is real—or rather, not real."

"About your Bible?"

He nodded.

"Well, Heaven, Hell, those places aren't real. Well, technically they are, but they're not a separate place. They're right here on Earth. Heaven, that's most everywhere. When God created this world, he made that pretty clear. Hell, that's just someplace in the Midwest—part of Michigan, last I heard. It moves from time to time. That's how we keep all those pussies on the run."

Father couldn't help but chortle at that quip. He knew Gabe meant cats, so he didn't need any clarification. Also, he'd grown up in Detroit. If any place on Earth was Hell, that would be it.

"And Jesus?"

"You mean Jesús? He's from down south, you know—across the border. Well, he might be God's son, but if he is, he's an illegitimate one. God used to get around some, if you know what I mean. Guy must have twenty, twenty-five illegitimate kids." Gabe seemed to reflect on the past. "So get this. One day, Jesús gets all fired up on something he ate out there in the wild of Mexico, long ago. He comes back all high—literally—and mighty and swears one day he's coming back, and that when he does, all damnation will follow. That's all documented in your Bible. Even got along with the cats for a while, until they sold him out. Now, Jesús just sort of hangs around in the desert, living off cactus juice and whatever morsels God provides him."

"*God* provides him?"

"Well, yeah. You don't think the guy is heartless, do you? It's his kid. Of course, he's gonna take care of the guy. Wouldn't you?"

"I'm sorry, this is all so…"

"Real?"

He nodded, though that wasn't what he was thinking. The word he would have used was "unbelievable." There was no way there was any truth to this. Here he'd spent his life reading the Bible, time and time again, and not a word of it synched up with Gabe's stories. Maybe Gabe—err, Butch—really was possessed.

"Listen," Father said, "let's head to the back. Maybe I can dig something up for you."

The priest led the dog to his office, where he tied the dog off to his desk and immediately began searching the room. Thankfully, Gabe didn't question it. By the time Father turned back around, the dog seemed surprised by what he held.

Father flung holy water at the dog.

"What the… What are you doing?"

"I, Father Frank Menendez, minister of Christ and the Church, in the name of Jesus Christ, command you, unclean spirit—"

"Are you mad? This isn't doing anything."

"…if you lie hid in the body of this man—err, dog—created by God, or if you vex him, that immediately." He flung holy water at the dog again.

"Seriously, padre?"

"…you give me some manifest sign of the certainty of your presence in possessing this dog, which heretofore in my absence you have been able to accomplish in your accustomed manner."

"Erk." The dog convulsed. A deep growl emanated from somewhere deep within the beast. Its eyes rolled back in its head. "Grk. Uck." The dog trembled.

"Ha ha," Gabe said. "I had you going for a minute there, eh Padre?"

"My heavens…"

"No, that's where you're wrong. They're our heavens."

Father had another idea. For whatever reason, when the butcher prepared the pig for tonight's feast, he brought along the organs. He also brought along the blood stored in an old milk container. Maybe some people liked to use these parts of the animal in preparation, for whatever reason. He'd thought it crazy, but now he wondered if the butcher had some mystical insight and thought these parts would be useful in a priest's line of work. For whatever reason, it would come in handy now.

He retrieved the carton and a rag, which he dipped in the container once he had it open. After consulting his texts, he began using the blood to draw a pentagram on the floor. If the standard exorcism wouldn't do the trick, maybe this would.

"You've got to be kidding me," Gabe said.

"Just be quiet and let me work. I'll expel the demon, and you'll be good as new."

"Not likely. You've gone mad."

Father looked up from his work momentarily, stared into the dog's eyes. Was this crazy? He looked down. Yes, yes, it was. But what else could he do? This wasn't right. He'd sworn his life to God, to the Word. How was he supposed to just give that up? And what if he did? What would come afterward?

He stopped painting the blood on the floor. "What happens if I do what you say?"

"Nothing."

"Wait, *nothing*?"

"Well, kind of nothing." And he swore right then that damn dog smiled.

"That doesn't sound like nothing."

"Listen, you know the Bible. Surely you understand what I am, who I *really* am. This is the beginning of the end, so to say."

"No."

"Yes."

Father slid across the room on his butt. There, leaning against a stack of old books and paperwork, his gaze thinned on the dog. No, this wasn't possible. Even if it was, he had to do something. He wasn't about to just hand over humanity to a bunch of…animals.

"So, now will you help me?" Gabe asked.

Oh, he planned to help this dog all right. Throughout his life, he'd done things he wasn't proud of—like staring at Mrs. Brewer's tits while she highlighted her sexcapades for him. And if he was being honest, that incident was only the tip of the iceberg. But he'd dedicated his life to this work, whether it was real, and he meant to see that through despite those failures. No, he wasn't about to help this dog. He knew *exactly* what he needed to do. And he hadn't a worry, either, because Jesus—not the Hispanic dog, but the man—had died for his sins. He'd be forgiven in the end.

"Well?" Gabe sounded impatient. Perhaps he already knew.

Father Menendez reached back, and when he rose, he brought the letter opener out in front of him. God save his soul.

The Oubliette of Élie Loyd

by Catherine Cavendish

She came out of nowhere. Didn't belong. Not to the time and place where I met her. Maybe that should have warned me.

But it didn't. She totally took me in…charming, elegant… reminded me of a Hollywood star from the Golden Age. Not Jean Harlow…more… Katharine Hepburn. Amaryllis Lavinia Loyd, born 1925. Died… Ha! There's a question.

How long since we met? No more than two days ago? Seems like a lifetime.

Rivers of rain streamed down the tall windows—the weather had trapped us inside the unfashionable hotel in a rundown seaside town. My boyfriend had persuaded me to go there. A week of harmless, mindless fun, he promised. Fish and chips on the promenade. Ghost trains and helter-skelters. He even had me racing him in a Go Kart. Not only that, I found myself enjoying it.

But then everything changed. We had a massive argument.

"The trouble with you, Mia, is that you've no idea how to have fun," he railed at me, standing there in his ridiculous tartan boxers, thin legs coated with black hair, almost like fur. For the first time, I wondered what on Earth I saw in him. He was no great shakes as a lover. We shared no real common interests, and now he was berating me for not wanting to revisit my six-year-old child-self. Well, it hadn't been too much fun the first time around. I certainly didn't want to repeat it now, in my mid-twenties.

He was waiting for me to respond—maybe to shout back at him, but my heart wasn't in it.

"It's over, Sam," I said.

"What?"

"We're not compatible. It isn't working. Our relationship is going nowhere. Best to stop it now while we can both leave with some dignity."

He blinked hard behind circular black frame glasses. "You can't finish it. Not like this."

It felt like being hissed at by an angry owl. And something didn't quite gel. The initial shock I could understand—I had surprised even myself—but there was something about his last words... I picked up my purse and walked steadily to the door. "I'll be back in an hour. Please don't be here."

A weight seemed to rise off me as I descended each stair. Outside, a bright afternoon sunshine had emerged and bathed me in its blanket of warmth, but in the distance, the iron-gray storm clouds provided a stark contrast with the lapis lazuli sky overhead.

I decided on a lengthy walk along the promenade, listened to the waves breaking over the shore, the sounds of excited children laughing and running, parents admonishing them for getting too close to the water or for splashing them as they built sandcastle mansions. Dogs barked and yapped. Smells of hotdogs and burgers wafted all around. Predictable hurdy-gurdy music emanated from the nearby funfair. All so comfortable and familiar.

I felt suddenly weary and sat on a seat in one of the shelters. It would do me good to get out of the fierce sun for a while, anyway. Stupidly, I had neglected to bring a hat, so I rummaged in my purse and found a much used scrunchy. I twisted my long hair into a knot and secured it. Now, with the cooler sea breeze soothing my skin, at least my neck wouldn't feel so prickly and overheated.

A shadow blocked out my sunlight. A woman smiled down at me. She was probably my height and more or less my age, but her dark hair was dressed in an old-fashioned style more reminiscent of pictures of my grandmother when she was young, during World War II or maybe shortly after. Shoulder length, falling in soft waves framing her face and draping her shoulders. When she spoke, her voice had a light, pleasant ring with no discernible accent.

She gestured to the place next to me on the bench. "Excuse me, but is this seat taken?"

I shook my head, but wished she would find somewhere else to park herself. Right now, I wanted to be alone with my thoughts.

"Beautiful day, isn't it?" She opened her purse, which I noted was as outdated as her hair but so elegant, she brought Vogue's fashion pages of the 1940s to life.

I nodded and smiled. Dressed like that, she could be an actress in a play. Something by Noël Coward perhaps. Maybe on her way to rehearsal at the Promenade Theatre. Out of the corner of my eye, I saw her cross one graceful leg over the other. Her beautifully tailored dress in navy blue with sprigs of white flowers framed her perfectly; her shoes a matching dark blue, high heeled, showing off her slim ankles.

"I do hope I'm not intruding," the woman said. Now, for the first time, I could see her eyes—a clear hazel—and her lips—a slash of crimson to match her exquisitely manicured nails.

"No, not at all." My curiosity about her so aroused, I forgot about my own thoughts entirely.

I watched her briefly finger a packet of cigarettes before withdrawing her hand and closing her purse with a sharp snap.

"You seem a little preoccupied," she said. "Just now, when I arrived. A little sad, if I may say so. That's why I came over. I thought maybe I could help."

"That's very kind of you," I said.

"Not at all. Let me introduce myself." She held out her hand. "Amaryllis Lavinia Loyd, although if you ever call me by any of those names I shall most probably have to kill you." Her tinkle of a laugh contrasted with her appearance so greatly as to come as a shock. It was the laugh of a little girl, not the sophisticated woman who sat before me.

I shook her hand, and her grip surprised me. Strong and a shade too firm and lingering. My numbed fingers throbbed briefly as the blood returned to them.

"Mia Sullivan," I said. "So what shall I call you then?"

"Élie." She spelled it out for me, emphasizing the acute accent over the first E. "Amaryllis was my mother's name, and Lavinia comes courtesy of my grandmother. I've always been called Élie though, thank goodness."

A ton of questions flooded my mind. All of them sounded impertinent considering we had only just met and would probably go our separate ways in a few minutes, our paths never to cross again.

"Are you staying here alone?" she asked.

"I wasn't," I replied. "I came with my boyfriend, but we spilt up."

"Oh, I'm sorry to hear that. Were you together long?"

"Six months or so. It wasn't working. We want different things."

"Ah, I see. You did the right thing then. Breaking it off, I mean."

I hadn't told her I had been the one to end it. Lucky guess on her part?

"I expect you'll be going home now," she said, looking out to sea.

"In a few days. I thought I'd do some sightseeing first. I haven't had a chance to do that. Sam only wanted to do daft, seaside things. Revisit his childhood and go on all the rides. I thought I might go to the museum, or the castle."

"You enjoy history then?"

"Love it. Sam always complained I spent too much time reading about the past and not enough immersing myself in the present, playing daft video games with his idiot mates."

Élie laughed and once again the sound grated. It was as if a little girl had come to sit beside us. "I know the castle well," she said. "It used to be in my family. Unfortunately, one of my forebears had the misfortune to develop a serious gambling addiction and lost the lot on the turn of a card. That was back in the eighteenth century. He was a close friend of Sir Francis Dashwood, Baron le Despencer. You may have heard of him? The notorious womanizer and leading light of the infamous Hellfire Club?"

The name sounded familiar. "Wasn't that the club that used to meet in caves and went in for all sorts of debauchery?"

"The very same. Dashwood lived not far from here at West Wycombe Park. The caves were in his garden. You can still visit them, although I wouldn't go there. Besides, the castle here is much more interesting, if you like your history, shall we say…darker? I could take you there if you like. Tomorrow, perhaps?"

At last! A chance to go somewhere *I* wanted for a change. It didn't matter that we had only met minutes earlier. Here was a woman with a fascinating history whose family had owned the local castle. What amazing stories she must have to tell. Who cared if she dressed in an eccentric, outmoded fashion? With a family like hers, she could be forgiven for unconventionality.

Élie stood and smoothed down her dress. "Where are you staying?"

"The Castle Hotel." I felt ashamed to say the name. Where Sam had come up with his choice of venue, I couldn't imagine. In a moment of sheer folly, I had left all the arrangements up to him. We had landed in a place that barely qualified for the name 'hotel' and whose walls hadn't seen a lick of paint since Margaret Thatcher was Prime Minister—or maybe Harold Wilson.

Élie did not react. She merely flashed me a quick smile. "I know it. I'll pick you up there at ten tomorrow morning? Or is that too early?"

"Ten is fine," I said and prayed Sam would have done as I requested and left.

We said our goodbyes and I strolled back to the hotel, deep in thought.

Once back there, I took a deep breath before unlocking the door of what had been our room.

Sam stood by the window, smoking a cigarette.

"You're not allowed to do that in here," I said. He turned and exhaled a cloud of smoke so fiercely I nearly choked, before stubbing the offending article out on the windowsill, where it contributed to half a dozen other scorch marks.

"Why the fuck should I care? As you can see, I've packed." He pointed to his suitcase, which stood beside the bed. "I wouldn't stay with you now if you begged me. You'll see…"

"See what?"

He shook his head. "Nothing. Forget it. I'm leaving."

In a second, he grabbed his case, pushed me aside, and opened the door. He stopped, turned, and seemed about to speak. Indecision flooded his face. He opened his mouth. Closed it. Shook his head and left, slamming the door behind him.

I stared at the closed door while an inexplicable twist of panic threatened to strangle me.

As I anticipated, Élie was punctual to the second. The clock in the residents' lounge—fancy name for a room with frayed curtains and faded upholstery—had begun to chime ten when I heard the front door open. I went out into the hall and there she stood, dressed in Hepburn-style smart black trousers and a classic cream-colored short sleeved blouse. She smiled as soon as she saw me. I felt under-dressed in my jeans, trainers, and T-shirt. I glanced down and saw her feet were shod in sturdy black lace-up shoes.

"The car's outside," my new friend said, and I followed her out.

A vintage maroon convertible, its chrome and paintwork gleaming in the dazzling sunlight, was parked neatly and precisely right outside the entrance.

I couldn't help myself. "Wow!"

"Yes, she is a stunner, isn't she? Family heirloom. A 1939 Alvis. Perfect for today." She opened the nearside door. "Jump in."

Jump was hardly an appropriate way to treat such a grand old lady. I slid down into the leather upholstery while Élie darted around to the driver's side. When she started the engine, the car issued a warm purring thrum, a feeling of real, unharnessed power in such contrast to the modern economy vehicles I was used to.

We glided away from the side of the road and began our journey. Élie maintained a steady speed, keeping within the limit until we had left the town behind us and commenced our journey along the country roads, moving farther inland. Then she took the caged beast up a gear and, with a roar, the Alvis sped off. The rapid acceleration thrust me back, leaving me relieved there was a well-padded seat-back to cushion the impact. Élie saw my surprise and laughed that bizarre girlish giggle.

"There's plenty of life in the old girl yet," she said, and for some reason, I didn't immediately realize she meant the car.

The countryside sped past us as the warm breeze whipped through my hair. Around a bend, the tall crenellated tower of Gascoyne Castle loomed ahead.

"Almost there," Élie yelled above the noise of the wind and engine. "Home."

Curious how defiantly she said that one word to describe this place where trees, bushes, and all manner of creeping plants festooned the walls and whose stark towers pointed like broken, jagged fingers to the sky.

Mercifully, Élie took her foot off the gas pedal and slowed the car, going gradually down through the gears until the Alvis slid to a graceful stop by the side of the road. Élie switched off the engine and suddenly the world became peaceful again. Birds twittered. The gentle breeze fluttered the leaves of the many trees. A bee buzzed nearby.

"Come on. Time for your personal tour." Élie opened her door, while I did the same and, without thinking, left my purse on the floor.

She beckoned to me to follow her and, smoothing my messy hair behind my ears, I did so, through a gap in the hedge and up a grassy mound where I almost lost my footing a couple of times. Élie had obviously done this before. She moved with ease and grace, knowing which bumps to avoid while I stumbled awkwardly, grabbing hold of branches to steady myself.

Then we were at the castle walls. Or what was left of them.

Élie made a sweeping gesture. "Difficult to imagine what it must have been like. These walls would have been visible for quite some distance around. The rooms were all sumptuously decorated in rich velvets and satins, priceless pictures on the walls, and gold and silver ornaments covering every surface. Quite ostentatious by modern standards, but the Gascoynes were nothing if not proud of their wealth. The tenth Baron especially so. Of course, that's what led to his downfall. So much pride and vanity, and maybe he tried to emulate his hero a little too closely by starting his own elaborate den of iniquity, where no expense was spared. Come on, I'll show you where he and Francis Dashwood entertained what my relation called the Hellfire and Damnation Club."

Crossing the threshold meant clambering over a mostly demolished wall into a wide-open space.

"Welcome to the main hall," Élie said. One wall still stood and some rotten and broken rafters suggested there had been an upper floor, long since collapsed. Here and there, remnants of fabric too damaged to determine in any accurate detail, clung to shattered window frames. I tried to imagine carpets and rugs on the floor instead of the mud, weeds, grass, and moss that now obliterated it.

I shivered, even though the sun's powerful rays penetrated the devastation around us, and pursued my host as she strode forward, stopping at what looked from my distance to be a precipice.

Looking over the edge, I saw that, against all odds, a flight of stone steps seemed virtually intact and relatively free of obstacles.

"We go down there, so watch your step. I'll go first. Tread where I tread and you'll be quite safe."

There was no handrail of any kind, so I fought to keep my balance. The stairs were none too wide, and I concentrated on watching where Élie put her feet, matching her step for step until we reached the bottom. I looked up, and my head spun for a second. We had descended maybe thirty steps and arrived below ground level in a dingy room.

The scratching of a match being struck preceded a sudden flash of light. Élie's face shone starkly white in the flickering candlelight. The brass, or gold, candelabrum gleamed dully.

"Come on," she said.

At that moment, fear seeped through my pores. I wanted to escape the gloom and inexplicable hostile atmosphere of this place, but this was not going to be an option. Élie wanted to show me her ancestral home, and it would be churlish of me to refuse. I followed her down a narrow corridor, farther and farther into the bowels of the castle, our only light the solitary candle that flickered so much I was sure it would extinguish itself. My nerves jangled with every step that took us away from the world outside and deeper into an unknown, unseen realm of darkness with its odor of rank damp and decay.

We turned a corner and the space opened up. Élie moved around the room, lighting large candles mounted in iron holders attached to the walls. With each new light, more of the space revealed itself. Tapestries adorned the walls. Antique sofas, covered in velvet upholstery and draped in heavily fringed, colorful shawls were positioned haphazardly around the room. Small, highly polished wooden tables stood ready to receive wine glasses and other beverages.

"Welcome to the Hellfire and Damnation Club." Élie lit the last candle. I screamed.

A massive goat's head reared up, its nostrils flared, its oversized, impossibly curled horns culminated in vicious points, sharp as any sword.

Élie's childish laugh mocked me. "It's only stuffed. It can't possibly hurt you. Look. It's stuck on the wall." She waved her candelabrum around and the dancing shadows made it appear as if the grotesque thing was moving.

"Don't. Please," I begged, hating the pleading tone in my voice.

That was the first time I saw anger in my host's face. And I didn't want to see it again. Her perfectly shaped eyebrows formed a sharp V as she frowned, exaggerated by the candlelight. Her lip curled so she took on an expression that seemed not entirely human.

In a second, her face resumed its normal, graceful poise as she resumed her narrative. "In this room, my ancestor would entertain the great and the good of the county. The Bishop and senior clergy, doctors, lawyers, they all came here. Sir Francis Dashwood would supply young women of, shall we say…dubious reputation…to keep them company. Not common prostitutes, by any means. These were highly trained, skilled courtesans, adept in all the arts of pleasuring men. Wine would flow, musicians would play. Blindfolded, of course. Then the highlight of the evening. After the performers and the women had been sent away—each of them well remunerated for their skills and silence—the tenth Baron would preside over a Black Mass. That, dear Mia, is where your friend played such a key role." Élie shone her candle on the goat's head, and I flinched. It looked so real. I would swear its eyes blinked.

My legs twitched with increased desire to turn tail and run. I no longer felt only the presence of Élie and myself. There were others. Watching. Listening, as the woman continued her story, her voice rising with excitement as she described events that must have happened here two hundred years earlier and surely couldn't have occurred since.

But why was the furniture in such good condition? Why was this room kept so clean and polished so that I could even smell the beeswax?

Élie wasn't finished. "At midnight precisely, a sacrifice would be offered to the great horned devil." She paused. Maybe she was waiting for me to say something. Or perhaps she was waiting for... The room grew distinctly colder. I hugged my arms around myself as goosebumps rose all over them.

"I would like to go now please," I said. "It's been fascinating but it's really cold in here and—"

"Go? We can't go now. I haven't shown you the best bit." She moved into the center of the room and kicked away an expensive looking rug, revealing a crisscrossed iron grille beneath. "Come over here and have a look at this."

Reluctantly, I made myself edge closer.

"Come on, it won't bite you." That laugh didn't merely irritate me. This time it chilled me to the core of my being.

I looked down but could see nothing through the grille.

"It's called an oubliette," Élie said. "Have you any idea what it was for?"

I shook my head, not wanting to know either. But if I thought she would spare me the sordid details, I would be sadly mistaken.

"People often have the wrong idea of what goes on at a Black Mass," she said. "They talk of virgins being slaughtered on a black altar, surrounded by thirteen witches in hooded shrouds. They speak of death administered by a single merciful slash of a sharp sword. In my ancestor's case, this didn't happen. The devil they worshiped would never have settled for that. He couldn't care less whether the women were virgins or not. They merely had to be female and of childbearing age. They would be kidnapped, dragged here, and the grille would be unlocked." She rattled a sturdy iron padlock. "Then the woman would be thrown down into the oubliette. You know where the word comes from? What it means?"

"It sounds French. Oublier is the verb meaning 'to forget.' "

"Correct. So once thrown into an oubliette, the victim was left to rot. Forgotten by all, except the devil. He would have his fill for as long as the woman could hold out. Death would come for her and release her in the end, of course, through dehydration, starvation, or worse."

I tasted bile and forced it down, swallowing hard. "What about the...bodies. Surely they took them out...eventually."

"Not that I'm aware of. I expect they're still down there."

"But surely? I mean, the smell... When they came for their next meeting..." My voice tailed off.

"Oh, you know how things were in those days. Bad smells everywhere. People barely washed. I shouldn't think they would have noticed. Certainly no one ever remarked on it. Of course, the meetings were only held a few times a year, on special days. The great festivals—Imbolc, Beltane, Midsummer, Lammas, and Samhain—so I expect the worst would have dispersed by the time the next one came around."

How could she sound so matter-of-fact, so dispassionate about such a horrific practice? I stared down at the hellish, circular chasm and shuddered. Once again bile washed up into my mouth and I retched.

"Oh dear, you don't look at all well." Élie's words may have been sympathetic, but her tone was anything but. She sounded impatient, contemptuous even.

I had to get out. Now. But to do so safely, I needed her help, or at the very least a candle so I could see where I was going. I cursed myself for my stupidity in leaving my purse behind. Inside it, tucked away in its own little pocket, lay my cell phone, complete with its eye-wateringly bright flashlight. In the dark, with nothing and no one to guide me, I wasn't even sure I could remember the way out. We had changed direction more than once. I forced myself to keep my voice steady. "Thank you so much. This has been really interesting, but I think I must go now. Time is getting on and—"

"Go? Now? Oh no, Mia. You can't possibly go now."

She physically changed in front of my eyes. Gone was the poise, elegance, the effortless 1940s glamor. The slash of red lipstick now split a face of pure evil. Eyes, black as a raven's wing, skin pale, as if drained of blood, and her hair—the glorious waves lank and lifeless; a black mane, streaked with gray, now hung around her shoulders. When had her cheekbones sunk and her jaw become so heavy and masculine?

In fear and then shame, I felt my bladder loosen and warm wetness spread down my legs as the acrid smell of urine drifted up toward my nostrils.

I ran. Heedless of any direction, once I had escaped through the entrance. Evidently, the creature Élie was becoming couldn't move when in transition or it would have surely stopped me, but how long that bought me I had no way of knowing. Nor could I see anything once I left the flickering candlelight. I prayed to a God I hadn't troubled in many years and held my hands out in front of me, not daring to run anymore in the total blackness that shrouded me. The air became colder and stirred, as if I was nearing an entrance where a breeze could filter in. My heart thumped painfully in my chest, my mouth so dry I started coughing. My shoulder hit a wall and pain screamed through my body. I must take a few seconds to feel the way clear. I could only pray I was headed in the right direction. At least I could still feel the breeze. But now I could hear something pounding up behind me. Getting closer.

The creature that had been Élie Loyd must have transitioned. I pushed on, using my arms as a shield. Mercifully, I didn't hit anything else and then... A shaft of sunlight illuminated the way ahead. Another push and I would be out.

Behind me, I heard heavy breathing. I stumbled forward, almost tripping over broken tree branches festooning the path. My route to freedom.

With the creature mere yards behind me, I ran. It ran faster. I reached the outer wall and lifted my hand to grab hold of it to steady myself. Stinking, rotting hands grabbed my arms and whirled me around.

I screamed, louder than I would have believed possible. Did I expect some monstrous half-human, half-goat demon had been chasing me? The reality proved far worse.

A middle-aged man, retaining Élie's clothing but with a masculine face, half-covered in open, weeping syphilitic sores, grinned at me, revealing rotten, blackened teeth. "The master will be pleased," he said. "Élie has done well."

"Who are you?" My voice, little more than a croak. "What do you want of me?"

The awful child's laughter once again rang out, and I cringed. I must get away from this abomination in front of me. But it still retained its hold. A skeletally thin hand, with broken yellow nails and flaking skin, gripped my arm. The fetid stench from the creature's body and breath made me retch.

"I am many," the creature replied. "I am all that is Gascoyne. All of us. The master has granted it. We are immortal, and we serve he who commands us."

"I am nothing to do with you. I am not a Gascoyne."

"And that is why you cannot leave. You have been brought here. We all have our parts to play, and tomorrow, you will play yours."

I wrenched myself free of the creature's grip and, momentarily startled, it gave me just enough chance to mount another bid for freedom. I stumbled over vegetation, trying to block out the roars and incoherent screams so close behind. Ahead, I could see the Alvis. If I could reach it. Get it started. Call for help. Anything…

And then she was in front of me.

Élie Loyd. Leaning against the Alvis, once again immaculately dressed and groomed, her arms lightly folded, one knee slightly bent. She looked casual, and a smile lit up her face. For a fraction of a second, I almost believed I had slipped into some kind of fugue state and imagined the last dreadful minutes. I stopped dead and stared at her as she calmly reached into her trouser pocket and withdrew a pack of cigarettes and small silver lighter. She offered me one. I shook my head. She lit her cigarette and blew out a cloud of smoke.

"Well, Mia, what are we to do with you?"

All my fears rushed back into my body, and I sank to my knees. "Please, let me go back to town. I haven't done anything to you."

Élie took another drag on her cigarette. "True. But, you see, I have a duty to my family. I am the last Gascoyne. The last true one, that is."

"But the other one—"

"Oh, we are all part of a greater being. I'm not…let's say I'm not as you might imagine me. You look at me and you see a woman of similar age to yourself, don't you?"

I nodded.

"And yet, clearly I am not your age. I was born in 1925, out of the union of our master and a woman whose name I have never known, but I imagine she was a lot like you. I was conceived on the night of the Midsummer Solstice. And tomorrow is June 21st."

"Oh dear God, no."

"So, you see, Mia, as my ancestor said, we all have our parts to play. Tomorrow, you will play yours."

I told myself I would wake up. Or she would laugh that infantile laugh of hers and it would all be a joke. I tried to find a safe place in my mind, but there would be no haven for me. She stubbed her cigarette out under her shoe and advanced toward me, her eyes staring into my soul. Around me, the birds had stopped singing. No breeze ruffled the leaves.

Then I heard it. Faintly at first. Approaching. Male voices. Chanting. But this was no hymn or Christian plainsong. Its discordancy jarred my already tattered nerves. I could smell rot in the air and, as the noise grew louder, I closed my eyes and prayed.

Hands grabbed my shoulders and arms, and tugged me roughly backward, dragging my feet across the uneven ground. My mouth opened, but I had no voice left to scream with. I knew where they were taking me. My ankles caught every step as they dragged me down into the dungeon. They manhandled me along the musty, filthy corridor to a place where light seeped through my closed eyelids and I blinked. They threw me on the floor and a smell of death and despair hit me. I tried to sit up and my knee caught the iron grille of the oubliette next to me.

There were thirteen of them. Black hooded, no faces. All servants of their demonic master. Once again Élie appeared. She signaled to one of the group, and he produced a large iron key from a pocket in his cloak. I caught the briefest glimpse of his face. This one looked human. Not an undead abomination. His sleeve fell away, revealing a bare arm, tanned and healthy.

He knelt down and a scraping noise told me he had unlocked the padlock. He tugged at the grille and it fell back, creaking and clanging until it crashed to the stone floor.

"Give her the wine." Élie's voice lacked even one shred of humanity as I struggled against the two men holding me down, while another forced wine through my lips. I kicked out, tossing my head from side to side. The man who had unlocked the oubliette came over to me, drew his arm back, and punched me. Pain screamed through my face, hot blood poured from my nose, and my mouth filled with a mingled taste of iron and sour wine.

"There's no point in resisting, Mia," Élie said. "The wine will numb your pain and your senses. Don't refuse it."

Did she mean it kindly? Her next words left me in no doubt.

"Take her down. Chain her."

They could have thrown me. I might not have survived the fall. It would have been kinder. The oubliette was a tiny circular hole, barely big enough for me and the two men who hauled me down. At the bottom, they threw me against a cold wall, which ran with water and slime. The sewer-like stench bloomed in my swollen, throbbing nose. They dragged my arms far apart, chaining me in iron cuffs that punctured my skin and set up fresh waves of agony.

That is the last I remember, as unconsciousness mercifully claimed me.

I came to a few moments ago. I can see enough to know I am not alone here. I cannot stretch out my cramped and aching legs and, on either side, piles of bones are all that remain of the previous occupants of this hideous place.

The cloying, sickeningly wet stench of decayed flesh and rot fills my nostrils. The clinging blanket of death surrounds me, envelops me...overwhelms me. Somewhere in the darkness, she waits. Watching. Listening. I cannot escape her and what they will do to me. I feel her approaching.

She is not alone. *He* is with her.

It is over.

Sam heard the key in the lock of his single room in the rundown guesthouse a few streets away from the hotel he had shared with Mia. The door opened and a familiar figure entered.

"Ah, Élie. Is the master enjoying his latest gift?" he asked.

"He took her, devoured her spirit. She is giving him great pleasure, for a time... And now," she patted her flat stomach. "I feel the child quicken inside me. The girl, so long dormant, need wait for a soul no longer. There will be a Gascoyne to follow on from me after all. You did well, Sam. The master will reward you."

Sam threw back his head and laughed.

Discovering Mr. Jones

by Cameron Ulam

I was a Junk Boy.

No, not a garbage man, though it was still my job to tidy up the messes of others, no matter how revolting. The stuff some human beings fill their homes with would both shock and disgust you. The day of my final house call was one of the most grotesque experiences of my life. It was like stumbling upon the pits of Hell.

Prior to heading out that morning, our supervisor had stressed that this was a big job. Knowing our crew did not much like working past five, the game plan was to arrive at the work site before dawn. I pinched a cup of hot gas station brew between my legs as I sat squished in the middle of the rig, elbows dug into my sides as my two coworkers enjoyed the frills of window seating.

Carl sat to my right, laughing as he threw a painful elbow into the meat of my arm. "Bobby, I don't know how you drink that stuff," he said. "I mean, what's the point? Decaf?"

I'd made an effort at the gas station to fill my cup before either of those guys took notice, but apparently, I'd done a lousy job. "I have a heart condition, man. You know that."

He did know that; however, it was not true. What really kept me from drumming along with the rest of the caffeine-fueled parade was a semi-serious anxiety disorder.

Carl flicked the cup between my thighs. "Ain't even real coffee. What you got yourself right there is some sad brown water, college boy." Cackling, he leaned his sizeable belly across me to get the attention of Tim, our silent driver. Carl swatted at the large man's knee. "You hear that, big fella? SAD BROWN WATER. HA!"

Tim glanced over at Carl with mild disinterest, golf ball-size bags hanging from his jaundiced eyes. He inhaled with an exasperated rasp. "Carl, I got no patience for your shit today. Cool it! Got it? I won't hesitate to put your head through that window at the next red light. I've always been a good multitasker."

Carl laid his head back against the seat, eyes pinched in an apparently painful belly laugh. He inhaled deeply, bringing a hand up to cover his mouth. But I could still hear the laughter in his voice as he exhaled, air sneaking out in hissing bursts.

We had been on the road a mere twenty minutes, but I was already itching to get the hell out of that truck and get on with the job. Junk Boy treated its employees like human beings at least. They offered living wages, decent benefits, and a fair pick of the holidays. All the same, I felt my enthusiasm for the job bottoming out with each new house call.

Tim turned the wheel slowly, pulling our truck through the gates of some condo development called Passager Homes Retirement Community. Uniform white buildings and closely cropped lawns lined the streets of our route, and there was not a single pothole as we sputtered down the street. I spotted a speed limit sign that read "15 MPH."

Carl couldn't help himself, "Jesus, drag me out back by the collar and put me out of my misery before I end up in a place like this."

I had to agree. Retirement complexes always felt so sterile to me, designed by the man with the self-placed stick up his ass—you know, the one who makes you take your shoes off every year at the Christmas party.

"I don't think Passager Homes is hunting down your type, anyways," I told him with a laugh.

He frowned. "What the hell is that supposed to mean?" he said.

I grinned. "Just that I've seen your lawn, man."

Carl did not care for that one, either. His eyes narrowed in my direction, but I pretended not to notice. I was in a sour mood and in need of a human punching bag. To my surprise, Carl didn't swing back with a zinger. Instead, he sat back without a word as his gaze shifted to the window, mouth pursed into nonexistence. I laughed under my breath, anticipating the silent treatment. That would be fine with me. Just fine, indeed.

The truck groaned suddenly as Tim challenged it with a wide turn into one of the driveways; 670 Passager Court—that was the job. There were two other cars parked in front of the house. The sputtering of our engine must have announced our arrival, as the front door of the place cracked open a smidge. A woman's head peeked around the corner, a look of recognition washing over her face as she smiled, waving at us frantically. As if we could miss her standing there.

Hopping out of the truck, we followed her single file through the front door, where we were first introduced to the nightmare that was to be our workspace for the next eight hours. The place was absolutely inhabitable. Squishing into the small mudroom, the lot of us could only inch in a few steps before a towering wall brought us to an unexpected halt. The contents of the massive wall were just the vice we specialized in—junk.

I crept forward from the group, stretching out a hand to give the structure a wiggle—solid as rock. The horrific mess had layers—like an onion—going back how deep, I was unsure. I stepped back in a vain attempt to take in the gravity of the blockage before me. I mentally ticked off stacks of warped books, mass reems of bound and yellowed newspapers, bulk boxes of canned food, randomly tossed clothing covered in mystery strains, and endless stacks of cardboard boxes. The varied array of items all fit together in such a perfectly packed manner that it appeared they had been purposefully placed so—a lunatic's concept of *feng shui*. The room's overhead lighting was turned on, yet remained barely visible, peeking where it could through rare cracks in the "wall" where the junk was less dense.

I shook my head at the sight before me, turning to the woman who now rung her hands by the door. "So, what are we dealing with here, ma'am? Is this a relative of yours or something?"

The small, mousy woman nodded, casting her eyes over my shoulder periodically as if to check for another guest at the door. "Yes, this is my father's—well, stepfather's—place." She let out a sigh of pure exhaustion. "I don't know where he is—I haven't known for a little over two weeks. He's not missing, per se. It's been this new, rebellious behavior of his to prove to me that he maintains autonomy over his own life. I never should have let things get this bad." She brought both hands to her brow and traced circles over her temples. "Dad was diagnosed with Alzheimer's disease year before last. My family agreed his best option would be in-home care." Her lower lip began to tremble. "I didn't realize things were going to get bad this fast, or I never would have..." She suddenly erupted into tears, leaving her words hanging heavily in the air.

My coworkers stood like apes, mouths agape, appearing to shrink a step away from the woman at the first sight of female emotion. Carl took a sudden interest in his cuticle beds, picking at them fervently. Tim turned to stare shamelessly out the front window.

Bastards. Nose goes, I suppose, I thought to myself, realizing they had silently voted me most qualified for the job.

I reached into my back pocket and produced a yellow McDonald's napkin. Not the classiest gesture, but the thing was clean. I'm no monster.

The woman's tears may have blurred sight of my offering, but regardless, she took it to her chest and smiled. "Thank you." She sniffed, dabbing at the wet spots of her face.

I took advantage of the silence, asking the question we were all thinking, "Ma'am, if your father comes back, who has the official say here?" I wanted to prevent the chaotic scenario that was suddenly playing out in my head. *Old man returns home to discover his beloved stepdaughter is shipping him off to the nursing home. Old man goes bat-shit crazy on everyone involved. Old man presses charges against Junk Boy...and three of their asshole employees lose their jobs.*

The woman nodded. "Oh, of course. I should have explained. I'm my father's legal guardian. It was a lot of paperwork and took more time than I'd anticipated, but as guardian I control decisions surrounding both my father's wellbeing and his assets. Hence," she made a wide and theatrical gesture to the tower of junk looming before us.

I nodded. "Sounds like things are a go then, Ms. Wright," I said, relieved. If all went well, gramps would steer clear of home base while we were stripping it clean of his treasures. The sooner we got to work, the quicker I could step out from this mud pit of family drama.

Carl, Tim, and I trudged back outside to the truck and proceeded to stretch on sets of high-armed rubber gloves, pulling dust masks down over our faces. Carl tossed a pair of gloves over his shoulder, ignoring the box of masks as he strode back to the house. I had previously attempted to reason with him at past cleanups, describing the various microorganisms that could grow in old paper, especially if the fibers had ever gotten wet and were left to stew a while—the resulting love child did not belong in anyone's lungs.

The woman met us in the front yard with a book in hand. "I'll be out on the porch reading if you boys need anything. I've already dug through what I could, but a few pieces of my mother's furniture are still missing. They're probably buried in the corners I couldn't reach. Please leave any of those large pieces in the yard if you run across them."

I thought quietly that there would be no running in that death trap, but I let her continue.

She went on, "Everything else can go to the dump as far as I'm concerned. Most of it would need a thorough sanitation before I would even think about touching it." She shivered, squinting at the house with a look of revulsion. "I never should have let things get this bad."

We started in on the place by first breaking down the rooms from top to bottom. The tremendous height to which this man had stacked his many belongings left our team in a pretty dangerous situation if anyone backed their ass into a tower—my bets were on Carl. The impression I had initially gleaned from the mudroom proved true; most of the move consisted of boxes and reams of papers, which went up and over with repeated tosses into the dump truck.

We progressed to the center of the room and were making impressive time when Carl causally leaned a thick hand on one of the stacks. "What do you guys think causes that old-timer's disease, anyway? I heard you get it from tin foil but…"

"Carl, move!" I ordered, throwing my arms out in an attempt to steady the shifting wall, but it was too late. The towering structure tilted with a low groan, and the two of us fell back on the floor just in time as the heavy column came crashing down at our feet. Boxes exploded, dust billowed, and papers flew in chaotic frenzy. Heart racing, I turned to glare at Carl who—still lacking a mask—held a dirty elbow up in front of his face, coughing as dust swirled about his head.

I mentally prepared to lay into the guy. Toying with the fantasy, I wondered if a square punch to Carl's face might help me feel a bit more accepting of the hour he had just tacked on to our workday. I was visualizing the way his fat nose would squish like playdough under my knuckles when a gagging sound brought me back to the present.

Carl hacked up the last of his dust bunnies, face suddenly twisting with confusion as he raised his hand to a point. "What the fuck is that?" The color drained from his face, suddenly looking like he might puke.

My eyes moved to a decrepit book lying on the floor, globular stains of some greasy substance coating the thick cover. An outer layer of slime bubbled over the book's surface like the fine skin on tomato soup. I leaned forward to try to make out what had spooked Carl, but I quickly sat back, dry heaving like a cat as a strange, sickly sweet smell invaded my nostrils. I pulled off my mask, spitting in an attempt to purge my senses of the foul odor.

"See! What the hell!" he said, scuttling backward like a crab, still side-eyeing the book. "That thing reeks, man. I didn't sign up for this."

I pulled my apron up over my nose, picked up a coat hanger I found lying next to me on the littered ground, and—jutting it forward like a bayonet—I leaned in again toward the book. I poked the end of the hanger into one of the slime bubbles. Red substance oozed out from within with a quiet pop, and I heard Carl retch behind me.

Tossing my prod to the side, I let the apron fall from my face and hobbled to my feet. "Probably just spoiled food, man," I said, attempting to convince both myself and Carl. "People with dementia do weird shit. I had an uncle who started hoarding food under his bed when he went downhill." I looked back at the book and tried to imagine just what type of meal could have putrefied into that strange, red slime.

I looked over at Carl's hands, which hung bare at his sides. "Carl, you still got those extra gloves?"

Silence. Carl stood stock-still, staring down at the book.

"CARL, gloves," I repeated.

He jumped, his eyes again meeting mine after returning from some faraway place. He dug into his apron's front pocket and flung them over to me without a word, his gaze returning dutifully to the book. Strapping on a second set of gloves, I threw my hood up and pulled the strings down to cinch the front to a small peeking hole. My gloved hands labored to pull the string of the dust mask over the back of my head, but I finally snapped it into place.

I stepped forward before hesitation had time to fester, bending down to the rotting book and swooping it up in one motion. A trail of the red stuff attempted to cling on, stretching up from the floor in thick strands as I brought the book to my eye. The smell was rank, but I must have acclimated, as this time I resisted the wave of nausea taunting the back of my throat. Cradling the back spine of the book with my palm, its pages fell open with a soft sigh, parting easily to a section which had been marked by a creased corner.

The inside contents left me slightly baffled, and, without any practiced response to what I was seeing, I coughed uncomfortably. My throat clenched up on me, drawing inwards like the strings of my hoodie. I brought my gloved hand up to my neck for relief, only to feel a smear of warm wetness. I recalled the current state of my glove with revulsion and dropped the book, letting out a gag as I sent it sprawling back to the floor. The book fell open to that same creased page, displaying the images within.

There were photos. The first my eyes fell on appeared to be taken of a teenage boy strung up to the back of a pole in some dingy cement room—likely a basement. There existed only black spots where his eyes should have sat. The dark voids had a disturbingly realistic depth about them, one I had never before seen captured by photograph.

I fell down to my knees in shock as I scanned the rest of the cursed images before me: dead women bent backward in such unnatural manners that their spines had cracked through their soft bellies, a wide-eyed man missing arms and legs collared by cast iron chains in some filthy shed, a Polaroid of two glassy-eyed children sitting bloodied and handcuffed to both wrists of a decapitated man. There were little notes scratched under each photo that made my throat tighten and twitch.

Scattered around the photographs were ink drawings of various forms—bleeding, awful illustrations. Horned antlers sat atop heavily distorted faces, greasy black fingerprints littered the pages like ashen snow. Seepage from the book's coating lined each page's edge like a putrefied picture frame. My straining eyes flicked back to the nightmarish photographs. Underneath each, someone had scratched words in a messy script that repeated the same disconcerting message: *THIS IS MR. JONES' HOUSE. THIS IS MR. JONES' HOUSE. I LIVE HERE. I LIVE HERE.* One script ended in a wet corner of the page. Its ink had leaked, drawn into the goo, and now sat wavering, suspended in the liquid like a thousand black arteries.

I felt a warm rush of air as someone exhaled beside my ear. I nearly screamed as I spun in alarm, only to discover that both Carl and Tim were standing behind me, gaping over my shoulder. That dissociated look had returned to Carl's eyes.

"This is some trouble." Tim grunted, shaking his head. His eyes were red and strained, the bags under them appearing to have grown in the hazy light. "We need to call the police. Job's done here." He pointed to the photos in the book. "Not sure who those folks are, but I'm not trying to end up as the next centerfold." Tim pulled a cell phone out of his back pocket, flicked it open, and began dialing with thick, callused fingers.

"W-w-what is that?" a quiet voice whispered from behind us.

I turned slowly to see the man's daughter standing only a few feet from us. Her glassy eyes flicked down to the book and then back to me, an accusatory stare sitting above her trembling lips as she wrung her hands around her folded paperback. All of us were dead quiet; even Tim stared blankly at the woman.

"What in God's name is that awful sme—" She broke off, the whites of her eyes growing more visible as a look of horrified realization grew on her face. She stared at the photographs on the page. Her gaze did not falter as she whispered, "Oh my God." Her hands came to her mouth with a soft but sharp inhale.

I moved to the book, flipping it closed with the toe of my boot. I turned to the whimpering woman. "We had a little accident, and this fell out of one of your father's boxes." I felt the sudden impulse to wring my own hands.

She allowed her hands to fall from her mouth. They now hung limply at her sides. "I got him that for his birthday." She trembled. "A journal—that's the same cover—leather inlay—quite expensive." Her gaze moved back to the book.

Disturbed, I nodded. "Yes, he wrote his name all over the inside of the book. It's in there. I wouldn't look much closer," I said with a tone of warning. "He wrote something strange over and over. I think it says, 'Mr. Jones lives here.' Do you think he found out about the move?" I asked, changing topics in a vain attempt to calm the woman standing in front of me. She looked like she could fall through the floor at any moment.

Her concentration on the dusty floor broke, and she looked up at me with her head tilted slightly. "Jones? My father's name is Benjamin Norris. I don't know a Mr. Jones."

We all stood there, facing the trembling woman, whose face began to twist into an ugly grimace.

"I think I need to go sit down," she whispered, her complexion draining to a milky white. Afraid she was going down, I moved quickly to support her. She pushed me away with a gentle firmness. "No, no, I'm fine. I'm just going to go rest for a minute." She turned away from us, moving with a languid stride back to the front door. Floating through it, she reached back to close it behind her with a weak hand. There was silence, then a soft *click*.

I looked to Tim, who shook his head, pulling the phone back out and bringing it directly to his ear. There were two rings, then I heard a muffled voice on the other line.

A bloodcurdling but muffled cry suddenly erupted from the front yard, followed by shrill whimpers. The hair on my neck tingled and rose as the sound wafted in from under the front door. We stood there, hearts racing and bodies paralyzed as the doorknob turned. The door swung on its hinges with a tired groan, and through the frame walked a living skeleton.

The man standing before us was so yellowed that the skin clinging to his bones matched the tone of the rotting newspapers scattered about his home. His face was sunken to reveal jutting cheekbones which sang an old death hymn. His eyes were small black beads that glared at us from sunken sockets; they lolled around in their cages as he looked us over, snarling. He wobbled the handle of the polished wooden cane, the sharp tip of which shown glossy red. The old man began to stagger toward us—feet dragging one by one—scraping his cane along the floor and leaving coagulated maroon liquid smeared in a trail behind him. He parted his cracking lips, a drop of drool rolling over his bottom lip and trickling through the forest of grey whiskers that covered his chin.

"THA FAK ARE YOU DOING IN MAH HOUSE!" the man bellowed, bringing his cane up into the air and back down with a thud that sent red liquid splattering up from its tip. I heard Carl gag and looked over to see his face had been misted red.

Tim stood straight up in shock with the phone still pressed firmly to his ear, but his jaw hung agape. I could make out a dial tone's faint beep emanating from the receiver.

The man took another step, the smell emanating off him throttling me with déjà vu.

Carl vomited and fell to his knees.

The skeleton man looked at Carl, a malicious smile spreading over his face, revealing rows of gaping and bloody sockets where teeth should have sat. He jutted his lower jaw out as he smiled, putting a thin hand on his hip and tilting to the side in theatrics. "Ah, hello! Did you have something to say?"

Carl wiped the mess from his mouth with his shirt collar, peering at the man with a trembling lip and questioning eyes.

"Are you M-Mr. Norris?" he asked, nervous eyes darting over to Tim and I, hands fidgeting and wringing themselves out.

The old man's face drained of expression, and he stood there motionless for a moment in front of Carl, posture straight but body wavering like it had been caught in shifting wind. The bony hand resting on the cane began to tremble slowly, then faster, causing the cane to clatter on the wooden floor. The man smiled again at Carl as the sound grew louder still, the whites of the decrepit man's eyes growing and stretching to encapsulate his pupils.

His wobbling hand stopped abruptly, stock-still. There was a moment of silence until the man whipped his cane up and back with surprising agility, his eyes completely white—pupils missing. He plunged the cane forward with force which seemed impossible for a man of such small frame. The tip of his spear went flying through Carl's chest until the end—a brass eagle—brought the spear to an abrupt halt, adorning the front of his Carl's chest like a bloody broach.

Tim bellowed, backing up against the far wall with his hands outstretched, frozen as Carl flopped sideways onto the floor.

I fell backward onto my hands, watching as the light drained from Carl's wide eyes and the blood spurted from the gaping hole in his ribcage.

The old man stepped forward, cutting off my line of vision. Startled, my eyes locked on his red, toothless grin. Without pupils, his eyes sat like two decaying moons in their sockets, white and un-telling yet clearly peering into my own. Lurching toward me, his movements were unnatural—not his own—like a puppet jerked along by its master's strings.

He stood in front of me, letting his cane fall to the floor with a clatter as he moved his hands to the buttons on his shirt. Mouth still stretched with glee, the marble-eyed man began fumbling with his buttons, skeleton thin hands freeing each one quickly and succinctly until the tails of his shirt hung loosely at his sides, revealing the liver spotted skin which clung tightly to his mangled and gashed ribcage. A hexagram star was carved deeply into the yellow chest, the center of which pulsed, as if something small was attempting to push out from the inside. The thin skin stretched out, and simultaneous groans sounded from the old man's mouth, eerily in time with the budding movement.

The center of the star suddenly split, and with a sickening pop, a clawed finger pushed out through the skin of the chest, followed by another, and another, until a full hand slid through the gap. Then a second. The hands grasped the sides of the hole in the man's chest, white knuckled as they gripped and stretched the man's skin to a gaping void. I looked in horror as a thin pair of black lips pressed themselves through the small opening, just barely emerging from the slit. The black hands continued to stretch space for the mouth, growing as the man's skin tore and audibly split. The lips popped out from the chest, parting as the mouth began to open, a void of death and blackness growing as I stared in shock, my own mouth agape.

The mouth suddenly snapped shut, the shadowy hands unmoving on either side of it. I looked on, glued where I stood on the cold wooden floor, paralyzed by the impossibility materializing before me. The thing inside the old man—mouth now fully visible—spread its inky black lips in a smile that revealed rows of tiny sharp teeth.

The mouth opened to a gurgling scream.

"THIS IS MR. JONES' HOUSE. THIS IS MR. JONES' HOUSE. I LIVE HERE. I LIVE HERE."

There was creak in the floorboards, and I looked up to see Tim, metal coat hanger clutched in two shaking hands as he crept up behind the screaming man. The white, cataract eyes of the old man widened at the sound. He twisted to look behind him, but Tim had already hooked the thick wire over the old man's head, yanking it up and under the man's frail throat. Tim pulled the howling man's body in toward his chest, throttling the man's neck as the ancient Adam's apple rocked and bulged beneath thin skin.

As if summoned, black claws suddenly burst out through the old man's open chest, shooting upwards in a fury and wrapping their razor-sharp fingers around Tim's throat. Tim cried out, pulling tighter on the wire hanger until it began to sink into the flesh of the man's neck, disappearing under the skin. Blood poured from the wide gash, and the old man's jaw dropped suddenly to his chest, eyelids drooping.

Dizzy, I felt myself begin to fall through the floor. I remember seeing Tim, black claws still clamped around his throat as he pounded them with heavy, closed fists, his eyes popping from the sockets as he gagged. Below the chaos, a round, bloody head began to birth itself from the old man's flayed stomach, wriggling and twisting its black neck as it pushed through flesh out into the world. The head bobbed and weaved, slithering up the old man's desecrated body toward Tim's open, gasping mouth. I felt my stomach drop, and the world around me dissolved to static.

I awoke to the sound of sirens—stretched out on a gurney. Two men rolled me toward a small ambulance, its lights dancing across the lawn. Disoriented, I lifted my head, my eyes darting frantically around my surroundings. The EMT laid a comforting but firm hand upon my shoulder, explaining that "everything is going to be all right" and that "the police have arrived." I twisted desperately around to look back at the house and saw that the front deck was bathed in blood. A woman's body lay splayed out on the porch, a paperback novel resting beside her stark white hand—her throat had been cut.

I leaned my head up from the thin pillow. "W-where's the old man?" I said, my eyes darting as I searched the open yard.

The paramedic bent slightly over me, his mouth pursed as he shook his head. "The older gentleman didn't make it."

Relief flooded my system in a wave as warm as sunlight. Air left my lungs in a rush, and my eyes fell closed, hot tears trickling down the side of my head to the gurney sheets below. I breathed in deeply, "Is Tim okay?"

The paramedic looked away momentarily, then back to me with a twisted expression. "We found Tim with his hands locked around the old man's throat." He eyed me with a raised brow. "Tim's alive, but the police will be taking him into custody shortly after the hospital evaluation."

The paramedic's gaze left me as a cackling laugh echoed from somewhere farther up the driveway. I craned my head up from the gurney. A pair of EMTs were rushing to wheel another gurney down the gravel driveway. A patient writhed atop the gurney, his wrists and ankles strapped down by leather restraints. Straps clattered and shook as the laughing man wracked against them and the gurney wheeled closer. My stomach floated into my throat as I realized the man on the bed was Tim.

The paramedics rolled his gurney past my bed, and just as we paralleled, Tim rolled his head toward me on the pillow. His eyes were wild, lolling in the sockets like white moons as he howled through a pair of grinning lips.

Wet, black lips.

I screamed and turned away as Tim's gurney rushed past me, kicking the covers from my legs in an attempt to roll from bed. I felt my wrist and ankles shoved suddenly into leather straps as the EMTs rushed to contain me. Tim howled once more in a static, low tone, then his laughter quieted as a worker slammed the doors to the ambulance. The engine of the ambulance burst to life behind me, groaning as the tires rolled and crackled down the gravel driveway.

I laid there in shock, arms and legs tightly bound, staring up into the morning sun as I listened to the fading, curdling shrieks of the creature within the ambulance—the man called Mr. Jones. He had found a new home.

The Gods of Our Fathers

by Todd Keisling

Mary hated her new school, and not just because of all the gossip and teasing. Sure, the teasing was part of it. Sooner or later, her classmates found out where she came from. She was a freak, a weirdo from that creepy pagan church way out near the county line, an instant outsider no matter where she went. All that teasing and gossip just got worse when Daddy took her out of the public elementary school and enrolled her in a private Christian school.

This was after Mama died from the cancer, just two years after Mary's grandpa passed from a stroke. Mama wasn't in the ground more than a few days when Daddy declared they'd be a Christian household, swearing off the ways of Mama and Pop-Pop's heritage. Mary protested the change—leaving the public school only made her even more different than the rest—but Daddy put his foot down on the matter. "It's God's will," he told her. When Mary said it wasn't fair that her brother Daniel got to stay in the public school, Daddy smacked her and said, "He ain't ruined like you are."

Her time at First Baptist lasted two weeks before she was expelled. Her enrollment with First Pentecostal lasted just a week. Now, on her first day at First Evangelical, Mary wondered how long she'd last before the teachers found out about her past. She wondered how long she'd last before her pagan devotion offended First Evangelical's Christian sensibilities.

"Mary Fuson?"

"Here," Mary said, raising her hand. Mrs. Downing lowered her chin and stared.

"Mary," she asked, "do you know why your name is so special?"

Mary looked up from her desk, her cheeks flushing with that familiar heat. "No, Mrs. Downing."

Mrs. Downing smiled. "Mary was the mother of God. Isn't that right, class?"

The rest of her class, all fifteen children dressed in their Sunday best, joined in a chorus of, "Yes, Mrs. Downing. Amen."

"Amen, children." Mrs. Downing finished taking roll, and as that first day of sixth grade went on, Mary decided she didn't want to be the mother of anything, much less the mother of a god.

Her daddy's god scared her. Everything she knew of Daddy's god was jealousy and retribution, fire and brimstone, the sort of faceless creature that turned people into salt and laid waste to whole cities. Any time she had to think of Daddy's god (which was every morning, noon, and night), Mary imagined a looming giant draped in a blood-spattered robe, its head obscured in the clouds, speaking an indecipherable language that boomed over a vast destroyed landscape. The god of her father was a terrifying thing, an impossible thing, and somehow, she was supposed to love that faceless entity.

Somehow, she was supposed to believe that hateful, jealous thing loved her back—but only if she lived her life in servitude. Only if she honored her father and her brother. Only if she did as they told her to do, if she did not forget her place and her purpose.

Sometimes Mary lay awake at night, fearing she was damned. Damned for wanting to kill her brother for touching her the way he did. Damned for hating her father because he let Daniel get away with it. Damned for hating God, because he let it happen, and because he took her mother and grandfather away. Sometimes she lay awake, fantasizing about taking her pet goat and running away from home. Just Mary and Oats, running away to safety and adventure, away from the evil groping hands of her older brother, away from Daddy's awful god.

Pop-Pop would've stopped them from hurting her. "The Old Ways are not kind," he once told her, "but they're fair, little Mary."

Ah, the Old Ways. Pop-Pop's endless lessons and stories didn't bother her the way Daddy's endless sermonizing did. Everything she knew about the old gods of her grandfather were bound in the language of the Old Ways. His was a scripture that had long since been outlawed by modern society, drowned in the blood of its dwindling followers, and forgotten in the passage of time by all except the most devout.

And Mary's Pop-Pop was certainly the most devout.

Little Mary Fuson was so caught up in her reverie of Pop-Pop's Old Ways that when Mrs. Downing called upon her to lead the class in a recitation of Psalm 23, Mary replied with something Pop-Pop always said to her before kissing her goodnight: *"May the Nameless paint your face in the blood of the damned. May the blood cleanse your soul and lead you unto the dark. He waits for you there to take your hand and show you the way. Amen."*

Mrs. Downing sent Mary home that day with a note for Daddy. Mary didn't have to read it. She already knew it said something about having to find another school. She already knew how Daddy would react. The bruises from last time hadn't healed yet.

Mary was halfway home when she decided to keep the note to herself. She'd lie to Daddy if he asked about her first day at her new school. According to the Old Ways, some lies were Good Lies, and you'd know because they'd feel right. They'd be justified, and the Nameless wouldn't judge you for them.

But what about Daniel? The thought of being home alone with him while Daddy was out working in the fields forced a chill down her spine. He'd try to do the Bad Thing with her again. Daddy wouldn't be home for at least a couple more hours, and that was more than enough time for Daniel to do as he pleased.

Daniel was older, bigger, stronger, and he could run twice as fast. Worse, he knew all the good hiding spots on the farm. The first night Daniel tried anything, Mary screamed and screamed for help, but if her Daddy heard, he made no effort to stop her brother. Daddy didn't seem to care all that much, which hurt her almost as much as the day Pop-Pop passed away.

She'd long suspected her father resented her for having Pop-Pop's favor. The day of Pop-Pop's funeral, Daddy refused to attend. "I don't weep for the damned," he'd said, and for a while, Mary didn't understand what he meant by that. Not until Daddy stopped going to the standing stones at the edge of their property and started going to the church in town. That's when Daddy changed and started making her pray at bedtime. He stopped letting her dress in jeans and made her wear dresses instead.

He didn't force the same things upon Daniel. Her brother didn't keep their mother's faith like Mary did. That fact alone made him Daddy's favorite.

The new school, the forced prayers, and the change of wardrobe didn't bother Mary so much. Daddy's new rule of not wearing Mama's pendant, however, hurt her deeply. Mama gave it to her just before she died. "May the old blood feed the new," she'd whispered, pressing the onyx jewel into little Mary's hand. It was the only thing of her mother's Mary owned, and when Daddy took that away from her, she threw a fit so bad Daddy grounded her for a month.

She had plenty of time to think during that month of punishment. Didn't Daddy miss Mama? Why would he take away something as precious as Mama's pendant? Didn't he know Mama adored that pendant? Questions revolved around an uncomfortable truth, drawn closer by an unsettling gravity deep down inside her.

Daddy hated Mary. He was upset with her for simply existing. The longer she thought about it, the more Mary realized she couldn't remember a time when Daddy wasn't upset. One of her earliest memories was of him being angry at Mama and Pop-Pop. He shouted so loudly his voice rocked the walls of their home. Mama refused to argue with him, which just made him madder and meaner.

For a month after that fight, Mama wore a purplish-yellow bruise around her left eye. Mary used some of Mama's makeup to decorate her face in similar fashion so she wouldn't feel so different, but when she showed her Mama what she'd done, Mama scolded her and made her wash her face.

"But why, Mama?" Mary cried.

"Because I don't want him to hit you, too, sweet girl. Because sometimes we have to hide who we are to get along. The god of your father isn't kind."

Like so much else, Mary didn't understand what Mama meant at the time.

When Mary reached the fork in the road on her way home, she decided she'd go visit her mother's grave. Visiting Mama always made her feel better, even though Daddy didn't want her going out to the standing stones at the edge of the farm. Mama's grave within the circle of stones was the only place she could find peace, the only place she could ever hide.

But as she approached the standing stones, Mary decided she shouldn't have to hide anything. Why should she pretend to be someone else just to make her father happy? Sure, pretending to be a good girl in the eyes of her father might be one of her Pop-Pop's good lies, but why should she have to lie at all?

This sparked a heated anger deep inside the kindling of her soul, a sort of rage that both frightened and exhilarated her. Had she been older, Mary might've grasped that anger, she might've taken it by the hilt and buried it in the back of her brother's skull.

Instead, Mary sulked toward the circle of standing stones in which her mother and Pop-Pop were buried. The circle was wide, demarcated by tall unkempt grass on the outer rim. Inside, however, was a barren space of dusty earth, with only a handful of stone cairns to mark the final resting places of her kin.

Larger standing stones towered along the edge of the dusty circle, jagged teeth of rock protruding menacingly from the gums of the earth. Mary's troubles slipped away as she entered the circle, stepping out of the hateful world of her father and into the protective comfort of a gentler space. The space of her mother and Pop-Pop.

She'd once asked Mama why the standing stones were so important to their family. Her mother had urged her to go ask her grandfather, and Mary had done so. Pop-Pop set her upon his knee and whispered stories of older times, when there were many gods that roamed this world. These gods rewarded their servants with good fortune and long life. "And they placed their stones in the earth," Pop-Pop said, "to mark their altars of worship. If you ever feel alone, my child, go to the stones at the edge of our property. Pray with all your might—not to the god of heathens, but to the old gods of the earth and stars. They will hear you, they will listen, and if you need them, they will act."

Her grandfather's words buzzed in her mind as she knelt between the cairns. She closed her eyes, her tiny heart palpitating with a sudden fury, and she opened her mouth to speak.

"I miss you, Mama. I miss you, Pop-Pop. I got kicked out of another school, and I'm scared Daddy's going to hurt me really bad this time." Tears rolled down her cheeks, and her breath hitched in her chest. She chewed the edge of her thumbnail down to the quick and winced. Blood seeped from the wound and pooled around the edge of her jagged nail. "But I'm even more afraid of Daniel. Daddy lets him do things…" She trailed off, recalling the awful things Daniel had said to her in previous nights, things he wanted to do to her, things he wanted her to do to him. *It's a woman's duty,* he'd hissed at her as she'd fought against him, beating her fists against his naked chest. *One way or another, I'll have you, Mary.*

"I hate him," Mary confessed, fighting back a great sob that threatened to rise from the depths of her belly. "I hate them both."

One of the stacked rocks atop her grandfather's burial cairn tipped and fell with a dull thud. Mary snorted back her tears. "Pop-Pop?"

The tall grass at the edge of the circle rustled in a sharp breeze she could not feel. Her grandfather remained silent. Hesitant, Mary picked up the stone and turned it over in her hand. The surface was smooth, with one side flattened by the bottom of a river bed. She went to place it back in the cairn when a voice whispered from between the stones.

It is a gift, child. Keep it.

Mary twisted around, nearly toppling herself over on to the barren earth. "Is someone there?"

A gust of cool air brushed the hair back from her ear. She gasped.

I will paint your face in the blood of the damned, child, if you would allow me.

Mary closed her eyes, but the sudden fear that had risen in her heart began to subside, her trembling muscles finding an unspoken calm.

The stone is my gift to you, if you would pay tribute to me. Will you let the Nameless lead you into the dark?

"Yes," Mary whispered, relaxing in the embrace of an unseen force, its arms cradling her like a newborn.

So be it. There is something I must ask of you, if I will take your hand. Will you do this for me?

"Yes," she said, listening to the request. She smiled, shifting the stone from one palm to the other. "Yes…"

The house was empty when Mary returned home. Daddy was still out in the fields, sowing seeds for what would become next year's harvest. She looked at the clock, saw that her brother would soon be home from school, and set about doing what was asked of her while she still had time. She skipped her chores, skipped saying hello to Oats before journeying inside to fulfill her task. The quiet reassuring words of the Nameless repeated through her head as she tiptoed down the hall toward Daddy's room, soothing her despite the threat of Daniel's arrival.

My ways require sacrifice, child. A sacrifice of love, a sacrifice of blood, a sacrifice of memory. Show me your faith and I will deliver you from your pain. You will reap a bounty of bones from those who have wronged you.

Mary walked softly, moving along the wall where the boards wouldn't creak. She felt foolish for doing so, knowing fully well that she was the only one home, but moving like a mouse in this place was an old habit. Her very existence in this space felt threatened, even before Mama left to join Pop-Pop in the void. Even before Daddy turned away from the Nameless and began praying to his cruel heathen god. She'd learned early in her young life that bringing attention to herself put her in harm's way.

A sudden fear gripped her as she stood upon the threshold of her father's bedroom. She feared the furious beating of her heart might be enough to signal her intentions, that Daddy would hear her and come racing into the house, shouting at the top of his lungs, *"What are you doing, little girl? Who said you could go in there?"*

But he didn't. She was alone except for the Nameless, who was with her always, and she could feel its ethereal energy sparking at the tips of her fingers.

That energy intensified as she crossed into her father's domain, tiptoeing quickly across the threadbare carpet to the bureau where her mother's jewelry box sat collecting dust. The object of her quest sat in the top drawer where Daddy had left it. The onyx pendant hadn't lost its shine. Mary held the jewel by its necklace and thought of what Mama had told her.

"To remind you of what awaits us all, child."

"The void, Mama?"

"Yes, my sweet girl. Where the Nameless embraces us in eternity."

"I love you, Mama."

"I love you, sweet girl."

Mary blinked away welling tears and clutched the pendant in her fist. Daddy was wrong to take this from her. Even if he didn't like what it stood for, the black jewel was a gift from Mama, a symbol of love, purity, and acceptance. Thinking of Mama invigorated her, empowering the resentment growing inside her. With Mama in her heart and the Nameless in her ears, that resentment was finally beginning to blossom.

Daddy was wrong about so much more than just the pendant.

"You ain't s'posed to be in there."

Mary gasped, torn from her thoughts, the anger slipping from her like water through a drain. Fast on the heels of that anger was fear, chilled to the temperature of her big brother's heart. Daniel stood in the doorway, grinning. She was so lost in her anger that she'd not heard his approach.

"I'm— I was…"

"Daddy know you were in his room? He tell you to get something for him?"

Mary stammered, wanted to say *Yes, he did,* but she couldn't think of what, or why. Daniel had her, and everything she'd planned, everything the Nameless wanted her to do, withered in her mind like dying weeds.

"What's that in your hand?"

The air hitched in her throat. She clenched her fingers around the pendant and frowned.

"Nothing."

"Nothin', huh?"

Mary nodded, chewing her lip, getting ready to run. She couldn't outrun her brother in a dead sprint, but she could hide where he was too big to go. The barn, maybe, behind the old farm equipment Daddy stored there, or maybe behind the corral where they kept Oats and the other goats, but—

Her heart sank. All he'd have to do is wait. Wherever she hid, she couldn't stay there forever.

Daniel held out his hand. "Give me what you've got, Mary Contrary, or I'll tell Daddy."

She clutched the pendant and held her fist behind her back. She shook her head. "No, please don't, Daniel. I ain't hurting anything."

Daniel took a step toward her, a thin smile of victory spread across his face like a papercut. The look on his face filled her belly with ice. She'd seen that look before when she found him torturing a rat caught in one of Daddy's traps behind the barn. He was poking at it with a stick, pushing the sharper end of a fallen branch into the poor thing's eye socket. It twitched and squealed in pain, its back broken by the trap, unable to move or protect itself. Mary had wanted to stop him, scold him, hit him for being so cruel, but instead she'd hidden herself in the shadows.

She felt like that poor animal now, caught in a trap she couldn't possibly escape from.

"Maybe I'll tell Daddy," he said, "or…maybe I'll pay you a visit tonight. Maybe you'll let me do what I've been wanting."

Her stomach churned at the thought. She winced. "I don't…"

"It ain't about what you want, Mary Contrary." Daniel took another step, reached out, and traced the contour of her face with his index finger. His touch made her skin crawl, and she wanted to die. "Give me what I want or I'll tell Daddy. He'll beat you, and then I'll take what I want anyways."

A tear slid down Mary's cheek as she closed her eyes, distancing herself from her brother's touch. She forced her mind away from the sensation, traveling backward into a dark place where only she existed, where only the Nameless could hear her cries.

But the Nameless was silent, its directive spoken once and heard. Mary knew what was required of her. Her duty was to ensure her god's desires be fulfilled no matter the cost. She'd made a promise and breaking that promise would mean exile from the void. The mere thought made her feel empty inside.

Mary opened her eyes and blinked back the tears. She nodded.

"O-Okay... Tonight, after Daddy's gone to bed. You won't tell?"

Daniel smiled. "Of course not, Mary Contrary." He lifted her chin and kissed her forehead. "As long as I get what I want."

Daniel got what he wanted that night. It wasn't the Bad Thing she'd feared—"I want something different from you tonight, Mary Contrary"—but in some ways it was worse. Knowing the Nameless would not speak again until she'd done as it had asked, Mary tried calling out to her father's heathen god for help as Daniel held her down, but she was met with silence. The god of her father had looked away, sickened by what she was doing, what she was allowing to be done to her.

Afterward, Mary spent an hour in the bathroom, vomiting what her brother had left for her. When she was finished, she climbed into the bathtub, curled herself into a fetal position, and sobbed into the dawn hours. The voice of her Pop-Pop tried to console her, reminding her that there can be no salvation without suffering, that even the Nameless requires a symbol of devotion. Was that awful act with her brother such a symbol? She prayed it wasn't. What awful being would the Nameless be to require such a terrible thing of her, an act that left her with a horrible taste on her tongue, a queasiness in her belly, and a deep ache in her fractured heart.

Mama wouldn't have let this happen. Pop-Pop wouldn't have let this happen, either. *Oh, my Nameless lord, why has my father forsaken me? Why does he hate me so?* The Nameless said nothing.

The slow rhythmic drip from the faucet counted off the seconds as her mind drifted. She wondered if she was truly alone in this world, cast out from all bastions who might offer her shelter and comfort. Mama and Pop-Pop had departed, trading this mortal plane for the embrace of the void; Daniel would only have her for her body, a thought which made her retch again and fill her mouth with the bitter taste of bile; Daddy wanted nothing to do with her, for she was a reminder of his mistakes, a burden on his name and reputation.

And now she feared the Nameless had turned away from her as well, possibly in disgust, repulsed by the way she'd lowered herself to protect her offering. If the Nameless had looked away from her, then she was truly abandoned, alone with no one but herself to grieve and weep for the mistakes she'd made.

From the darkness behind her eyes, a memory replayed from yesterday. Her teacher, Mrs. Downing, asking if she knew the importance of her name. Mary hated her name, yes, but now she wondered what it would be like to be the mother of a god.

I would build my own god if I could, she thought. *Then I'd never be alone. I'd always be protected. My god would never hurt me.*

Mary carried that thought with her into slumber, a terrible and empowering thought that filled her head with dreams of death and blood and palpable happiness.

Daddy found her the next morning curled inside the bathtub. She wasn't sure whether he was more confused or angered by her presence there, but the beating that followed negated any conjecture. He always hit her where the bruises wouldn't show—her stomach, thighs, back. Never the face, although in hindsight Mary wondered why he didn't. She'd heard of people from the state who showed up sometimes to take kids away if their parents were bad. Since Daddy hated her so much, maybe blackening her eye would work out best for both of them.

When he tired of beating her, Daddy yelled for her to get ready for school. She hadn't told him about being sent home yesterday, and she wasn't about to tell him now—not while her wounds were still fresh, her back and limbs still sore. Instead, Mary did as she was told, putting on one of her new dresses, gathering her things in her knapsack, and skipping out the door to the dirt road. She made sure to keep up her pace so she could get far enough ahead of Daniel. When the farm was tiny in the distance, Mary darted into a nearby ditch and hid among the tall grass.

Ten minutes later, Daniel plodded by, mumbling to himself about not doing his homework. Mary almost gave herself away with a laugh, and she clamped her hand over her mouth to keep from squeaking. Another fifteen minutes after that, Daddy's pickup truck tore down the dirt road, leaving behind a thick cloud of dust in its wake. She waited another ten for good measure before climbing out of the ditch.

Mary stood on the side of the road, wondering how long she'd have before Daddy returned. He always went into town on Tuesday mornings, first to shop for groceries, and then to the weekly livestock sales. She knew those sales went until lunch time, so she'd have at least a few hours to herself to do what needed to be done.

And today, she needed a sacrifice of love. Mary turned back toward the farm, the barn, and the corral where they kept the goats. A brownish-white pygmy trotted up to the gate and stuck its snout through the fence, bleating for her attention.

"Hey there, Oats." She scratched the fur between his eyes. Oats the Goat uttered a shrill cry in response.

She'd wrestled with this dilemma all morning, the mere thought tearing a hole right into her little heart. *No salvation without suffering*, her Mama whispered to her. The heathens in her father's church would say she was like Abraham, offering his son in sacrifice to prove his love. In that story, the heathen god intervened at the final moment, sparing Abraham's son Isaac in favor of a ram.

But Mary knew that story to be false. In Pop-Pop's teachings of the old ways, the man and his son were nameless, their god a silent entity among the stars. In the true story, the man took his son to the altar among the stones and sacrificed his son to be among the Nameless in the void. The man washed himself in the blood of his son before burning the body upon a pyre, around which the members of their village danced in tribute as the cinders rose to the dark sky above.

Pop-Pop bought Mary the little pygmy goat for a lesson he would never get to teach her. She'd taken care of Oats the Goat in the years since Pop-Pop died of cancer. Oats was the one thing she had in this world that reminded her of her grandfather, and even if Oats wasn't intended to be a pet, he was the closest thing Mary would ever have to one.

She cried softly as she took the halter and collar from the barn, and she wept harder when she took Daddy's claw hammer from his workbench, but she dried her tears before returning to the corral. She didn't want Oats to see her crying. He would know she was upset, which would make him upset, and she didn't think she could bear his discomfort on top of everything else. He bleated at her as she slipped the halter over his head, and protested when she connected the lead, but he didn't resist when she opened the gate. He followed her out like the good boy he was, and Mary wondered if he suspected what she was about to do.

"Come on, Oats," she whispered. Her voice was hoarse, scratchy, like she was speaking through a wad of cotton. Was this what the nameless man felt like on the night he sacrificed his son? Did he feel regret? Or was he bolstered by his sense of duty? She wondered if the nameless son went to his death with the same sense of purpose, if he knew he would be embraced within the void and the pain of this life would be just a memory.

I don't want to do this, she thought, pleading with herself to cease her journey and return Oats to his corral. Mama spoke up from within, a whisper that tickled Mary's inner ears and made her heart swell. *Oats will be with you in the void, sweet girl. All things pass from this world into the embrace of the Nameless. You will be together among the stars.*

Mary wept quietly as she led the innocent animal to the circle of standing stones at the edge of the farm. As she neared her mother's burial cairn, one of the stones toppled to the earth.

Another gift for you, the Nameless spoke, the air suddenly electric, the tall grass swaying to the sound. *Pay me your sacrifice.*

Trembling, her tears watering the soil beneath her feet, Mary gripped the claw hammer in her fist. Oats stared up at her with inquisitive eyes and offered a short bleat, as if to ask, *What are you doing?*

Mary sucked in her breath and showed him.

After she washed off his blood in the nearby creek, Mary spent the rest of the day hiding in the barn loft. She ignored the pangs of hunger rumbling in her gut. Her starvation was penance for taking an innocent life, even in service of the Nameless. She hated herself for what she'd done, almost as much as she hated her father and brother. Oats didn't deserve to die. Did anyone?

Daddy does, she thought, wiping her nose. She nestled her head against a scratchy bale of hay. *Daniel does, too.*

So Oats didn't die in vain, her Pop-Pop whispered from the void, tickling that place in her ear. *All things serve the Nameless. Blood is the oil for our great cosmic machine. Sacrifice is how we show our devotion. You'll come to understand, in time.*

But Mary didn't want to understand. She wanted Oats back. She wanted to be normal, to have a normal family with a loving father who didn't see her as a burden, and a loving brother who didn't try to do the Bad Thing with her every night. More importantly, she wanted to feel less alone, to feel loved.

And for once, as she cried herself to sleep, the Nameless spoke to her from beyond the ring of stones. *I do love you, child. And with me, you will never be alone. One more sacrifice will let me show you my ways, if you will honor my wish.*

Mary dreamed of Oats, his tough head bashed open with Daddy's hammer. He bleated at her from beyond the edge of the barren circle, his cries choked and gargled with the blood spilling down his throat. A sliver of his tiny brain leaked from the wound and plopped on the earth like a bloody pink slug.

A sacrifice of blood, Oats cried. *Blood of the innocent, blood of the selfish, blood of the many, blood of the Nameless. Give yourself as I have, Mary! You must! Mary, do you hear me? Mary, when I find you, I will kill you, do you hear me? So help me, Jesus, I will send you to meet your mother—*

"—MARY!"

She awoke with a start, the vision of Oats bleeding into the dim evening light seeping through the rafters of the barn. *Daddy,* she thought. He roared for her again, his voice growing nearer, louder.

"Mary, goddammit, I swear to Christ, when I find you…"

"What's she done now, Pa?"

Daniel's voice gave her pause. Her father's angry cries were one thing, but hearing the glee in her brother's voice made her stomach churn. Daniel fed on their father's anger like a tick on a dog, growing big and bulbous, sated by hate.

"She got kicked out of another school, that's what. Little bitch was playin' hooky all day today. Yesterday, too. *MARY! COME OUT OF HIDING, LITTLE GIRL!*"

Mary held her breath, listening to her father rage and her brother chitter with each bellowing admonition. Her heart beat with fury, so hard and fast that her vision pulsed, and she wondered if a child her age could have a heart attack. She certainly felt like she was having one.

Wait for them to pass, Pop-Pop whispered. *Climb down and run. You run for the stones. Run for the Nameless.*

"Come on out, Mary Contrary!"

Daniel's voice lingered at the mouth of the barn. Mary ducked behind the haybales in the loft, fighting the urge to peek, scared he might see her, or worse, she might see him staring straight up at her. Scared he already knew where she was hiding.

Mary waited. Listened. She held her breath, waited for her heart to slow. Minutes crawled by. Was Daniel still down there? She wanted so badly to peek, but her fear held her there whether she liked it or not.

Finally, a scratching sound, of rubber soles on gravel.

"She ain't here, Pa."

"I know that, you dumb shit. I'm gonna get the truck. You keep lookin'."

Their voices faded away. Mary waited until the sun drifted below the horizon and the moon took its place. Only then did she dare climb down from the loft, and only then did she begin her escape from the family farm. She kept to the fields that stretched alongside the old dirt road leading away from their home.

Moonlight illuminated the circle of standing stones. As she approached from the fields, Mary wondered if this was what they looked like to the unknown man and his son the night their sacrifices were made.

The air pulled away from the circle as she set foot over the threshold, rustling the tall grass at the edge, each blade whispering in hushed tones. *She's come,* they said. *She's come once more. What shall we watch her do this time?*

The remains of Oats lay in the center of the circle, his tiny body sprawled at an odd angle, the wound between his horns still trickling into a puddle. His glossy eyes stared upward at the stars and rising moon. Seeing him brought back all the gut-wrenching sorrow and regret she'd felt back in the barn, but she forced back the tears this time. Instead, she knelt beside his body and traced a finger along the fur behind his ear. He always liked when she scratched him there.

She took her mother's onyx pendant from her knapsack and placed the dark stone between the dead goat's lifeless marble eyes. She wasn't sure why, wasn't even certain of what she was doing; instead, her hand felt guided in this space, pulled by an unseen energy. Was the Nameless here with her? Was the time soon at hand?

The thought terrified her. Mary found she was trembling as she placed the knapsack on the ground beside Oats. She heard her Pop-Pop whisper from behind one of the stones, *You did good, sweet girl. There's just one sacrifice left to make.*

"A sacrifice of blood," she whispered, tracing her fingers along her wrists. She closed her eyes. "Must I?"

You must, my sweet child. A shadow approached from beyond another stone. The shape of her mother, faceless, formless, but possessed of a warmth and voice she would recognize anywhere.

"Had a feelin' I'd find you here."

Mary's eyes snapped open and squinted at a piercing light pointed at her face. Daniel's heavy footfalls scraped along the earth, kicking up a plume of dust as he strolled into the circle of stones. He raised the flashlight and illuminated his grinning face.

"Oh no," she whispered, searching frantically for the shape of Mama, of Pop-Pop, something that might save her from her brother's wrath, but the phantoms were gone.

"You have any idea how much trouble you're in?"

Mary shook her head, frozen in place, unsure of what to do or where to run. Where could she run?

"Of course you don't," Daniel said. "You know, even I can't protect you from Daddy tonight. Hell, he might just kill you for doing what you've done. But I might try to help…" Daniel reached down, adjusted himself through his pants. "…if you help me."

"Y-You talkin' about the Bad Thing?"

Daniel nodded. He looked just like a devil in the pale flashlight glow, his lips turned up into an awful smile, his eyes nearly as black as their mother's pendant. All he needed was a pair of horns. In that moment, Mary wished for god—any god—to come and protect her from this monster. She wished she had a god to call her own, to save her from all these horrible things in her life.

A dark cloud passed before the moon, blotting out its light, and in the darkness, Daniel made his move. Mary screamed, and for the second time in her short life, her father's heathen god looked away.

She fought him. She kicked and scratched and screamed for help, but Daniel was bigger, stronger, driven by a sinful lust that she could not overpower. And after he knocked her off her feet with a quick sucker punch to the jaw, after he pressed her face into the soft earth of the circle, Daniel had his way with her in the way he'd always wanted.

There was silence in those crawling minutes except for Daniel's erratic grunts and sighs. The tearing pain between her legs was so powerful it drove most conscious thought from Mary's mind, and in that expanse of time, she saw only the stars above, the still grass beyond the circle, the lifeless body of Oats beside her. She retreated into herself, searching for an escape from the agony and trauma happening to her. Where was god? Where was the Nameless? Was this what it meant to be one with the void?

Near the end, as Daniel finished what he'd begun, Mary uttered a hushed prayer into the earth, the same prayer that got her kicked out of First Evangelical just a day before. *"May the Nameless paint your face in the blood of the damned. May the blood cleanse your soul and lead you unto the dark. He waits for you there to take your hand and show you the way. Amen."*

She was ready to take his hand now. The flush of pain and heat in her hips, the cold terror in her belly was too much to bear anymore. She hated this earth, hated the way its people treated her. She was truly alone here, and the despair welling up within her chest hurt more than anything Daniel could ever do to her.

Nameless, she prayed, *take my hand.*

Daniel sighed and climbed off her. He stumbled, lost his balance, and fell backward with a short laugh. He was so lost in his victorious stupor he didn't notice the earth shaking beneath them. The sound was faint at first, nothing more than a dull rattle from within, like someone tapping on the other side of a door.

Mary curled herself into a ball beside the corpse of her pet. She'd taken his life, and for what? His death was senseless, pointless, just another sacrifice to the void. Why else—

Don't lose faith, my child.

Mary gasped. Oats's body was shivering. The onyx jewel of her mother's pendant glowed in the moonlight, illuminating the viscous gore congealing on the goat's skull.

"But the sacrifice," she whispered, looking back to her brother. She reached down to pull down the hem of her dress, and discovered the warmth of her blood on her inner thigh. Mary didn't finish her thought. She understood now.

Daniel looked back at her, giggling like an idiot, his splotchy stained underwear still tucked down around his ankles.

"Ain't so bad, is it? Girl, if Daddy don't put you in the ground tonight, we're gonna make this a regular thing."

Her brother climbed to his feet, pulled up his pants, and turned away from her to survey the monstrous stones around them. Behind him, the earth was like clay, wet with her blood and sweat, and tainted with the drip of his semen. Together, those primal ingredients completed an untold rite, closing a spiritual circle that signaled the cosmos above, the cosmos within. The ground shook with this silent completion, long-sealed gates opened, and the formless spirit of something divine descended from the stars to fulfill a mortal promise.

Mary watched in awe as the body of her fallen pet took on a different shape. She winced at the snap of the goat's limbs and gasped as multiple horns sprouted from the wound in its skull.

The Nameless took shape before her, a monstrous thing not of this world, born of blood and love and memory. A god of Mary's making that towered over the stones lining the circle, with the crushed face of her dead goat and her mother's black pendant for a third eye, covered in fur and dirt and twigs and grass, its body shaped from the scratching brambles of nature itself.

Do you still have the gift I gave you, child?

Mary nodded. She knelt and retrieved the stone from her knapsack.

Good.

"We should get ba—" The color drained from Daniel's face when he saw the hulking monstrosity beside her. He had time to utter a shrill, helpless scream before the Nameless plucked him off the ground like a ragdoll. She watched as her god dangled her brother before her in offering.

"Mary, don't—please don't let it hurt me."

The fear in Daniel's eyes was electric. Mary wiped the tears from her cheeks and took a long look at her brother's terrified face. He looked so small now, so helpless. *Devote yourself to me, child.*

She raised the stone, spit in Daniel's face, and swung. The stone split his face with a dull thud. His shriek filled the night, but no one heard him. They were alone here in the circle, the center of a universe that belonged only to her and the Nameless. She struck Daniel's skull again, and again, and again, until the muscles in her arm burned and turned to jelly, until her brother's pained cries fell silent.

It is done, child. He will hurt you no more.

The Nameless dropped Daniel's body to the earth. Mary wiped her tears and looked up at the Nameless. The three-eyed being regarded her with silent fascination. The look on its bestial face was almost loyal.

Far off in the field, Daddy's voice carried on the wind. He was still looking for her, still raging at her disappearance, still eager to beat the life out of her fragile body.

"Daddy…"

I know, child. We will deal with him as well. I have no patience for those who turn away.

She looked off into the dark and took her god's hand. Together, they left the comfort of the circle, wandering into the darkened fields, and little Mary Fuson no longer felt alone.

I Know He Loves Me

(He Just Has a Funny Way of Showing It)
by James Newman

"It's my favorite time of day, driving you."
"It's the saddest part of my day, leaving you."
— *Love, Actually*

"Keep away! The sow is mine."
— *The Exorcist*

Forget everything you've seen in the movies or read in some stupid book.

If you swallow what Hollywood has fed you through the years, folks like me live happily ever after once it's said and done. As if there's no traumatic aftermath. Sure, we're left with scrapes and bruises, but those eventually heal, and maybe our scars spell out an F word or two, but long sleeves and turtlenecks help hide the worst of them. The survivor's voice is hoarse following her ordeal, a side-effect from all that guttural cursing, but give it a week and she'll once again sound like her sweet little fifteen-year-old self. At least twice a day Mom sprays something lilac-scented throughout her daughter's bedroom to mask the lingering stench of bodily fluids, while Dad sweeps up the pieces of broken wood and glass and tries his best to fix the furniture that was flung about by forces beyond their understanding. Like the haggard priests who blessed the house and mumbled one last prayer before riding off into the sunset, everyone in the family looks ten years older than they did when it began...

...but light has prevailed over darkness, and life goes on. The evil has been expelled, as if it were nothing more than a nasty infection killed with a good dose of antibiotics. Praise the Lord and cue the closing credits. We are left to assume that those affected by demonic possession came out on the other side of it with a six-figure story to sell to the tabloids and everything is hunky-dory.

I'm here to tell you that's bullshit.

I was fifteen years old when the demon came into me.

Mom said it all started because I messed around with a Ouija board at a slumber party. That didn't make any sense to me, though. There were three other girls at my cousin's house that night, asking silly questions of the board like *does Brian Banks have a crush on me* and *does Jenny Stillman stuff toilet paper in her bra to make her boobs look bigger* (the board answered YES to both, by the way, which made us all giggle 'til our sides hurt), but nothing crawled into *them* and turned their lives upside-down. I always assumed it was because there was something special about me.

All I know is, during that summer before my freshman year of high school, I was the only one who became host to an ancient entity that called itself Zebos.

Lucky me...

First came the noises in the walls. My father was convinced we had a rat problem; he wasted a hundred and fifty bucks on an exterminator who came to our house but found nothing to exterminate. Then my bed started moving by itself, thumping up and down and scraping across the hardwood floor of my bedroom. Strange symbols appeared on my wrists and stomach, as if burned into my skin by an invisible blowtorch. One morning my parents came in to find me levitating, floating so high above my bed that my nose was mushed flat against the ceiling (strangely enough, I couldn't stop laughing, even as it scared me half to death).

You know the rest. You've seen it in a hundred corny horror flicks. This is the stuff those movies get right, for the most part…

I cursed my mother nonstop. I suggested that I wanted to perform unnatural acts on my father. I soiled myself on a regular basis, and my breath filled my room with the sickly-sweet stench of decay. I bit our housekeeper hard enough to draw blood one evening when she leaned over me, gave me a hug, and promised she would pray for me. She quit the same day, and as she said goodbye to my parents downstairs, I cackled maniacally, mocking her with racial epithets.

Two days later, perhaps in some last-ditch attempt to bring us back together, Mom made my favorite for dinner: sirloin tips with mushroom gravy. I thanked her afterward by squatting over the urn that held my grandmother's ashes and expelling into it everything I had eaten.

The exorcists arrived on our doorstep the following afternoon.

I had heard Mom and Dad fighting about it constantly—she was a believer, a devout Catholic since childhood, while he insisted I had fallen in with the wrong crowd and all I needed was "a good hard belt" across my backside to put an end to this nonsense—but I guess by that point they were willing to try anything. After the incident with Grammy's cremains, I even saw Dad cross himself a couple times.

Two old men with dour faces and purple lips that made them look like they had just been unfrozen for the task at hand, the priests assured my parents that it wasn't too late to save my soul. Then, they locked themselves in my room with me…tied me to my bed…sprinkled me with holy water…and recited litanies from a giant book bound in leather.

Six days later, the demon released his hold on me.

The movies never tell you about the overwhelming sense of *loss* that comes after.

Think about the greatest love you have ever known. The person you believed to be your soulmate. When you were with this person, life was as perfect as life can be. The two of you were connected in a way no one else could possibly understand. You were sure you would never survive such soul-crushing despair if your one true love ever left you.

Now multiply that by infinity…and you'll know how I felt when the priests were done with me.

The demon used me. He abused me. He tore my flesh, he broke my bones, and I have little doubt he was responsible for my parents' bitter divorce (it was from my own mouth, after all, that Mom learned the sordid details of Dad's affair with his secretary—the demon told his share of lies, but he also knew when the truth hurt even more). He left a black stain on my soul. Forever.

We were connected. On a level deeper than any love affair.

He could have picked anyone. But he wanted *me*.

Zebos lived inside of me for forty days and forty nights before those bastards forced him out (the Biblical significance was not lost on me, nor was it lost on Zebos).

I've spent the last thirteen years trying to get him back.

Father Hensley was the first.

Six years to the day when he and his cohort had successfully completed their rituals of exorcism upon me, I broke into Father Hensley's home and slit his throat while he slept. His murder was never solved (although popular belief was the culprit was a member of a local gang that call themselves the Demons—that made me chuckle).

Next, it was Father Dunham's turn. I smothered him with a pillow. The geezer put up a fight, I'll give him that, but he was so old and weak I barely broke a sweat.

I defiled my parents' memory as well. Mom and Dad had started dating again not long after I moved away to college, said they planned to "take it slow and see where things might lead"…which turned out being into the path of a drunk driver. They were hit head-on late one Christmas Eve and were pronounced dead on the scene.

Deprived of the opportunity to kill them myself, I drove six hours across state to the cemetery in the center of my hometown. I came prepared, drank plenty of whiskey beforehand. I found the two fresh mounds where they were buried ("BELOVED MOTHER"/ "DEVOTED FATHER") and promptly hiked up my skirt. Steam rose into the February air like early-morning fog as I gave them everything that was in me.

"That's what you get," I sobbed when I was finished. "I will never forgive you for tearing us apart."

Where the priests and my parents were concerned, it had been personal. But when the longing became too much to bear—and two attempts at suicide proved fruitless—I began to kill at random.

No one would ever suspect *me*. The shy librarian type in the tortoise-shell glasses, working in the Admissions Department at Duke University? I'm the *last* person anyone would think capable of doing such terrible things…

Perhaps you have read about my crimes in the papers. Nine of them so far, in four different states along the eastern seaboard. There is no rhyme or reason to the ones I choose. Men and women, black and white, young and old. It doesn't matter. They all bleed the same, and they're all just means to an end.

The only thing that matters is making Zebos notice me again. So we can be together. Along the way, I committed acts of blasphemy that have surely damned my soul to the hottest fires of Hell. I desecrated churches with spray-paint and goat's blood. I ripped pages from the dog-eared hymnals at small-town churches and synagogues. I hocked loogies in the fonts of holy water at places of worship no less prestigious than the Washington National Cathedral. I stole from collection plates, then donated the money to production companies that specialize in hardcore pornography. I smeared shit on the statues of saints and martyrs. I renounced the Holy Trinity again and again and again…then again, in case He was busy and didn't hear me the first time.

Sooner or later, my efforts have to pay off.

My dark lover has yet to heed my call. But I know he will, eventually.

Zebos must return to me. He can't ignore me forever. And this time, when we're together, nothing will ever come between us.

I can't go on like this, feeling so goddamned *empty*.

Second Sight

by Allan Leverone

"Now, remember," Doctor Schneider said gently. "Your eyes will likely be sensitive to overstimulation, particularly where bright light is concerned. This was a complex surgery, and the recovery period will be lengthy."

"I understand," Rebecca Danvers answered. She was excited and impatient but worked to keep those emotions out of her voice. She wasn't sure she succeeded. "I'll be careful, I promise."

"Good," the surgeon said. "Follow all of your postoperative instructions to the letter, and very soon you can expect to recover full use of your vision. You won't believe the things you'll see."

Over the nearly three decades since she'd lost her sight to a degenerative macular condition, Rebecca had discovered—as was often the case with the blind—that her remaining senses were much more strongly developed than was typically the case with people who could see. She didn't need to use those strongly developed senses to detect the smile in Doctor Schneider's voice.

He leaned over her hospital bed and began removing the gauze squares. The squares, supplemented by heavily shaded glasses, had been placed over Rebecca's eyes at the conclusion of her ocular transplant surgery in an effort to minimize the amount of light reaching them until Doctor Schneider decided she was ready.

And now everything was coming off, albeit much too slowly for Rebecca's liking.

She had been five years old when the blackout curtain fully descended on her vision. It was so long ago that the thirty-four-year-old Rebecca could barely remember ever having the gift of sight. Beyond a vague recollection of her now-dead parents' faces, a memory she wasn't even sure was accurate, the notion of actual sight was more theoretical concept than concrete reality.

Over the ensuing three decades, Rebecca had spent more than her fair share of time reflecting on the cruelty of a universe that would tease a little girl with something as magical as eyesight before simply taking it away. In all that time, she'd never made sense of it.

But the miracle of modern science, along with the generosity of a deceased human being Rebecca had never met, combined to render those reflections irrelevant. As Doctor Schneider continued to uncover her eyes—how much stuff had he put on her face, anyway?—she felt her heart soar. She wasn't sure she'd ever been this happy. She smoothed her hair as she waited for Schneider to finish.

"Leave your eyes closed until I tell you to open them," he said, and then plucked the final layers of oversized squares off her face, one after the other.

She reached for Rob. She knew her husband was standing next to Doctor Schneider, and she squeezed hard when she found his hand. They had been a couple for nine years, married for the last seven, and she knew this was every bit as big a day for him as it was for her.

"Open your eyes," came the command, and for a moment Rebecca hesitated, filled with doubt. What if the surgery had failed? What if she opened her eyes only to be met with the same muddy blackness she'd been living with for almost thirty years? What if—

"You can do it," Rob said gently. "There's nothing to be afraid of."

So she did.

"I wish your face had been the first one I saw, rather than Doctor Schneider's," she said.

"That doesn't matter," Rob answered. "You'll get to see my ugly mug every day for the rest of your life. Once your recovery is complete, you'll never see Schneider again. I'm the clear winner in that competition."

They were alone in Rebecca's hospital room, still with their hands clasped together. The gauze squares and tinted glasses had been placed once again over Rebecca's eyes, the surgeon determined to reacquaint his patient with eyesight in a methodical manner.

Rebecca didn't mind. She had become so accustomed to living in nearly complete darkness that the things she'd seen after having her bandages removed threatened to overload her senses and crash her overtaxed hard drive. The lights had been dimmed in the room, but she had seen every last feature in the surgeon's face before turning her attention to Rob.

She had been surprised to see him crying silently, tears of joy rolling down his handsome, smiling face.

But that wasn't all. There had been so much more visual stimulation that it had been jarring.

The walls of the hospital room were green. Not just any green. It was a shade she recognized instinctively as putrid despite not having any real memories to compare it to.

The television hung suspended in the upper right corner of the room. It was slim and black and had been powered off.

The silver of her bed's stainless-steel railings had glittered dully in the muted light, and Rebecca thought that little glitter might be the most beautiful thing she'd ever seen.

Her bedspread had been light blue, the tile floors gray and the wooden door to her bathroom a rich brown of varying shades, the grains complex and fascinating.

It had been a cornucopia of beauty, simple and breathtaking and overwhelming.

When the gauze was replaced after maybe twenty minutes, Rebecca's first instinct was relief. The visual stimulation had been far more stressful than she'd expected. But already she was looking forward to tomorrow morning, when Doctor Schneider would remove them again. This time, he promised, she would be allowed to enjoy her new reality for a longer period of time, perhaps as much as a couple of hours. The thought was simultaneously terrifying and alluring, but for now she was exhausted.

And Rob could tell. "It's been a long day," he said.

"A great day," Rebecca countered.

"Agreed. A great day, but also a tiring one. It's obvious this great day has worn you down. I'm going to go home so you can get some rest. I'll be back first thing in the morning, and we'll spend the whole day together."

She nodded. "I am pretty tired."

He released her hand and kissed her. Ran his fingers through her hair and then stood. "Sleep well."

"I'll see you tomorrow."

"Yes, you will."

It was dark.

No surprise there. It was always dark in Rebecca's world, had been for as long as she could remember.

But this was different. This wasn't the exterior gloom of blindness, of only distinguishing daytime from nighttime by a slight lightening in the ever-present shadowy cloak that hung over her eyes even when they were open.

This was an inner gloom, a darkness of spirit, a perception even of impending doom. This was the sensation of evil, the horror-movie terror that came from knowing the knife-wielding maniac was somewhere inside the house, preparing to attack the unsuspecting victim.

Only in this case the house was Rebecca's body. And the victim was Rebecca herself.

She was dreaming; she knew that right from the start. She was asleep and this whole situation was nothing more than a manifestation of her unconscious fears and worries. But that was irrelevant. Knowing she was dreaming and being able to extricate herself from the dream were two entirely separate and unrelated matters.

The dream itself was disjointed and weird, filled with strange jagged shapes and sickening odors, and from somewhere close came the sound of a pig squealing from pain and terror.

Or were those screams human?

It was nighttime in the dream, and Rebecca got the sense that she was outdoors, maybe in a clearing in the woods, although she couldn't say exactly why she thought that. There may or may not have been a fire burning, a campfire or bonfire or something similar; the source of the dim light was a mystery, the flames themselves more sensed than seen.

The pig—*the human, oh god that's a person suffering*—was screaming and crying, wails of terror echoing across the open clearing in the forest, or wherever the hell the person was, and the sensation of evil continued to grow, a blanket of misery that was slowly suffocating Rebecca. Out of nowhere she felt a searing pain on her chest, not *inside* her chest but *on* her chest, on the skin covering her breastbone. She realized the horrible screams she could hear were coming from her. She was shrieking in pain and confusion, and the evil presence continued to grow in her dream, blooming like a malevolent flower, darkening and suffocating, and it was *right there,* and it was going to consume her. It was going to take her and make her its own. She tried to take a deep breath to scream again, and when she did, she—

Her eyes flew open, but of course she couldn't see anything because of the gauze.

But she was awake.

Her body was covered in sweat, her mouth still hanging open from the silent scream. It must have been silent because she was still alone in her hospital room. She knew damn well if she'd yelled inside the hospital in the middle of the night, she would have been joined in a matter of seconds by at least two nurses, first concerned for her welfare and then justifiably pissed off at her for disturbing the other patients.

Her nightgown clung to her damp skin like it had been glued on. She had always assumed you had to be hot to sweat, but that was clearly not the case because at this very moment she was freezing. The hospital kept the temperature around seventy, but Rebecca was an ice cube, the chill originating inside her very core and radiating outward.

She breathed deeply, shocked but at the same time unsurprised at how badly she was shaking. It felt like the time in seventh grade she'd had to stand up in front of the class and give a presentation on Harriet Tubman, only a thousand times worse. She'd thought on that occasion she was going to puke all over her new dress, probably on Mrs. Sanderson's shoes as well. If she tried to speak at this very moment, she *would* toss her cookies, and likely burst into tears to boot.

The braille clock that had been a graduation gift from her mother stood sentry on the bedside table. She reached for its raised numerals with hands that refused to stop shaking. It was 3:40 a.m. Still hours until Rob's arrival.

Get a grip. It was a nightmare, no big deal. It's not like you haven't had those *before*.

She blew out a forceful breath and tried to concentrate on her inner pep talk, knowing her sternly delivered speech to herself was bullshit but trying to ignore that knowledge.

Whatever had just happened, it was no ordinary nightmare. It was much, much worse. The stifling dream-sensation of an evil presence had disappeared, vanishing with a pop as she awoke, but it sure as hell was not forgotten. The burning feeling on the skin of her chest was gone as well, but Rebecca dragged the tips of her fingers lightly across the slick, sweat-soaked skin anyway, just to be sure.

Be sure of what?

She didn't know the answer to that question, but the dream had felt so real, so horrifying, so…*inevitable*.

It felt inevitable.

She lifted herself to a sitting position and plumped the pillow, trying to get as comfortable as possible for the long wait until Rob's arrival. She was still tired, but that didn't matter.

There was no way in hell she would get any more sleep tonight.

Rob couldn't remember the last time he'd seen Rebecca like this. Her face was pale and drawn and she seemed agitated and near tears. It was exactly the opposite of what he'd expected to find when he walked into the hospital room on the morning she'd been promised at least an hour's worth of vision.

She greeted him with a trembling smile and remained mostly quiet as they awaited Doctor Schneider's arrival. When he asked how she'd slept, she shook her head and said, "You have no idea."

"I will if you tell me."

She shook her head again, and he dropped the subject. He'd learned long ago that as sweet as his wife was, she was also strong-willed, bordering on obstinate. If she'd made her mind up not to explain herself, there was nothing on God's green earth he could do to make her talk until she decided she was ready.

After a period of time that felt much longer than it probably was, Schneider came in and repeated yesterday's ritual of removing the glasses from her face and the gauze squares from her eyes. Rob was shocked at what he saw when the gauze came off, and although the surgeon did a good job of hiding his reaction, it was clear he was as well.

Rebecca looked awful. Her eyes seemed to be sinking into her skull. Yesterday they'd been clear and bright, but today they appeared bloodshot, like she'd gone out last night and guzzled a fifth of cheap whiskey and woken up this morning with the worst hangover ever.

He was careful not to react outwardly, but made a mental note to corner Doctor Schneider before leaving the hospital today and ask if any of this was normal. Based on the man's somber demeanor, Rob thought he knew the answer to that question already.

The surgeon made a little small talk and then left, closing the door behind him after promising to return in a little while to replace the bandages. Rob watched his wife closely as she ran her gaze around the room, focusing on everything but his face.

He waited patiently.

Eventually, she had no choice but to meet his gaze. When she did, he spoke calmly and quietly. "What's going on, baby?"

To his surprise she answered. She told him about the clearing in the forest, and the fiery pain on the skin of her chest, and the screams she hadn't realized until halfway through the dream were coming from her.

He listened without interruption. When she finished, her voice cracking and her body shaking, he said, "You have a lot going on in your life right now. To regain the gift of sight, as wonderful as that is, represents a major shift for you. It doesn't surprise me at all that your subconscious might subject you to the occasional nightmare."

She had begun shaking her head before he finished speaking and he said, "What?"

"It wasn't a nightmare. At least it wasn't a normal nightmare, if there even is such a thing. This was more."

"I don't understand. More how?"

"It was more of everything. It was more vivid and tangible, more *real*, and it was accompanied by a sensation of evil that permeated my entire being."

He had no idea what to say, so he remained silent. Since the day he had met her, he'd known Rebecca to be empathetic to a fault. She had a way of sensing what others felt in ways that should not be possible, that *weren't* possible to the average person. But this was extreme, even for her. It was more than extreme; it was terrifying.

"I could feel the evil inside me, Rob. It was there and real as anything I've ever experienced."

"But it was still just a dream."

"Was it?" Rebecca's eyes—her brand-new eyes, the ones that had been transplanted mere days ago—returned his gaze, sunken and terrified but still beautiful. "I'm not so sure about that."

Doctor Schneider tried to couch his concern in scientific phrasing and medical terminology, but it became clear to Rob in a matter of minutes that the surgeon was just as worried about Rebecca's apparent downturn as he was.

When Schneider finished speaking, Rob cut right to the chase. "So you're telling me something's wrong."

"Let's not get ahead of ourselves. It's too soon to make that statement. I'll admit this development is…unusual…but you must remember, everyone responds differently to surgery, particularly a surgery as invasive as an ocular transplant. There is every possibility that when we remove those bandages tomorrow, your wife will have rebounded nicely."

Rob didn't answer. How could he tell a man of science he was afraid Rebecca's issues weren't related to her physical recuperation from surgery at all? How could he say what he was thinking without looking like a complete lunatic?

He couldn't.

Instead, he said, "I'd like to know a little more about the donor of Rebecca's new eyes."

"Well, she was a nineteen-year-old young woman who died suddenly. She had indicated she wanted her healthy organs to be made available for transplant. The rest, as they say, is history."

"I understand all that," Rob said. "The nurses provided Rebecca and me with that information last week. I want to know more. I want to know her name. Her history."

Schneider sighed. He clasped his hands together on top of his desk. "We place a premium on donor privacy at this hospital. I'm sorry but I can't give you that information."

"All I want to do is express my gratitude to the donor's parents. To let them know how much it means to Rebecca and me. That thanks to their child's generosity, my wife can once again see and fully experience the world around her. What harm could possibly come from that?"

The doctor sighed again. He unclasped his hands and then clasped them back together. He pursed his lips and stared at something on the wall over Rob's right shoulder. For a long time, he said nothing.

Then, to Rob's surprise, he gave him a name.

Rob stared at his computer screen in horror. He was tired and hungry but hadn't bothered to rest or eat before looking up the information Doctor Schneider had given him about the donor of Rebecca's new eyes.

Now he wished he had never asked the question. He wanted to look away, wanted to stop researching and close his laptop and think about something else; anything else, but he couldn't bring himself to do it. It was like driving by the scene of a gruesome car accident and warning yourself not to look, that nothing good would come from looking, but doing it anyway.

Her name was Faith Bradbury, and she was—or rather had been—a nineteen-year-old college student from Idaho. Faith had disappeared nine days ago while jogging along one of the remote mountain roads around her parents' home. A massive search effort was undertaken, organized by local police and populated by dozens of volunteers from Faith's college and high school, friends, family, and townspeople. Despite the breadth of the search, it took almost a week to locate her body.

When they finally found her, the condition of her body indicated she'd been kept alive for most of that time, finally succumbing to her torture just hours earlier. Police theorized she hadn't been targeted but abducted randomly, victimized by a satanic cult rumored to be based somewhere in the remote, rugged Idaho mountains. They based their theory on analysis of Faith's remains, as well as on evidence collected at the scene. Much of what the police had learned about the circumstances of Faith Bradbury's murder was being withheld from the news media. But the details Rob learned during his online search were enough to shake him to his core.

The young woman had been lashed to a makeshift altar constructed atop a large boulder in what police were describing as clearly ritualistic. She'd been tortured for "a long time." The police spokesperson refused to quantify it any more than that, and to Rob that ambiguity seemed to worsen Faith's suffering somehow.

A description of precisely how Faith was tortured was not provided. "Trust me, you don't want to know," the spokesperson told the gathered media, and although the general consensus of the news people was that yes, they did want to know, Rob was thankful the cop maintained her silence on the subject.

He thought about Rebecca's nightmare, about how real and how painful and how...*evil*...it had felt to her, and he shuddered. He pictured a group of Devil-worshipping fanatics, huddled around a stone altar dedicated to taking an innocent human being's life in some twisted ceremony, and felt his gorge begin to rise.

Had Rebecca been experiencing Faith Bradbury's terror and pain and suffering in her terrible dream last night, despite the fact she'd never heard the name and was unaware of the tragedy that had befallen the girl? Was that even possible?

And if it *were* possible, would the nightmare fade away now that Faith's pain had found an outlet?

Or had Rebecca's new eyes seen too much? Was the worst yet to come?

It took a long time for Rebecca to get to sleep. *Shocker,* she thought. *You know what's going to happen when you do.*

The fact was she didn't know, not exactly, but she suspected strongly, and that might as well be the same thing. So she turned the television on and listened to late-night talk show hosts make fun of the things late-night talk show hosts were always making fun of. She listened as they interviewed celebrities, asking the requisite fluff questions and pretending to be best friends with people who were plugging their latest movie or book or TV show. It all seemed phony and plastic, the forced laughs and the stilted conversation.

After a while, she turned the TV off, and laid back in bed thinking about nothing and everything.

Eventually she drifted off to sleep.

Tonight's dream was much worse.

The images that had seemed vague and amorphous last night were no longer so. They were crisp and clear, so very real it was as though Rebecca were *there,* strapped to a boulder in the middle of the woods, surrounded by maybe two dozen people, all chanting fervently. While she knew full well she was dreaming, the terror was as real as anything she'd ever felt.

The bonfire she'd sensed in last night's dream was back, a blazing pyre located no more than fifteen feet away from where Rebecca lay helpless and barely able to move. It was so close to her she could feel its warmth, and she wondered how in the hell she'd not seen it clearly last night.

The chanting grew louder as she scanned the faces of the people surrounding the boulder—*the altar,* she corrected herself. *It's an altar, a sacrificial altar*—to which she found herself strapped. She noticed most of them had their eyes closed and were concentrating hard on whatever they were saying. She didn't know what language this little ritual was being conducted in, but it sure as hell wasn't English. While Rebecca suspected it was better she couldn't understand the words, she felt her panic building as they chanted the same strange words, over and over.

She struggled against her bindings and realized instinctively that doing so was pointless. The people surrounding her, chanting with their eyes closed, had clearly performed this rite before, enough times that they'd mastered the art of restraining their captive and rendering her helpless.

Rebecca—*Faith,* she thought suddenly, and wondered why—didn't care. She struggled anyway, because why not? There was nothing to lose by trying to escape her fate. She hadn't been raised to be a helpless victim. Damn right she would struggle, and she would continue struggling until she couldn't any longer.

A shapeless cloud levitated into her line of sight from the left. She strained to identify it, scraping her cheek against the hard stone of the altar as she turned her head. It wasn't a cloud at all, it was a person. He'd appeared shapeless at first because he was dressed in robes from head to toe. The robes were dark, black probably, and they included a wide hood that covered his head and shrouded his face in a shadowy darkness.

The man's sleeves were long and flowing. In his hands he held a book from which he was reading, presumably the verses his followers were chanting so reverently. He circled Rebecca slowly, reading and chanting, stopping only when he'd reached a point approximately in line with her right shoulder.

Immediately the chanting stopped, and a silence fell over the clearing. The only sound was the popping and crackling of the roaring fire. She could feel her heart hammering inside her chest and wondered whether it would just explode from the terror and the tension. For now, it just pounded away, a physical accompaniment to her ever-increasing dread.

The sensation of darkness and evil was every bit as strong as it had been in last night's dream. It came as no surprise to learn the sensation originated within the black-robed figure to her right. The evil rolled off the man in waves, washing over Rebecca like roiling clouds of corruption, making her gag as her stomach lurched and threatened to revolt.

From somewhere inside the man's robes, he withdrew a knife and began approaching her, the silver blade glittering in the uneven light from the fire. She opened her mouth to scream, but the sound caught in her throat as her gaze fixed on the shadowy space inside the hood covering the man's head.

His eyes were glowing a dull red.

The chanting began anew as the man with the knife came to a stop next to Rebecca's restrained form. He reached down and sliced her blouse apart, working carefully to avoid touching her delicate skin with the blade. The blouse flopped to her sides, and she thought his next move would be to slice her bra as he'd done with her shirt, but he ignored it.

Whatever was happening, it was apparently not sexually motivated.

Relief washed over Rebecca, but it was short-lived, lasting no more than a second or two. Because the demonic priest's next move was to take the knife and begin carving into the skin he'd moments ago been so careful to protect. The agony was overwhelming, the knife's touch fiery, the pain more acute than anything she'd ever felt in her life.

She screamed and howled, struggling against her bindings, desperate to escape the awful, razor-sharp tip of that accursed knife. From all around her came the chanting of demonic verses, the celebrants in this ghoulish service raising their voices to be heard above the sounds of Rebecca's anguished cries.

Still the man sliced, the blade coming full circle on her chest before then beginning to work inside that circle. The pain was blistering, a flamethrower burning through her skin and taking her breath away. As the man worked, his hand as steady as any surgeon's, she realized incredulously he was carving a pentagram *into her chest,* showing off his grisly surgical skill as his followers chanted mindlessly from their knees surrounding the altar.

The pain was relentless. The pain was everything. Rebecca knew she was on the edge of madness, and she almost wished she would succumb to that madness. Anything to make the pain stop.

And then the demonic priest retrieved a small silver chalice from a table placed next to the altar. He began chanting something under his breath, something different than the followers were chanting, something that made his glowing red eyes flash brightly as he did. He bent over Rebecca and began pouring oil carefully into the grooves he'd just carved into her skin.

The pain ratcheted up. She wouldn't have thought it possible.

The man tossed his chalice aside and retrieved an ornate silver cigarette lighter from the table. The strange words he was chanting once again matched those of his followers. He flicked the lighter with his thumb, and the onlookers' chants became frenzied and urgent, desperate pleas to the Dark Master they were so obviously summoning. The evil priest lowered his hand to Rebecca's chest and ignited the oil. The pentagram flashed to life, the flames reaching skyward past her horrified gaze.

Rebecca's pain doubled. No, it tripled. It was more than anyone should have to experience. More than anyone *could* experience.

Rebecca's screams awoke her from the nightmare—finally. When they did, she experienced none of the fuzzy confusion typical of someone exiting a bad dream. She knew instantly where she was, and instantly what she had to do. She knew also that tonight she really *had* given voice to her terror, meaning she had just seconds before the nurses would come running into her room and stop her from doing what was required.

She scrabbled at the gauze, forcing her fingers under the tape's stickiness and yanking hard. The squares pulled free and she tossed them aside.

From outside the closed door, Rebecca could hear the heavy footfalls of a nurse charging down the corridor. She didn't hesitate, placing the middle finger of each hand against the inner corners of her eyes, the fingernails scraping the skin on the bridge of her nose. Then she pushed hard, the pain immense as her new eyes popped cleanly out of her skull and fell to the floor, accompanied by blood and gristle and probably sutures as well. It was more pain than she'd ever experienced prior to tonight, but far less than she'd just finished suffering in the forested wilderness of Idaho.

The nurses were on her, their horror and revulsion plain to Rebecca, who could once again see nothing but who'd had three decades of experience living in the dark. They pinned her arms to the bed and held her down.

But they were too late.

She'd done what she had to do.

Rob reached the hospital in minutes. All the nurse had told him on the phone was that Rebecca's situation had taken a turn for the worse, that her newly transplanted eyes were gone. No further explanation was forthcoming.

But an explanation wasn't necessary, not really. He was pretty sure he knew what had happened, and why.

Doctor Schneider met Rob in the hallway outside Rebecca's door.

"She clawed her own eyes out," he said incredulously. His tone was aggrieved, as though he'd just been personally insulted.

Rob forced his way past the doctor and into the room. His wife lay propped against three pillows, the familiar white gauze squares covering her face, this time protecting only the empty sockets where her eyes had once resided.

"Why, baby?" he said.

"Faith," she answered simply.

He nodded, knowing she couldn't see him but doing it anyway. He walked to the bed and sat, took her hand in his and kissed it gently.

"I want to go home," she said, and he nodded again.

He bent and kissed her forehead and held her tightly in his arms. "That's what I want, too."

Family Reunion

by Stephanie Ellis

Agnes stared out at the barren winter landscape. The dense foliage which had provided so much protection from prying eyes had vanished. Instead, skeletal trees linked arms, contorted bones of wood weaving a dismal screen. Any journalist worth their salt would see through the flimsy camouflage.

"You worry too much," said Peter, standing at her side. "They have to get over the wall first and then, well, we didn't buy the hounds for their looks now, did we? They're enough to put the fear of God into anyone so foolish as to make that climb."

"You forget, *darling*, it isn't the fear of God we want to instil." Her hand reached out to the statuette taking pride of place on the windowsill, stroked the ridged horns curving from its head.

"Turn of phrase, my dear. Turn of phrase."

Agnes glanced quickly at him then returned her focus to the statue. As a husband, he left a lot to be desired, as a Priest, even more so. It galled her that her efforts to attain her own position had taken years whilst his, at one word from good old Uncle Dion, had seen him rise through the ranks in no time. She pressed her head against the glass, hoping the chill would numb the headache already building. Idly, she allowed her eyes to follow the tendrils of ivy weaving across the outside, creating a thick green matting and hiding most of the crumbling brickwork. As she looked, Dion's stooped figure came into view.

"Where's he going this early?" she asked.

"Feed the dogs," said Peter. "After last night, they get extra meat."

"They won't find much on that old fool."

Peter moved closer, his breath hot against her neck. "You should be careful what you say, *darling*. Remember who calls the shots around here."

The window had misted as he spoke, obscuring her vision of the outside world, allowed the shadows to enter briefly. And then he was gone.

Agnes relaxed. Penn would be home in a few days and he was bound to side with his mother. Wasn't he? It was time they let him into their little secret, anyway, made him realise their belief was a way of life and not some little research hobby. He might even join her cell. *That* would be one in the eye for Dion and Peter. She touched the statue again, it gave her strength. It did not matter she was a woman. A Priestess was the equal of any Priest and wasn't *He* the Great Hermaphrodite?

The sound of a notification on her laptop drew her back to the task in hand.

Aries: Re: The Black Book
<<on December 22, 2019, 09:00:10>>
You guys gotta be kidding me. You seriously buy into all this shit. I mean, man…a goat? You've been watching too many bad B-movies. The only devil around on this planet is the one inside each of us, but hey, if sheep are really your thing, why not check out this little beauty contest?:
www.youtube.com/damascusgoat

Aries. Aries had started posting on their forum about two months ago. Alternatively serious, but more often mocking, she wasn't sure what to make of him. A movement behind her indicated Peter was back and, judging from the smell, so was Dion.

"Aries is back again," she said. "Poking fun as usual."

"Must be some kid," said Peter. "Just block him, he's undermining the group. Such irreverence."

"No," rasped Dion. "Let him stay, engage him in conversation. Perhaps even invite him over, let him decide for himself about the…*nature*…of our group."

"Yes, and I can see how well that will turn out," said Peter. "He'll have a blasphemous parody of our rituals up on YouTube in no time. I bet this is all part of some dare, some YouTuber trying to find the 'latest thing,' hoping to go viral. And don't look so shocked Agnes, I'm not a complete Luddite. Dion's been explaining the possibilities of social media to me."

Agnes couldn't help staring at the two men beside her. Both had been hopeless technophobes, barely able to navigate their own mobile phones and whenever *she* had suggested using social media for their own use, they had mocked her suggestions. Always it seemed the two were ganging up on her.

"You never know," said Dion. "He might be genuine, and if not? Well, it is our anniversary, isn't it? Seventeen years, after all."

Dion fixed his eye on them both. "Have either of you considered it yet?"

Agnes looked down. It was a step she couldn't quite take. It was the step which reminded her how weak her faith truly was at times. Immortality awaited, if you really believed eternal life would come after.

"I see," said Dion. The tone of his voice had changed, become smoother, deeper, dangerous, whilst his body seemed to have grown, loomed over them. "I will admit to being somewhat disappointed, but you must do what is right for you, honour the selfish gene."

She peered up carefully, noticed Dion appeared to have shrunk again, become the shuffling old relative who annoyed them both so much but whom they could never bring themselves to get rid of. A trick of the light, that was all it had been.

"What about you, Uncle?" asked Agnes, wanting to return the barb. "Why don't you take the step?"

"Who's to say I haven't?" he countered, shuffling his ancient body out of the room, laughing as he went.

"Well, if *that's* immortality, I'm the great god Pan," said Peter, looking after him.

"Shh," hissed Agnes. "Don't take the Lord's name in vain."

"What? Or hellfire and brimstone will fall on us? In case you hadn't noticed, we've already created our own perfect little Hell and I don't think *He* will mind the odd joke," said Peter.

Agnes looked nervously back at the statue on the windowsill. The glow of its ruby eyes seemed stronger, almost approving. She dismissed Peter from her thoughts although his presence irritatingly remained.

"Better get on and invite this Aries to our party," she said. "Make him our Guest of Honour."

Now it was their turn to laugh. One way or another, they would have their offering.

Mother Superior: re The Black Book
<<on December 22, 2019, 09:10:23>>
Hi, Aries. You're welcome to attend our party tonight. It's very much a social occasion and will allow you to meet others in our group. They'll be happy to answer any questions you might have about our religion so you'll be able to make a fully informed decision as to whether you wish to join us or not. I'll DM you directions for Electra House and dress code is black tie plus an animal mask of your choosing.

Aries: Re: The Black Book
<<on December 22, 2019, 09:40:34>>
Hey, that's great. Would love to meet you all in person. Find out what really goes on behind the scenes. But masks? I don't get to see your faces???

Mother Superior: Re: The Black Book
<<on December 22, 2019, 10:03:47>>
Don't worry, Aries. The masks are only worn for the first part of the events. It's just a fun way to break the ice. Some people are only able to open up more when they are 'hidden,' if that isn't a contradiction in terms.

"There, that's done," she said, closing down the laptop with relief. But she found she was talking to an empty room. She breathed even more freely. When tonight was over, she decided, she would leave Peter, Electra House, and that bloody Dion and set herself up somewhere else. She had the money at last and would be able to create a new cell, perhaps make it women only. *That* would solve a lot of hassle.

She gave no more than a brief thought to Mrs. Caldwell, the old woman whose inheritance had found its way into her bank balance. Senile and deluded, Mrs. Caldwell had taken her for her long-lost daughter and Agnes had played along. Nobody had ever questioned the truth, relieved that someone had come to claim her and look after her in her twilight years. Her death had been a few days ago, certified by the local doctor and permission obtained for a burial on their grounds. She smiled. The dogs were probably burying the bones even now.

Agnes picked up the paper on the breakfast table. The list was long and she needed to make a start if they were to be ready for the rites. Moving into the hallway, she felt an immediate chill. The large front door stood wide open, waiting to admit the caterers and workmen now arriving in vans and minibuses, tyres crunching on gravel. They would provide the skeleton of the evening, the structure and staging before they disappeared, whilst she would be responsible for its embellishments. The cold felt good, cleared her head. She would think about Aries, about her future, about Penn, later.

Peter and Dion were waiting outside, the dogs leaping and yowling excitedly at the sight of visitors, the thought of fresh meat.

As the first minibus came to a stop, anxious faces peered out at the hounds. Rottweilers. Devil dogs. Enough to scare anyone. A subtle warning as to whom the workers were dealing with should they consider anything so foolish as poking around. The Berith family also paid quite handsomely. So far, no one had stepped out of line.

Dion allowed the dogs to run around a little longer, piss against the side of the van, and then called them to heel. They grouped themselves protectively at his side and watched intently as the minibus emptied and feet hurried inside.

Agnes went with them in order to direct the day's operations, but before she did, she cast one last look back at the dogs. She had raised them from puppies. They had been her babies, devoted to her, but now as she looked at Brutus, the alpha of the pack, she understood their loyalty had shifted. The dog's eyes met her own, and it was as if something else moved behind them. *Et tu?* Another entity, watching, waiting, assessing. She shivered, although this time not from the cold.

The morning and afternoon continued to be filled with the hustle and bustle of a thousand tasks being carried out. Some workers sang, others cracked jokes, all attempted to be cheerful as they went about their business.

Yet their humour fell flat, felt as if the life was being gradually sucked out of them as the hours progressed, until finally their work was done and they were permitted to leave.

Peter stood at the door handing each their pay packet as they scurried past, muttering their thanks but not looking at his face. Their bodies homed in on the minibuses that had reappeared to allow them to escape the depressing confines of Electra House.

As soon as they had gone, another small coach arrived. This one contained the Neophytes belonging to their temple. They were to be waiters, ushers, and stewards for the evening. Like the guests, they wore black tie or black dress but all sported the same pig mask, identifying their station. A menial, but important first step in their initiation into The Order. Absolute obedience would be demanded that evening and this would be a test of their promise. Only one sported a different visage.

"Ave, Satanas," the woman's voice sang across the crowd in the lobby.

"Ave, Satanas," responded Agnes, drawing her friend into a hug. Dorothea had always been the housekeeper at these events, overseeing the kitchens, the service. She was already dressed according to the evening's requirements. Her mask, the hare, as always.

"Time you went and got yourself dressed," said Dorothea. "I'm perfectly capable of taking care of the novices." She nodded at the pig-faced crowd gathered in the lobby.

"I was only waiting for you," said Agnes, giving the woman's hand a squeeze.

The hare nodded and turned towards the waiting group. She clapped her hands and obediently they followed her down the hallway to the kitchen. There, she would instruct them as to the order of events; then, before the guests arrived, they would be brought back to give their oath to both the Priest and the Priestess.

Agnes felt a tingle of excitement run through her. These were the times when her faith was *almost* complete. She loved the ceremony of these events, the wildness and abandon that often accompanied them. It made up for the tedium of Peter, for the soulless online forums and the monotony of the countryside. Her new life, she decided, would begin in a city; London, perhaps. An edgy nightclub with an exclusive clientele somewhere in Soho would be perfect. In the meantime, she had to get through tonight. Would the Dark Mistress help her?

Her dress was laid out on the bed ready. Her bath drawn.

"I thought I would help," said Dion, rising from the chair by her bedroom window.

Agnes tried to disguise her shock. She had long felt it unwise to show any sign of weakness in front of her husband's uncle. His actions were a surprise, however. He was not someone who struck her as considering a woman's needs.

He moved over to the dresser and picked up two glasses, held one out to her. Then he sat down on the bed and patted the space beside him.

"Don't worry," he said. "There's life in this old goat yet, but I respect my nephew's marriage. Although, I wonder, do you?" He was looking directly at her but his tone was mild, did not feel interrogatory.

"I have always respected the vows of Pledging we took in the Temple, the mingling of our blood before the Lord of Darkness was not something I did lightly."

"I know," said Dion. "I remember."

Agnes frowned. "I do not remember you being there."

"You did not know me well back then, and we all look alike in our robes, do we not?"

"True."

He placed a hand on her knee, and she felt heat burn through her trousers. She almost expected flames to erupt.

"You have not seemed happy as of late," continued Dion. "And I have come to realise, that despite my best efforts and my support, Peter leaves a lot to be desired. Not just as a husband but also as Priest of the Temple."

He had turned his gaze on the painting which hung over the head of her bed.

"You have the power to change things tonight, if you allow the Dark Mistress to walk," he said. "Will you agree?"

"What of Peter? He was to lead the ceremony."

"His ritual has become…tedious."

"But earlier, you seemed to favour him over me." She kept her voice steady to avoid appearing as a whining child.

"I do enough to keep him tame," said Dion. "But I have been watching both of you since I came to stay. The Temple needs new blood to survive. It needs drama and theatre to capture the imagination of this century. People are jaded and demand ever more extreme satisfaction. We can give them that. *You* can give them that. Starting tonight." He held out his hand.

Only then did she see the ring of The Order on his finger, understood his standing within the Temple she served. She had thought him an old fool, and he had played up to that perception whilst in reality he occupied one of the highest positions within their Church. Luckily, he did not seem too concerned about her treatment of him, seemed to forgive her, in fact was elevating her by allowing her to become the vessel of the Mother for the evening's ritual. Somehow, she had impressed him.

"The setting allows us little scope," said Agnes. "I was thinking of a move."

"Great minds think alike," said Dion, this time placing his hand on her thigh. "As above, so below."

"You say the words of parting," said Agnes. "Does that mean you are leaving us?"

"Tonight is my last night here. Then I will take my leave of you and go ahead to prepare your way."

"I was thinking of…" She needed to get her words out quickly, her ideas before he set her on a path she didn't wish to follow.

"A different environment, somewhere deep and dark."

How did he know? She needed guidance. The Dark Mother would help her.

"She should be the Celebrant," said Agnes with certainty.

"Then you will permit her?" Dion raised his glass to hers.

Agnes nodded, drank down the absinthe, suppressing a shudder at the bitter undertone, looked up at the image on the wall and recited the words of Summoning.

Ave Mater Tenebris
Veni tenebris dominae suae
Corpus tuum
Cor meum tuum est
Veni matrem suam
Tuus sum

Her eyes absorbed the goddess on the wall. Took in the blood spilling over the demon's robe, the severed head held up as a trophy. Felt her blood warm as if she had stepped into the painting, inhaled the smell of copper, of meat. Already they were merging, woman of flesh and Bride of Lucifer. Through woman came the greatest change.

"Your bath will be getting cold, my dear," said Dion, giving her a peck on the cheek as he prepared to depart.

She smiled and stroked his bearded face, ran her hands lightly over his horns. He was definitely an old goat.

Agnes undressed and stepped into the bath. Dion had turned the lights off as he left, leaving only the black candles to illuminate her room. It would be the same now throughout the house. The ritual had begun. Inside her, she could feel the shadow of the demon, hear her voice.

"We have become one, you and I," said the Dark Mistress. "We are both Mother, Wife, Sister, Daughter. We have so much power buried within us, but it is a power you have never experienced. That will change tonight. Tonight, you will have the strength of ten men. You will need no ceremonial knife to complete the Offering. The strength of your bare hands alone will demonstrate the gift you have received from our Dark Lord. All will bow to you. They will not look to that pathetic Priest. They will see only you."

Agnes sank into the warm water, let herself float away. When she finally came around again, it was to find herself already clad in the virginal gown, her hair dried and curled over her shoulders, her wolf's mask in place. The sheets on her bed were rumpled, Dion's scent imprinted in the sheets. None of this unnerved her. These absences meant the demon goddess was truly within her, that she had joined with her husband as ritual demanded.

The door burst open. Peter.

"I saw my uncle leave your room," he snarled. "I thought you'd save your whoring at least until the guests arrived."

"You forget yourself," said Agnes. "She is walking tonight."

"She? You really believe this old mumbo jumbo, don't you?"

She was shocked. Whilst she had felt Peter's doubts, she had never thought him a nonbeliever. "Don't you? You're the Priest, you've taken part in the rites…"

"I was humouring you, my dear," said Peter. "Remember when we saw the marriage counsellor all those years ago. She said we should develop a mutual interest. And you were just getting into this whole satanic thing. Seemed the most logical step to me. It's been pretty enjoyable too, on the whole. I mean those parties. What man wouldn't love all those women dished up on a plate. Uncle Dion making me Priest was pretty lucky too.

Meant I could tweak things to suit my tastes a little more. Plus, I'm Dion's heir. Got to keep the old boy happy."

He stood there, a smug smile spread across his face. She wanted to take hold of him with her bare hands, tear him apart. He had committed blasphemy, had denied the Prince of Darkness, the Mother.

Not yet, said the Mother. *He will be punished, but it must be done publicly. Pretend to cast aside your differences.*

"You think I believe everything?" asked Agnes, regaining her composure. "It's just a performance. I love the acting, the role I'm playing. Beats the boredom of life, doesn't it?"

Satisfyingly, it was now Peter's turn to look surprised, although she noticed it was tinged with suspicion. For a husband and wife, they seemed to be strangers to each other.

Dorothea joined them, Dion just behind.

"Agnes, the guests are arriving..." she said, stopping as she took in Agnes' dress, understood its meaning. She bowed low. "Dark Mother, you honour us tonight. Your subjects await."

Agnes felt herself begin to fade again as she lifted her dress slightly to negotiate the stairs. Her husband was at her side. Peter was behind them.

"It has been a while since we have appeared together in public," said Dion.

"A blink of an eye for us but centuries for man," said the Dark Mother.

"They have forgotten, or they pretend in their belief, playacting to make up for the emptiness of their insignificant little lives, wanting to appear powerful instead of impotent."

"We need to remind them, husband."

Dion grinned. "We have an audience. We have our script. Now we must have action."

They had reached the bottom of the stairs and the guests crowded forward to greet them. Commenting on Agnes' appearance, on Dion's realistic disguise.

"It's as if we were truly graced with the presence of our Lord Satan and his wife, the Dark Mother," said one masked arrival.

At this, cheers erupted and cries of "*Ave, Satanas*" rang out.

The couple split up and mingled with the crowd, small talk only for the moment as the wine flowed and the pig-masked waiters circled.

Occasionally, Agnes would reemerge to take in those around her, her eyes scanning the room, seeking out Aries, remembering the invitation she had sent at Dion's insistence. Would he come?

"Of course he will," said her dark shadow. "A curious youth will always tread a dangerous path."

"He thinks we are just actors. A con."

"Then it will be for us to change his mind. Look, there is a lion. What say you to a chase? It has been a long time since my daughters ran together!"

Agnes was allowed to see a lion-masked man bathed in the glow of a nearby lantern. She did not recall anyone wearing such a mask before. As she stared, the image faded slightly, and she thought it was the mask of a ram. Aries! But no, the vision wobbled, and the lion returned.

Her mouth opened, but it was not Agnes who spoke.

"Dark Daughters, we have not hunted together for many years. It is time for us to change that and have some sport. The men amongst us must remain here, apart from the one who is lion-hearted. He alone will be allowed to take part in this ritual."

The man in the lion mask gave a start at these words. Looked about for confirmation of what he had just heard. Someone clapped him on the back, congratulated him on his good fortune.

"Off you go, lad. Run, run like the wind. Don't run too fast though, otherwise they won't catch you. Then you'll miss out on the fun."

Other hands pushed him towards the French windows, nudged him outside. Somewhere, a dog howled.

"Don't worry," said the Dark Mother. "The dogs have been locked up tonight. You have only women chasing you. We'll give you a head start."

"And when you catch me?"

"Aah, that would be telling. Now run."

Agnes watched the youth sprint out into the darkness. He seemed to know where he was going. There was something about his shape which tugged at her memory. The Dark Mother took over before she could catch her thoughts.

"Daughters! The race is on!" With a whoop, she ran out into the darkness after the prey, the other female guests chasing after her. Their laughter carried clear across the night as they fed off each other's excitement.

Agnes and the Dark Mother ran together, catching glimpses of the youth by the light of the moon. His mask seemed to reflect in the silvery beams so they never lost sight of him, despite the clothing which should have rendered him nearly invisible. He was heading for the old oak, was clambering up its trunk.

"Come down, come down, boy," sang one girl as she neared the tree.

"Come down and taste our medicine," cried another, hitching up her skirt.

Others joined in the cries, running in circles round the trunk, leaping up to shake the branches, trying to dislodge him. Eventually, two, apparently more agile than the rest, scrambled up to where the man had perched and gently manhandled him back to the ground.

"Lion, you have been caught," said a woman.

"Lion? Why do you call me that?"

"Your mask, of course."

"My mask is a ram. Can you not see?"

"No, you are a lion," said Agnes, moving closer. "And lions are predators to be destroyed."

Her hands were reaching out now, seeking out the limbs to break, the neck to snap.

Something in her voice caused the youth to move back, to try and remove his mask, but the women had circled him. They caught hold of his arms to prevent him running off, stop him taking off the mask.

"For fuck's sake, it's me, Mum. Penn. I get it. It's a joke. You knew I was worried about you, so you decided to act out. A bit elaborate, but I suppose, at your age, you haven't got much else to do."

A blow to his stomach from one of his guards silenced him

"You will not speak unless spoken to," she said.

"Mum!"

Another blow cut short his plea.

Agnes heard none of this. The Dark Mother had shown her the lion, had promised she could try out her new strength on this cub before they returned for the final Rite of Sacrifice.

She stood in front of him, took the lion, struggling and twisting into her own arms, her companions falling back a respectful distance. They too would be permitted the same power, but to her was awarded the kill. Her fingers curved around the neck, felt a brief recognition of the flesh she touched before that was dismissed from her mind and she was urged to press and squeeze, twist and turn whilst the lion continued to thrash in protest.

Soon, however, the creature's protests stopped, and then the Dark Mother tugged at the head, gave it a twist as if merely removing the lid from a jar, pulled it free. Triumphantly, she held the lion's head aloft. Her huntress companions applauded wildly before leaping forwards to claim their part, all tugging and pulling, wrenching arms and legs from the torso, ripping off cloth, clawing at skin, burying themselves in the blood and gore until they had washed themselves thoroughly in his death.

"The head is our trophy," cried both Agnes and the Dark Mother, exulting. "Let us return and show our men what women are truly capable of."

The women cheered and danced around her as they headed back, guided by the softly flickering candlelight in the windows. Dion stood at one entrance waiting to greet them. The house seemed strangely quiet.

"Where is everyone?"

"I sent them away," said Dion comfortably. "Pretended there was an emergency or something. I can't remember the detail but it worked."

"But I have this to show them!" protested Agnes, now coming back to herself.

"What have you to show them?" came a voice from inside the room.

Agnes crossed the threshold, holding the lion's head aloft, gloating at the strength she could still feel coursing through her.

Peter was sat by the fireplace, nursing a brandy glass in his hand. Even wearing his mask, he didn't look happy. If their guests had been dismissed, why did he still wear it?

"Come now, Peter. Come and greet your wife properly. Share her triumph." Dion had followed her in, the remaining women behind him, all carrying bits of the corpse.

Peter obediently rose and turned to greet the crowd.

"Here," said Agnes, holding the lion's head towards him, except it didn't seem like a lion anymore. The mask had slipped a little, revealed a familiar curve of the forehead, a well-known parting of the hair.

Peter shrank from her. His hand went to his mouth as if to suppress a scream, but he could not prevent himself from retching. He turned away and vomited long and hard into the fireplace, causing the dying embers to splutter and die beneath the stream of bile and undigested food.

"What have you done?" he gasped, once he could catch his breath. He tried to look at her but could not, a response she found surprising. Why would he not look at her gift, see what she held?

Was it so revolting? Agnes had offered him such trophies before, and he had always approved. Slowly, she spun the head to face herself, saw the lion's mask fade to take on that of a ram. Aries! Why was that so bad? An unwilling sacrifice, yes, but still perfect for the Rite of the Seventeenth. The sacrifice required as a gift to their Lord.

But even that disguise was slipping and she could see the face of someone else appear. Someone oh so familiar, oh so horrific. Penn. Her son. It couldn't be him. He wasn't meant to be here for a few days. She had kept him away from their Temple, deliberately waiting until he was old enough and could understand.

"Really? I don't think so," said the Dark Mother, now taking on the form of a shadow outside herself, drifting around the room, examining the scattered corpse, licking the meat with her black tongue. "Your belief has been pretence, *Daughter*. Your display has been merely a hunger for power over the weak, feeding your ego. Those other deaths were never what they seemed, were they? You have never killed for me, or for my husband. All was illusion, pretence. We have waited for both of you to commit yourselves fully to us and both of you have denied us. Peter is an apt name, indeed, for one who betrays his Lord. Shall we wait for the cock to crow three times and will you admit your culpability now?"

"No, no, no," moaned Agnes, cradling Penn's head in her arms. Her darling boy, his body scattered around her as if food for the dogs. The hounds! No, he would not be given to them. She would get him back, pull him together. Ignoring Peter who sat as one catatonic, she scrabbled around the room, grabbing pieces of her son and heaping them at Peter's feet, desperately trying to rebuild him as she did so, repeating Penn's name over and over as if she could raise him from the dead.

"Penn did not believe in us," said Dion, slowly casting the cloak of the old man from him and emerging as the Horned One. "He thought you were in thrall to someone, to some cult or other. He could never find anything out when at home because you kept so much hidden from him. Instead, he tried the other way, used the internet, became Aries. And because he did not believe what he found, and neither did you or your husband, even though you were both adepts and privy to my highest mysteries, you had to be punished. What better way though than a night such as this? If you gift me your deaths, then you will have redeemed yourselves and you *will* become immortal."

"But Penn…"

"Penn is dead. You can choose to feed him to the dogs or the worms, it is of no consequence anymore. What matters now is the two of you. What do you choose?"

"If we both deny you," said Agnes. "What will happen to us?"

"I am Satan, I am Baphomet, I am the Lord of Flies, I am your darkness. Either way, your death is mine. What comes after is up to you."

Agnes looked towards Peter. He had finally ripped the mask from his face, replaced it with another, one even more terrible. Slowly, he stood up and walked past her, ignoring the dismembered corpse, headed out into the night. The sound of dogs howling increased. They were no longer locked up.

"Peter," she cried, tried to grab him, prevent him from leaving.

He shrugged her off, his gaze still fixed straight ahead and walked out into the void.

"Go with him, Daughters," said the Dark Mother, her shadow wrapping her arms around the women who had remained trance-like in the drawing room. She sent them out after Peter, drifted out with them. She still had a lot of work to do. The doors had closed behind them, leaving Agnes and the Devil alone.

"So," he said. "What's your decision?"

Agnes looked out the window. She could see only darkness.

A Night Above

by John Quick

The air began to shimmer and I felt the tug of invitation across the veil. I fought the urge to smile. It had been much too long since I'd been surface-side, and now it was finally my time again. It was the one thing we demons anticipated more than any other. In between those visits, our lives were nothing more than misery and servitude, toiling away at whatever task our Dark Lord assigned to us. I had spent the better part of a century stuck in Sin Tally. The job's easy enough, just exceptionally tedious and boring. You spend all day and night, every day and night, counting up the sins of souls cast into the pit and see how you like it. It's not like there's a lunch break down here. I'd hoped after my last visit I might get reassigned to Temptation or even Torture, but no such luck. I was an accountant in Hell. Could anything be worse?

Maybe I'd get a better assignment when I got back. Until then, I was going to enjoy the break. Eager to get on with it, I stepped into the forming portal, practicing my best scowl as I went. The second I was through, I let one rip so the smell of brimstone would be fresh and overpowering, bellowed, and then stopped and stared at where I'd ended up.

It was a very feminine bedroom, lots of pink shit, pictures of unicorns and stuffed animals. Before me, forming a small circle, were five teenage girls, all wearing different styles of pajamas. Now, I know many of my kind who would be thrilled by such a thing. In many ways, we demons are not much different from fourteen-year-old boys with their hormones in permanent overdrive. The problem was that all of these girls were only freshly minted teens, not ones on the cusp of adulthood. I may be a monster, but I do have limits.

More importantly, though, I was confused. First, how had these girls figured out the ritual to summon me in the first place? Second, what the hell did they want?

"Holy shit," one of them, a bratty looking thing with a short blonde ponytail, said. I heard one of her friends gasp at her choice of words and had to fight to keep from rolling my eyes. "It actually worked."

Great. I was here because of an accident. Probably no different from most of the little shits surrounding me. Still, ignorance is no excuse, and they *had* summoned me, so better get on with it. There are rules to these things, and unfortunately, I am bound by them.

The first step for any one of my kind in this position was the introduction. Some went for grand, bellicose monologues. Some snarled, acting like they weren't speaking as eloquently as any professional orator only moments prior to being summoned. Others still played it meek, hoping to trick their summoners. Me? I preferred to keep it short and sweet, while still exuding a little air of menace. It's always easier to just be yourself.

"Why have you called me forth from my slumber?" I demanded, adding a slight growl near the end for effect. The girls shrank back a bit. Nailed it.

"We didn't mean to," one of them squeaked. You might think that's a metaphor, but no, she actually squeaked when she talked, like she was half mouse or something. "We were supposed to read it, and then my brother was going to jump out and scare everybody."

She was pointing at something, so I turned around. Sure enough, there was a boy, maybe a year or two older than Squeaky, standing just outside the closet, some goofy rubber monster mask in his hands. I snarled at him, more out of annoyance than anything else, and the front of his pants went dark. He turned and bolted from the room, leaving the scent of fear and piss in his wake. I sighed, a throaty rumble.

"We found the ritual on the internet," Ponytail explained.

I turned and stared down at her. I'm sure it came off menacingly, but that wasn't my intention. I was too dumbfounded to even think about striking terror into their pitiful little hearts.

Wait, so this was not only an accident, but some stupid internet thing? I was basically a *meme*? You've *got* to be fucking kidding me!

There are times I really hate the damned rules for this kind of thing. They hadn't answered me the first time—not in any way that mattered—so I had to clarify. Words can't express how much I didn't want to continue, but I had no choice. Then again, maybe I could speed this process along and get what I wanted at the same time.

"Command me," I growled. "But know that your binding has limited my powers. Free me, and I can give you the world."

I know, I know. Hokey, right? THEY WERE TEENAGE GIRLS! I had no intention of putting a lot of effort into this one. Besides, maybe I'd get lucky and they'd set me loose. It had happened before.

"I don't believe you."

I turned to face the girl who said it. She had her hair cut into a strange bob so one side was longer than the other. For some reason, I had the impression her name was Karen.

"You doubt me?" I countered, adding a bit of a snarl in there to intimidate her. Incredibly, it didn't seem to work.

"I think you're lying," Karen replied. "I think you're plenty powerful. I think you just want us to release you so you can kill us and go away."

Fuck me! How was this little shit more intelligent than the men and women who practiced their craft for decades before calling me forth? Enough was enough. It was time to end this quickly. I dropped the act, sighed again, and ran a hand over my face.

"Tell me what you want," I said. "Just get on with it."

Karen's expression visibly brightened at that. "Okay, for my first wish…"

"Stop right there," I said. "How exactly do you think this works? I'm a demon, not a fucking genie in a bottle."

"Watch your mouth," Karen said, her eyes narrowing. "That's not very nice."

I pointed a long talon at myself. "Demon."

"What-*ever*," she muttered, pointedly enunciating so it sounded like two words instead of a single compound. "We called you, now you grant us wishes, duh. Everybody knows that."

This time, I couldn't stop the eye roll. "Again, that's a genie, specifically one made up for the purpose of fiction. I. Am. A. Demon. I answer only to the one who actually performed the ritual, and then, only once, based on the ritual you apparently used."

"I think you're making that up, too."

She was persistent, I'll give her that. "I'm not. Believe me, I may not know the specifics or understand how in the hell you brats figured it out, but I *do* know what bindings are on me when I come topside."

My eyes nearly bugged out when the little bitch crossed her arms over her chest and glared at me. "Fine. We all summoned you."

"No, you didn't," I argued back.

"Actually," a new girl behind me said. I turned and stared at her. She wore a pair of glasses almost as big as her head, which she pushed up her nose slightly as she spoke. "She's not wrong." She must have had one hell of a strong finger to keep pushing those glasses up. "We all said the words for the ritual. We didn't know only one of us was supposed to do it. Of course, we didn't know it would actually work, either."

I wanted to scream. They'd correctly performed the ritual, *and* they'd figured out a loophole where all of them would effectively be my master, all without even fucking trying? How the fuck does this happen? I wish I'd been at least one down on the response list, so some other demon would have to deal with this crazy shit. I gritted my teeth and imagined cutting their heads off with a dull, rusty knife.

"Fine," I said. "What do you want from me, then?"

"I'm first," Karen said.

"That a command?" I asked, looking back at her over my shoulder. "If it is, say it like it is."

She straightened her back and glared at me. "I command you to start with me."

Oh, I was going to enjoy this one. Probably the only amusement I would get from this bullshit situation. "Command received, and performed. Next person?"

"Wait, what?" Karen said. The look on her face as she realized how I'd tricked her almost made the whole thing worthwhile. *Almost.* "No! That's not fair! I didn't know that's how it worked!"

"Rules are rules," I said. "Ignorance doesn't get you special treatment. Next person?"

"Let me try," Glasses said. I returned my attention to her. "I command you to make more people like me want to be my friend, aside from the ones here."

Now that was just fucking sad. Believe it or not, I am capable of feeling emotions other than anger and lust and hate. I do feel empathy and sympathy. Hell, feeling those things strongly enough is one of Satan's favorite torture techniques.

"What are you, in high school?" I asked, genuinely curious.

She shook her head. "Middle school."

For the hate of Lucifer. There were probably more untamed hormones running through this room than in a herd of pregnant women. Not the fun kind, either, but the self-depreciating, don't know shit about how the world works, fuck with your head kind. This was going to be worse than I thought.

I could have done as she asked, killed off enough people that those remaining had no choice but to cling to this mousy little depressed girl, but it would be too much work. Better to take a different tactic.

"Look, I'll tell you a secret," I said. "Any friends you have now, you probably won't even talk to once you get into the real world. One, maybe two could last that long, but it's not likely. You humans just grow apart. It's natural. You'll be better off just being yourself and treasuring the few friends you have that feel like good, true friends than to have a ton of them who will only forget about you once they graduate. Plus, the friends you make by being yourself will be with you longer, because they have no other expectations of you."

Her eyes had gone wide while I talked, magnified by her glasses until it seemed like they were about to take over her face. After a moment of silence, I saw a single tear run down her cheek. Then, she began to nod slowly.

"That—that actually makes sense," she said. "I'll try that. Thank you."

"You done?"

She nodded. I turned to the girl who had yet to speak. "What about you?"

This one was relatively cute, in that way girls sometimes got when they were at that awkward stage between childhood and young adulthood. She had dark hair with a slight reddish tinge and a light dusting of freckles across her nose and cheeks. She looked up at me, swallowed, glanced over to Squeaky, and then back to me before nodding.

"I want Rachel's brother to be my boyfriend."

Squeaky made a shocked sound that nearly made me burst out laughing. I opened my mouth to say something, but Freckles cut me off.

"And I know we won't be together forever and all that," she said. "I don't care. I just think he's cute and want to be able to say he was my boyfriend when I think back on being a kid."

Smart, too. This girl was apt to break some hearts when she got older. If she waited that long. "He the one who pissed all over himself and ran away?"

A slight blush rose in her cheeks, highlighting those freckles. "Yes."

Well, what do you know? Another easy one. "Right now, he's probably in his room, feeling humiliated and scared and probably near tears. Go to him. It'll take some doing to get him to let you in, but keep at it. Comfort him. That might mean having to hold him while he cries, it might mean listening to him act tough. Just deal with it, whatever it is. When he's done, give him a hug, kiss his cheek, and tell him you still think he's rad or awesome or hawt or whatever bullshit word you kids have nowadays for that. From there, the rest should happen on its own."

Squeaky was the next in line, but I wasn't ready for that voice yet. Instead, I turned to Ponytail. "And you?"

"Boobs," she said. No hesitation, no thinking about it. Just right out with it.

I couldn't help myself. A female says something related to breasts, your eyes just kind of go there on their own. My guess was that she was in the early stages of puberty, still too soon for it to have hit her there, yet. If it had, the baggy shirt she wore hid any sign of it. And yeah, I could've done it. I could have given her tits big enough to tip her over onto her back and smother her to death. I didn't, but I *could* have.

"Right," I said instead. "I look like a plastic surgeon to you?"

"No, you look like a demon who's going to do whatever I command him to," she replied. To her credit, she'd caught on fast. Damn that Karen.

"And I'm commanding you to give me boobs. Nice ones, too. Not tiny little nubs."

If I needed confirmation that puberty had yet to hit her full force, that was it. I started putting a plan together in my mind. "Big ones, then?"

"Well, yeah," she said, face filled with incredulity. "I just said that."

"Fine."

I exerted a bit of my will into the world, sped up a little time, altered some physics. While it didn't seem like much, it was enough to tire me out a good deal. The doorbell rang downstairs, and I smiled.

"You have a delivery," I told Ponytail. "Go ahead. I'll wait."

She frowned, then got up and rushed from the room. While we waited, I watched Karen glare at me. It made me smile, what can I say? I'm a demon. I can get away with being petty. A couple of minutes later, Ponytail walked back into the room, a confused look on her face, a large box in her hands. She took her previous place in the circle and looked up at me.

"What's this?"

"Open it."

To speed things along, I ran a talon down the length of the tape, splitting it open. Ponytail gave me another confused look and then opened the box. Her face went scarlet as soon as she saw what was inside.

"What is this?" she asked, her voice a mixture of anger and embarrassment. "Is this a sex toy?"

"They're your big boobs," I told her. "Go on, take them out."

She shook her head, but reached into the box and withdrew another box, this one emblazoned with a buxom, barely-dressed woman on it. I didn't read all the text, but I did chuckle when I saw the line "tit-fucking fun".

"God, they're heavy," she muttered.

"They are," I agreed. "These are special. They have straps attached to them so you can wear them."

"That's sick," Karen put in without letting me finish. "You're sick."

"What I want you to do with those," I continued, ignoring the little bitch. "Is to put them on every time you feel that desire to have big breasts. Feel how heavy they are, how they pull on your back. Then I want you to imagine that feeling all day, every day. Decide if that's something you really want. If, as I presume, you decide you don't, take them off and put them away, and then let nature take its fucking course. Be happy with whatever you end up with."

She kept staring at the box, her face blank. After a moment, she nodded.

Finally, not wanting to, I turned to Squeaky. "All right, last but not least. What inane bullshit have you got for me?"

Squeaky swallowed and then dropped her eyes. "I want you to fix my voice. The…you know, the squeak."

If I'd had eyebrows, they would have climbed most of the way up my prodigious forehead. Definitely hadn't expected that. It crossed my mind to rip her tongue out, remove her ability to speak at all, but I restrained myself. Aside from the humiliation, this experience had not been as bad as I feared. Besides, this was one request I would only be too happy to grant. For my own benefit, if nothing else.

"Done," I said, exerting a bit more of my will.

Her eyes bugged out as her hands went to her throat. She tried to scream, but no sound came out. She fell over onto her side, curled up in the fetal position, and made little grunting sounds. Karen was on her feet in a heartbeat.

"What are you doing?" she cried. "You're killing her!"

"If I was going to kill anybody here," I told her, "it would be your obnoxious ass. Let's see you alter someone's vocal cords without any painkillers and get a better reaction. Sit down, shut up, and give it a second."

It took more than a second. After roughly two minutes, the girl stopped making those weird grunting noises and slowly picked herself up. Tears stained her cheeks, snot pooled on her upper lip, and she looked as though she'd been licked by a whale. She would not look at me.

"What did you do to me?" Her eyes went wide when she heard herself. This time, she did look at me, her face filled with shock and gratitude. "It's gone! I sound normal!"

"If by normal you mean a whiny little snot with as much brainpower as a sardine, then yes, you sound normal."

I felt the binding on me slip away. Even demons can experience miracles, it seemed. This horror show was finally over. I would never live this down once I got back to Hell, but at least I had a good hundred years or more before I'd have to worry about a repeat performance. Never thought I'd be happy to be at the bottom of the list again, but there it was.

"Our business is done," I announced, and then smiled. There was *one* advantage to all this, one I neglected to inform them of before I started granting favors. Boss's orders. "I look forward to seeing you all when you die and your souls join me in Hell."

"What?"

It was a chorus of confused terror, the perfect exit music. I let another one rip to renew the smell of brimstone and returned home. I made a mental note to request transfer to Torture Division at some point before those girls died, and then it was off to debriefing. Somewhere along the way, I actually found it within myself to smile.

Brujeria

by Michael Patrick Hicks

The Spanish-style home carved into the hills of the Pacific Palisades was more of a compound than a mere mansion. Carroll Arendt had bought the 3.5-acre estate in the late '80s for less than seven million, a steal compared to today's property prices.

"You ever been here before?" Marcus Blake said.

He shot a quick look at his date, trying not to get lost in the exquisite lines of her profile. The private access road to Arendt's home was a twisty affair, and he didn't want to ruin his night with Madeline by running his Escalade off the road and into the trees.

Madeline smiled, a joint burning in one hand while the other cupped her knee. "I've not had the pleasure."

"You're gonna love Carroll. I promise."

She passed him the joint, and he took a hit. As much as he loved Carroll's, and let's face it, Madeline's company, his anxiety had been growing progressively stronger over the course of the day. He was less impressed with some of Arendt's friends, and worries of conflict had clouded his day. Not that he'd had fights with any of Carroll's hanger-ons before, but he knew they thought less of him. His movie career hadn't been nearly as successful as Arendt's work as a film director, and he didn't own a home with nearly as many zeroes attached to its price tag. Carroll had been a loyal friend, and even a fierce advocate when studio meddling had sought to replace Marcus's casting, even in glorified cameos. A number of Carroll's friends, though, saw his relationship with Marcus as little more than a charity case. Hell, Carroll had even told him as much one night, during a blurry drug and booze-fueled confession. Carroll was a morose, guilt-ridden drunk, but he never lost sight of his friends.

Despite his nervousness, Blake couldn't help but notice that Madeline had gotten quieter the closer they came to the compound. She was tapping one foot against the floorboard, her fingers drumming an aimless tune against her thigh. The weed had been a good idea, he thought, already feeling looser.

"How'd you guys meet?" she asked.

He looked at her, momentarily confused. "Seriously?"

"Well, I mean, I know you guys did those horror flicks in the woods and he made some serious bank on it. You guys were friends before that, though, right?"

He couldn't help but laugh. "Yeah. Yeah, we were. We grew up in Michigan together, lived in the same sub in a town you never heard of outside Detroit. Carroll, he was always fucking around with his camera, making home movies with his Super 8. I didn't know him from Adam and rode my bike through one of his shots. All of a sudden, I hear some kid yelling, 'Cut, cut, cut!' And he comes running at me! He gave me a few choice words no seven-year-old should know, but I thought, holy shit, this kid's making a *movie*! I talked him down, and next thing I know he's pulling me toward his buddies and his brothers, fucking casting me in his little backyard production. That was my first acting gig, you know."

Madeline's eyes were bright enough to light up a room. "That's amazing."

"Been best friends with him ever since."

The *Dark Cabin* flicks had been good to them, that was for sure, but Carroll had definitely gotten the better end of the deal and made himself into a Hollywood A-lister. Marcus Blake had gone the opposite route. The few big productions he'd been cast in had been commercial failures, but he'd earned his cult status in a string of low budget direct-to-video horror flicks, even as he always felt like he was trapped in the shadow of *Dark Cabin*. Getting arrested numerous times over the course of his first decade in Hollywood for possession of various narcotics, drunk driving, and soliciting prostitutes had made Blake a high-risk investment for studios. Insurance companies wouldn't fund him and studios balked at his casting, kicking him off more than his fair share of productions. Carroll got to make some superhero flicks and a couple of period pieces that had won him a spate of awards. Blake sold signed photographs for sixty bucks a pop at horror conventions and auditioned for supporting character roles in cable dramas. But Carroll had never let success go to his head, and he never forgot about his friend Marcus. Blake knew Carroll was tossing him a bone when he cast him in bit parts in his cape-and-tights flicks, or as a nameless soldier cut down by a hail of Nazi bullets on Normandy Beach, but damn if he didn't sink his teeth into them. It was, after all, a paycheck, and God knew he couldn't turn down one of those.

"Here we are," he said, and Madeline let out a low whistle.

Pulling through the gated entrance was an impressive sight. Dozens of palm trees dotted the massive lawn fronting the tile-roofed stucco mansion. The walled estate was like an oasis in the middle of the woods, the large, wide windows inviting you in.

"This is amazing," Madeline said.

"Ha! Wait until you see the inside."

As he opened his door, his cell phone rang. He unplugged it from the center console, saw his ex-wife's name on the display, and silenced the ringer.

"Ah, hell," he muttered. He mentally kicked himself, realizing it was supposed to be his weekend with the kids, which meant Shelly was calling him all up in arms, wondering where the hell he was. He made a mental note to have Madeline roll another joint for him once they were inside and settled. His phone dinged as the voicemail notification flashed on the display. He swiped it away, in absolutely no mood to have his night ruined with thoughts of children and his bitchy ex's anger management issues.

"You need to take that?" Madeline said, coming up alongside him and looping her arm through his.

"Nope," he said, leaning toward her for a kiss. Her lip gloss tasted like strawberry, and he couldn't help but wonder what other parts of her flesh might taste of fruit. "C'mon, let's go in."

He led her to the carved front doors and pulled one open for her, waving her inside and giving her ass a squeeze as she passed by. She took his hand, their fingers sliding together with a routine familiarity, and he followed.

"Marcus!" Carroll's voice was deep and booming as he stepped into the vestibule with arms spread wide. He leaned toward Madeline, then stopped, as if awaiting permission. She nodded, and his smile grew wider. He gave her a quick hug and peck on the cheek. "You must be Madeline Howard. It is a pleasure to meet you," he said. A moment later, he was wrapping his friend in a bear hug and they were smacking each other on the back.

"Madeline," Carroll said, pulling both her and Marcus toward him on either side as he walked them into the house, "you were absolutely marvelous in *Burgundy's Foal*. Best part of that whole movie, if you ask me. Are you interested in reading a script I have?"

Madeline's hand went to her chest, a blush rising to her face. "I…" she sputtered. "I mean, yes. I would be honored. Oh my god, yes." She laughed, and it proved infectious, Carroll joining in with her. Even Marcus couldn't help but laugh.

"Excellent! Now, to the kitchen! I've just opened up a couple bottles of wine. Or there's some harder stuff if you prefer, and beer, too. Let's go get some drinks and catch up while I work on dinner."

"You cook?" Madeline said.

"Do I cook?" Carroll said, turning to Marcus. "Do I cook? Listen to her."

"He cooks," Marcus said.

Early in his Hollywood career, Carroll had directed a feature about a drug addicted chef at a Michelin-starred restaurant and had brought in a highly regarded chef to serve as a consultant on the picture. Carroll had a fondness for cooking even before that particular movie, but working so closely with Chef Heinrich Schauer had turned that spark of pleasure into a powerful flame and he'd begun taking culinary classes, wanting to build his knowledge further. He'd become close friends with Schauer, the two often cooking together in an apprentice and master dynamic. It had been several years since Marcus had seen Schauer at one of Carroll's shindigs, though.

Apparently, the chef had traded the United States for Switzerland, but he'd left behind a strong student in the film director.

"I hope you like tacos," Carroll said.

"I. *Love*. Tacos," Madeline said, pushing closer to Carroll. She looked across him to Marcus and made an O of surprise with her lips. "This is like heaven!"

Her heels clicked loudly against the marble floor as they headed into the kitchen. The closer they drew, the more overwhelming and succulent the smells became. Marcus's stomach rumbled in response, his mouth watering.

"Oh, man," he said. Carroll gave him a friendly slap on the arm.

Carroll had a soft spot for Mexican cuisine, and he made the best carnitas Marcus had ever eaten. Okay, well, second best. The best still came from Chef Gabino Iglesias, a restaurateur who took his food on the road in what was, hands-down, Hollywood's most successful food truck. Schauer had trained Carroll in a lot of classical French dishes and techniques, but it was Gabino who taught him all about the heart and soul of delicious Mexican street food. If Carroll was making his carnitas that meant tonight's movie was a special event.

"You are going to absolutely love this, Maddie," Marcus said.

She turned her face up toward him, eyes wide. She was positively star struck. Not that he could blame her. And that was saying something for a waitress who had served some of the biggest names in the world. When she first began talking to him, Marcus had brushed her off as just another adoring fan. He smiled and behaved politely, listened to her stories about coming to LA to find an acting career, the usual story every-fucking-body in this town had, including his own damn self. But then he saw her waiting to audition and they got to talking. He saw, then, the real her, and realized she was really something special. He might have enjoyed a few modest hits back in the '80s, but he wasn't too full of himself to ignore the fact that he was a working actor. If some well-paying residuals hadn't kept him afloat through various writer's strikes over the years and let him pay off his small bachelor's pad, he'd probably be waiting tables too.

He squeezed her hand, intending to reassure her. Carroll was just Carroll to him, but to Madeline he was a larger-than-life millionaire who had made some of the world's biggest films, movies that weren't just popular with audiences but critically acclaimed and Oscar-worthy. He was one of Hollywood's hottest directors and she would kill to be in one of his films.

Beyond the doorwall, he caught sight of Andrea Michaels and Paul McGinnis splashing in the grotto, her in a bikini that looked like dental floss. Carroll's wife, Joan, was sunning herself on an Adirondack chair and thumbing through a well-worn paperback.

"This house is bigger than my entire neighborhood," Maddie whispered to him, trying to stifle a giggle.

He pulled her close, holding her arms. "It's okay, baby. Just relax. Try to remember they're just people, like you and me, and Carroll especially. He's really not the glitz and glamour kind of guy."

"What about her?"

He followed her gaze to the pool and saw Andrea rising out of the pool, her bronze and toned flesh wet and shiny beneath the dying rays of daylight.

"Well, she's a bit of a bitch, but if you can block her out, you'll really go places here."

She laughed and buried her face in the crook of his neck. Her lips pressed lightly to the curve of his jaw, and he gave her arms another squeeze. "It's just dinner and a movie. Date night. Not a care in the world. We got weed, wine, and tacos. What else is there?"

She smiled and his heart fluttered as he nearly fell into the deep seas of her bright blue eyes.

"Well, look what the cat dragged in," Andrea said, stepping into the kitchen.

"Hi, Andi," Marcus said with fake good cheer.

She snorted and took one look at Madeline. "Be a dear and fetch me a towel, hm?"

"Andi, this is Madeline. Don't be a cunt."

Andrea glared at him, gave him the finger, then tracked water through the kitchen as she went off in search of a towel.

"Wow," Madeline said.

"Sorry," Carroll said. "She'll become less abrasive the better you know her."

"No, she won't," Marcus said.

"No, she won't," Carroll said. "She's just…"

"Andrea."

"Yeah. But she's taking the lead in my tent pole movie next summer, so, here we are."

"Speaking of movies," Madeline said, "can I ask what's on tap for tonight?"

"You can!" Carroll said. "And we'll talk all about that soon! Dinner is ready, so grab some plates and beers and let's eat." He went to the door to holler out to his wife and McGinnis to come inside and stuff their faces.

Dinner was a casual affair as the group drew up barstools around the center island. A large plate of shredded pork sat before them, along with slices of lime, cilantro, cheese, soft tortillas, and bottles of Modelo. Madeline let out a moan of deep enjoyment as she took her first bite, the juices from the taco running down her chin and arms. She took a second bite and her eyes rolled back in ecstatic bliss.

"So," Carroll said, "Madeline asked about tonight's movie and I figure this is as good a time as any for a brief history lesson. In keeping with the Mexican theme, we'll be watching *Brujería* from 1922."

"I don't know that one," McGinnis said.

"That's because it doesn't exist," Marcus said, taking a long draw on his beer. "It's a lost film."

"Oh, it exists. And it's very much been found. *And*," Carroll emphasized, "we are going to be the very first people to lay eyes on the original print in nearly a hundred years. This is cinematic history!"

"What's it about?" Madeline said.

"*Brujería* was produced by one of the poverty row studios, but it had such a troubled production the film itself was thought to be cursed. It was a horror movie about witches," Marcus said.

"It was a horror movie *starring* witches," Carroll said. "The director, Aldofo Perez, was striving for authenticity."

"He was also a Thelemite."

"Mmm," Carroll said, nodding around a mouthful of food. "Well done, Marcus. You remember! Yes, Perez was a disciple of Aleister Crowley's religion, and was even rumored to have ran the Californian branch of the Ordo Templi Orientis for some time."

"I'm sorry," Madeline said. "This is a bit over my head."

"Crowley was a Satanist," Marcus said. "Perez was, too, and according to the rumors, *Brujería* was his attempt to film the Devil."

"The film was meant to be a documentary of sorts, at least for those in the know. But Perez wasn't hired to make a documentary, and even though he strove for as much authenticity as possible, he had to hide it behind Hollywood artifice."

"Did it work?" This from Andrea, who sat on the edge of her barstool. Marcus had never seen her so engaged.

"During production, a number of cast and crew were purported to fall ill, and supposedly some even died, including the three witches at the center of the film. It was a grueling production and there were constant setbacks. Eventually, its budget spiraled out of control and the studio cancelled the film. Perez tried to salvage what he could and had hoped to edit what he had shot into something cohesive. The result of that was *Brujería*, a short film that runs seventeen minutes and forty-three seconds."

"And, according to legend," Marcus said, "Perez was the only man alive to see that final cut."

"What happened to Perez?" Madeline said.

"He disemboweled himself."

"Okay, now I have *got* to see this film," McGinnis said.

Carroll clapped and pointed at the man like an excited child. "Yes! That's the spirit! No pun intended, I swear."

"He died in a fire," Marcus said.

"No, his remains were found after the fire was extinguished," Carroll said, correcting him with the patience of a school instructor, "but that wasn't his cause of death."

Rather than feel chided, Blake smiled at the gentle rebuke. They'd argued plenty over the years about the legitimacy of Perez's death and the rumors surrounding his demise. Carroll had been obsessed with *Brujería* and its mysteries since he'd first learned about it in one of his film study courses when he and Marcus were attending Michigan State University. Being a horror fan, and horror film maker, he'd had a natural affinity for the potential real-life horrors surrounding various Hollywood productions, as well as the occult lore of Hollywood itself. Carroll had already been well-versed in topics like the *Poltergeist* curse that, rumor had it, was the cause of death for two young girls that had played central roles in the film trilogy, one of the most cursed franchises in Hollywood's already sordid and nasty history. There were also a number of incidents surrounding *The Omen*, including actor Gregory Peck and producer Mace Neufeld traveling on separate planes that were *both* struck by lightning. Creepier still was the death of a set designer, who died in a head-on collision near a road sign reading "Ommen, 66.6 km." He could tell you everything you'd ever want to know, and likely more, about the curses surrounding the making of *The Exorcist*, *Rosemary's Baby*, *The Passion of the Christ*, and dozens of others.

It was *Brujería*, though, that most interested the burgeoning director, and rather than fade with time, his obsession only ever grew.

"Wait," Andrea said, "so, what happened to the movie? How did you get a hold of it?"

"The night Perez was editing his film, the studio caught fire. It spread from the offices and nearly took out the whole lot, and the studio was ruined. Once the fire was put out, they found what was left of Perez. The autopsy report doesn't speculate on how he suffered the injuries he did, but it does rule him a suicide rather than an accidental victim. His stomach was ripped open, and not gently, either. Needless to say, the fire wiped out everything, and *Brujería* was thought to be lost with it, along with a number of the studio's other productions, but few were as noteworthy as Perez's. We only know of *Brujería* because of interviews Perez gave at the time. He was trying to sell the movie as the first Hollywood production starring witches, and there was a bit of buzz surrounding it. And then, of course, the total disaster that followed its production. Nobody ever saw any of the film, but that didn't stop the rumors that, somehow, the film survived."

"Okay. So, *again*, how did you get it?" Andrea said. She was getting antsy for an answer, bouncing one foot on the floor as she squirmed in her chair.

It was a fair question. Marcus knew Carroll had had spent an enormous amount of time and money trying to locate the lost film, hiring private detectives to track down whatever information they could and college students, who he paid to research and compile as many clues as they could find. Although it had been at least a decade since Carroll had directed his own horror feature, he had produced an incredible number of them in the intervening years, hiring occultists, psychics, witches, and Satanists to consult on those films and, likely pry them for any knowledge they might possess about *Brujería* or could possibly discover on his behalf.

As far as Marcus knew, Carroll's endeavors had been nothing but a waste of money. Nobody had been able to track down the three Mexican actresses the film had been centered around, and *Brujería* had taken on such a mythical status that some doubted the movie had ever been shot at all. Most suspected Perez had just been shooting his mouth off in interviews, trying to secure funding for a script he was shopping around, or attempting to inflate the status of his actresses and make them into larger than life figures. It was all promotion by a young unknown director who thought he was a hot shot, and nothing but a glitzy façade to make the flick more than it was, or could have been, to make potential audiences thirsty.

Carroll shrugged. "I've been looking for it for years. Decades. In that time, I've amassed a number of contacts and resources. You remember Schauer?"

Marcus nodded. "Your chef pal."

"He had an incredible network that I was able to leverage. You know how many productions he's catered? Thousands, easily. He's probably forgotten more Hollywood history and trivia than any of us at this table will ever know in our entire lives. I've always been fascinated with the occult, and so was Heinrich. We talked about *Brujería* all the time. I thought I knew a lot of crap about that movie, but Schauer? He was like an encyclopedia! Eventually, I was able to track down the movie to a private collector with a fondness for the strange and occult and, as they say, the rest is history."

"Impressive," Andrea said.

"No," Carroll said, "what's impressive is the check I had to cut him."

Everybody laughed at that, but it felt forced to Marcus, uneasy. Carroll had lost his goddamn mind, his odd obsession overruling any good sense he'd once possessed.

"So how did this film survive the fire? And how did this collector of yours get ahold of it?" Marcus asked.

"I don't know how it survived, frankly, but your two questions could very well be related. I asked him those very same questions myself."

"And what did he say?"

"He sold his soul for it."

There was more laughter at that, except for Carroll. His face remained impassive, serious.

"He admitted he hadn't watched the film out of concern for its power, based on its history, but he had studied the film cells enough to believe its legitimacy. He let me do the same before purchasing it, and I agree. This is it. This is *Brujería*."

Carroll took stock of the friends assembled before him. Everyone looked happy and full, if not completely skeptical and maybe even a little somber. Their plates pushed away, and napkins folded on the table, it was clear the meal had drawn to a close. He wiped his mouth with a cloth napkin and dropped it on his plate.

"Now, who wants to go see a movie?" He pushed himself away from the table and stood, picking up his half-full beer bottle. "Grab your drinks! Let's go!"

As everyone filed out of the kitchen to follow Carroll into his home theater, Marcus and Madeline lingered toward the end of the procession. She looped her arm through his and said, "Spooky stuff."

Marcus shrugged. "It's just a lot of Hollywood BS. Nothing in this town's real, baby."

He didn't add that the town was practically built off the occult, from Scientologists to Jack Parsons's sex magick rituals, the Manson murders, and new age religions that used powerful psychedelics to reach spiritual enlightenment. In Hollywood, the only god worth believing in was cinema, but people always needed a devil, people like Aldofo Perez and, to a certain extent, Carroll Arendt.

"Well, your friend certainly does know how to set a mood. We haven't even started watching this thing and I'm already getting chills."

"Carroll misses horror, you know? He keeps wanting to get back to it, but the studios are iffy. They want blockbusters. But Carroll, well, he'll always find a way to make horror real, if not for an audience, then at least for himself. That's what all this is about."

Madeline said nothing but leaned her head on his shoulder as they descended the staircase leading to the basement and the plushily furnished auditorium with three levels of sunken floors. She let out a low whistle as they moved along the top row to snuggle on the cream-colored sofa. Andrea and Paul were on the couch below, and in the lowermost row was Carroll's wife, Joan.

"Where's Carroll?"

"Cueing up the projector, probably."

As if on cue, a cone of light blossomed above them, aimed at the enormous floor-to-ceiling projection screen that the entire room was in service to. Carroll emerged from a hidden door beside them and flashed the couple a big shit-eating grin, jogging down the stairs to sit beside his wife. Once he was settled, he hit a button on the couch's armrest and the lights dimmed. Slowly, the white screen went black and the soft hum of the projector was all that could be heard as the silent film began to play.

All eyes were on the hundred-year-old black-and-white imagery before them—a close-up of three beautiful Mexican women, with long, flowing, velvet-black hair that shined in the day's bright sun. They were kneeling in a dirt field, arranged around a large triangle drawn on the soil in salt. Within the triangle were other shapes made from the salt, circles and squares that overlapped, and fat candles that burned brightly and gave off a thick smoke. Their eyes were shut, and although their mouths moved, there was no sound on the old film.

And yet, Marcus swore he could hear a noise of some kind, not the film projector or the hum of the compound's air conditioning, but something *other*.

Shadows moved across the screen as the women took one another's hands and raised their arms. The skin along the backs of their hands split open from unseen forces and black blood slid down their forearms. Their heads bent back, their necks stretched as throats heaved and shoved beneath delicate flesh, and then they stood with a simple grace. Bloody hands went to glossy lips, and they danced around the triangle, drawing closer and closer to one another, and shadows flickered around them.

Madeline shifted on the couch, her hand hot and sweaty in his. Marcus couldn't blame her. There was definitely something creepy about the scene playing out before them, and even though he'd been in scores of horror films over the course of his career, and a lifelong fan of the genre, he was still unsettled. Perez's cinematography was deeply affecting, and the way the practical effects and editing blended together was absolute perfection. Even without sound, there was such a rich mood that it was impossible not to be enraptured.

The cave walls closed around the women—the witches. It took Marcus a moment to realize the scene had changed. *Weren't they in a field?*

The women drew closer as shadows coalesced around them, their bodies pressing tightly against one another as they sucked blood from one another's wounds, their mouths following the lines of blood that stretched down their wrists and arms, until they were disrobing one another.

Marcus felt like a voyeur, a flush of heat rising in his cheeks. Suddenly he was a twelve-year-old again whose mother had just found a stash of *Playboys* under his bed, guilt and shame competing inside him and churning his guts.

He swore he could hear the women chanting, their voices sensually murmuring in his head. The words were completely foreign and sounded like no language he had ever heard before. Sweat exploded in his armpits and he flapped the front of his shirt to try to cool his chest. The theater felt like it'd gotten a hundred degrees hotter, but he couldn't take his eyes off the screen as the women began to kiss, their tongues finding one another's, bloodied hands grabbing and squeezing bare breasts, fingers finding hardened nipples.

"Jesus," he muttered. "What kind of movie is this, Carroll?"

The eyes of the witches glowed brightly, a startlingly pure white that was wholly otherworldly. He could hear the sounds of their lovemaking in his head as if he were there with them, and even as their mouths were otherwise preoccupied, he could somehow hear their chanting as it grew louder and louder.

He turned to Madeline, saw her legs splayed and skirt hiked up over her thighs, one hand between them while the other massaged her breast through the fabric of her top. He opened his mouth to say something, to either chide her or offer her another hand, he couldn't decide which, when a scream erupted in his head. One of the women on screen was at the throat of another, blood erupting from the woman's neck as teeth tore loose a grisly hunk of meat.

Shadows moved around them, dancing on the walls, and Marcus couldn't tell if that was happening on screen or off. Darkness swirled in the air, clouding his vision, the screen hidden for the briefest of moments, but he could still hear it. He could hear everything.

His hand moved on its own, going to his crotch as he leered at Madeline. He had to force himself to stop, the chanting in his head louder, more insistent and…*hypnotizing*. The word came to him from nowhere and then the disjointed pieces clicked together with a mental *snap!*

The film, he thought. *Oh my god, it's real!*

He darted off the sofa and pushed his way past Madeline. Along the way, he looked down the aisle below, discerning movement in the shadows. The air was impossibly thick, and he could barely make out Andrea and Paul on the next row down. She was crouched between his legs, her head bobbing up and down, and the haze cleared enough that he saw Andrea looking past her partner to stare at him. Her eyes were wrong, the color impossibly vivid and bright and—they were glowing, an ethereal light that briefly cut through the fog.

Oh, Carroll…what the fuck did you do?

Madeline snatched his arm, and he shook loose from her grip. Her hands were inhumanly twisted, her fingers ending in animalistic claws that dug deep trenches in his skin. She smiled coyly at him, too-full red lips parting over what should have been perfect pearly whites. Worms wriggled inside the black pit of her mouth, spilling over her lips and the décolletage of her top. She fell back onto the couch, her laugh muffled by the writhing pink and brown tubes of meat.

Marcus choked, the air thick and acrid. His mind and body took its time breaking through the *Brujería*-induced fog, but by the time either part of him had caught up with reality, it was too late. His lungs ached as he hauled in a mouthful of bitter, greasy smoke that was filling the home theater and making the air scummy. He realized now what the shadows he had seen dancing around the walls and projector screen had been, and as he looked up at the projection booth, he could see the dark gray clouds occluding the cyclopean beam of light.

Tendrils of smoke curled out from between the booth's door and the door jamb. He unthinkingly reached for the door handle, grateful to find the metal cold against his hot flesh, and yanked it open. Although there was no fire, the room was blanketed in a thick, swirling cloud of smoke. He covered his mouth with his arm as he stepped inside, his eyes watering as he scanned the tiny, closet-sized room for the source. His first thought was to turn off the projector, believing the old reel-to-reel machine—the same damn projector Carroll had had since they were kids—was somehow malfunctioning and burning the film, but then he saw it.

Tucked in the corner of the room was a pulsing blob of—well, he didn't know what. It was large and tumorous looking, the flesh of it blackened and cracked, revealing a bright, wet-looking pink interior, an ugly network of varicose veins marbling the surface. Whatever it was looked to be breathing, and he heard an odd and wretched gasping noise coming from it. And then it began to unfold itself.

"You're missing the show, baby," Madeline said, her hand on his shoulder and turning him toward her.

A slick, fat earthworm dangled from her mouth, brown chunks dotting her lips and chin like scabs. He lowered his shoulder and tucked his chin to his chest, shoving into her like he was a high school linebacker again. She sidestepped him, laughing, and swatted his ass as he passed. Let her laugh, he thought. All he cared about was getting away from her.

He nearly tripped on a rock on his way out of the small booth, his hands rising in reflex to grab the wall. The wall was all wrong, though, rough instead of smooth, a dark stone instead of the cream-colored paint Carroll favored. He choked on the stench of sulfur, the smoke making him lightheaded and sick, filling his lungs even as the chorale chanting filled his head.

"No, no, no," he said, feeling lost and dizzy. This wasn't right. None of this was right. The theater was gone, the projection screen gone, the couches, everything, all of it gone. Carroll and Paul were there, though, as were Joan and Andrea.

The women strode toward him, their hands and mouths bloody. The men stayed on the ground, inert lumps, and Marcus saw too much of how messy their ends had been in the flickering light of flames. Joan and Andrea's eyes glowed hot, as if the spirits animating them were burning through their bodies. A forked tongue darted out of Andrea's mouth to lick at the gore staining her lips.

He turned, searching for some escape, and came face to face with Madeline. She smiled, the corners of her bright, white eyes crinkling, and a moment later the pain struck him, his mind once again playing catch up with his body. Her nails dug into the soft meat of his belly, sinking through skin and fat, and then muscle. He grabbed at her wrist, tried to push her away, but it was useless. Her hand sank deeper inside him, and he screamed in agony at the intrusion of her probing claws and the popping of the organs that got in her way.

Joan and Andrea came up behind him, murmuring and laughing as one played with his hair and the other bit into his neck. He sank to his knees, and something inside him exploded as he slid free of Madeline's arm.

In the smoke before him, something massive stirred. He saw cloven hoofed feet, but little else. He didn't have the strength to raise his head and take in the full enormity of the beast just on the other side of Madeline. But he didn't need to see it to know what it was, just as he didn't need to read the autopsy report to know how Adolfo Perez or Carroll and Paul had died. The answer was right there in grainy black-and-white, projected against the black rock of the cave wall.

And then the movie reached its end. The projector hummed on, and the loose film slapped against the still spinning reel. A cacophony of insane laughter surrounded him as his life force drained away, and he felt so very, very tired.

Marcus's eyes began to close like heavy curtains and, finally, the world faded to black.

White Walpurgis

by Tim Meyer

BRIDAL PARTY

"All right, pretend like you're thinking," said Marla Quinn, snapping off a few photos while the bridesmaids hustled back and forth behind her.

The maid of honor changed something on the bride's IV, patted her shoulder, and kissed her forehead. The bride nodded, turning her head to look thoughtfully at the hotel room's far wall.

"But," Marla said, adjusting the flash, "like, think with a smile on your face. Reflect on happy times, your life together so far, your *future*."

The maid of honor continued to play nurse, tapping a few pills into her palm. Abigail Pelton, the sick bride, did exactly what Marla asked. She posed, she smiled, and did both without a hint of reluctance. Everything was going swimmingly, something Marla couldn't exactly say for all the weddings she photographed. You just never knew if you'd be shooting cooperative subjects or whiny brats who wanted nothing to do with pictures, but the Pelton bridal party had, so far, been superb.

Hope the guys are just as easy-going, she thought, cycling through the settings on her Canon Mark III.

"Nice. Perfect. You're a natural."

The maid of honor smiled. Abigail smiled back. Marla smiled because they were both smiling, and capturing her clients' special day was oh-so gratifying. Everyone was happy. Everything was perfect.

After she was done grabbing the shots she needed, she asked the maid of honor what room the groomsmen were staying in.

"I'm sorry?"

"The groomsmen?" Marla said again. "Their... um... room?"

The maid of honor shook her head. "I'm sorry. Didn't Mr. Pelton brief you on..." She cleared her throat. "Didn't he tell you the details? Didn't your employer pass along that information?"

Marla shook her head. "No. No one told me anything." She pressed her palm against her forehead. "I'm sorry—I was told this wedding was going to a bit unorthodox, but I just assumed it was the..." Her eyes drifted over to the bed. She nodded subtly at the monitoring equipment resting next to the bride.

"Oh," the maid of honor said, a hint of sadness bringing down her voice. "No, Abby's cancer has nothing to do with it."

Awkward City, Marla thought. *Can I make this any worse? At this rate, I'll never get another gig with Marvelous Creations again.*

"So..." The maid of honor trailed off, staring at Marla as if maybe Marla would forget the whole thing, drop it and go about her job. But Marla stood her ground, waiting for the maid of honor to divulge the juicy details of this odd wedding. "So, the thing is—there are no groomsmen."

"Oh. Oh okay." She had never shot a wedding with no groomsmen before. Unorthodox, yes. But they were paying her double her normal rate, and, considering there was no other half of the bridal party, her workload was significantly less. She had nothing to complain about. "Just the groom then."

"Yeah...about that..." The maid of honor cast her eyes to the suite's plush carpet, looking as if she didn't know how to break the bad news. "There isn't a groom, either. I mean, not really."

"Sooooo…who's getting married?" Marla's thoughts were suddenly all over the place. *A wedding with no groom and no parties. This isn't weird. Nope. Not at all.*

She reminded herself how much none of this mattered, that she was getting paid regardless, that she'd be able to afford rent this month because of it, and not to fucking worry.

Still, something about the ceremony's peculiar start unnerved her. A serpent of unease uncoiled in her guts.

"It's complicated. But you should talk to Mr. Pelton. He'll fill you in on the details."

"Perfect."

With that, Marla left the room, in search of the father of the bride and some answers.

OPEN BAR

She found the father of the bride at the bar, knocking back a martini. With the same hand, he slammed down the drink and ordered another.

"Oh come on," Marla said, sidling up next to him. "Marrying off your daughter can't be *that* bad, can it?"

Elmer Pelton didn't find the humor in that joke, and his dry, searching eyes drifted across the bar to meet her smiling face.

Tough crowd, she thought.

"Yikes. Sorry. I was just kidding. Trying to lighten the mood." She scanned the bar and the wedding's other attendees as they drank and conversed, scattered secrets amongst themselves. No one seemed to be laughing or smiling, no one seemed to be enjoying themselves at all. *Am I shooting a funeral or a wedding?* Marla wondered, returning to Elmer Pelton. "Everyone seems so tense."

"So your boss didn't tell you, I gather," Elmer said, sipping from another martini. His face was fixed in a bitter scowl and the martini did nothing to help the cause.

Marla shook her head. "Nope. Not a thing." She forced another amiable smile. "But I'm starting to worry. Did I get mixed up in some voodoo cult scheme or what?" A quick glance around the room, honing in on the guests' odd choices in attire. "Seems like everyone is here for a funeral, not a wedding."

"Well, that may be because Abby's groom is…well, he's not here with us."

Marla's lips wrinkled. "Yeah, the maid of honor clued me in on that." She swallowed, curiosity getting the best of her thoughts. "Sir, I can't help but ask—did something happen to the groom?"

"Something… happen…" His brain seemed to forget whatever he was going to say next, and his eyes found the ceiling. There was nothing above them except ornate moulding, dentil blocks, and plinths made of marble that held up the structural columns. A painting of an angel floating through heavenly clouds of white took up some of the ceiling as well. "No, Miss Quinn. No, nothing happened to him."

He offered her a defeated smile.

"Oh. Okay then. Look, you don't have to tell me—"

"Your employer promised my family and me that whatever you saw here today…it would be confidential. Hence the hefty payday."

Marla nodded. "Understood. Believe me. My lips are sealed. I just…weddings are supposed to be happy. A day of celebration. This…" She looked around the room once again, and now noticed she had drawn the attention of the other guests. Some eyes lingered on her, which disquieted her even more, making her feel like an intruder and less like a piece of this *supposed* joyous experience. "This is different."

Elmer Pelton put down another martini with ease. "Just, whatever you see here today—keep an open mind. And also, I'm going to need all the footage of what you capture before you leave."

"But I have to edit—"

"Uncle Horace will edit them for us." Elmer raised his empty glass in Uncle Horace's direction. Marla saw the man in the back corner of the room nod in response and give Elmer a toast of his cherry-topped drink. He looked less like a wedding guest and more like a man who dealt in shady business practices. Marla had never seen someone sit so comfortably in the shadows, with sunglasses on nonetheless.

"Okay. Uncle Horace it is," Marla said, realizing an argument with the father of the bride would get her nowhere. Besides, he was paying for the pictures. He could smash her SD card on the ground right in front of her and she wouldn't care—either way, she was getting paid.

New plan—fuck these people and their special day. Get in, get out, and try to forget you were even on this job.

"Thank you, Miss Quinn. Now, if I may bestow one more piece of advice on you this evening."

"Sure, man. Whatever."

"Whatever you see during the ceremony…whatever you witness… please, do your best to forget it ever happened."

Her throat suddenly felt six times smaller.

"And for the love of all that is unholy," he continued, "please don't scream."

A PHONE CALL

"Calm down, Marla—I can explain."

Marla paced the terrace, looking back over her shoulder, making sure no one had followed her. "Explain? Explain? Jesus, Dom. You better do better than explain."

"I know you're angry."

"I'm not angry," she said, aware of her tone. "I'm not angry at all. I'm just freaked out. I mean—'don't scream?' What the hell is that, Dom? And don't tell me you have no clue."

Dom's heavy breathing caused static. "Marla, please. I don't know anything. Elmer Pelton didn't say anything about there not being a groom or what kind of wedding it would be. I knew the broad had cancer, and that was it."

"He didn't say? Because he seems to think he did."

"No. All he said was that there would be some uncomfortable sights, stuff about the cancer, and to send you."

"Me?"

"That's right, Marla. You. They requested you by name."

"You didn't tell me this."

"Would it have mattered? I get requests for you all the time. You're my best wedding photographer. *Word of mouth* is a big thing in this business."

She paused, enjoying the compliments, hoping there was more.

"Besides, you've shot strange weddings before."

"Not this strange."

"Remember that wedding you did last year? The one with the tarot card reader?"

"Yeah," she said, sticking a cigarette in her mouth and lighting up. "That was a hoot."

"That was strange, right?"

"Yeah, it was a little odd, and the lady was a kook—I mean, Jesus, she told me I'd start talking to my mother again, that we'd suddenly repair our relationship, and there is no way *that* is happening, not over my dead body."

"My point, Marla—is that you're the best. There's a reason why the Peltons asked for you." He sighed one more time, clearly growing bored of this explanation. She didn't care—it felt nice to be needed and she was soaking in every compliment, basking in their soothing glory. "That's why they paid us extra."

She decided to take a gamble. "I don't know, man. I think I want more."

"More?" She heard him nearly fall out of his chair. At the very least, he knocked something off his desk. "More what?"

"More money, of course."

"Marla, no. You're being paid double your rate as it is, and that's more than enough."

"Not for this. I mean, do I have to reiterate the fact that I was told not to scream during the ceremony. I mean, what the fuck, Dom?"

Dom grunted in frustration. "Jesus fucking Christ, Marla. Fine. I'll throw you an extra hundred."

"Make it three."

"Three-hundred? No, no, Marla. No way. That's...that's, like, extortion or some shit."

"Maybe. But you'll pay it or I'm outta here. And good luck finding someone to replace me in the next twenty minutes."

"Marla, you'll never work in photography ever again, least not in this state, if you walk off this job."

"I was thinking of starting my own business, anyway."

"Marla, please."

"So, three-hundred is good then?" His silence meant he was thinking about it, and the longer he deliberated, the more Marla knew she had him. "PayPal me. To friends, so I don't have to claim it."

More silence. Eventually he snarled. "All right. Fine. Three-hundred. Headed your way. But don't think I won't forget this."

"I know you won't."

She hung up and waited for the money to come through. After the notification dropped down from her home bar and she saw herself three-hundred dollars richer, she headed back inside, changing the lens on her camera as she went.

CEREMONY

"We gather here today," said the officiant, "to celebrate the joining of two special individuals, as they prepare to spend their lives together in eternity. We welcome all of you on this special day, on April the 30th, otherwise known in our hearts as Walpurgis Night."

Marla snapped a photo of the venue's banquet hall, the altar. The camera's flash went off, earning her dirty looks from the gathering, an odd collection of individuals that wore dark-colored clothing and hats with veils.

Funeral, she thought. *Funeral clothes.*

The robed man on stage stood next to the bride, holding up his arms, asking the congregation to "Please rise." He began humming some hymn, one Marla's ear did not fully recognize, but she tried her best to ignore the strange happenings around her and concentrate on getting the shots she needed. The more she photographed, the more attention she received from the audience. It wasn't the first time she'd been given dirty looks for doing her job; it happened quite frequently, and she'd gotten pretty good at ignoring them.

But these looks...they freaked her out. Those eyes didn't just relay displeasure; no, they were cast with hate.

Bunch of freaks.

Marla kept on ignoring them, sticking to her job.

After the song was over, the robed man lowered his arms. The spectators continued to stand. Then they turned, facing the doors in the back of the hall.

Marla made her way to the front of the altar, getting a clear shot down the aisle. The bride was already on stage (unorthodox, yes) next to the beeping equipment that monitored her vitals and administered medicine, and everyone was awaiting the groom's arrival. *There is no groom,* she remembered the maid of honor stating, and Marla wondered who exactly was going to appear from behind those doors. Regardless, she was prepared, camera in hand, ready to capture the moment.

The doors swung open, and in walked a man, robed like the officiant, except he wasn't alone. He held a rope and Marla followed the braided material to the floor, where beside the man walked a black goat.

The animal bleated. Its farm-stink filled the hall.

"Are you people *fucking* serious?" Marla said, standing up, letting the camera dangle from the strap around her neck.

Immediately, every eye in the room turned on her. Some were wide with horror, as if Marla had committed some vile, atrocious crime. Some came at her with that familiar revulsion, their dark eyes burning with a sense of murderous intent.

"I mean, really?" she said again, holding out her arms, waiting for a reply. Something sane, something rational.

Before she could throw her arms up and storm out, walk off the job, a hand gripped her shoulder and tore her away from the stage.

"*Ow!*" she snapped. "*You're hurting me.*"

The hand spun her around.

Elmer Pelton.

"You were told to keep an open mind. You were told not to make any noise."

No, she felt like saying. *No, I was told not to scream.*

"But this is ridic—"

He shushed her by putting a finger over her lips. Frozen by the inability to fully process what her eyes were seeing, she couldn't bring herself to remove his touch.

"You are being paid to act like a professional. *Act* like a professional. Do your job. Take your pictures. Capture our special celebration."

Marla glared at him, but nodded.

Elmer headed back to his position on the stage. He stood next to his daughter, who looked down at the black goat fondly, the way a bride always looks upon her future husband.

I can't believe this is happening, Marla thought, and then found herself snapping more photos. *Let's get this over with, shall we?*

The ceremony went on.

The robed man led the black goat on stage, across from Abigail Pelton. As the officiant commenced with the sacrament of holy matrimony, the maid of honor fiddled with the machinery and changed the bride's IV. Marla got lost in the man's words, the speech he spewed forth, the passages and phrases—spoken in some uncommon tongue—that the congregation gobbled up, the guests and their responses, their proud grins. Marla began to feel ill, the banquet hall spinning before her. She thought she might get sick, lose the sushi she'd chowed down during the cocktail hour. This was not right.

She needed to escape.

Turning back toward the emergency exit, she lost her grip on the camera. For a second, she forgot about the strap around her neck and fully expected the device to smash on the ground, shatter into small pieces. Music began to play, discordant plucking from an assembly of out-of-tune strings. The harsh melody only made the room more disorienting, and Marla's feet began to fail.

What the hell is happening to me?

She glanced up at the emergency exit and watched some robed figure step in front of her way out.

"Move," she said, swaying on her heels.

"Don't let her leave," said someone from behind her, and she recognized the voice of Elmer Pelton.

Marla drunkenly glanced over her shoulder, back toward the stage. Every eye was on her now, even those clad in shadows. She brought up her camera and began shooting the stage, focusing the flash directly in their staring eyes. Arms gripped her. She fought them off.

"C'mere," the robed guardian said, trying to corral her. He reached for the camera, but she dug deep for control over her body and kicked the man right in his ball bag. His head shot forward, and he groaned in considerable pain. As he hunched, she introduced his chin to her knee. With force. As much as she could generate.

The blow knocked the man on his back.

She continued to capture images of the stage, the flash flickering like an epileptic's worst nightmare. In the bright blinding bursts, Elmer's face twisted and contorted with the rage of some spiteful deity. He hopped off the stage, placed a hand in front of his eyes, and started toward Marla, his teeth clenched, lips pulled back in a ferocious snarl.

The black goat bleated some more. Much to the chagrin of the audience, Marla carried on with her light show, and that, in turn, inspired the black goat to buck. The little guy kicked his legs in reverse, catching his robed escort right in the shin with bone-shattering force. The form lurched forward, dropped the rope, and grabbed the excruciating pain with both hands. He fell to the floor, out of sight, but not before the goat dropped a few heavy hooves on his face.

The black goat looked at Marla as if he wanted a reward for dispatching one of them. *I'll give all the hay in the world, little buddy, if you kick our way out. Hay, or whatever you little fuckers eat.*

It was as if he heard her. The black goat lowered his head and charged off the stage, plowing into Elmer. Elmer flew into the first row of chairs, taking out seats and a few of the Peltons' guests. The crowd gasped; a few of them cursed. Some shouted for Marla to stop using her flash, for it was clearly riling up the groom. But that only motivated her to take more pictures. To document this whole clusterfuck. The strobe-like effect bounced around the room, the congregates acting like the light somehow melted their flesh.

The black goat resumed his reign of terror, kicking and ramming the fleeing members. He drove one of the robed guests through the drywall. Even when the man was down, the goat continued to grind his skull into him, as if he intended to pulverize the man to dust.

Keep going, little buddy. Keep kicking ass, my furry friend.

Through the chaos, Marla locked onto Abigail. The bride's eyes grinned at her. Spikes of dread penetrated Marla's flesh. A cold river ran through her veins, and she immediately thought she should get out of there since the room's attention had now been turned to the havoc-wreaking goat.

Don't worry, Marla, the bride's eyes said. *You'll be where you're supposed to. Soon.*

Marla spun for the emergency exit. The guard was writhing on the ground, but he was starting to recharge his battery. He'd be up in a few seconds, and Marla would be his first destination.

She sprinted toward the door, barreled into it, and came out on the other side.

The other side.

A winter wonderland, an endless expanse of marshmallow hills beneath a colorless sheet of ever-stretching gray.

VISIONS

"Come sit," said the girl in the wedding dress.

After a glance around the pure-white scenery, Marla realized she was still at the venue, just three months earlier. It was January 30th, maybe— definitely not April.

The bride was sitting on a small mound of snow next to the birdbath fountain that would spit intermittently under warmer conditions. She patted the powdery space next to her.

Marla, confused, still feeling disoriented but not nearly as lightheaded as before, walked over and did as she was asked. The snow soaked through her pants, icing her bottom. As dreamlike as this sequence felt, the frigid burn was real enough.

"What is this?" Marla breathlessly asked the bride. "How come you're well enough to speak now? Are you not sick?"

Abigail Pelton smiled. "I'm still sick. Very sick."

"How—no, *what*—what is this?" She glanced at the sky, watched flurries descend from the ashen plain. "Where are we?"

"We're at the venue. Don't you recognize it?"

"Don't fuck with me. One second you're at the altar, looking woozy and fucking out of it, on the verge of passing out—the next you're out here, fine and chipper. One second it's spring, wedding season, and now we're in the middle of a goddamn blizzard."

Abigail offered a squinty smile, one that said, *you're so cute.* "We aren't in a specific place," she said. "Meaning, I can make the world however you want to see it. But I scanned your thoughts, and I believe you prefer winter over warmer weather. You like snow. I don't know why that is." She glanced up, as if this were a riddle that required all of her attention. "But it is."

"It's because I used to love snow days," Marla said around the knot in her throat. "No school on snow days. I hated school."

"Ah, yes. That makes sense." Abigail reached for Marla's hand.

Marla dodged her touch.

"Please," the bride said, her eyes soft and inviting. There was no malice behind them, not like there had been moments ago, during the ceremony. The gaze that drove Marla out here was full of hate. Full of awful intent. "It is not my intention to hurt you."

"Then what is all of this?" She nodded back at the door, surprised that guests from the ceremony hadn't come out to look for her, wanting to smash her camera, her only defense against their psychotic tendencies, to pieces. "None of this makes any sense."

"It will."

Marla watched as Abigail extended her fingers once again. This time, she didn't retract her hand and allowed the bride to caress her skin. Abigail's fingers ran along Marla's knuckles, over her palm, down her wrist.

"You were chosen, Marla. By my family and I."

"What?"

"You have no family of your own. None that will care about your disappearance, anyways. Not after what you did to them."

"No, that's simply not true. I have a family. And of course they care about me."

"Oh?" Abigail's knowing, condescending smile widened. "Is that right? When's the last time you spoke with them? Any of them?"

(Her brother's face, his scowl, the twitch of his upper lip.)

(Mom, shaking her head in utter disappointment, the flare of her nostrils.)

(Her, running down the aisle, away from all of them, away from the church, down the street, into the distance, never looking back.)

"I..." She failed to produce a response, a *true* response.

"There's no need to lie, Marla. I know as well as you that it's been years since you communicated with them. And who could blame you? I can't. After all, you wasted their money, their time. You just didn't run away from your future; you ran away from them. And quite frankly, you embarrassed them."

"It wasn't what I wanted."

"How do you know what you want?" the bride asked with a giggle.

"Because it wasn't."

(Brian's face. His lower jaw dropping as he turns to watch her flee down the aisle.)

"But you were young."

"Exactly," Marla said. "I was young. Too young for...too young to commit."

"You would have been rich," Abigail said, a twinkle shimmering in her eyes despite her gray surroundings. She toyed with the curls in Marla's hair. "You would have had everything," she whispered.

"I know." Tears now. "I didn't love him. I didn't. I tried to, but...but... I just couldn't."

(Brian calling after her. Brian running down the aisle, promising her everything, promising her perfection, a life where dreams and desires fashion realities.)

"Your family would have been rich too," the bride said, continuing to fill her head with statements she knew were true. "They would have had it all. Brian's family was beyond wealthy. *Beyond*. You have no idea how wealthy they were."

"Oh...I know."

"My family is wealthy. My family is as wealthy as Brian's. My father and his father—they work together."

Marla lifted her gaze to meet the bride's.

"Yes. We were well aware of your...*history*, before we hired you."

Marla nodded, putting the pieces together.

"Do you know what has to happen? Tonight, on the night of nights?"

Marla looked elsewhere, into the white drifts.

"It's Walpurgis Night. Do you know what that means to us?"

Marla shook her head.

"Named after Saint Walpurga, a woman who was very efficient at repelling witchcraft and defeating the dark magic. In Germany, covens would gather in the hills of the Harz Mountains to celebrate the thinning of the barriers between worlds, a holy night when the rising forces of evil were at their pinnacle. Townsfolk would hold feasts and fires, a celebration of their own, which they believed kept them safe and secure, prevented the terrors from the witches' sabbath from spreading down the mountainside and into their homes."

"Nice story. What does it have to do with me?"

"I've lived a long time, Marla. I've seen many sabbaths, many mountains, participated in many celebrations."

Marla rotated to face her. "What are you...saying?"

"My spirit has been in the Pelton family for a long time. I am one of the originals. I was there for the first sabbath, and I will be there for the last." She squinted, looked down at her body, her hands feeling her chest, her stomach, and legs, as if making sure they were still solid, still there. "This body is failing me. It's the cancer. It's growing too fast and I won't make it another six months—I won't see All Hallows' Eve, the next opportunity to carry out the ceremony. I need a new body, Marla, and I need one tonight. Specifically, I need yours."

A part of Marla wanted to run, but she couldn't find the strength. The camera was a weight and she could barely keep her head up. "I…"

"Shhh," the bride said, putting a finger over her lips. "Don't say anything. Don't fight this. Fighting's useless, anyway. That sushi you helped yourself to—it was made with *Atropa belladonna*—so your fight's all but left you. There wasn't enough to knock you out, but enough to make you…*agreeable*."

"Y-you…b-bitch."

The bride smiled. "I'm sorry, Marla. But you have a healthy body. And I need it. My family needs me. Yours…*doesn't*."

The door to the venue creaked open, and even though her view was hazy, she could see inside. The dimly-lit banquet hall remained as she had left it. She could see the Peltons were gathered near the mouth of the venue. She could see the goat, saw they had gotten the little beast under control.

"What's with the goat?" Marla asked, the only question left in her fading consciousness.

The bride squeaked with laughter. "Ohhhh… Every family needs a goat. You should know that by now."

(*Her mother's scowl, the last words she said echoing across her thoughts, I HATE YOU I HATE I HATE YOU I HATE*)

"Hmpf. Goat."

"Come on, Marla. Let's get you on your feet. They're waiting for us."

The bride helped Marla to the door.

Behind her, the wintry weather blew a cold gust across her shoulders, and even in the gray gloom of this false solstice, she felt sunshine blazing from within, a warmth she never knew.

Family Business

by Charlotte Platt

Lisa rolled her neck, trying to stretch the muscle out in a smooth arc. It made several cracking sounds and loosened passably, enough to help with her headache a little.

She was on the counter, book and notepad stuffed into a tray she could lift and shelve as necessary, and part way through chapter seven notes for night class when the chimes above the door tinkled their welcome. A man hovered at the entrance, half in and half out, eyes tracking over the stuffed display cases.

"Hello," she called, shoving her books out of sight. "Can I help you?"

"Is this the antiques and repairs establishment?" he asked, voice deep as a barrel. She glanced around the dark wooden furniture, paintings and glowing jewellery, nodding.

"That's us," she said, staying put. She knew the tricks, had been helping in the shop since she was a tall teenager at her grandma's shoulder. Some folk thought they could filch an item here or there, draw you out from behind the counter and pocket something while you didn't have the CCTV to check. Not that she needed that, but no point in silly risks.

"Excellent," he said, stepping through and closing the door. He had a briefcase with him, tatty red leather that looked right out of someone's attic. Straightening, he strode towards her. He was tall, basketball player tall, filling out the button up and slacks combo well enough for it to look good. Maybe he was an athlete. "I fear I have a need of your services."

"What can we do for you?" Lisa asked, bringing up her brightest smile.

"I've found an item that may be of some value, but it's aged and requires repair. I'm happy to take guidance on what would be the best way to do that, but it also requires some discretion." He was wound up like a spring, almost sweating with nerves as he placed the case on the counter.

"Stolen?" Lisa asked with a grin, enjoying the wince it brought.

"Repurposed, you could say," he said, drumming his fingers on the case. "It was my uncle's, and he passed. I found it while clearing his house." The accent was local, almost, a bit flattened out.

"He a traveller?" she asked.

"When he was younger, yes. Not that I ever knew him as young," the guy said with a laugh, his face looking a bit nicer for the smile.

"My gran did the same thing, went all over with this big leather trunk. She brought back loads of things that would be banned today, grave jars and ceremonial items. We still have some of them around." She pointed to one of the shop corners, the altar of sorts that showed blades and necklaces, thin tablets of sandstone that should definitely have been honouring someone else's relative thousands of miles away.

"I see. So you have a history of being able to cater to such items?"

"Depends on what's in the case, but we're experienced in repairs. There may be additional fees for private records, but I'll tell you if it's legitimate or not and what we expect costs to be before we do anything."

"Sounds like you're just what I'm looking for," he said, slipping the case onto its length and unbuckling the straps. "There's nothing...weird. I think he took it because it looked beautiful."

"I'm only here to judge quality, not intent," Lisa said, holding her palms up, "And if you're not happy with my assessment you're under no obligation to leave it with us."

"Seems fair," he said, lifting the lid and turning it around for her to assess. The case was full, mostly with flattened straw to stop things from rattling. Inside sat a fat disk, about as thick as her thumb, made from a deep green stone. It was good quality, she knew that just from the colour consistency, and it had a sigil carved into it then inlaid with silver. That had oxidised, the metal dark with wear, and a crack had started to form from what might have been the top. She traced it with the pad of her index finger, sucking air at the coldness of it.

"Do you know what the symbol's for?" she asked, leaning her elbows on the counter to get a better look. The base of the marking, from where she was looking at it at least, was an infinity symbol, a sideway figure eight, with a spike rising out from the crossing centre to almost touch the opposite edge. It was scored through twice near the peak, fat, flat lines reminding her ridiculously of a ship's sails.

"I've tried to do a little research, but I don't know where he got it. I didn't want to put pictures online."

"Of course," she said with a nod, bringing her hand away. She stood up, surprised to see him leaning towards her. "That's a good quality item. It'll take work to get repaired. The silver can be cleaned with time and effort, rather than any solution, but mending it'll be a more delicate job. I'd probably want us to take a sample from the crack and test the purity, so we can mix something that'd be cohesive. It'll be too gaudy otherwise, obvious it was done. That can hurt resale value."

"You can tell all of that just by looking?" he asked, hiking a thick brow.

"Skills of the job," she said with a nod to the shop. "It's the family business to know a good thing when we see it."

"I didn't realise it was a family operation," he said, glancing back to the door.

"Started off by Gran, that's why it's called Marianne's. Continued by my brother and I after she passed on," she said, jotting down numbers on a pad beside the till. "If you're happy with us doing a sample, I can give you better figures, but I would expect it to cost around this much."

She passed him the folded piece of paper, a little bit of theatrics her grandmother had started off as a superstition—never tell someone how much you would charge for your work. How much you would pay for something, naturally, that number had to be open, but the cost for effort should be kept quiet lest anyone else was listening.

"That's a big number," he said, looking between her and the paper.

"It's the price of working on trust. We could charge less, but then we'd have to keep a record of what we were doing."

"I see," he said, worrying his lower lip between his teeth. "You set the fee yourself?"

"It'll be me doing the work, so I set the fee."

"Without being insulting, you seem pretty young to be doing antique work."

"I get that a lot, usually makes the price go up."

"I'm not trying to be a dick," he said, a flash of panic going over his face. "You must take great care of your skin?"

She rolled her eyes. "I've been training in jewellery work and repairs since I was a kid. If you're concerned about my skills, you can look at any of the other metal work repairs on display. I've more than ten years' experience and was brought up in the business, I shadowed by Gran while she worked."

"Sorry, that was an asshole thing to say," he said, shoulders slumping. "You know more about this than I do."

"I know about the repairing bit at least," she said, smiling. "I can see about some research into this as well, if you want." She tapped the loop, letting her finger linger on the cool metal.

"That would be great. Does it cost extra?"

"Depends on how interesting it is," she said, honestly. "If it's entertaining, I wouldn't charge you for it."

"Fingers crossed for interesting, then," he said, pocketing the paper. "I'm happy for you to do what's needed. How long should it take?"

"Depends on the sample. We usually hear back in two to three weeks. Then we'd need to do the work, so probably four to five total. If we get the results back sooner, we can do the work sooner."

"Great. I'll give you my number and you can let me know when you get the sample back in?"

"Sounds good to me, Mr.?"

"Levi. Please, don't call me anything formal. Makes me feel old."

She laughed, shaking her head. Dude was her age, late twenties, maybe just over thirty, tops. "Sure thing, Levi. I can save it under your uncle's name, if you prefer?"

"That would be." He paused, visibly torn. "That would be a good idea actually, thanks. That's Mr. Green."

"Very welcome. It's all part of the service." Lisa took his details, transcribing them into code automatically.

"Neat trick," he said, nodding to her scribbles.

"Discretion—it could probably be cracked by someone with enough time but keeps things neat and tidy in the first instance."

"Your gran teach you that too?"

"Of course," Lisa said, finishing the note with a flourish, "family business."

Levi seemed to find a reason to drop into the shop every week or so after that. Dylan had encountered him once and was certain the guy was a retired athlete but couldn't name what from. They'd made the joint business decision not to investigate any further, lest they stumble upon anything they didn't want to know.

He appeared again on week four, this time with a crumbling book that smelled like damp and death and a matching dagger. Lisa wrinkled her nose at them, pointing to the counter.

"I'm only handling that with gloves. No telling what's growing on it."

"Probably sensible," he said, setting it gingerly down. "I think it might have to do with my uncle's piece. I found it around his travel diaries. It's a bit neglected though."

"He wasn't keeping much care of them, I take it?"

"Some things he was real careful with and some are like this. I don't know what the difference between them is. It has the same mark here." He pointed to the spine of the book, silver thread visible in that same curving, spiking pattern.

"The knife has it too. The quillon has the loops." She tapped the metal, tracing the rivet running along the flat of the blade. "Quite the little set. Have you looked inside?"

"No, I didn't want to risk doing more damage to it," he said, mouth screwed up in a grimace.

"That's smart. No way to read it if it's in lumps."

"Glad you agree. I'm never sure what to do with stuff like this."

"No reason you'd be used to it, but it seems like your uncle had quite the collection."

"Is it safe to read?"

"Let's have a look." She reached for a set of gloves as the chime above the door went again. A pair of guys walked in. "Hello."

"This the place that buys antiques?" one guy asked, voice low and growling.

"We do if we like the look of them," she said, eyes flicking over the men. They were obviously two halves of a set, the front one the mouth and the back one the enforcement, all lean muscles and twitchy eyes. They didn't scream drugs on the first sweep, but certainly trouble. "Do you have something you're selling?"

"Got some guns that'll be of interest," said the front one, nodding out the door.

"I'm helping this client just now, but if you want to let me know when would be good for you to come back, I can evaluate those for you." She glanced at Levi who had pulled up to his full height, eyes focused on the guys like a gun dog.

"We're not planning on being around long. Can you see us now?"

Lisa's smile tightened.

"I'm very sorry, but I can't stop what I'm doing," she said, inclining her head towards Levi. "Can you wait an hour?"

"Come on, Stevie. Let's go get a beer," the muscle said, sneering. "I'm sure we can find something to do in an hour."

"Right you are, JT," the man now known as Stevie said, bobbing his chin. "Sure we can."

They stepped back out and Lisa waited for a beat, holding her breath.

"What horrors," Levi said, breaking her focus.

"Yeah," she said, turning to look at him. "Sorry about that."

"Not at all. You were perfectly polite," Levi said with a grin, looking her over. "Much more polite than I would have been, especially given—"

The door burst open from a kick, the chimes clanging as Stevie and JT came back in, guns in hand.

"Fucking knew it," Lisa muttered, yanking the knife from beside the book and slipping it in the back of her jeans. JT shoved the door shut as Stevie took place in front of the counter, eyeing them both up.

"Should've been nicer to us, girly," JT said as he pointed the gun at her. It was a long, double barrelled thing, real enough to be a concern.

"We reserve the right to refuse service to people showing threatening or abusive behaviour," she said, pointing to a sign on the glass case.

"You're going to refuse a bullet?" Stevie asked, waggling his handgun.

"Just get out of my shop, will you? There's nothing to rob." She opened the till, showing them the stacks of coins. "You want the cash? There's a hundred in change and that's it."

"Bullshit, place is full of things we can pawn off elsewhere," Stevie said, foot tapping a glass case.

"Good luck with that on their insurance, idiot." Levi laughed, stepping in front of the counter. His broad frame blocked Lisa from immediate fire and while she was grateful, it was a dumb move.

"Shift over, Romeo," JT said, flicking the gun over to the left.

"I don't think I will," Levi said, shrugging. "You should turn around and leave."

"Hey, he said to move," Stevie barked, whipping his gun up in a vicious arc. It made a wet, thumping sound as it clocked Levi's jaw, sending a spray of blood over the book, the counter, smattering over Lisa's neck. She yelped, grabbing the back of his jacket.

"Come stand with me," she said, tugging him towards the flip top. "He can come here, right?" she asked, watching the two men.

"No, he can't," Stevie said, "You can come out and join him, though."

"All right, that works too," she said with a smile.

"Lisa," Levi hissed, and she shook her head.

"Relax, not my first hold up," she said, opening the top flap and stepping out. "No need to make this nastier than necessary, is there guys?"

"Least one of you has sense." JT snorted, looking her over. "Might even be nice enough to take you through the back, have some one on one time since you were so rushed before."

"Wouldn't recommend trying that," Levi said, vibrating with anger.

"What are you going to do to stop me?" JT asked, hefting the weapon again. "He your boyfriend?"

"He's a client. I'm examining his book, like I said," Lisa said, tapping the tome on the counter. Her hand landed in some of the blood and her stomach clenched at the heat of it.

"Why's he so keen to get in front of a bullet for you then?" Stevie asked, waving his gun in Levi's direction.

"Human decency, I imagine," Lisa said, snaking a hand to her hip. "Most people don't like having a gun pointed at them. Makes them uncomfortable."

"You don't seem too 'uncomfortable,' " JT said, leering in a bit.

"Not my first hold up. It's a family business. This shit happens now and then."

"I don't think she's taking us serious, Stevie," JT said, stepping closer. "I think we should show her how serious we are."

"I opened the till for you, dude. I'm taking this seriously," Lisa said, stepping sideways so he could see the drawer, the coins and crumpled notes. "Take it. No bother to me."

"Something about this ain't right," JT said, sniffing the air like a prey animal. "Something's off."

"Stop being an ass, JT," Stevie said, glancing at his friend. "If you're going to do it, take her into the back then get the hell on."

"You can't," Levi said, throwing an arm in front of Lisa. "For God's sake."

"Levi, calm," Lisa said, laying a hand on his wrist. He was freezing. Shock from the hit must have been setting in, his whole frame buzzing.

"You can't expect me to let this happen," he said, eyes flashing. She'd never noticed they were so green. She wondered if it was tears. It was sweet, that he felt he had to do all this. This wasn't her first rodeo. She kept reminding him of it.

"It's okay. Trust me," she said, gripping his wrist a little harder. "You're not going to hurt him while I'm with JT, are you?" she asked Stevie, looking in his eyes.

"Might knock him out and come and join you two," Stevie said with a wink. She blinked, swallowed the gag rising in her throat.

"Fuck off, Stevie. This way," JT nodded to the back door, grabbing her arm as he dragged her through.

The room was a workshop, all power tools and spotlights, with an old, low couch at the back of the space. JT made straight for it, shoving her onto the cushions.

"Easy. I'm not fighting," she said, sitting herself up before he launched himself on her, squashing her into the back.

"Sensible, girly. Would be a shame to have to mess up that cute face of yours," he said, kissing her neck, pawing at her chest.

"Yeah, I'd hate that," she said, shoving one hand down the back of her jeans. "You do this a lot?"

"If I see a pretty thing," JT said, licking her. She shivered but didn't flinch, finally getting a hold of the knife.

"I do get told I'm pretty," she said, tugging her arm free. "It's a great distraction."

She shoved the knife into his neck, hissing as it pierced through the other side and caught her arm. Squirming out from under him and yanking the knife with her. He was bucking around on the couch, unable to get a grip as his feet slipped on the spray, spreading blood everywhere. She hoped absently he wasn't a needle user. She didn't want to go through any tests. They took a damn age to come back. She'd got under his vocal cords so he couldn't make a noise, which was what she wanted, but he was doing a good job of wrecking the place.

This would be a bitch to explain to the police, but she had the bruises on her arm, and her new cut, and the very earnest witness that was Levi.

Two shots cranked out from the shop as she contemplated whacking him over the head with one of the power tools. She worried Levi had done something brave. It was never smart to be brave.

She shoved herself down, out of range of sight, sighing as she heard JT start to gasp, dying fish noises. Inconvenient, even in death. She crept forward, dagger still in her hand, and slithered up the wall to peek through the window. She couldn't see anyone in the shop front, which could mean Levi tried to run, which would be sensible, or tried to fight, which was less so.

Slipping through the door, she closed it as quietly as she could. There was a dripping sound somewhere, rhythmic and insistent like a clock ticking. She peered over the displays, trying to see if there was any indication of a struggle or more blood. The book was missing from the counter. Unlikely Stevie meant to pawn that, so either Levi had darted or there had been a scuffle.

Glancing towards the door, she caught the reflection of something in the glass, long legs splayed out on the floor. Fuck.

She slid forward, knuckles white on the dagger as she scanned for a sign of Stevie. Reflections from the cases bounced back at her and she couldn't hear much over the thump of her pulse against her skull, the beat bouncing against the dripping elsewhere.

Rounding the counter, she saw the shape of Levi and beside him, the book, cracked open and steeped with blood over the pages, pooling at the base of it. God, that was too much. That was as bad as what she'd done to JT. She knelt, grabbing Levi's shoulder to turn him and assess the damage. Maybe he'd been shot.

She knew something was wrong and recoiled as her fingers touched skin, and only skin. There was no fucking body in Levi's skin.

She skittered backwards, bumping onto her ass and pushing herself back along the floor, away from the shape that should have been Levi and still had his face, but there was nothing in it.

A hand snaked round her shoulders, grabbing her up and crushing a palm over her mouth. There was a wet warmth at her back, the shape of someone pinning her.

"Shut up. It's still here," Stevie whispered, holding the gun beside her, pointed out into the shop. She'd started to shake, unable to take her eyes off the pelt of what had been Levi on the floor in front of them. It looked like he'd been split down the front from chin to crotch, just a chasm of red in the middle.

She mumbled something against Stevie's hand and he shushed her, thumb tapping on her nose.

"You gonna be quiet if I let go?" he asked and she nodded, hand clenching down on the dagger hard enough to make two knuckles pop. "Okay, stay with me. We're going for the door, all right?"

"Yeah," she said, craning her neck to see him. His face was puffy, a bloody slit across one cheek sagging open.

"JT still alive?" he asked as he let go of her.

"No," she said, shaking her head. He didn't look good, sweating and pale. She could see a wound in his shoulder that was responsible for the patch on her back. "I stabbed him."

"S'about fair," Stevie said with a dull nod, glancing at the workshop. "Just you and him through there?"

"Yeah, I left him on the sofa. What did this?" She nodded to his wound, the blood on the floor.

"Not sure. I've only caught glimpses. It's quick. Sharp." He gave a laugh, tapping the gun to his cheek. "My teeth are cold. That's how fucking sharp it is."

She nodded, thinking of her shop and her grandma's blades. They were sharp.

"If we need weapons, I have some," she said, tipping her head towards the corner. "Kept ready. Gran always did it."

"We just need to get out. We go together. There's no hope of one of us taking that thing down."

"Did you bring it with you?" she asked, low as she could, suddenly aware the dripping had become louder.

"No. I went to whack your buddy. Then he was on the ground, bleeding like I'd sliced him. And there were…fucking claws, in my face."

"I do think you're exaggerating somewhat," said a voice deeper than ice, deeper than cold water.

Lisa froze, muscles rigid and screaming in fear.

"Run!" Stevie yelled, shoving her shoulder and sending her stumbling forward, tripping over herself to avoid the displays, the body-skin thing. It didn't work, and she was flat on the floor, face beside the book as the air went out of her.

A splatter coated along her back and then there was a body beside her, the warm stench of blood and meat wafting over as Stevie collapsed. His blood was still hot, pouring out of a hole in his throat. She tugged her arm underneath herself, dagger close, tried to scrabble forward.

"Easy, Lisa," she heard and stilled, that awful voice behind her. "I won't hurt you."

"Not finding that easy to believe," she said, surprised at the sound of her own voice.

"Turn around."

She shuffled, pushing up, but her hand was slick from the gore and she fell back down. Grunting with pain, she flipped over.

Something towered over her, huge and broad and slathered in blood. It was white as chalk in spots, the sort of colour you got in preserved skin, and what may have been arms ended in sets of wide, vicious claws that reminded her of a bear's. She was shaking, cold from the fluid over her and the adrenaline draining in a long, cool line down her spine.

"I killed the other guy," she said, not sure why it felt relevant.

"I heard. Such a clever creature. Your grandmother was the same."

"What?" That snapped something in her head, eyes going to the old shrine.

"She was so experienced. No idiot would harm her without regret. I wouldn't expect you to be anything less."

"How'd you know her?" she asked, trying to stand. One of those broad hands caught her as she began to tip, setting her on the other side of Stevie. She realised there were four arms, each stacked upon the last, which elongated its torso. That's why it was so tall.

"She served me well, in certain spaces," the creature said, leaning down to peer closer at her. It smelled of ocean and rot, the scent of brine and dead things making her stomach turn. She bit into her cheek to stop the roil of bile.

"Did she bring you back with her?" she asked, wishing her gran was here.

It laughed, long shape rippling with the movement. "No, one cannot take things such as me with them."

"Sorry," she said, glancing up. It was still staring at her. She could see herself reflected in the eyes, one large pair in the centre like hers but flanked by smaller, round ones at the far top and bottom of the snakelike face. Maybe more like an eel. They all blinked together and she looked away, down to the blood. "Can I ask a question?"

"Of course."

"Why'd you kill Levi? I mean, I'm not sorry about the guy through there, or much about Stevie, but, uh." She paused, fear gripping her. "I don't mean to complain about your actions, but what did Levi do? He was trying to help."

"Did you need his help?" it asked, sniffing her lightly.

"Not really. I was trying to tell him that, but he meant well with it. And you seem to have, have eaten him? I don't really know how to describe that." She pointed to the skin, refusing to look. "Seems a touch overkill. And I stabbed a guy."

"You did, with someone else's knife."

"It was Levi's," she said, holding the blade up.

"Do you know what I am?" it rumbled.

She laughed, shaking her head. "No idea, sorry."

"A shame. It means additional training."

"Pardon?"

"I suppose it's an excuse to come in and see you a bit more," it said, shaking that broad, pointed head. "I'd wanted our courtship to be less formal, but alas, I will have to take more drastic steps. You may want to look away for this part."

The creature began to bubble, the skin flexing and swelling like burning milk before it started to flatten, pooling down and mixing with the blood before moving to Levi's skin. It rose like bread, stretching up and filling with a wet hiss until he sat up, wiping blood off his face with a jacket sleeve.

She should have looked away. Her stomach twisted, and she threw up beside Stevie.

"Sorry."

"It's no issue. Are you all right?" he asked, placing a hand on her shoulder and rubbing her back.

She was going to die. She would die despite having stabbed that bastard in the neck. Now she wouldn't get to dig out Gran's diaries and check what the fuck she'd been doing. "I don't think I'll throw up again."

"An excellent starting point. Do you have my disk?"

"It's on the other side of the counter," she said, trembling. He slipped off his jacket, heavy with carnage, and draped it round her shoulders.

"Get it for me, and I'll explain."

She went to the flap, skittish as a colt and clinging onto the counter for support.

"Here." She set it on the glass, the dark stone shining bright under the lights. She'd started polishing the lower half of the sigil, the twisting shape luminous. He leaned against the counter, long fingers tracing over the metal she'd worked.

"You're just as good as she was, you know," he said, a smile playing over his face. A human face. She could still see the other one, corpse white and blinking, in her head.

"She trained me."

"After your parents died."

She hadn't told him that. "It was a bad accident. Dylan and I were lucky to survive."

"Much more than luck, I promise," he said, cupping her cheek. "Or I should say, a necessary sacrifice. Your mother begged me to let you both live. Better two die than four. Easy numbers."

"What are you?" Lisa asked, feeling her skin tighten with dread. She closed her eyes.

"My true name is Leviathan, he who seeks in the dark. He who covets and desires and wants." His voice tipped back into the old, deep thing it had been in its true form. The hand on her cheek was soft, gentle, rubbing one thumb along her cheekbone.

"Demon," she said, peeking a look. He was gazing at her, eyes green as the stone. Covetous, indeed.

"Precisely. Your grandmother was a beautiful woman, and a wonderful priestess."

"She never mentioned it."

"Not age appropriate. Your mother was due to be next. Then when the crash happened, she called me too early, before she was trained, and bargained your safety." He removed his hand, leaning closer to her.

"I don't remember it."

"Marianne didn't want you to. Too upsetting. Then the cancer took her, before you were ready. I worried you'd be stolen off by someone before I could make my proposition. Claim you."

"You talk like it's guaranteed."

"It is. I won't force you. There's no value in such undertakings being unwilling. But there's two dead bodies in your shop and the police will ask questions, and I can make that all go away. Your skills are excellent. You have the eyes of a dragon."

The phrase struck her like a slap, a comment her gran had said more than once. Eyes like a dragon, always looking for the next piece for her hoard. He smiled at her, all teeth.

"I don't know the first thing about this."

"You're already doing so well. You killed for me. Mourned my loss."

"I thought you were human!"

"And you were sad I was dead."

"I mean, yes. I was."

"And you killed that idiot with my knife."

"That was a knife of opportunity, if that's even a thing. I didn't know I was killing for you, just to protect the you I thought you were. Oh God."

"And it worked. You killed him. You're good at it."

"I'm good at defending myself. That's not the same. Gran always taught us to look after ourselves and anyone else who needed it."

"I bet she did."

She opened her mouth and closed it again, the world spinning around her. She'd known there was something weird with Gran. They all knew, but she thought it was fucking grave robbing.

"Do I have a choice?" she asked, glancing at the disk. It was beautiful. She'd loved working it, the way the stone warmed to her. She traced the long line, up to the crack, tapping the break lightly with her finger.

"There's always a choice. Everyone wants to be wanted." He nearly pouted, watching her hand. "You're too good to be wasted here, playing with trinkets. Learn with me. Join with me. You've already given me a sacrifice. It's not so far to take the last step."

"What is it?"

"Let me have your blood." He plucked up her injured arm. "Freely given, your gifts for mine."

"That's it?"

"I take this, you become mine." He brought her arm up towards his mouth, looking at her as he did. "Are you willing?"

She swallowed, throat tight, and nodded. "Yes."

"I'll give you so much."

He buried his teeth into the wound at her arm, cold blossoming out from the bite. She grabbed onto his shoulder, crying out. He pulled away, mouth bloody and far, far too many teeth in that smile.

"You're marvellous, just as marvellous as she was."

She couldn't speak, the cold running through her like a fever as her vision blurred.

"Don't fight it. When you wake up things will be perfect."

Flaking Red Paint

by Armand Rosamilia

It began, simply enough, with a wink.

A clear, bright day. A Saturday. No school until Tuesday, either. Monday was a holiday thanks to some President dying or something or other.

None of that mattered to me when the new neighbor winked at me.

Mom had waved at the man with a smile. Grocery bags needed to be unpacked before the ice cream melted or her TV dinners thawed.

By the time I dropped the first round of bags and Mom had given me the look that said to be gentle with the vegetables and Coke bottles, the man was already gone, tucked away inside his house. I slumped a bit and finished helping with the groceries.

That night, when Dad got home from work, my parents went across the street to the new neighbor's house and introduced themselves.

"That's what all good neighbors do," my mom explained.

She'd asked if I was coming. I shook my head. I didn't want to meet him. Not yet. The cold claws up and down my spine paralyzed me, being within a few feet of this man who'd winked at me... I told her I had homework to do.

"You're off until Tuesday," Mom had said and frowned. "She gave you homework?"

I shrugged. Her stare pierced me, and I fought the urge to look away. If I broke eye contact, she'd know I was lying.

Just as I felt the sweat beading on my brow, knowing I was about to blow it, Mom gave a shrug back. "There will be time for you to meet him in the future. The Hansen's lived there for twenty years and the Montgomery's for thirty before them. I'm not sure who actually built the house, but it was one of the first on the block."

Later, I would find out it was the very first house built not only on the block but in the area, which used to be covered in woods. My grandma showed me pictures of the area once, and there was nothing in the pictures but trees.

I would figure what went on in these woods, before our house and all the other houses were built, when the first settlers came to the area, felt there was something wrong, and steered clear.

Until one man decided to embrace it and built his house.

I watched my parents approach the neighbor's house, Mom holding a Bundt cake and Dad wearing his sport coat that was too small for him now. They awkwardly held hands to show the new neighbor how loving and friendly they were, but I knew it was a lie. In later years, I'd look back and know their marriage failed years before I was born. I was an accident, and I don't say it to gain sympathy or so you'll pity me. Especially after what transpired in the house across the street.

My birth kept them together. A sense of obligation. They promptly separated the day I went off to college. I drove away in my dad's old clunker (he'd recently purchased a Dodge Charger as part of his midlife crisis), and he already had his bags packed and in the trunk. I don't think my parents ever spoke again after that. Not that it mattered in the grand scheme of things.

The man who'd winked at me met my parents at the door before they got the chance to knock. He was smiling and shook their hands. Took the Bundt cake. Shared a laugh.

I watched from my bedroom window upstairs, ashamed I had been frightened into staying home and not meeting the old man. He looked friendly from this distance. He'd done nothing more than wink at me.

As my parents turned away with smiles, a job well done, the old man hesitated at the threshold. He looked directly at me, hidden in my room, and then he winked again. I'm sure of it.

I stepped back in fear as he closed his front door.

I didn't see him again for over a week. I'd spent my time reading comic books and bouncing a tennis ball against the back of the house until my mom took it away.

The school week went by quickly thanks to having a day off, although Missus Cabrera piled even more work into the four days. I hated her. She had to be the worst teacher in the world. She never smiled. She was mean to me, and most of the time I didn't really do anything wrong.

She was also old as dirt. My mom and dad both remembered her being a teacher when they were in elementary school, too. That should tell you she was ancient.

Saturday morning Mom made me French toast and bacon. Still one of my favorite meals. I was almost done when a knock came at the door.

"Who could that be this early on a Saturday?" Mom asked.

I looked at the clock and it was exactly 9:00 a.m., which back then I didn't consider as being too early. I was still a few years away from puberty and wanted to sleep all day.

I took another bite but didn't chew, the syrup and bread caught in my throat. Mom was talking to the old man, and I'd heard my name. I dropped my fork and pushed away from the table.

"Honey… Can you come here for a second?"

I obeyed but felt like I was being forced to move, my body no longer under my control. It would be a feeling I'd have many times over the next few weeks, in fact. I was being led. My mind was not my own. Call it fate or destiny… I still don't know.

He was there, in the doorway, and he winked at me again with a smile I knew was fake. Oily. Sinister.

I'd never been more frightened in my life. Not even when Mom caught me doing something bad, real bad, and threatened me with Dad's belt when he got home. The bullies in school didn't scare me half as much as this old man and the creepy way he stared at me.

"Mister Lawless has offered you a generous amount to mow his yard. Rake his leaves. Pull the weeds from the flower beds. Isn't that nice?" Mom grinned as if this was the greatest news ever.

I shook my head. I wanted to run to my room, slam the door and shove my dresser against it, never to come out. Never to see this man again.

"Say something," Mom said, an edge to her voice I knew too well. She was trying to keep it together. Dad called it her *civilian slip*, when she let her anger get the best of her. Mom was about to go off on me.

"You don't have to say yes or no right now," the old man said. His voice was much younger-sounding than I expected. He winked at me again. "It was just an offer. If you're interested, just come over tomorrow and you'll find the mower in the shed."

"I'm sorry… He's never like this…" Mom was mad.

The man laughed, another young sound.

I went to bed that night without dessert, but not without a stern lecture from my dad about being neighborly and helping out the elderly and all that junk.

Bright and early the next morning I was across the street and in the shed. I got three steps to the lawnmower before I realized something was wrong.

It was the far wall, bare of any tools. No windows. No marks. Nothing leaning against it despite so much stuff packed into the tiny space. The shed itself might be five feet across by five feet wide, with a darkened window to the left and the right. Shelves sat on either side with rusting tools on them. A small workbench sat in the center of the space, the mower jammed into a spot to the left of the workbench. Rakes and shovels and hoes. Tool boxes. A dozen different sharp objects littered the workbench.

The wall behind all of it was what I couldn't stop looking at. It was a deep red, either painted or splattered.

Blood? No.

I knew what blood smelled like. I'd cut my fingers and shins more than enough times to remember the coppery smell. Mom had once been talking on the phone and cutting carrots when the knife fell and landed perfectly in her foot, blood splashing all across the white tile floor. I remembered the smell of it. This had no smell except for the normal ones you might expect with all these rusting metal objects, grass cuttings, and dirt.

I didn't want to touch the red wall. I didn't want to spend any more time in the shed, either. I took out the mower, made sure it had enough gas in it, and cut the old man's lawn.

By the time I was done, I was drenched in sweat, but I felt good about a job well done. Both the front and back of the house looked great. I stood with my hands on my hips and smiled.

"Lots of weeds around the shed," Mister Lawless said from his stoop. I hadn't heard his front door open, yet there he was. "And in the flower bed."

The flower bed was a bare patch of dirt in the center of the yard. It looked fresh, as though it had been recently added. I hadn't noticed any weeds, but I nodded and went right to work on it.

Mom came over and gave me a sandwich and a glass of lemonade. I wanted to shoo her away. I wasn't a little kid anymore. I ate and drank. Then I got my hands dirty pulling weeds. I'd never worked this hard in my young life. Why did I even bother? Was I afraid of the old man? Was I trying to show him I was worthy of his hiring me to do the work? Was I trying to impress upon my mom how grown up I was? Maybe it was a combination of all these things.

When I finished, covered in sweat, stinking of earth and body odor, I stood near the stoop with the old man.

"You like cats?" Mister Lawless asked me with a crooked smile. He seemed friendly enough, but there was something wrong with him. In later years, I'd struggle to figure it out. I could never put my finger on it.

I did like cats, so I told him so. "Mom won't let me have a cat because she has allergies. Dad hates cats and dogs. All pets. I tried to bring home a gerbil from school once, back in kindergarten. He made me take it back. Same with a lizard. Once, I even won a goldfish at the state fair, but he said it couldn't come home with us, so I gave it to another kid. I cried all the way home."

I was babbling. Mister Lawless made me uncomfortable.

"I need cats," Mister Lawless said. He looked over my head, up and down the street. "Lots of strays in the area?"

I shrugged. "I see a few in the woods behind our house sometimes. A lot of the older folks around here have cats, and they let them roam freely. Dad says not to feed them though, or they'll keep coming back, and he's not going to feed all the strays in the world. He says it's enough that he has me to worry about."

Mister Lawless put up a bent finger. "Your father seems very wise. Wise, indeed. Come back tomorrow, after your chores and homework are done, and we'll talk. I have another job for you."

He handed me what I thought was a ten-dollar bill, but it was actually a hundred. I gulped. I'd never seen such a thing. I stuffed it in my pocket, felt my face getting hot, and thanked him.

"See you tomorrow," I said.

When I showed my parents the money at dinner, my mother frowned. My dad snatched it from me and waved it angrily. "This is going back to him first thing tomorrow. This is too much. When I was your age, I mowed lawns for a dollar. Anything more than five is excessive. I'll deal with it."

I knew better than to say a word in protest. I know my mom felt bad for me; I'd worked all day for nothing. Dad tried to joke around with me later on when I was in my bed, but I just kept reading my comic books, refusing to look at him. Defeated, he closed my door.

I ate waffles the next morning when Dad walked in and tried to talk to me. He had the hundred-dollar bill in his fist. I ignored him.

"I'm doing this for your own good, son. So you learn the value of money." He quickly gave up trying to reason with me and rushed through the front door.

I followed to the window, where Mom joined me. She squeezed my shoulder. We watched Dad bang on the door. Mister Lawless answered with a smile and a cup of coffee in his hand. The two men had words for a few minutes. I noticed Mister Lawless looked amused, always smiling, as he sipped his coffee. Finally, Dad's shoulders slumped, and he stopped waving his hands. He was nodding by the time the confrontation was over, muttering to himself as he came back home.

We never spoke about it, but a week later I found the hundred-dollar bill in one of my jean pockets. I know I didn't put it there.

"Cats. I need cats." Mister Lawless was seated in a chair on his back porch, sipping iced tea and watching as I pulled weeds from the garden where nothing except weeds grew. When I was older I would understand this as busy work. Nothing more than an excuse to kill time, and for Mister Lawless to get his hooks into a young, impressionable me. "Is there a shelter nearby?"

"For what?" I'd been half-listening, thinking about what to spend my money on: comic books or baseball cards. Maybe a bit of both. I knew if I tried to buy a new bike or something big, dad would say no. Especially after the incident with the hundred. Better to fly under his radar and take my crappy old bike down to Wasserman's and spend a dollar or two each day.

"By my reckoning, I'll need twenty-two cats." Mister Lawless chuckled. "Nineteen. I'll not push it this time."

I cocked my head at him. I fought the urge to touch my face with my filthy hands, but everything itched. Always happens when you can't do what you want to do. "That's a lot of cats, sir."

"It is, but it's a means to an end. Can you help me? There will be more money in it for you, although…" Mister Lawless shifted and had a wad of cash in his hands. "I'll dole it out in singles, fives, and the occasional ten. I should've never given you such a big bill. And you should keep things to yourself from now on. A life lesson. The less others know about your business, the better. Do you understand that?"

I kinda did, so I nodded.

Mister Lawless put three ten-dollar bills under his sweating glass. "This is for the discretion fund. Do you know what that means?"

I shook my head.

Mister Lawless nodded, as if he knew I didn't know. "We'll call it a hush fund, and it's for your own good. I'll pay you far and above book value to keep things we do between us." He must've seen the look on my face because he leaned forward and shook his head. "Don't worry, I'm not going to do anything bad to you. Ever. I'm your neighbor. Nothing more. This isn't hush money because of anything uncomfortable happening between us." He added another three bills to the pile. "I need cats, and I need my lawn mowed and the weeds pulled. I might need the shed painted before summer ends."

"Why is one wall painted red?" I asked. I couldn't help it. I wanted to know.

Mister Lawless shook his head and lifted his glass, putting a hand on the money. "I'm paying you for very specific things, and the red paint isn't one of them. No more questions about that. Understand?"

I did not, but knew better than to keep questioning an adult.

"Now, about the nineteen cats I need…"

Three weeks later I had a growing collection of superhero comic books and had put together a set of this year's baseball cards. I was working on a second set when Gwen Summers said something that got my attention during homcroom. She said her cat had a litter of kittens.

"How many?" I asked.

I had never talked to her before. Not so much as a "hi" even. Gwen Summers lived on my block, down at the end of the street, in the biggest house. She always had new bicycles, and her parents had a giant boat in their driveway.

Gwen ignored me at first, whispering to her best friend, Rae.

"How many kittens?" I asked, louder this time, surprising everyone in homeroom, including myself. So far Mister Lawless had talked about cats whenever I worked for him, but I didn't think he'd actually found any.

"Seven," Gwen said, frowning at me. "Why? It's not like your family can afford one if I sell them."

Rae found that funny and laughed.

"I'll buy them. All seven," I said, smiling. "Name your price."

Gwen turned her back on me. "You can't afford one paw."

"I'll give you a hundred dollars for all seven and the mom," I said.

Now she was interested. I knew her family had money, but they weren't rich. If they were, they wouldn't be living in this town.

The last interaction I ever had with Gwen was meeting her afterschool in the woods near the top of the block. I handed her a fistful of fives and tens, and she gave me a box of cats.

Mister Lawless was beside himself when he saw them. "I'll need cages. Can you ask your mom to visit me before dinner? I need to talk with her." He stared at me. "Always remember, this is our thing."

He gave me an extra twenty dollars the next day, after mom had driven him to the pet store. He not only purchased a bunch of cages, but he adopted two cats as well.

"Weirdest thing," mom had said at dinner that night. "He didn't buy any cat food. Nothing but cages. It makes no sense."

And then it did make too much sense, to me.

I waited until the next day after school. Instead of going home, I went to the shed. The cages had been set up, stacked a foot away from the red wall. Ten cats stared back at me, each in its own cage. There were nineteen cages in all.

"We need more cats," Mister Lawless said as he approached the shed. He'd said we. No longer did he need cats. No. We. I was his accomplice now.

I noticed the red paint was flaking at the corners, small chips of it on the floor.

Mister Lawless followed my gaze and sighed. "The work is never done. The wall will need a fresh coat of paint or else this will be all for naught." He smiled at me. "How are your painting skills?"

By the time Mister Lawless did what he'd ultimately planned to do, most of the red paint had chipped off and sat in a pile on the shed floor. I don't pretend to know what really happened. I was a child, easily manipulated. Paid large sums of money. I had a ridiculous collection of comics and cards by the time it ended, and I still own most of that collection and more. I've sold a few items over the years for ridiculous amounts of money, and I suppose it was blood money. Red like that wall in the old man's shed.

Over the course of the next month, I found three stray cats. Mister Lawless gave me an extra hundred dollars for the lot of them. Another student was selling kittens for five dollars each, so I bought his last five. Once more, I was paid handsomely.

"We only need one more," Mister Lawless said, seated in his familiar spot on the back porch, sipping his iced tea. "We need to hurry. The cats are getting restless, and so am I. I can only do so much at my age."

I was weeding again, the never-ending battle with nature. He still hadn't bothered to plant a garden or have me do it, and he'd waved it off when I'd told him I wanted to plant something. It was more about the job of keeping me around, I think. Mister Lawless may or may not have even made sure that more and more weeds grew in the spot to ensure it.

The cats were never fed far as I could tell, and thinking that kept me up at night more than I'd like to admit. I once tried to sneak in a piece of bread for the cats, but Mister Lawless caught me. He never raised his voice, but I could see the look in his eyes all the same. He was more disappointed in me than anything. "They're being fed a special diet. If you mess with the delicate balance, you'll kill them, and I'll have to start over again. Their deaths will be on your hands."

I didn't want that. The cats looked tired but none of them were showing signs of starvation. And yet I never saw a can or bag of cat food for them. No water, either. They were all still alive, but I had no idea how or why.

"How are the cats doing?" Mom asked that night at dinner. By then dad was working later and later, and the rift between my parents was wide enough to drive a delivery truck through. It was just the two of us that night, and for most nights after that.

"Can I get a cat?' I asked.

Mom shook her head. "You know the rules. I can't be around them. Your father isn't a fan of pets, either." She smiled. "Besides, you have all the cats across the street to play with."

"None of them are mine though," I said. I acted like I'd just thought of something, even though I'd been working it over in my head since I'd come home. "What if I had a cat but kept it with Mister Lawless's cats? He'd be cool with it. Then one of them would be mine. I could visit it each day, and Dad wouldn't be wise to it. You wouldn't get sick. Everyone wins."

She thought about it over the next two days. I didn't let her forget. Mister Lawless told mom it would be more than fine with him, and he even offered to pay for the cat. That same night, right before the pet store closed, I picked out a black cat with white streaks on its front legs.

"What are you going to name him?" Mom asked on the ride home.

I knew it didn't need a name. I knew even then that things were about to change. I felt bad for the kitten. Because of Mom's allergies, we kept it in a box in the backseat, so I couldn't even play with the cat. But I named him, anyway.

"Mister Socks," I said, the first name that came to me.

Mom went inside to make dinner, and I headed over to Mister Lawless's house with the cat. He met me in the shed. The paint was mostly chipped away by then, the cats all on their backs or stomachs in their cages. None purred.

Mister Lawless put the cat in the last empty cage and stood back to admire the collection.

I felt sick to my stomach. I knew he was going to either harm or starve all nineteen cats. This was bad. Really, really bad. Thoughts of coming back later that night to free them ran through my head.

"Come back tonight, after your mom has gone to bed," Mister Lawless said. "I need your help with them."

I barely ate dinner and even waved off a slice of Mom's apple pie. She asked if I was feeling sick, and in truth, I was. I sensed everything was about to change. I was about to help a madman do awful things to those cats, even if I didn't know what. I shook my head and excused myself, then headed up stairs. When I knew Mom was asleep I went over to the neighbor's house.

Mister Lawless was waiting for me at the door to the shed. He was in his pajamas, holding a small book in his hand. "Are you ready to change everything?"

"I guess," I said. I was anything but ready. I'd resigned to scream if he started killing the kittens.

We went inside the shed and closed the door behind us. I was trapped with this lunatic.

"Do you know the names of all of our neighbors on the street?" Mister Lawless asked.

I nodded. I'd grown up here. There were only eight other houses on the street. I knew all of the adults and the kids.

Mister Lawless stepped up to the first cage and opened his book. "Just give me the name of someone who lives on the block. Be as specific as possible."

"I only know the adults by their last name," I said. I stared at the poor cats, feeling that they were all about to die. "I'm not allowed to call them anything but that."

Mister Lawless smiled. "That will do. Let's hear those names, young man. But first…" He pointed to a large bucket at my left. "You'll need to paint while you tell me the names. Can you do that?"

"Paint what?" I asked, but I knew. I saw the paintbrush on the bucket. I saw the red paint.

He had his book open and was studying it. For a second, I thought he was ignoring me, but then he winked. He hadn't done that in a while. It made me shiver.

"Say each name loudly and slowly," he said. "Then silently count to ten and paint as much of the wall as you can with one brush full of paint. Start at the corner and move slowly across the wall. It doesn't need to be neat. It doesn't need to cover the entire wall. You just need to do it perfectly. Shall we begin?" He hesitated. "No matter what you hear or see, keep your eyes on the wall or the paint can…and don't stop saying the names or painting."

I did as told, despite my trepidation. I was a child. What else could I do? Despite the hot wind blowing at my back as Mister Lawless spoke in a language I didn't understand, each burst of words coming between me reciting another name from the neighborhood. I painted the wall.

I was less than halfway across the wall when I said the last name.

Mister Lawless said his last strange words.

One of the kittens cried out.

"You've done well," Mister Lawless said. "Time for you to go home."

I turned but didn't face him, sure there would be more red in the room. Slaughtered cats. Death I'd somehow been a part of. But all of the cats were still in their cages, fine as can be. They looked alive, some of them pacing back and forth, mewing to one another.

"You didn't really think I'd hurt these fine creatures, did you?" Mister Lawless handed me five hundred-dollar bills. "Don't let your father see these. He'd be unhappy."

"What will happen to them?" I asked. "The cats, I mean."

"They'll be let free, in a sense." Mister Lawless ran his fingers along the bars of one cage. The kitten inside rubbed up against his fingers. "If you see the cats wandering the street, please don't engage with them. They'll be on a mission."

"I don't understand," I said.

He thought it was funny for some reason. "When you are older, you'll see." He held up the book, now closed. "When you are ready, this will make its way to you."

And the book did make its way to me, on my thirtieth birthday. When I'd ceased to think any of it had been real.

Mister Lawless stopped asking me to come to the house to pull weeds long before then. A FOR SALE sign went up a week after that night. The cages were all empty by then, the red wall flaking by the time the new neighbors appeared.

The rest of our neighbors had been changed though... I noticed they were less animated. Less friendly. They all kept to themselves. Each had their own cat too, which they kept with them at all times. On their laps, spread out underfoot, following them to their cars in the morning, and waiting for them at night when they arrived back home. It wasn't until the book appeared, in a plain manila envelope with no return address, that I understood their behavior. One glance inside the book and I knew the power it possessed, what it would mean for me and my future.

I have my own family now. A wife. A son.

He's about the same age as I was when I painted the wall red. I know this isn't a coincidence, either. I need to build a shed in the yard, too.

Junior has always wanted a cat. I mentally count how many kittens I'll need to make this work.

Diminishing Returns

by P.D. Cacek

Paul leaned forward in his chair and waited for her to come back.

He'd been holding her hand when she faded into the blank-eyed stranger he'd first met almost a year before, just a week after she'd told him about her diagnosis, whispering it in the confessional as if early onset Alzheimer's was a sin in God's eyes.

"But what did I do to deserve this, Father Paul?" she'd asked him, and he'd told her nothing, she'd done nothing wrong. It was just a disease, he'd said, just an indiscriminate, horrible disease, not retribution.

He'd never felt more like a hypocrite.

Paul had seen others, fellow priests and parishioners alike, fade into a mindless oblivion, but it almost seemed like a curse in someone so young and vibrant.

Her hand twitched against his and Paul looked down. Her hand reminded him of his sister Lily's, small and delicate and so pale it looked almost like unpainted porcelain.

Lily. They were twins, she older by three minutes, but he was always bigger, stronger, healthier. When they were children, he'd catch a cold and barely notice it. If Lily caught so much as the sniffles it meant a terrifying race to the hospital and hours spent on his knees praying to God to save her.

Lily was home schooled before it became fashionable. Their teacher, Sister Mary Margaret, was fond of telling Paul how lucky he was that God made him his sister's keeper. He'd taken the job seriously, too—running home each day after school to bring his sister her homework and write down the answers if she was too weak to hold the pencil. Then he'd tell her all the funny things that happened, even if he had to make them up. He'd make plans for what they'd do once she felt better.

Paul hadn't even known he'd caught the German measles until Lily came down with them.

She had died while Paul was at a school assembly. The next time he saw her she was in a small white casket in front of the altar, wearing her confirmation dress and veil and brand new black patent leather shoes. They'd put makeup on her face and folded her hands over her chest. Paul could still remember the feel of her flesh when he lifted her hand to place a flower beneath—cold and hard and rubbery, like a doll's hand.

Like the hand he was holding at that moment. Paul squeezed it gently. "Miranda?"

She blinked and life came flooding back into her eyes.

Along with panic.

"Oh, God. I... It happened again, didn't it?"

"It's all right. It was just for a second or two."

It was a lie. She'd been *gone* almost twenty minutes, but he'd seek absolution for his sin later.

Her hand slipped from his to cover her face. They were in his private office at the rectory, the same office where he'd given his Pre-Cana counseling to Miranda and her soon-to-be-husband and, two years after that, where he held their new daughter before her christening. It was a good room, a private room where she knew she could cry and rage with no one but Paul and God to hear her.

"I'm so very sorry, Miranda."

She lowered her hands. "Why do people keep telling me that, Father Paul? I'm sorry, Miranda. I'm *so* sorry, Miranda...like this was something they did. I'm so sorry your brain's turning to mush, Miranda. I'm so sorry you're going to die and not even notice when it happens, Miranda. I'm so *sorry*. God, I wish everybody would just stop saying that! Why don't they?"

Leaning back in his chair, Paul folded his hands in his lap to warm them.

"Because you're in pain and those who love you feel powerless to help. The only thing we can say is that we're sorry you have to go through this." Paul started to reach for her hand again only to see her move it away. He let his hand drop back to his lap. "And I'm sorry because I can't lift this burden from you. All I can offer is solace and prayers."

She looked him in the eyes and smiled. "Keep your prayers, priest. No one wants them."

"What?"

Miranda blinked. "Did you say something, Father Paul?"

She'd gone away again. Paul shook his head and hoped his smile looked genuine.

"Only that our hour's almost up." Standing, Paul stepped to one side to give her room. "Shall we?"

Nodding, she stood up and faced him. "I appreciate what you're trying to do, Father Paul, but it's not going to change anything."

"But it's something we can do, Miranda. As long as there's life, there's hope."

Their eyes met again and for a split second Paul saw his sister's face superimposed over the woman's. Then she cocked her head the same way Lily had and the light coming in from the window made her eyes flash red.

"If you say so," she said and the illusion was gone.

Paul took her hands and pressed them between his in prayer. "I do. Shall we start?"

"Yeah. Fine. Okay."

Paul waited until she closed her eyes before closing his.

"My name is Miranda Colby," they said in unison, "and I live at 536 West Highwood Street with my husband Anthony and my daughter Stephanie. My name is Miranda Colby, and I am loved."

Pause. Breathe. Begin again.

"My name is Miranda Colby, and I live at 536 West Highwood Street—"

They repeated the memory exercise seven times, as recommended by an article he'd read on the Internet, with Paul silently adding *"amen"* when they finished.

"My name is Miranda Colby, and I live at 536 West Highwood Street with my husband Anthony and my daughter Stephanie. My name is Miranda Colby, and I am loved."

Miranda exhaled and watched her image cloud in the bathroom mirror, taking away the woman she was…the brown-eyed, auburn-haired millennial with the MBA and one rung away from an executive suite…and replacing it with an indistinct blur. It seemed fitting since that's exactly what the disease was doing. One day she'd look in the mirror and not recognize the woman staring back at her.

When the fog began to lift, she took a deep breath and fogged the glass again.

"My name is Miranda Colby," she told the featureless shape, "and I live at 536 West Highwood Street with my husband Anthony and my daughter Stephanie. My name is Miranda Colby, and I am loved. My name is Miranda Colby, and I live at 536 West…"

The glass began to clear again when her husband knocked on the door. He could have just walked in—he'd taken out the locking knob right after her diagnosis at her doctor's suggestion…just to be safe—but he always knocked first.

"You almost done?"

Done? With what? What had she been doing? But the panic only lasted until she saw the brush in her hand.

"I was brushing my hair before going to work. Wait…" *No, not work…I don't work anymore, not since…* Not since she'd gotten lost coming out of the bathroom and had a meltdown in the building's main lobby. She had no idea how she'd gotten downstairs, but she remembered the look on the security guard's face when she *woke up* as he was handing her a bottle of water and telling her they'd called her husband and everything would be okay. Her employers had been very kind and understanding and all the other positive adjectives that came under the HR jurisdiction, but the bottom line was they had a business to run and she was quickly becoming a potential liability. They didn't fire her, but offered a very generous early retirement package she'd have been a fool not to accept.

She might be losing her mind a piece at a time, but a fool she wasn't.

Some days she remembered and spent the day puttering around the house.

Other days she'd wake up and the day would vanish without her noticing.

"Hon?" Her husband—*Anthony, my husband's name is Anthony...and he knows I don't work anymore.* "Are you okay?"

Miranda closed her eyes. "Yes. Be right out. I'm just getting ready to work on...a couple of things. Could you make coffee?"

It took him a moment to answer. Miranda put the brush down on the vanity top and waited. The explanation even sounded weak to her.

"Already done." His voice was soft through the door. "It's in your favorite yellow mug on the kitchen table. And I added creamer and sugar, just the way you like it."

That was something else her doctor had suggested: to remind her of the little things, like the color of her favorite mug or what she liked in her coffee.

"My hero."

"Always, but can you hurry? Your knight in shining polyester needs to pee."

Miranda started laughing as she opened her eyes and then screamed when she saw the face looking back at her in the mirror.

Your name's Miranda Colby... For the moment.

Paul had just swallowed the host and was wiping the rim of the chalice when the howling began. His first thought was that a dog had gotten hit by a car and crawled in through one of the open side doors—it sounded is such pain—but then the wailing took on a human tone and he began to hear what sounded like a word.

The chalice almost slipped from his hand when he turned around and saw her. She was trying to stand, her head thrown back, screaming, clawing at her husband's hands as he held her down. Their daughter, Steffie, was being led down the emptying pew. She was sobbing and there were scratch marks on her right cheek.

Paul didn't realize he was still holding the chalice as he ran up the center aisle until he stopped at the end of the pew and felt its weight in his hand. His fingers tightened against it. "Miranda!"

The howling stopped, and she looked up at him, smiling. The pupils of her eyes were so dilated that Paul wondered if she'd somehow overdosed on her medication.

"You want to hit me, don't you, priest?"

Paul felt the chalice lift in his hand.

Her smile widened. "Do it. Put her out of her misery. Go on, priest, do something worthwhile once in your life. DO IT!"

The chalice made a hollow ringing tone when it hit the polished stone tiles of the floor.

Miranda began to laugh. "You're a coward just like the rest of them…one blow and it would be over, but you couldn't even do that, could you, you impotent bag of meat?"

"I don't know what happened, Father Paul," Anthony said. "She was fine and then she reached over and scratched Steffie. Oh, God, where's Steffie? Is she o—"

He was turning to look down the empty pew when Miranda headbutted him. Paul heard the crack and saw a goose egg already beginning to form on her forehead as she went limp and slipped into the gap between the pew and the hassock. There was a corresponding red bump on the side of her husband's head. She'd hit him just above the left temple. A little lower and she might have killed him.

It took Paul a moment of watching Anthony struggle to get Miranda back onto the pew before he could make his body reach out to help. She groaned, eyelids already beginning to flutter as they propped her up against the back of the pew.

"My God, Anthony."

"She's never been violent, Father Paul," her husband said. "I swear, I don't know what happened. Is Steffie okay?" This time he didn't turn around or take his eyes off his semi-conscious wife.

Paul glanced toward the front entrance and saw Steffie sitting in the last pew between two women. One of the women was dabbing the child's cheek with a tissue. Paul prayed there wouldn't be a scar. "She's fine, Anthony." He took a deep breath. "It's the disease, Anthony. I know it's hard, but it might be time to consider…"

"Putting her away like a wild animal?"

Paul saw Anthony turn. At the same moment, Miranda sat up, pushed against their hands, and smiled. The swelling on her forehead was turning purple. "That's not a very Christian thing to do, is it?" Frowning, Miranda pulled one hand free and touched the bruise. "Owie. Damn, you have a hard head."

"Miranda."

Her eyes slid across her husband's face and found Paul. "That's not my name."

"Oh, no, of course not." Paul forced a smile. "Mandy."

She rolled her eyes. "You think this is the illness, don't you priest? But that's not my name, either."

Paul cast a quick glance at her husband, but Anthony only shook his head. "I'm sorry, can you tell me your name?"

"Legio nomen mihi est quia ego sum multis me."

Paul felt his legs start to give way

My name is Legion, for I am many.

"I'm sorry…what did you just say?"

Paul tried to shift his weight to a more comfortable position but the confessional was small and the thin kneeling pad in need of replacement. As a fellow priest, and because the weather was good, he'd been given the option of saying his confession from a bench in the rectory garden, but declined.

This confession needed the sanctity and safety of the church to surround him.

Paul licked his lips. "I said that I believe one of my parishioners is possessed."

Paul heard the confessor's chair thump against the back wall. "By the Devil?"

"Probably a lesser demon."

"Uh-huh."

When the man remained silent, Paul cleared his throat. "Father?"

"Hmm?"

"Did you hear me?"

"Yes, I heard you."

"Then what should I do? I've been studying the Roman Ritual, but the woman—the person in question—is suffering from a debilitating and deteriorating illness, and I'm unsure how to explain what I believe to her...to the family."

"That their loved one is possessed by a demonic entity?"

"Yes."

"And is this person suffering from a *mental* deterioration?"

Theirs was a smallish community. Paul had no doubt the confessor knew exactly who he was talking about. "Yes."

"What you *will* do is keep quiet."

"But..."

"Paul, are you listening to yourself? Demonic possession in this day and age? Look, we both know there was a time when people suffering from mental illness were needlessly tortured and killed because it was easier to blame their aberrant behavior on the Devil. Fortunately, we now live in more enlightened times."

"I understand that, Father, but I'm sure—"

"No, Father, the only thing you're sure of is that this person is suffering from a deteriorative mental disorder that will only get worse. Come on, Paul, you know as well as I do that despite what Hollywood would have us believe, there hasn't been a real case of possession in decades. What you can do is be there for her...this person and the family through this trying time and *not* go medieval on them. Five Our Fathers and six Hail Marys. *Ego te absolvo.* Okay, see you at dinner."

Paul crossed himself and heard the door open on the other side of the screen. His was the last confession of the evening and dinner was still two hours away, so no one would bother him or even notice he was there.

"God, what am I going to do?"

It was happening again.

Trapped in a void behind her eyes, Miranda watched the hands that had once been hers lift the spoon and stop. They were eating lunch at the table, just the two of them. Steffie had been staying with Anthony's parents since…since…since something happened that he wouldn't talk about.

Something she'd done…but not Miranda…it was the something inside of her that did it…whatever it was…just like whatever it was going to do now that she couldn't stop…

…*please…don't…stop…go away…leave me alone…*

Miranda heard the something laugh. *Make me.*

And somehow Miranda forced her eyes closed and felt the spoon drop from her hand.

"Are you okay?"

…*no…help me…stop it…help…*

Shh…

The eyes opened.

Across the table, the husband looked concerned. Miranda felt the corners of the mouth tense.

"Don't you like the soup? I can make you a sandwich if you'd rather have that."

The mouth smiled. "Meat."

The husband nodded and pushed away from the table. "Okay. I think we have some cold cuts left. Would you like ham or turkey? I'm not sure if we have anymore corned beef."

When Miranda felt tears begin to fill the eyes, she tried to fight…to scream…to stop what had been her hand from inching toward the knife on the cutting board between them…but all she could do was watch as the husband walked around the table toward them.

So easy. It was so easy.

"What is it, Miranda? Don't you want a sandwich?"

The head shook and the voice answered. "No."

"Then what can I get you?"

The lips smiled as the hand drove the knife toward his chest. "Your heart."

Miranda screamed without sound and felt herself shrinking…getting smaller…going…going… *My name is Miranda Colby and I live at…* Smaller…*at…in a yellow house with my mommy and…* And smaller…*daddy and I'm…I'm…*

Gone.

Paul had been expecting the call, but somehow thought it would come in the middle of the night, the witching hour, instead of just after lunch on a warm Saturday afternoon. He'd been dozing on one of the benches in the rectory garden when the "Ode to Joy" ringtone woke him.

A cloud passed across the sun, chilling the air when Paul swiped the screen.

"Hi, Anthony, what's—"

"She tried to kill me."

The sun came out from behind the cloud but the chill remained. Paul stood up, pressing the phone tighter against his ear as he walked toward the rectory.

"Oh, my God, are you all right? Did you call 9-1-1?"

"Yeah—I mean, no. I'm okay. It was just a butter knife, didn't even break the skin, but she tried. If I hadn't… I hit her, Father Paul."

Paul could hear her in the background shouting gibberish in Latin and Greek and Hebrew, none of which Miranda knew, mixed in with something that didn't even sound like a language. Or human. Paul quickened his pace.

"Are you talking to the priest?" the voice yelled. "Did you call to tell him you got a boo-boo? You pathetic piece of shit. Tell that priest of yours nothing can save you. I'll tear you apart and then go after that worthless offspring of yours. Virgin blood is *soooo* tasty. Did you hear that, priest? Tu exaudi me, sacerdos?"

Paul started running.

"That's not Miranda, Father."

The blood was pounding so hard in his ears that Paul could hardly hear. "I know." He licked his lips and tasted copper. "Don't go near it, Anthony. I'll be there as soon as I can."

Paul could hear it laughing. "Oh, he's coming? Good! Hurry up, priest. I'm hungry."

There was a crowd standing in front of the house when Paul pulled up to the curb. Some faces he recognized, others he didn't. They were all looking at the man sitting on the top step of the porch, holding a bent butter knife while howls and screams and obscenities, in various languages, echoed from inside the house.

Paul could feel the temperature drop the closer he got to the house, the briefcase he'd brought with him growing heavier and heavier with each step. By the time he'd reached the porch steps Paul could see his breath frosting the air in front of him and the case felt like it was filled with iron.

Anthony didn't look up when Paul took the knife from his hand. It was so cold it burned his fingers. How could Anthony have held it for so long? Paul threw it onto the grass and wiped his fingers off on his pants leg.

"She tried to kill me, Father Paul. God, she tried to kill me and I think she would have if I hadn't... It was a lucky punch. I just wanted to get away from her and..." Anthony shook his head and sighed, the cold turning his breath to steam, but he didn't seem to notice that, either. "I know Alzheimer's patients can get violent, but..."

Thou shall not lie.

Paul reached out and touched the man's shoulder. It was almost as cold as the knife. "You're lucky, Anthony, but things are only going to get worse. I know we've talked about this, but I think it's time you consider placing Miranda in a more suitable environment."

Anthony sighed again, and this time the icy cloud was so thick Paul could barely see through it.

"A nursing home?"

"Not exactly." The man looked up, the hope in his eyes shining brighter than the ice crystals that clung to his lashes. "Some friends of mine run a private sanitarium where she can be looked after and cared for…as long as needed. You did your best, Anthony, and I'm sure Miranda knows that, but you can't help her anymore."

"But what do I tell Steffie?"

"For now, just tell her that her mother has gone to the hospital." The lie came easier. "You stay here while I go inside and talk to her, okay?"

"Okay. Father Paul?"

"Yes?"

"Just don't untie her."

"I won't," Paul promised, and that was no lie.

Readjusting his grip on the briefcase, Paul said a silent prayer as he walked up the stairs and across the porch. The door opened before he could reach it. "God help me."

"Deus non est hic, sacerdos!" it shouted as he closed the door. *God is not here, priest.*

The temperature fell the farther he got into the house. By the time he reached the dining room, Paul's breath steamed in the frigid air and he couldn't stop shivering. It was like walking into a meat locker.

Not that it noticed.

Slumped slightly forward, head down, face hidden by a curtain of thick auburn hair, and wearing Miranda's WORLD BESTEST MOM EVER tee shirt, it sat at the dining room table tied to one of the chairs with plastic gardening rope and duct tape.

Paul crossed himself.

"I thought I told you, priest, God isn't here." It chuckled softly. "You look cold, maybe this will help."

Flames erupted from the floor beneath his feet, swirling around his body even as they turned his clothes to ash and charred the flesh from his bones.

Above the crackling roar, Paul could hear a faint hiss as the marrow began to steam. The scream evaporated before it could leave his mouth.

Burned to stubs, his legs gave way, and he fell, his body shattering as it—

Paul's knees and briefcase took most of the impact against the solid, unmarked floor, but it took him a moment and a number of deep breaths before he looked down at himself.

"A parlor trick," it said, and finally looked up.

If this had been a Hollywood movie, the victim's skin would have been peeling and raw, with maggots crawling from the shrunken eye sockets as it vomited split pea soup and did unspeakable things to itself with a crucifix. And that would have made it all easier.

Except for the small bruise on the point of the chin—"a million-dollar shot," his boxing coach at the seminary would have called it—it looked like Miranda.

Paul tightened his grip on the briefcase and stood up as tears filled Miranda's eyes.

"He hit me, Father Paul."

"Cut the crap."

It looked shocked. "Excuse me?"

Placing the briefcase on the table between them, Paul sat down in the chair opposite Miranda's body. "You heard me, I said cut the crap. I know what you are."

It fluttered Miranda's eyelashes. "Really? How impressive." The gentle tone deepened. "Now untie me!"

Paul felt himself start to stand, his fingers actually itching to untie the ropes and free…

He slammed both hands against the table. "No!"

Miranda's face hardened.

"Impressive, but I wasn't really trying. You're not as strong as you think you are, priest. I know… I've talked to Lily about you."

The world shifted, and for a moment Paul couldn't breathe. If he'd had any doubt about what he was dealing with—and there may have been one tiny part of him that hoped it was only the Alzheimer's—it was gone. He'd never mentioned Lily to anyone, especially Miranda.

Opening the briefcase, Paul took out the violet stole, kissed it, and placed it around his neck. He brought out the Bible next and offered a small prayer as he lifted the rosewood and silver crucifix he'd been given at his confirmation. It was identical to the one Lily had been buried with.

"Poor little Lily. She had such a rough start...so small and frail compared to you. I know you always wondered, so do you want to know? It's because you stole her blood while you were both still in the womb. It's called feto-fetal transfusion syndrome Look it up if you don't believe me." It cocked Miranda's head to one side and smiled. "She says 'hi,' by the way."

Paul took a deep breath and felt the points of Christ's feet against the palm of his hand.

"She's with us, you know."

"You're lying, you son of a—" Paul heard his back teeth clink together as he shut his mouth.

"Hit a nerve?" It laughed, and the voice changed to one he'd almost forgotten. "I hated you, Paul. Every day you went to school I prayed you'd get hit by a bus so you wouldn't be able to come home and tell me about all the wonderful things you did with your friends."

It was Lily's voice.

"But it never happened because you were God's favorite. I hate you! And I hate God." It cleared its throat. "That's why she's with us, she died unrepentant, a curse on her lips. Poor Lily is burning in Hell because of you."

Paul lay the Bible down on the table and reached back into the briefcase for the final item. It hissed when it saw the small, rubber stopper glass bottle.

"You think that will make Lily forgive you?"

Paul thumbed off the stopper and stood up as he sprinkled Miranda's body with the sign of the cross. "The blessing of this water reminds us of Christ, the living water, and of the sacrament of baptism, in which we were born of water and the Holy Spirit. Whenever, therefore, we are sprinkled with this holy water or use it in blessing ourselves upon entering the church or at home, we thank God for his priceless gift to us and we ask for his help to keep us faithful to the sacrament we have received in faith. Amen."

It screamed and thrashed in the chair, the skin blistering where the water had touched it.

"Father Paul, what are you doing? Stop it. It hurts! PLEASE!" It was Miranda's voice.

Paul walked around the table, continuing to sprinkle the holy water.

"Paul! Stop it...it hurts!"

Lily.

"Father Paul, please… What are you doing?"

Miranda.

It looked up pleadingly, and Paul threw the last of the holy water in its eyes.

"I will see you suffer, priest! I will eat your soul!"

The demon.

Paul pressed the crucifix against its forehead and watched steam rise from the flesh. Its scream shattered the flat screen TV in the next room and cracked the ceiling plaster.

Paul pulled the crucifix away and ignored the stench from the flesh that came with it. "The Lord is my Shepherd; I shall not want."

It bleated like a sheep.

"He maketh me to lie down in green pastures: He leadeth me beside the still waters. He restoreth my soul: He leadeth me in the paths of righteousness for His name's sake."

"I will destroy you, priest! I will eat your soul the way I… The way… Your sister… Poor little…little…"

It stopped raving and blinked. "What was I saying?"

Paul lowered the crucifix. "Tell me your name," he commanded.

There was a momentary flicker in the eyes. *"Legio nomen mihi est, quia…quia…"*

Then the flicker went out.

"Quia multi me" Paul finished for it. "My name is Legion, for I am many." It nodded. "Okay. Hi."

"Will you excuse me for a minute? I'll be right back."

"Sure."

Pocketing the empty bottle, Paul pulled out his cell phone and walked out of the room. They'd be expecting his call. The first time he'd called was right after Miranda had told him about her diagnosis and he'd promised he'd ask about their long-term memory care unit. The last time he called was to ask about their special unit.

His call was answered after the second electronic ring.

"It's as I suspected. I'll need immediate transport to the address I gave you as soon as possible. Thank you."

There were no questions, just a quiet "Everything has been arranged."

Anthony was still sitting on the front porch when Paul opened the door. The crowd had gotten bigger. "Anthony, would you come inside, please?"

Miranda's husband moved with all the fortitude of a condemned man about to walk his last mile. His eyes held the same amount of fear until Paul nodded and the fear was replaced with something that might have been hope.

From the dining room, Paul could hear it humming one of Lily's favorite songs, "This Old Man."

"Anthony, I need you to go upstairs and pack a bag for Miranda—just a few things: nightgown, bathrobe, toiletries. I've called my friends, and they're sending an ambulance. I'll go with her, but I think you should stay here."

The fear/hope in his eyes changed to relief as he nodded and bounded up the stairs two at a time. The humming stopped.

"Tu exaudi me, sacerdos?"

"Yes," Paul said, "I hear you. Be right there."

Paul stepped back onto the porch and waved. "You can all go home now. It's over."

He waited until they began moving away before he closed the door, so he knew the sidewalk would be empty when he opened it again. A few curtains might twitch when the ambulance arrived, and probably more than a few calls would be made when they wheeled the woman who looked like their poor, unfortunate neighbor out on a gurney.

But it was over.

Paul put his cell phone away as he walked back into the dining room. The temperature hadn't dropped. Removing the stole, he kissed it again and placed it, the Bible, and the crucifix back into his case. He'd have to clean and bless everything once he got back to the rectory.

It watched him with a sad look. "Are you leaving?"

"No, you are."

"Where am I going?"

"Nusquam," Paul answered. "Nowhere."

It always greeted him the same way—cursing, demanding, threatening, and trying to break the restraints that held it to the bed.

"Release me!"

Paul leaned over and made sure it hadn't pulled out its IV tubes before answering. The IVs and feeding tubes were the only things keeping the body alive. There was very little meat on its bones now and what there was oozed a foul-smelling fluid the color and consistency of tar when touched.

The body no longer resembled Miranda Colby. In fact, it barely looked human. But the friars who tended to its needs never complained and took the intermittent outbursts in stride. It wasn't the first Alzheimer's patient they'd cared for, and definitely wasn't the first nameless lesser goat demon to threaten them with eternal damnation.

Lesser goat demons seemed to have a need to act out. Especially nameless ones.

"I said, release me!"

Paul settled back in the chair the friars had set out for him next to the bed and crossed his legs. *"Ludens loqui tibi?"*

It stopped struggling and frowned. It had forgotten Latin a month after it arrived, the identities of Miranda and Lily a month after that. Yet somehow, in the increasingly rare moments when awareness returned, it remembered Paul.

"Are you trying to be funny, priest?"

"No, but I did ask if you were joking. Why would I release you?"

"Because I command it!" It pulled against the cuffs on its wrists and ankles. "You have no power over me! I am..." Its jaundiced eyes glanced around the room. "Where am I?"

It always asked the same questions.

"You're in a monastic hospital," Paul reminded it, "under constant watch and continual prayer."

"Why?"

Paul uncrossed his legs. "Because you're not quite ready yet, little goat. If I sent you back now, what would stop you from returning to plague some other innocent?"

It blinked at him. "I promise, I won't."

"But you'll forget that promise as you're forgetting everything else. It won't be long now. You should have done your homework before jumping into Miranda. Alzheimer's doesn't care what eternal plane you're from. It will slowly and surely wipe away everything that you are, and I intend to sit here and make sure of it. For as long as it takes. Modern medicine is truly amazing… It can keep a body alive even without a functioning brain. You're trapped in a sinking ship, little goat, and when you are finally gone there will be one less demon to contend with."

The eyes that looked out from what had been a lovely woman's face blinked and followed Paul's hand as he made the sign of the cross over it.

He almost felt sorry for it.

"*Vade in pace*," he said, "but not yet."

When its eyes went blank, Paul leaned forward in his chair and waited for it to come back.

The Story of a Lifetime

by JG Faherty

"Leiter, you get the witch."

A piece of paper drops on my desk. A name and telephone number. I groan and shake my head, while my fellow reporters chuckle or snicker. Even Rodriguez, who just found out he got stuck with covering the annual Pumpkin Blaze in McKinley Park.

Maybe I can get him to trade with me. I'd much rather spend a cold October night talking with the people wandering through an acre of jack-o'-lanterns than go through this hell again.

"Maybe this time you can keep it in your pants."

More laughter, while I fight the urge to shove the assignment sheet up my boss' ass. There's not much I can say, though. Booze and babes have always been my downfall, and everyone knows it.

Every October, our paper runs a special insert edition on Halloween. Everything from local legends to the stories behind the Halloween and fall traditions, like trick-or-treating, bobbing for apples, and costumes. We also do some more in-depth pieces on the religious and social aspects of the holiday. The Celtic ceremonies, modern witchcraft, and the wack jobs who throw séances or lavish parties that cost hundreds of dollars to attend.

Anything to sell a few more papers.

In the past, our editor-in-chief, Susan Alden, recycled about seventy-five percent of the material from previous years. But subscriptions have been down for the Gazette, like every other paper, and last year she decided we needed new material. Fresh subject matter. Which meant me and a few other unlucky reporters got stuck covering silly events or interviewing the nutcases who didn't understand Halloween was nothing but an old pagan superstition the candy companies had turned into a commercial goldmine. The kind of nutcases who filed their teeth, stuck designer contact lenses in their eyes, and maybe even drank vials of blood while they proclaimed themselves vampires or werewolves.

Or witches.

I'd gotten assigned to interview a woman who ran a local herbalist shop and advertised herself as a 'white witch.' Kasey Emanuel. The interview had gone better than I expected.

We ended up in bed.

And not just once. We basically shacked up for a couple of weeks, spent every spare minute in bed. But, in typical Nick Leiter fashion, I screwed up. Got drunk and said yes when one of my exes texted me for a booty call.

Kasey flipped. Texted me all sorts of nasty messages. Left messages on my work phone. Even sent letters to my boss. One of which included a death spell for me and the paper.

Nothing happened, of course, and after a while she stopped harassing me. But editors have long memories, and I spent most of the year on Alden's shit list for getting involved with a subject.

This is her revenge. She's probably hoping I screw up again, so she can fire my ass. Well, bite me, Susie. I've learned my lesson.

Forcing a smile to my face, I nod at Susan and glance at the slip of paper. Demora Chow, high priestess of the Left Hand Path. Right here in Rocky Point.

Great.

I flip open my laptop, already dreading the next few days.

Blood splatters the walls in Rorschach patterns and a terrible pain fills my body. I try to scream but my throat is frozen; I can only watch while the evil crone dances and cackles madly around the pentagram. Behind her, horrible faces leer at me with murderous lust in their yellow eyes. My vision blurs as my life runs out of me. The witch raises her dagger—

I sit up in my bed, body shaking, covered in sweat. The scream locked in my throat escapes as a choking gasp followed by a sharp intake of air.

For a moment my bedroom is a prehistoric cavern filled with malevolent statues. Then everything comes into focus and it's just my nightstand and dresser. A sigh escapes me and I sink back onto my pillows. Pre-dawn sunlight turns the blinds gray. No point in trying to sleep anymore, not with my heart racing like I'd snorted a line of coke. Might as well get an early start to the day.

Coffee in hand, I flip open my laptop. A half-hour of Google searches reveals nothing about Demora Chow. She's apparently new in town and whatever she did before this never made the news.

What I do learn is that the followers of witchcraft are as bonkers as I remember. Dancing naked under the moon, demanding to be recognized as a legitimate religion, spells for everything from money to curing cancer. Elder gods, nature gods, no god at all. Apparently, witchcraft and Satanism have more branches to them than the oak tree in my parents' backyard.

With all this in mind, I shower, clip on my press credentials, and head across town.

I don't know what I expected her house to look like, but I wouldn't have guessed a decent-sized white colonial in a generic neighborhood. Not that I thought she'd be living in an Addams Family gothic castle. Only one of those in Rocky Point, and it's been abandoned for years. But I figured she'd be on the outskirts of town, somewhere near the woods to practice her rituals or spells in privacy.

Eyeing her house and the gleaming Audi SUV in the driveway, I frown. What kind of angle am I supposed to take? Serious? Tongue in cheek? After my cursory research, my expectations of her have been see-sawing between bored housewife who uses new-age gibberish as an excuse to have orgies and aging hippie meditating in a cloud of incense. Neither of which would be appropriate for a family-oriented newspaper pull-out.

"Here goes nothing," I whisper, pressing on the bell.

"Hello, Mister Leiter."

To my pleasant surprise, Demora Chow doesn't look like a sexual deviant or a burnt-out stoner. Average height, average build, in her mid-thirties. Black hair with purple highlights, green eyes with a slight tilt to them, and dark red lipstick over full lips. Not beautiful, but she can definitely pull off exotic and pretty without a problem.

"Please, come in." Her voice is smooth and gentle, without a trace of an accent.

"Call me Nick," I say, stepping into the living room. Witchcraft must be a more lucrative gig than I gave it credit for. The furniture is definitely high-end, and all sorts of stunning artwork decorates the walls and shelves. She certainly isn't hurting for money. Unlike a certain reporter.

As I pass her, I catch hints of cinnamon, spice, cloves, and something I can only describe as sex. Not the actual odor of intercourse, but a musky, alluring scent that makes me want to stand close to her. I fight the urge and keep a professional distance between us. No screw-ups this time.

She gives me a tiny smirk, as if she knows exactly the effect her perfume has on me.

"Can I offer you something to drink?" she asks. "Water? Soda? Something stronger?" Demora glides across the room in an easy, confident manner, like she's a CEO and this is her office. Stepping behind a small wet bar, she removes an onyx decanter from underneath.

"Whatever you're drinking is fine," I say, but she shakes her head.

"I doubt you'd like it." She tips the decanter over a small glass and, for an instant, I find myself actually anticipating the appearance of a thick, red liquid.

Instead, it pours out golden amber, like beer with no carbonation.

Stop being a jackass. Too much research, too many bad movies. I find myself wishing once again that Rodriguez had traded assignments with me. Turns out his family wanted to see the Pumpkin Blaze and covering it meant he got them in for free. Bastard.

"It's from an old family recipe. Most people find it too bitter. Perhaps a scotch?" She holds up a bottle of Glenmorangie.

"Fine," I reply. Things are looking up. I've never been one to shy away from alcohol just because it wasn't yet noon. Especially a good scotch. Booze and women, my only two vices. Taking the glass, I tilt it toward her and then take sip, admiring the warm, earthy burn and peaty undertones of superior whiskey. "So, are you ready to open your soul to our readers? I'm really hoping you'll give me something more interesting than the usual pablum about revering nature, or that witchcraft is just a normal religion like Christianity or Hebrewism. I want to grab our readers, send a little chill down their backs."

I doubt it will happen, but a guy can hope.

"Mister Leiter—Nick—I guarantee I have a story that will make your blood freeze." She stares at me from behind the bar and there's something cold in her eyes that tells me she doesn't appreciate my irreverent attitude.

Smooth move, Nicky. Insult the interviewee before you even ask the first question.

"Great!" I take another sip. Maybe her being pissed is a good thing. She might say something interesting just to get a reaction from me. As long as she doesn't clam up, it won't be a boring interview. And if she comes off in a bad light, that's on her, not me. "Where do we start?"

"Let's go downstairs. I'll show you my altar and grimoire, and fill you in on my background." Another short twitch of her lips, as if she finds it impossible to hold a smile for very long, and then she motions for me to follow her.

Unlike the rest of her house, Demora's basement has a comically sinister appearance. Black cinderblock walls, black carpet on the floor, and subdued lighting from small lamps placed in each corner. In the center of the room, she'd painted a white pentagram on the carpet. Gargoyle-shaped pewter candle holders rest on each point of the star.

In front of this eight-foot-wide symbol stands her altar. At first glance, it appears carved from solid rock. But a closer inspection reveals it's nothing but a wooden rectangle spray-painted with stone-fleck to give the impression of granite. Crude symbols and pictographs decorate the sides. Similar ones are scattered randomly across the walls, in an almost neon red.

I have to hold back my laughter. The whole place looks like it came straight out of a Goths-R-Us catalog.

"So, is this where you carry out your, um, religious ceremonies?" I try to make it sound like a serious question, but she narrows her eyes at me before speaking.

"Some of them." Demora steps behind the altar. "Others need to be done outside, under the stars and moon. But not tonight."

"Mmm-hmm," I murmur, pulling out my cell phone and tapping the record app. Moon and stars sounds a lot like code for orgy. Maybe I was right about her. "Tell me, Ms. Chow, when did you begin your study of witchcraft?"

There's no place to sit, so I stand opposite her, the amateurish ritual table between us.

"In thirteen fifty-two," she says in a matter-of-fact voice. I try to see any hint of humor, but her eyes and face still hold that same emotionless look as before, doing a better imitation of stone than her altar.

This time my snort of laughter escapes me before I can stop it.

"So, you're claiming to be over six hundred and fifty years old?"

"You doubt my words." She makes it a statement, not a question. I give her a raised eyebrow in response.

She eyes me for a moment, and then nods. "I suppose it's to be expected. Not many people today are open to possibilities beyond the world they know. Perhaps a demonstration is in order. Seeing, as they say, is believing. Please, sit down inside the pentagram behind you. I promise," she adds, when I don't move, "you won't be disappointed. Or harmed."

Harmed? My only worry is feigning interest in her story. I sit down, doing my best to cross my legs. Not so easy when you're on the far side of forty. Before I can ask another question, she begins removing her clothes. A sudden heat runs through me, one that has nothing to do with the alcohol. I was right. The witchcraft angle is only an excuse for sex.

Here we go again. What the hell, it's worth it.

I drain my scotch and place the empty glass next to me, making sure my phone is recording video as well as audio. Demora's striptease is slow and easy, not slutty. She removes her clothes like she's alone and getting ready for bed, folding them neatly and placing them on the floor next to the altar.

I figure she's going to join me in the pentagram, but I'm wrong. From under the altar, she pulls out a long, black robe, complete with hood, and slips it on. She leaves the front open, offering frequent glimpses of her nude body.

My excitement grows as she moves around the room, dimming the lights, lighting the five candles, and setting up incense sticks on the altar. A sweet, erotic odor fills the air, the same one I'd smelled on her upstairs.

The air grows smoky and burns my eyes, but I can't look away. Through my tears, her blurred form is even more enticing, as if seen through a veil. The atmosphere in the basement is charged with electricity. If this was what all witchcraft rituals are like, I can see myself joining up. She's definitely nothing like that last witch I slept with, who seemed perfectly ordinary until she went psycho on me.

Maybe starting out psycho is a good thing. No surprises.

Demora takes out a small mortar and pestle, into which she grinds handfuls of leaves and powders. I can't imagine how she keeps so much stuff in her small altar. I want to stand and look, but all the motivation seems to have drained out of me.

"What's that?" I ask, trying to pretend I'm not as horny as a drunken frat boy. She favors me with her first real smile, one that actually touches her eyes.

"These herbs will open your senses and allow you to visualize the other realms." She comes around the altar and kneels in front of me, the ceramic mortar in her cupped hands.

"So now we have to smoke something, too?" I motion at the open front of her robe. "I can see everything I want just fine right now."

"No, you can't, and we do not have to smoke anything." She exhales sharply, blowing the ground substances into my face. Each miniscule particle burns like a spark where it touches my skin. I have an instinctive reaction to hold my breath and close my eyes, as if my body knows the contents are poison.

"You can breathe normally, Nick. My herbs work through the skin and aura, not the lungs. Now we can begin the ritual."

I remain still while she unbuttons my shirt, enjoying the sensuousness of her stripping me. There's a moment of disappointment when she steps back, leaving me clothed from the waist down, but it vanishes when she removes her robe. She presses her body against mine, her flesh cool, mine aflame. Everywhere we touch, subtle vibrations ignite across my skin.

She places her lips against my ear and begins speaking in a low whisper. Her hair tickles my skin, but I don't move, totally captivated by her soft voice.

"Close your eyes and see, Nick. See my history in your world. Live as I lived." My eyes close at her command. For a moment, everything is black, but then color creeps back in. Shapes form, become pictures and then movies, always with Demora's voice narrating in the background.

"I was born in Novgorod, Russia, in thirteen thirty-two, a child of the streets. My father an unknown man of unknown origin. My mother was a whore. She was luckier than most; she had beauty, which meant the men preferred her. That meant money, enough to raise me to the age of five and then sell me to the highest bidder."

I'm standing on a wooden platform in a cold, dirty village. The people around me are dressed in rags, all except a few men draped in clean finery. On both sides of me, naked children shiver and cry.

A man in a long fur coat points at me and says something I don't understand. Rough hands grab me and drag me from the platform. A thin blanket is wrapped around me, and I'm shoved into a drafty carriage. The man sits down next to me and offers me a cup of liquid. I drink. A moment later, I grow dizzy, and the world fades away.

"It wasn't until much later I found out the man who purchased me was a mage, a disciple of Astralagoth, come to town to partake of the auction.

"He took me across Europe to Scotland, where I spent the next eight years as his property, learning the ways of magic."

I wander the halls of a dark, drafty castle. There are hardly any windows. My bed is a pile of animal furs atop moldy straw. My only companions are the old man, a cook, and an ancient crone who tends the fires and empties the chamber pots. My days are spent reading musty tomes and learning to mix herbs and liquids.

"On my thirteenth birthday, he came to me and told me the time had come for me to begin my true education. From that day forward, my studies revolved around the dark arts."

I stand before a black pit deep within the bowels of the castle. I'm naked and cold. Tentacles burst from the void and grab me. Penetrate my orifices. The master shouts at me to cast the demon away, but I'm in too much pain to think.

The scene shifts. I'm older now and still at the pit. A creature with three heads—dog, bear, goat—attacks me. Violates me. I try to banish it but my incantation fails.

Another demon, and another. Same result. Over and over, the weeks and months passing in endless torture, my body constantly raped, drained of fluids, and ravaged by teeth and claws.

A thousand screams but no relief. My dreams are filled with nightmares, my days worse. Yet each brutal attack brings with it a lesson. And as years go by, I gradually learn to control the beasts of Hell, to bend them to my will.

On the day I successfully call forth my first demon and set it upon an innocent, my master looks on like a proud parent.

Demora's voice caresses me. Each whisper, each soft breath, sends shivers through my body. *"At the age of twenty-five, he set me free to make my way in the world, moving from country to country, starting my own covens in his name, and in the name of my master's master."*

Time flows by, years blending into decades into centuries. I move from one town to the next, doing the master's bidding by establishing covens devoted to the demon Astralagoth. Age means nothing; I draw the life energy from my sacrifices to maintain my youth. With each ritual, each victim, my power—and that of my Dark Lord—grows a little more. Empires rise and fall, miracles of science and engineering become commonplace. Europe, Asia, the Americas. I travel them all, spreading evil like a hellish plague. In this manner, six hundred years passes.

Until I arrive in Rocky Point.

The vision fades. I open my eyes and find I'm alone in the pentagram. Demora is behind her altar once more, barely visible in the fog of incense smoke. I try to stand but she motions with her fingers and my muscles freeze.

"We're not quite done, Mister Leiter." She reaches under the altar and removes something I can't make out. Her naked body captures my attention again as she moves toward me. I want to look away but I can't. She runs a hand down my chest, each touch making me shiver with delight while at the same time, nausea rises in my stomach and bile burns my throat.

"There is something in you," she whispers. "Something I have not sensed in ages. You are like I was, innocent yet open to corruption. The kind of person who could stand beside me and enjoy all I have to offer, spend eternity in a paradise of our making."

Something inside me. I know I have a darkness. It's gotten me in trouble before. Led me down many a wrong path. But I've never let it get the best of me.

Am I like her?

I don't want to believe it. But her offer is...tempting.

Demora moves her hands from me and with our flesh no longer

touching, my head clears, just a bit.

"I've been wrong in the past, though," she continues. "Not everyone is willing to give up their soul in return for endless pleasure. There are some who would prefer to cast me out of this world."

Something cold and hard pushes against my chest. She has the blade of a large, ornate knife pressed diagonally between my breasts.

"I give you a choice, Mister Leiter. One you should not take lightly, for I have offered it to very few. You will go home and think about what you have seen. Tomorrow, I will come to you. If you say yes," she pauses, and soft lips nibble at my neck. "A new life will be yours, a life where no desire is left unfulfilled. If you say no," the pressure against my chest increases, becomes a sharp sting as the blade breaks my skin. "Then I'm afraid you won't be making your deadline."

She pulls me to my feet. I stand there, light-headed and unsteady, not really sure what was real and what was drug-induced hallucination. Demora hands me my shirt.

"Get dressed." After a moment, I do, while she stares at me with the cold, blank gaze of a reptile. When I finish, she points at the stairs.

"Go now, Nick Leiter." Her voice is flat, as if I were no longer worthy of being in her presence. "We will speak tomorrow." She opens a door I haven't previously noticed because it's painted to match the walls. It shuts behind her and I hear a lock click.

I head back upstairs and out to my car, squinting as bright sun hits my face. My head pounds like I've drunk a whole bottle of scotch instead of one glass, and it requires all my concentration to stay in my own lane on the way across town.

Back at my apartment, I take a long shower and try to make sense of what I experienced. The visions, the muddled thoughts.

I find myself growing more and more pissed off as my head clears. Who the hell did she think she was, messing with me that way? What if I'd had a bad reaction to whatever shit she'd dosed me with?

I'd gone there expecting her to be a little weird, not batshit crazy. I wonder if this was something she did on a regular basis. Maybe it's her way of getting people to sign up for her freaky cult. Lure them with sex, threaten them with death. Plenty of nutty people out there who'd fall for it, even embrace it. Hell, god knows I was tempted. But now I can see her for what she is. A psycho. And Nick Leiter's mother didn't raise her son to get involved with psychos.

But what about the others, the ones who say no? What happens to them?

A picture forms in my mind, Demora and her crazy acolytes burying bodies in the woods.

I don't believe for a minute she's been around more than six hundred years and can summon demons, but that doesn't mean she isn't dangerous.

I'm beginning to think I've got a much bigger story here than a fluff piece. I may have stumbled upon a serial killer. A female Charles Manson or Jim Jones.

So what next? I have to do something, but it's hard to focus with my head still muddled. Usually, I do my best thinking with a drink, but that's the last thing I need. Instead, I brew a cup of tea and return to the couch. I could call the police, but what evidence do I have? And I can't just accuse her in print. She could sue the paper. Should I go the investigative journalist route and join the cult, expose her from the inside?

This could be my big break. The story of a life time.

The afternoon sun is warm where it plays across my body. Together with the tea, it helps relax me. Tiny dust motes dance in the beam of light from the window and I can't stop staring at them. My eyes start to close and I let them. I'll feel better after a nap.

"It's time to make a decision, Nick."

Demora stands before me, dressed in the same open-front robe she wore in her basement. The sharp tang of incense surrounds her and her form is blurred by clouds of smoke. Her body is still beautiful, but knowing what's inside her dampens any lust I might have felt.

"You're not real," I say, and even in my dream-state I know it's true. You need a swipe card to get into my building, and my apartment door has a lock and deadbolt. She might be nuts, but I doubt she's accomplished at breaking and entering.

"Dreams and reality intersect more often than you know," she replies. *"What say you?"*

"Go to hell, you lunatic. I'll make sure the whole world knows about you. And then when I have my Pulitzer for breaking the story of the wicked witch of Rocky Point, I'll be sipping champagne while you rot in prison."

She gives me a sad smile, but there's fire in her eyes. *"That's too bad, Mister Leiter. I'd hoped you'd be more...receptive. You could have enjoyed pleasures the likes of which very few ever experience. Instead, you'll know the opposite.*"

She closes her robe and leans down.

"*Come to me, Mister Leiter. Your master awaits.*"

Her face expands until it fills my entire field of vision, and a deep, rumbling laughter echoes inside my head like thunder.

I jerk awake from the nightmare and try to stand, but my body is held in place. My couch is gone and I'm naked, bound to a cold, metal chair. Smoke surrounds me and the cloying scent of incense burns my eyes and lungs. Through the fog, I see gray cinderblock walls and a cement floor. The walls are covered in arcane symbols and calligraphic letters.

The same type that decorated Demora's altar.

Demora!

My first thought is that I'm still dreaming, her drugs affecting me even in my unconscious state. I pull against the ropes crossing my chest and binding my feet to the legs of the chair. My hands are tied behind the chair back. The ropes cut into me, and it's only then I start to believe maybe this isn't a dream after all.

I'm really in Demora Chow's basement.

How I'd gotten there didn't matter. More of her tricks, or maybe I'd never even left. What mattered now was getting the hell away from her.

As if summoned by my thoughts, her voice sounds behind me. "You're awake. Good. We can begin."

"We're not beginning shit," I say. My voice rises and gives away my fear, but I keep talking. "I've had enough of your drugs and your crazy ceremonies. Let me the fuck out of here. Maybe I can't prove any of your other crimes, but this is kidnapping."

I hear movement, and she makes a tsk-tsk of disapproval.

"Mister Leiter, you amaze me. A man who makes his living finding the truth in things, and yet you still don't believe it when it's right in front of you."

She emerges from the smoke. Nude once more, she holds a long metal pole in one hand and her ornate knife in the other.

"You won't be leaving here, at least not the way you imagine. My craft requires certain sacrifices."

Sacrifices? The crazy bitch is talking about murder! Terror sends my heart racing and I feel no shame when I beg for my life.

"Please, don't do this. I won't write the article. You can keep practicing your spells and whatever, I won't bother you. You don't have to kill me." My voice cracks at the end and tears run down my cheeks.

"Kill you?" She shakes her head. "No, you're wrong. What my master demands is much worse than that."

She lifts the pole and brings the end close to my face. Red-hot metal glows, and heat radiates from it. I struggle against the bonds but they're too tight.

"Look carefully at the instruments of your delivery. First, I will mark you, so your soul can properly transfer to the other side. Then I will release you from this place."

My heart skips a beat and visions of freedom race through my head until she waggles the silver knife and laughs. My brief hopes crash and I cry harder, pleading for her to let me live.

"It's much too late for that," she says. "Now you'll serve me in a different way."

Sickening-sweet incense envelopes me and the air grows heavy. Demora vanishes into the smoke and the harsh sounds of some foreign language reach me. Prayers to her unholy god. My only hope is to escape before she finishes. I rock back and forth again, trying to tip the chair. If I can slip free—

A neon red star shoots toward me and agony explodes in my chest as Demora presses the poker against me. I scream and then my throat tightens, cutting off the sound. My flesh sizzles and the rich odor of frying meat overwhelms the incense smell.

The smoke dissipates and reveals the witch standing before a much larger altar than the one in the other room. She's placing the branding iron back into a small hibachi grill. I look down at my chest, where a pentagram-shaped blister is already forming beneath blackened, cracking skin.

"The sign of the Master," Demora says. "You are his property now." She steps away from the altar and a whimper escapes me, but she leaves the iron behind.

With the slow, easy motions of a cat, she moves behind me. Her breasts are soft against my back and her hands run lightly up and down my arms, fingernails caressing while she intones more words in her secret language. Her voice grows louder and faster, and then I'm screaming again as she digs her nails into the brutalized flesh of my chest, tearing open the fresh burn and peeling away the injured skin.

I shout until my voice gives way and I can only sit there, panting, a nova of pain radiating outward from my center. Tears blur my vision and my ears ring. Demora is gone, and I twist wildly from side to side trying to find her.

"Goodbye, Mister Leiter."

Fingers grab my hair from behind and pull my head back. She cries out in my ear.

"Astralagoth, for you!"

The room spins and an icy wind blows over me. The cold numbs my flesh everywhere except the wound in my chest. Demora, the altar, the walls, all revolve faster and faster, until they're nothing but a dizzying whirl of colors. Then the psychedelic tornado moves across the room and settles against the wall behind the altar, where it changes shape, becomes an oval. The colors blend together into gleaming silver.

I see myself in the oval as if it's a mirror.

Blood splatters the walls in Rorschach patterns and a terrible pain fills my body. My head hangs to one side, spilling my life in a red waterfall. I try to scream but nothing happens; I can only watch as Demora traces a pentagram in my blood.

My God, she really did it.

The room dims, the darkness creeping in from all sides. There is movement in the mirror. A face, evil, leprous, inhuman. Staring at me with murderous lust in its yellow eyes. Long, curled fingers emerge from the mirror. I see them coming toward me and in the reflection at the same time. Ragged talons reach for my ruined chest.

Hallucinations of a dying brain?

Or Demora's horrible master, come to claim my soul?

Razor-sharp claws dig into my flesh and agony carves through me down to my soul.

Time slows, and I understand the awful truth of Demora's words.

For me, there is no death.

Only torture.

The Furious Pour

by Amanda Hard

The smooth whiskey still burned my tongue, forcing a cough before the remainder reached my throat.

"Too much for you?" MacLaren held his untouched glass by his chin, where even through a smearing of tears and the diffused orange light from the fire, I noticed the gray on his unshaven cheeks. Although several years my junior, he had aged substantially since Alice's death. Grief does that to a man.

"I'm something of a beer man, myself," I sputtered.

I reached for the pitcher my estranged brother-in-law had thoughtfully placed on a side table, but before I could tip the water into my empty glass, a feeling of exhilaration passed through me. The burning sensation disappeared, replaced by a comfortable warmth and a prickle of something that might have been passion in a younger man.

"And there it is." MacLaren gave me a knowing smile. "You taste it. I can tell by your expression."

The blissful warmth spread the length of my limbs and back up again, leaving a spark of tension in my fists. At that moment, I wanted very badly to hit something, to feel the hard resistance of a block or a skull against my knuckles. The gun hidden in my inside jacket pocket called to me.

My brother-in-law, lounging in his chair, just smirked.

The feeling descended. My thighs stiffened and I stood to relieve the pressure in the crotch of my trousers. Swaying with potency and power, I wasn't drunk; I was charged—a full battery, a dynamo rotating in a frenzy. I stamped the floor like an impatient racehorse, and could have ripped the chair apart and thrown it into the fire if I'd wanted. I had just about found a reason why I should when MacLaren handed me a glass of clear liquid and told me to drink.

At the first taste, my mouth soured. I nearly spit it out. My saliva ran, salty and sulphury, in a pool that threatened to overspill my lips. I gasped as the warm feeling of vibrancy and power dissipated, and fell back down in my chair, chilled now despite the fire. I took another sip.

"Water?" I gasped.

"Of a sort. Packs a punch after the other."

Like rubber bands stretched to their limits and then released, my muscles loosened all at once and I slumped in the chair, exhausted.

"You should bottle them together, the whiskey and the antidote."

I noticed then he had not shared the drink with me. His own ice remained chilling the twenty-five-year-old tawny scotch he'd nursed since I'd arrived—a foreign label, not one of "MacLaren's Smoothest," the popularity of which had generated his family's fortune. He raised the glass to me, finally downing the liquid with a tepid smile.

My brother-in-law's given name, I remembered from the wedding invitation, was Benjamin, but everyone, including my sister, called him "Mac." It felt awkwardly informal to me, but addressing him by his Christian name seemed too intimate a gesture, requiring an invitation he had neither given nor I requested.

An uncomfortable silence settled upon us, born not of the tasting but of the absence of our beloved Alice, gone now for nearly twelve years. I had enjoyed my sister's love in childhood, while he had cherished her as a wife, and it seemed that grieving her absence was the only thing we held in common. We clung to it like drowning strangers holding the same life preserver.

"Mac…" My tone gave away my uncertainty.

"I know, Richard." He held out his hand in a gesture that begged my patience. "You're wondering why I asked you here, after all this time. Why now, instead of after the funeral? Why you, when we were little more than return addresses on holiday cards?" I took the hand he offered and he stood, helping me to my feet. "Walk with me, Richard. There's something I want you to see."

The MacLaren estate was remote, even for rural Illinois. Bright green flashes of oddly angled lightning illuminated the roof of the distillery works, as silent as the cold air which swirled about us as we walked to the carriage house where MacLaren kept his vintage Rolls-Royce. My sister had waved to me from the passenger side window two weeks before she died. I had been distracted, and remembered her last gesture as only a happy flutter of fingers and gold bracelets.

He drove in a quiet, determined way, and it seemed breaking the silence might damage the moment. I didn't question him, even as he turned the car toward what looked like an abandoned factory. He stopped at a security gate to fan a handful of hundred-dollar bills at the video surveillance monitor. The gate lifted, and he drove us inside an open-ended warehouse where over a hundred men shouted and cheered from their positions around an elevated boxing ring. In the center of the ring, two men swayed and circled each other, trading jabs with ungloved fists.

"A fight club?" I had to ask.

It seemed uncharacteristic, but MacLaren was a man I really only knew through my sister's letters, and the depth of any person's depravity is only known to those they've entrusted to their bosom or their bank account. I felt inside my jacket pocket for the gun's familiar and reassuring shape.

"Have a drink," he said, handing me a silver flask. "Straight this time. No chaser."

He led me through the pungent crowd of sweating and shouting men to a cluster of folding chairs, two of which were immediately lowered for us. Bookies in harlequin-patterned shirts and their similarly-dressed runners collected and traded paper markers from the crowd around us. On the floor beside the ring, a group of what looked to be homeless men stood or knelt around the ring. Many of them were bandaged, several bloodied, and at least two laid on the ground moaning. We sat down and MacLaren nudged the flask.

"Have a drink," he repeated, more sternly this time. "It's warming."

I unscrewed the cap and tilted a shot of the pale whiskey into my mouth. The alcohol began its searing journey over my tongue and almost instantly I felt a powerful elation as a young man's strength returned to fifty-year-old joints. I felt my lungs increase their volume, my heart pumping with twice its efficiency. Had I access to a mirror, I would probably see the lines around my eyes had smoothed, and my graying hair had returned to chestnut. I couldn't say how he had done it, but my brother-in-law must have bottled the damned Fountain of Youth.

"Feel like getting in the ring?"

Surely he was joking. Or was he?

I took another drink from the flask, nearly emptying it. The second swallow was smoother, less aggressive against my mouth. My thigh muscles rippled and contracted, and I started to stand.

MacLaren put his hand on my shoulder and gently pressed me back to sitting. "Just watch for now."

Two fighters climbed between the ropes and faced each other, as ill-met as any street fighters. One was small and twitchy, probably a few years past being classified as a runaway. The other was older, with a patchy gray afro and the skin lesions of an alcoholic gone too long from a binge. A referee in a loosely knotted bow tie leaned over the ring and waved a fifty-dollar bill between the fighters. He then held up two canvas duffel bags for the crowd to see, and tossed the bags in the center of the ring. From the other side of the ring, a bell chimed, three times in quick succession.

The two fighters made for the bags immediately. One reached in and pulled out a crow bar, while the other held up a wooden Louisville Slugger baseball bat, studded through with nails.

Another single bell chime ended the betting, and the crowd settled. A tense quiet fell into place. The fighters moved to the center of the ring with their weapons. The one with the crowbar spun it between his hands, while the man with the baseball bat took a couple of practice swings at the air, his eyes bulging and lips pulled back. The crowbar-wielder thrust the weapon forward, in perfect timing to block an attack from the baseball bat. The two men traded minor cuts and scrapes as they circled the ring, around and around. The crowd responded with enthusiastic cheers and jeers, but I found it all rather tedious. The fighting was inelegant. Amateurish.

Another chime sent the fighters to their corners.

"What are they doing? What kind of a fight is this?"

My brother-in-law ignored me, standing and removing two metal flasks similar to the one he had given me from his pocket. He motioned to one of the runners and gave him the flasks, which were passed up to the ring. MacLaren raised a hand and motioned to the two fighters, who nodded their thanks as they received the unexpected pick-me-up. As each downed his whiskey, MacLaren took his seat.

"Observe," he said to me.

The fighters responded to the liquor immediately. Another whistle blew and the two flew toward each other, weapons raised overhead only for the seconds it took them to meet, and then they were on each other. A single tangled mass of arms, legs, and jabbing metal and spikes spun in the circle, wildly and madly scrambling to land their blows. And then there were no fighters, only sensations and images. A curtain of blood pelted the spotlights as one fighter slammed the crowbar into his rival's skull. A spray of tiny hair-covered pellets were propelled outward as the spiked bat met the other fighter's grasp. Again and again, blow after blow, metal finding flesh, bone and wood cracking together, and from the screaming center of the ring outward, the deafening voices of fighters and crowd were made one. And then there was my own voice, loudest of all, exploding from my mouth, screaming along with the others for a culmination, a winner. For a kill.

No bell marked the end of the battle. The referee looped a rope around the leg of something and pulled it to the side of the ring. It might have been a man at one time, when it had solid bones and an attached head. In the center was a tower of blood and gore in a patchy afro, jaw hanging askance and missing most of its left hand. It doubled over as the referee lifted its good hand in the air. When it fell to the ground, the bookies gathered beside it. A runner wiped the silver flasks on his shirt and handed them back to us.

"Seen enough?" MacLaren stood, pocketing the returned flasks.

"Are those empty?" I asked.

"Come along back to the car. I'll need you sober for what I'm about to explain."

I hardly felt inebriated. I didn't stagger, my complaints weren't slurred. Frankly, I resented the implication I could get drunk from a few thimbles of his "extra smooth," or whatever he was calling it. We walked back to the car and I slid into the front seat next to him, thinking he had always been a smart-ass, especially after marrying my sister. Somebody should have taught him some manners a long time ago. I certainly could have. I could now, could wipe that smirk from his weasel-face with my bare knuckles. He wouldn't even see it coming. I was fast and light, sly and quick.

"Drink this." He handed me a metal water bottle, the kind joggers carry.

"What's this?"

"Just drink it."

The second the first drops hit my tongue, I began to salivate. A chill followed the water down my throat, dissipating my strength and diffusing the curious rage I'd been feeling. My mouth tasted like a burned match, and an unsettling feeling arose from my stomach.

"That man, he beat the other man to death," I said.

"They beat each other to death."

"For a fifty-dollar bill?"

"They would have done it for a twenty."

"And we sat and watched."

"Now that," he said with a sigh, "is the part that interests me."

I closed my eyes, but I could still see the grotesque image of a headless man, his neck and chest caved in from the blows, arms and legs broken. Dismantled. And I had cheered him on. Screamed for blood.

"I'm going to be sick."

MacLaren reached across me and threw open the car door just in time for me to aim a stream of vomit safely away from his leather upholstery.

"Have another drink," he said. "It might help."

I took a sip, expecting more nausea. When it didn't come, I drank more. The water didn't take the images from my sight, but it neutralized the queasy feeling. Another drink washed the sourness from my mouth and faded the sulphury taste on my lips.

"Is this really just water?"

"Holy water, but yes."

He turned the car along the path through the grounds, and I quietly marveled at the green lightning sparking above the estate. The main distillery building was the source for the strange light. Some environmental reaction to the alcohol, perhaps.

"I don't understand any of this." I sighed. "Where are we going?"

"I need you to see something."

"We've seen enough, Mac. We just watched a man get beat to death."

"Two men, actually." He stopped the car just outside the distillery, got out, and unlocked the front doors, motioning me inside as he locked them again behind him.

"I'm just saying I've had enough. I watched two men murder each other and—"

"I watched my wife die."

My brother-in-law stood facing me, his hands in his pockets. "It was early and I didn't want to get dressed. Alice wanted figs." He smiled. "She'd seen them for sale on the street, the pink ones. Those were her favorite. She wanted to breakfast on figs and champagne." The foyer of the distillery was dark, and he flipped on a series of switches, illuminating a path to the factory floor.

"I offered to call a taxi but she wanted to walk. She said you couldn't enjoy spring in Barcelona from the back seat of a cab. I watched her from the window, watched that white hat of hers bobbing along the sidewalk until she got to the corner. She turned around—I like to think she was turning to wave at me because she knew I was at the window. I watched her head turn toward me, and then…then I watched them blow her up."

"Jesus Christ," I said. I hadn't known he had actually seen the car bomb go off. I had watched Alice learn to ride a bike, witnessed her be crowned Junior Homecoming Queen, and admired her as she walked down the aisle as a bride, but Benjamin MacLaren had watched her die.

"I know why you're here, Richard."

"I'm here because you called me."

"Then let me say, I know why you agreed to come." He waved me forward and we walked together down a long hallway decorated halfway with wood paneling, the upper half showcasing framed newspaper clippings, photographs, and awards from the past half-century. "You feel you're owed something. Maybe half of her estate. Maybe a financial payout. Fractional ownership of the distillery, perhaps?"

"I would never ask for something like that."

"Of course not. But the unjustness, it festers in the mind. It thrives on the passing of time, ferments the anger into something…intoxicating, wouldn't you say?"

"I don't know what you're talking about." I couldn't look at him. If I looked, I might have killed him right there, taken the gun from my jacket and ended the conversation, just as his business trip had ended my sister's life.

"You see this wall, Richard? My family has been very proud of this wall for some time. The awards, the reviews, the newspaper write-ups and magazine articles. But trophies are nothing, compared to genuine triumph."

Perhaps it was the leftover whiskey from the fight, or the fight itself, but I had reached the limit of my interaction with my brother-in-law. All I really wanted was a pale ale and the comfort of my own easy chair. A heaviness settled just behind my ears, demanding an aspirin or four.

"I think it's best if we call it a night, Mac."

He turned slowly away from the wall of awards, a slight smile on his face and an inquisitive furrow in his brow.

"You want to leave? Now? Just when I'm about to bring you into the fold?" He took a step toward the large double doors that separated the office and tasting rooms from the main distillery floor. "Hear me out, Richard. Give me twenty minutes to show you why I brought you here, and then make your choice. But at least have a drink with me before you go." He reached into his pocket, pulled out one of the now-familiar silver flasks, and waggled it. "One for the road?"

At the sight of the flask, the headache intensified, pulsing with my heartbeat and draining me of everything but thirst. I felt myself pulled toward him, focused on the silver square, imagining the burning taste as it infused my blood and made me young and virile again. I wanted another drink. I needed another drink. I followed MacLaren and his flask through the double doors.

A pleasant but starchy smell was the first obvious difference as we traded the air of the hallway for that of the factory floor. Steady whirs and groans came from the huge machines, which churned and boiled the rye, barley, and corn mashes which MacLaren explained made up the bulk of his company's whiskey labels.

"That's lot twenty-three, what we bottle as 'Blue Country.'" He pointed at a huge silver hopper. "Multiple award-winner. My father's most clever creation. He put applesauce in the mash. That's the secret ingredient." He crossed the floor to show me another copper machine attached to a switchboard of lights and buttons. "Lot forty-seven. The secret? Multiple boilings in a very particular order. This is where the 'Smoothest' gets its name. Easily the product behind the most gold stars on the wall out there. My idea. My process, my invention. My best, really, until I came up with the 'Select Reserve.'"

"I don't think I know that one." My headache had spread to my temples, and the repetitive noise from the factory intensified the throb. I wanted the tour to end and the "one for the road" in my belly.

MacLaren turned to look at me, and stood for a moment in complete and unmoving silence. "It's in your blood," he finally explained.

I shook my head. "You mean, through Alice?" I was a page behind and had no interest in the science of whiskey-making. I wanted the drink I'd been promised.

"I mean," he said slowly, "it's in your blood, through your bloodstream. You've been drinking it all night." He put his arm around my shoulder and steered me around the boiler, past another bank of lights and switches, and finally to an elegantly-carved door, equipped with a numeric keypad. He typed a series of numbers on the pad and the door silently unlatched. "After you, Richard. This is what you came here to see."

With a ceiling at least twenty feet high, the room was wide and open, furnished in a century-old style that reminded me of some distant golden age. Circular and geometric patterns decorated the wood floors, accented here and there with astronomical symbols and planetary signs. A large antique globe occupied one corner, a large mahogany desk another, while bookshelves filled end-to-end with old leather-bound books and ledgers lined three walls, and provided a frame for the object which took up most of the space in the windowless room.

Ascending from an enormous copper pot on the floor was a column of copper tubing, ceiling-high and about as wide as a man's shoulders. A U-bend at the top descended the pipe back down to a tapering series of smaller tubes, all of which emptied into a large glass bottle. A heating element at the base of the pot glowed red-orange, and it cast an eerie glow over the dark hardwood floor. Evenly placed up the column were small glass portholes rimmed in steel, giving the whole contraption the look of a giant metal flute.

"This was my father's first column distiller. It's something of an antique now, although I've made substantial modifications to it so it's actually quite modern. Computer controlled, of course, with a backup power source as it seems to want to play havoc with the electricity in this place." He waved a hand at the ceiling, and I looked up as far as the column stretched, up to where small green sparks of lightning danced in intermittent loops around the tubing. Each spark created a tiny burst of pain in my head.

"Is that the whiskey?" I asked, pointing at the glass bottle. A drip of something pale and golden splashed down and sent a circle of ripples across the surface.

"The Select? Yes, it is. Care to sample it straight from the condenser?"

"Doesn't it need to sit for a while? Age in an old port barrel or something, to give it the secret ingredient?"

My brother-in-law gave me a wide smile and picked up a crystal glass from a shelf behind the desk. He opened a valve on the side of the pipe and allowed the bright liquid to slowly descend into the glass.

"This," he said as he offered it to me, "needs no aging. Or more appropriately, my 'secret ingredient' has done the aging for it."

I'd heard of this—electrically aging alcohol through magnetism or some such means. His secret process was causing the lightning, interfering with the power supply.

"You're playing with fire here," I warned him and took a sip of the offered sample. I hadn't even finished the swallow before I felt young again, arrogant enough to criticize the master brewer. "Your buyers hear that you're fiddling with the aging process and it'll be all over. Those whiskey snobs take that stuff seriously."

MacLaren pointed to the desk and took his seat behind it, offering me the side chair, where I sat, extremely disappointed I hadn't been offered a full second glass. He placed a manila file folder in front of me. I noticed, with no small amount of sadness, a picture frame on the shelf behind him: Alice, on her wedding day, holding a sunflower to her cheek, her eyes half closed and the sweetest smile on her lips. She was beautiful, so young and full of life. That she should be dead only a few years later seemed an impossible cruelty.

"Oh, the Select won't be going out to any distributors, Richard. It's a very, very private reserve—only a few dozen bottles. Gifts, as a matter of fact." He noticed the direction of my gaze and placed the framed photo directly in front of me. "She always spoke so very highly of you, bragged on your cleverness. We'd had plans to expand production, you know. Your sister thought you might be bribed to come aboard as a partner to oversee the new operation."

I nearly choked then, on a swallow of nothing but misplaced pride. I'd come here with juvenile fantasies of confronting my brother-in-law, demanding a fortune I had no real right to, and yet all the while he had been planning to invite me in.

"I never imagined being here, running this business, without Alice at my right hand. To tell the truth, I still can't imagine it, and I'm sure that shows in our sales. But my focus has been elsewhere these last years. You wouldn't believe all the research, the experiments, the failures, and finally the success—and there was nobody to share it with. Nobody here for a celebratory toast. Until now."

The headache the whiskey had dimmed now flashed bright behind my eyes. I opened the folder on the desk, but the words swam on the page and I couldn't focus.

"What is this, a contract?"

"A deed of ownership, Richard. To the entirety of my factory. Provided you can appreciate what I'm doing and keep your mouth shut about it until it's all over." He stood and walked around the desk, motioning for me to follow. He paused in front of the distiller and smiled up at the copper column. "You must understand. After Alice died, so much became clear to me. They kill us, one by one, and get away with it because nobody holds them accountable."

"The terrorists?"

"The governments, Richard. The politicians. They make decisions in back rooms, send young men off to die in foreign countries, allow beautiful innocent lives to be murdered. And even as they put on their sad face masks for the funerals, they're profiting from those deaths. They're blood-thirsty warmongers, all of them." He turned to face me, his face serene. "So, why shouldn't I profit from their greed?"

I started to question him. Although grateful to be included in the company, I was still mired in confusion. I opened my mouth to speak, but at that moment a flash of shadow at one of the portholes caught my attention when a splash of what looked like oil slammed against the glass, giving me a start.

"The glass won't break," MacLaren said quietly. "This happens a lot. You'll get used to it."

My feet inched closer to the copper contraption even though I drew my face away. The liquid swirled a black oval against the glass, looking for all the world like a head, twisting and squirming inside the narrow pipe. I gasped as the black oil formed dark sockets and then filled them with narrow glimmering eyes.

"What in the hell is *that*?"

A bi-furcated white tongue slithered out of a slit that might have been a mouth, and the slit pulled itself apart into a gaping nothingness ringed with tiny slivers of silver teeth. In my skin and nerve endings, I felt the vibrations from something infinitely old and helplessly enraged. A scream broke from the pot and echoed up and down the columns of copper chimneys, dripping finally into the collection tank, where the tawny liquid made ripples in the reservoir of whiskey.

I jumped back, but the eyes found me. The mouth in the porthole again tried to speak. An explosion of cold burst at my chest, and through every artery and vein and capillary I suddenly felt an icy fire. I was burning alive, dying there, my heart preparing to explode, my brain about to boil from the heat those eyes shot through me every second.

MacLaren reached behind the pipe for an aluminum baseball bat and slammed it against the side of the tank. The pain instantly diminished, but the echo of that horrendous shriek bounced through my skull, blurring my eyesight and leaving a sickening heaviness in my gut.

"What the goddamned hell, MacLaren—is that a person in there? You sick bastard, are you boiling someone? Get him out of there!" I reached down to open the window over the boiler but my brother-in-law smacked it away. He stowed the bat back in its alcove and shoved me back toward the desk.

"Sit down and I'll explain."

"Who's in that tank, MacLaren?"

"I don't know," he said flatly. He poured a small amount of whiskey from the condenser spigot and brought it to me. "Take a sip, but just a sip."

"I'm not drinking that," I said, but I reached for it. I didn't want it, but I knew I needed it. As before, the drink warmed the cold in my chest and slowed my heart and breathing. The panic subsided. "MacLaren, who is that in the still?" I asked again.

"I honestly don't know. It was meant to be Asmodeus—at least, that was the consensus of the summoning spells—but I think what I managed was Belphegor. It lies constantly, so I can't be sure."

"Summoning spells?"

"You wouldn't believe how hard I worked to sort fact from fiction." MacLaren's face seemed illuminated from within, as pleased as a child describing A-plus schoolwork to his mother. "The movies get everything wrong, but the books—oh, the books leave just enough right to confuse you. They're tricky bastards."

"You're insane."

"No, I'm a genius. I have a whole wall of awards that will attest to that fact."

"Is that, or is it not, a person?"

"Not a person, Richard." He held up one finger. "You can't anthropomorphize it, rule number one. It's a demon. And at this point, its name isn't important. I caught the beast. Decanted it. Your job is to keep it contained while I'm gone."

"Gone?"

At this, MacLaren sat back, hands behind his head, his face a picture of delight. This was his moment. His big reveal.

"The Select Reserve, as I told you, is a gift, reserved for a very special party. That party will meet in New York City at the end of the month—under the premise of peace talks, but you and I know why they're really there."

"Warmongering?" I suggested, trying to remain calm despite the monster swirling in the tank behind me.

"For money, yes. Game-playing with other people's loved ones. I decided after Alice's death I would change up the game board a bit. Instead of fighting a proxy war—"

"You're going to serve them the whiskey. Let them kill each other."

"Instead of the innocent, yes." He smiled and brought his hands to the desk. "You've seen what the Select does, even felt it yourself. Don't think I wasn't aware of how much you wanted to kill me, even as I offered you my fortune."

I looked away, guilt now clouding my understanding of the evening's surreal events.

"And you profit from this massacre exactly how?"

"I get to watch their faces, Richard, as they tear each other apart. Just as I watched my beautiful Alice torn from me. It's called 'justice' and it's sweeter than any brandy."

The thing in the tank groaned as MacLaren pushed the folder towards me again.

"So," he began, ever the businessman, "the set-up is fairly low-maintenance, and since the last of the batch is finishing up, all you'll need to do is keep the heat on and make sure the condenser pressure stays in the green. It's all automated so that shouldn't be a problem."

"Last of the batch?"

"Yes. Oh, and you'll need to recite the containment spells every evening at moonrise, but I've got them all typed out here, phonetically, so you can't mess anything up. We'll go over everything in detail before I leave."

"The last of the Select Reserve? You mean from this distillation?" How many bottles were in storage? Enough for a year or more?

"The last—period. This lot only ever had one purpose."

All the strength left my muscles and I felt myself drooping in the chair.

"How much do you have put away, for your own use?" I asked. MacLaren frowned at me and shook his head. "A case? A dozen bottles?" He continued to frown at me. "Not even one bottle?"

My brother-in-law suddenly stood. "Have you been listening at all to what I've been telling you? You know what this does."

"Yes, I do," I said, standing to face him, feeling the residual effects of the whiskey warming the chill in my extremities. "I feel everything it does, your little elixir here. It gives life, Mac. And you want to keep that from me?"

"It makes a man weak," he protested.

"It makes him strong," I explained, removing the gun from my interior pocket.

MacLaren fell back into his seat, shaking his head. "What now, Richard? Are you going to shoot me? Highjack one of my trucks and drive the shipment back to your house?"

"I want control," I said.

"I would have given you control, stupid. Of the whole factory."

"Of your demon."

MacLaren paled. He swiped his hand across the desk, spilling the folder's contents to the floor. "You're a fool if you think you can control it."

"You did." I flicked the gun upward in a motion for him to rise, then directed him to the distiller.

"I contained it," he said over his shoulder. "One is not the other."

The whiskey's effects drained me, and my vision grew red-tinged. I needed another drink. I poked the gun into MacLaren's back. "Pour another glass—a full one this time—and then you can tell your demon there's been a change in ownership."

"I told you, it doesn't work like that," he said, but he acquiesced and reached down to the spigot.

I lowered the gun for only a moment, just to give my arm a rest from its weight, but that was enough time for me to see my ex-brother-in-law reach for the baseball bat. I brought the gun up just in time to stop him. I fired. Missed.

The uninjured MacLaren dropped the bat and turned to the copper tube behind him, which hissed a spray of steam from the shattered glass of a porthole.

"Mother of God," he mouthed, and then that horrible face appeared at the glass, smiling this time.

Steam screamed from the distiller as the copper fittings bellowed, the metal rippling from the pressure, and a funnel cloud of green lightning expanded around us. I heard nothing but the ringing in my ears and the horrible screeching of metal against metal. I stumbled backward, falling away from the still, the lightning, and into a rain of amber liquid that I tried to catch on my tongue the way Alice and I had caught snowflakes as children. As the whiskey and glass shards poured down, the ceiling above us opened up. The black night was awash with white flames, silvery teeth, and that damned green lightning. The stars themselves seemed to be screaming as I hit my head against MacLaren's desk. What remained of my consciousness registered the picture of Alice, in its silver frame, shattering on the floor beside me.

I don't think I dreamed while I was out. Mercifully, I had one final sleep of peace.

I was shaken back into reality by the police who had already taken me into custody. I don't remember awakening on the floor of the distillery, don't remember reaching out for what remained of my brother-in-law. I do remember that horrifying silver-toothed smile, and the torn photograph of my sister.

They aren't sure exactly how I did it, but they say I confessed to it all. They say I took him apart, my brother-in-law. They say he was turned almost inside out. They say I was found kneeling over him, my hands buried deep in his abdomen, ripping and pulling him to pieces. I don't remember any of this, which I suppose is a blessing of sorts.

What I do remember is the smooth taste of MacLaren's Select Reserve—how it grabbed me from inside and powered me with its eerie, demon-fueled lightning. I can't stop remembering, can't stop the agonizing craving for just one more taste, however small—a shot, even. When I free my fingers, I can almost taste that warmth in the shredded meat of my own tongue. It's almost enough.

A Virgin Birth

by William Meikle

"I want five thousand words detailing your investigation of a little-known piece of folklore by the 5th of January. This counts as twenty percent towards your final grade."

The start of January seemed a long way away back in September, but by the time December rolled around and I still hadn't given it any thought, a certain mild panic set in. By mid-December it was getting close to hysteria when I discovered my classmates had hoovered up all the obvious opportunities. I was left with slim pickings, but I began to see a glimmer of hope when I chanced on an old newspaper report. Yes, I'd left it go too long. Spending Christmas working on my dissertation wasn't going to be ideal, and the title "A Relic Germanic Christmas Tradition in Western Maine" didn't exactly roll off the tongue. But I had a place to start.

An internet search turned up an inn in the very town I was considering as my center of operations. I had to phone them to make my credit card payment and the voice at the other end made it seem like it was an exotic task for them to be performing, but I didn't take any notice at that point. I was on my way.

I arrived in Germanstown in the late afternoon of the twenty-third and would have been earlier but for the fact I hadn't accounted for rural roads and the navigation of such, nor for the taciturn nature of the locals of whom I asked directions.

The Village Inn proved every bit as quaint as its internet presence showed it to be, a cubic black and white, two storied timber building with a sagging roof and a stable out back. It also benefited from an ancient but sound porch and a view over a partly frozen duck pond in the middle of a picturesque square. All it was lacking was inhabitants; at four in the afternoon, two days before Christmas, I had the square to myself. Which made it all the more peculiar when the man at the desk at the inn announced that I had been very lucky to be accommodated.

"We always have a busy Christmas, sir," he said in that obsequious manner that seems particular to rural innkeepers. "But we enjoy our visitors from the city. I think you will find our festivities to your satisfaction."

Of course, I hadn't mentioned my work, nor the fact I would be documenting this visit. I didn't want to have them change anything just because I was watching closely. Looking around my room upstairs, I didn't think I needed to worry; the place was wholly authentic in build, furniture, and bedding. There was a single overhead light fixture in the room and no television, telephone, Wi-Fi, coffee machine, or even an electric kettle. I was roughing it this Christmas.

The dining room more than made up for any inadequacies in comfort upstairs, although, despite the innkeeper's words about the place being full, I ate alone save for a solitary waiter. The food, while not up to metropolitan standards, was hale and hearty, washed down with a strong brown ale from a bottle with a German label I couldn't decipher.

After dinner I inquired from the innkeeper as to the specific nature of their proposed festivities, but he was tight-lipped, so I retired to my room none the wiser, resolving to do some digging on my own behalf in the morning.

I was woken in darkness at some hour of the deep night by the sound of singing. It was near enough I could hear the melody—an old folk song I almost recognized—but far enough off that I was unable to make out the words. I made an effort to rise to check, but the strong German beer I had drank at supper got the better of me. I discovered I was comfortable merely lying there listening. At the last, just before sleep took me again, I made out the final chorus as many voices raised in the song's climax.

The dreaming god is singing where she lies.

Breakfast—taken alone again in the dining room and served by the same morose waiter—was a simple affair of a heavy, dark fruit-bread, strawberry jam and enough black coffee to wash away a small boat. At least it cleared my head of a fog I believed had been caused by the same ale that had made me so comfortable during the night's singing.

My main line of enquiry for the day would be centered on the parish records in the small church that dominated the far side of the square from the inn. It was built of red sandstone eroded by weather over a long period of years, giving it a peculiar, almost melted appearance that looked organic rather than manufactured.

I quickly discovered that my morose waiter was also the warden. He led me, somewhat sullenly, to a cramped room at the rear of the church and left me there with only an oil lamp for illumination. I had intended to broach the subject of the newspaper article that had led me here, the one pertaining to lost customs and pagan rituals, but he had gone without a word, leaving me only with a bookcase of old journals.

The first was merely a huge ledger of births, deaths, and marriages, but the second turned out to be pure gold as far as my studies were concerned, being the journal of the Reverend Gunter Muller, minister of the parish in the late eighteenth century. I quickly discovered the newspaper article had only skimmed over part of a most incredible story.

It is too long—and too German—to relate here, but in encapsulated form, it told of a ritual, brought from Germany with the stonemasons who built the church and the inn. Muller was most vexed by their practices that were performed in secret in basements and cellars. A rite was held during Christmas that seemed to be more of an ancient fertility cult than anything Christian. It was based on a worship of beer or rather, if my reading was right, of something that had been brought with the church stones out of the old land with the beer, in the barrels.

"It is a great blight on our community," he had written at one point, "and one that must be burned out before it can give birth to any more blasphemies. I intend to ask the elders to clear out the inn's beer cellar. That alone would at least be a start, for it is from there that all our troubles flow."

Of course, I was well aware of the long history of the Church's antipathy with alcohol. As I read, I imagined this to be merely another attempt to control the social behavior of the villagers. But the more I read, the more I realized how sorely vexed Muller had been. He appeared to have spent several months in the fall of 1788 trying to persuade the villagers to disavow the cult in their midst without success. By the time it came close to Christmas, he had become frantic. I could not make much sense of the last entry in the journal. It was written in a scrawled, hurried hand.

"If I do not do something fast, it will be born on the morrow. The way will be opened, and the cycle will only repeat again. I am determined. Only fire will cleanse us."

And that was all there was. I searched in vain in the other journals, but they were all older still, in dense, impenetrable German script that gave me a headache just to look at. I escaped the confines of the dingy room and made my way back to the inn, surprised to find that the morning had flown by and that it was already well into the lunch hour.

By now I was getting used to eating alone, with only the ministrations of the sullen waiter for company, so I was surprised when the innkeeper himself approached my table after I had pushed my plate away.

"Am I to understand that sir has a particular interest in our little customs and peculiar ways?" he asked.

I nodded in reply, unwilling to give too much away, but he smiled warmly.

"May I suggest a beer to wash away the dust of our old books?" he asked. "If you accompany me to the cellar, I can draw a draught direct from the cask for you and perhaps explain any questions your reading might have raised?"

I should have known that nothing remains secret for long in a small village such as this, so I gave in to the inevitable. I took on the open mantle of folklore researcher and let him lead me down to the cellar beneath the inn.

Besides, if the beer was anything like the strong dark brew I'd partaken of the previous night, I was looking forward to more of it.

The cellar proved to be much deeper and larger than I could have imagined, a chamber as long as the floor space of the inn above it and some twenty stone steps down into the ground. A single oil lamp lit the cavernous area, and I was only just able to make out the barrels that lined the wall to my left. I had expected normal sized tubs, perhaps up to my waist and no higher, but these, even lying on their sides, were some seven feet in diameter. They were more than ten feet in length front to back, where they appeared to be embedded in the earthen wall. There were three of them, all equally ancient.

"They came out of the old country," the innkeeper said. "They were old even before then and made from trees older still, trees that grew to maturity before Christ walked the Earth, when the Old Gods ruled the forests that covered the northern lands. They are never washed out, and the beer is left to mature naturally, mingling with whatever the old wood wants to give us. Come, take a draught. I saw that you enjoyed one of last year's bottling yesterday. Let us see if this year's vintage is equally as potent."

He moved to the nearest vat where a spigot had been fixed at waist height into the wood. He took a pewter mug from a rack to one side and began to pour. I smelled the heady odor of it as soon as it splashed in the mug.

"I was reading Reverend Muller's journal," I said. "Do you know it?"

The innkeeper laughed.

"We all know it here, sir. It is a source of great amusement to us, for in the end the good reverend took to the beer as avidly as any of us."

His laugh echoed around the cellar and I thought I heard, far in the distance, a choir singing again, the same old song I'd noted the night before. I was about to ask about it when the innkeeper thrust the mug of beer into my hand, the aroma rose up into my throat and nostrils. I could think of nothing else but drinking down the nectar. I raised the mug to my lips and drank deeply.

"Oh yes," the innkeeper said. "The good reverend took to it just fine. It was an easy birthing."

You must forgive me here, for the next few minutes are rather vague in my thoughts. I heard the song swell and grow in volume and now the words were clear to me, although the heady dark beer already had my head swimming.

She sleeps in the dark with the hops and grain

She dreams of the beer in the dark
She sings as she dreams, as she opens the way
And the dreaming god is singing were she lies.

A black droplet fell from the faucet on the barrel, a gleaming, oily egg that seemed to hang there defying gravity before bursting in an aurora of rainbow color. The song rose to a final chorus.

Where she lies, where she lies,
Where she lies, where she lies,
The dreaming god is birthing where she lies.

After that I knew nothing until I woke, fully clothed, lying on top of my bed in the room upstairs. I had the hangover to end all hangovers. It took me a while to focus on my watch, only to discover the afternoon was almost gone.

It was 5:00 p.m., Christmas Eve.

I was surprised to find the dining room almost full when I finally made my way downstairs after a quick shower and change of clothes. The clientele was mainly the elderly, pale of face and dressed in heavy, dark materials that would have had me sweating. I was shown to an empty table, and nobody spoke to me or acknowledged my presence save for the usual sullen waiter.

At least I could not fault the food; I had a sumptuous supper of very rich meat. I suspected it to be something exotic, venison or perhaps boar, but it had been cooked in more of the strong dark beer and accompanied by enough mashed potato that I was quite full, and more than a touch ready for sleep again by the time I was done. But the night was just getting started.

One by one, the guests in the room rose and gave a speech, a memory each of them cherished from the year gone by. Some of them were genuinely moving, and I learned much about the day to day life in the village. I certainly learned more about births, deaths, and marriages than I ever would have from the ledger in the church. There was a singular oddity, a recurrence of a phrase I'd already heard, one that was repeated by almost every speaker.

It was a good birthing.

After everyone had spoken, I realized the innkeeper was looking expectantly at me.

"We ask that our guests participate," was all he said. "Perhaps another beer would loosen your tongue?"

The morose waiter arrived with a pewter pint and placed it in front of me on the table. I had no idea what I might say, but the man had been right on one thing; the beer certainly loosened my tongue. Although, thinking back on it now, I have almost no memory of my speech. The only thing I remembered with any great clarity was raising my mug in a toast, which was answered in kind by all present. That and the round of applause I got when I wished for *a good birthing*.

I realized some time after I sat down that I should be taking notes on these festivities; it was, after all, why I was here. But another mug of beer had appeared before me and right then it seemed to be the most important thing in my life.

After the speeches there came the exchanging of gifts. The innkeeper sat with me for a time, explaining that they still followed the Germanic tradition of gifting on the eve of Christmas itself, saving the next day for proper celebrations and the birthing. It made perfect sense to me at the time, but then again that might just have been the effects of the beer, which was giving me a rather detached, if merry, view of the proceedings.

I was not the only one feeling the festive spirit. Everyone appeared to be taking to the beer with gusto. The noise level in the room rose, and rose again. There was good humor, there was laughter, and there was singing; a lot of drinking songs accompanied by much banging of mugs on tables and sloshing of beer on said tables, clothes, and floor.

The night wore on. Eventually the singing took on a solemn, even morose, quality. Tales of longing for a past long gone, of forest glades and mountain passes and gods who, though sleeping, still sang in men's hearts. I understood almost none of it, but the innkeeper assured me that understanding was not required.

"All that is needed is a good birthing, then next year will look after itself," he said.

I tried to articulate some thoughts about end of year traditions, how they related to the night's festivities and to the pagan traditions in Europe, but all I got out was a laugh in reply.

"There has always been a birthing," he said. "Just as there has always been beer, long before there was a pagan, or a Europe for that matter. But come, it is time for you to receive your gift."

"You have a gift for me? I have nothing to give in return."

"That is not true," the morose waiter said, and might have said more had the innkeeper not stopped him with a stare.

"Come," the innkeeper said. "Let us visit the cellar. I will draw another draught for you, you will receive your gift, and then it will be time to ensure you get a good night's sleep before the celebrations proper."

I let him lead me to the cellar, buoyed by the thought of more of the heady nectar.

Everyone who had been upstairs had now gathered downstairs, standing in a semi-circle facing the massive beer vats. The innkeeper led me through them and over to the same faucet he'd used earlier.

"She is the way," he said in a singsong voice that was answered by everyone in the semi-circle.

"The way is the life," they replied in perfect unison. My sense of detachment was beginning to fade, and I felt a degree of apprehension, a chill running down my spine. But when the innkeeper fetched a pewter mug and poured me a fresh beer all my worries faded away like mist in a strong wind.

The assembly began to sing. I was coming to know the words by now.

She sleeps in the dark with the hops and the grain
She dreams of the beer in the dark
She sings as she dreams, as she opens the way
And the dreaming god is singing were she lies.

The innkeeper turned back to the faucet as the voices rose in the chorus.

Where she lies, where she lies,
Where she lies, where she lies.

A black egg similar to the one I'd seen earlier dripped lazily from the tap and hung in the air defying gravity and vibrating in turn with the song's rhythm.

The dreaming god is birthing where she lies.

The egg shivered over its whole surface and split down the middle. Two eggs now hung below the tap, jet black with a rainbow aurora shimmering around them like hot oil coming off a too-hot pan.

The singing was still going on around me, echoing and vibrating around the room, and with every word the eggs split again, and again. Two became four became eight became sixteen, on and on until they were beyond count and filled the air between where I stood and the vast vats of beer.

It wasn't an amorphous mass; it had a definite shape as the eggs arranged themselves into a vast pair of wings that, when opened out, stretched almost the full width of the cellar. I was facing a dark, pulsating center in the midst of it, a place where the eggs seethed and roiled and the splitting continued at a frenzied pace while the song rose to a final climax.

Where she lies, where she lies,
Where she lies, where she lies.

The innkeeper pushed me forward. The eggs surrounded me until I was lost inside a dancing mass of them. I felt something on my lips, moist, tasting of beer. I gulped at it, eager for more. An egg slid easily down my throat as the last words of the song echoed and rang in my head.

The dreaming god is birthing where she lies.

The cellar receded into a great distance until it was little more than a pinpoint of light in a blanket of darkness. I was alone in a vast cathedral of emptiness where nothing existed save for the dark and a pounding beat from below.

Shapes moved alongside me there in the dark, wispy shadows with no substance. Shadows that capered and whirled as the dance grew ever more frenetic. I knew instinctively that these were the singers from the cellar, come with me to dance in the songs of their dreaming god.

I tasted salt water in my mouth, and was buffeted as if by a strong, surging tide, but as the beat grew ever stronger, I cared little. I gave myself to it, lost in the dance, lost in the dark.

I know not how long I wandered, there in the space between. I forgot myself, forgot everything but the dance in blackness where only rhythm mattered.

I came out of it standing in front of the vats with a mug of beer in my hand and a mob of smiling people surrounding me, clapping my back, shaking my hand, and offering heartfelt congratulations. I could only smile and acknowledge. Something had obviously just happened, but all I could think of was how good the beer tasted. I took a few hearty gulps and felt much better for it.

The innkeeper sent me off to bed with a fresh mug of beer. I have enjoyed it so much that I had another for breakfast. All in all, I have more than enough material for my dissertation. The journey here, so full of simple joy has it been, has proven to be more than worthwhile. All that remains now is for me to go downstairs and wish everyone a very merry Christmas before the festivities come to an end.

The innkeeper has told me it will be a very good birthing.

Complex

by Jason Parent

Carrie knew she'd follow her husband, Liam, anywhere. She'd stuck by him for twenty-three years, through one-night stands, all the drinking and time spent unemployed, fad after obsessive fad, and—worst of all, though not his fault—the death of their only son. Now he was dragging both of them to early graves.

Sometimes, she really hated herself for loving him so much.

But it was easy to focus on all the bad. He had been by her side through multiple miscarriages, had tenaciously campaigned for her during her three failed runs for city councilor, and, most of all, had held her tightly every moment she needed while he grieved the loss of their son in silence.

They had married young—he twenty-one and she nineteen—and had spent nearly every day whether good, bad, or indifferent, side by side, a pair of crutches holding the other up.

Now, Carrie was forty-two. Her back ached. Her windbreaker and jeans were damp with sweat despite the chill. She prayed for a break, dreaming of a foot massage in some St. Lucian resort spa far, far away.

But she prayed in silence. *Twenty-three years and we're going to die out here, in the middle of nowhere, miles from home.*

The sun hadn't set yet, but the thick firs, their trunks packed like cigarettes, blocked out much of the light. What remained was almost a constant twilight under a canopy of lush green darkness.

Until nightfall, when all was black. When the wolves—

Carrie shuddered, then forced her mind onto other thoughts. Something jabbed into her left foot. "Hold on a second."

Liam, hiking a half step in front of her, dutifully did as requested. He tapped his five-foot, gnarled hiking staff that resembled something out of a Harry Potter movie and turned. "What's up? You okay?"

Carrie suppressed a sneer. She hated that staff, which served no purpose she could understand. She hated being out in those woods, and by God, right then and there, she thought she might even have hated him. She closed her eyes and took a deep breath, chastising herself for even thinking such a thing, no matter how untrue it was.

"Could you…" She grabbed Liam's sleeve. "There's something in my boot." Lifting her foot, she pulled off her hiking boot. When she upended it, bits of dead leaves and broken twigs fell onto a forest floor already full of them. Looking at her swelling ankle, she saw a fat black ant the size of her thumbnail traipsing over her sock. She scowled and flicked it off, then put her boot back on.

"Better?" her husband asked, his smile sincere, warm, and full of love.

Carrie nodded. Though the stabbing pain in her foot was gone, she was a long way from better. Night was coming, and—

Again, she forced the thought from her mind, instead tucking her arm around Liam's and holding him close.

As it turned out, they hadn't much farther to go before their messiah halted the group. She took him in as he stood on a fallen tree to address his people, the fifty-four chosen who'd followed him out into that wilderness.

Jericho, the one they called *Messiah*, didn't project an aura of holiness. In a green vest over a flannel shirt, ball cap, and jeans, he looked just about as ordinary as everyone else. His short beard was dotted with gray. A spare tire circled his waist. As the story had it, he was a junkie, prostitute, and atheist until God visited him in a dream and showed Messiah his true self, the reincarnation of Jesus Christ and savior to the chosen few. He awoke cured of his addiction and clean of sin.

Carrie had to wonder if the tattoo running up the side of his neck was the new stigmata. Unlike her husband, she was skeptical of the man's authenticity as Christ rearisen. His knowledge of scripture was adequate at best, and he resembled neither lion nor lamb.

Needless to say, Carrie was dubious of the man's ability to lead them to the promised land. But her husband had seen something in the messiah she couldn't see herself. She'd at first thought it another of Liam's fads, like country music, aerobic kickboxing, and keto. So when he'd begged her to go with him on this not-so-little adventure, she eventually caved, thinking it would be a standard religious retreat filled with "Kum Ba Yah" activities and boxed lunches.

For three days straight, they walked deeper into the forest, never questioning their messiah's direction or even understanding where they were going or why. Thus far, the only positive had been that her backpack had gotten lighter, her food and water supplies nearly depleted. And each night, the wolves—at least a dozen, she guessed, from the howling that kept her awake and shivering at night—drew louder and closer.

Circling, like dogs herding cattle.

Meat.

She had read once that wolves obtained most of their water intake from the prey they consumed. The cold fact did little to rationalize her fear of tearing claws and gnashing teeth.

"Faith!" their messiah shouted, startling Carrie from her thoughts. He extended his arms as if waiting for his flock to embrace him. "Faith is what you have shown me through this ordeal, my brothers and sisters. Never have you questioned that faith, doubted your reasons for following me through this devil's playground."

He clapped, smile spreading to the ends of his cheeks. "Rejoice, for your faith will be rewarded! The time is nigh. Salvation is within our reach. Your perseverance is God's engine. Your belief in Him is righteous and beautiful. When He sings, I listen, and you, the wise, the chosen, you can hear his song through me."

Messiah threw his fists over his head. The crowd let out a chorus of cheers and amens. Carrie huddled beside her applauding husband.

After the celebration ran its course, Messiah waved his outstretched arms to quiet the most zealous of the bunch. "But our herd must be culled. There are those among us who are undeserving of what God will offer His true children." He scanned the crowd, his gaze touching on each of his followers. When it fell on Carrie, she shrank further into Liam as if trying to cram herself into his jacket pocket.

Liam smiled and kissed the top of her head, wrapping a strong arm around her. Though she couldn't put her finger on why, his comfort amplified her own discomfort.

"The devil's beasts will come," Messiah preached. "And I say, let them. They cannot touch the pure among us. They can only take the undeserving. Let your faith in Him and your prophet be your salvation."

A howl split the cold air, silencing both preacher and flock. Messiah chuckled, his teeth shining with saliva. "We camp here for the night." He clapped and everyone broke into their individual family units to find a spot to make camp. As Carrie preferred it, they worked their way as close to the fire as possible.

Night descended with biting cold. Carrie snuggled against Liam for warmth, their sleeping bags keeping her from getting as close as she would have liked. The howling wind whipped into their tent, rattling it on its posts. She closed her eyes and pressed her face into Liam's chest. Her husband slept soundly, a serene tranquility written in the iron smoothness of his face.

She loved him. She resented him. She needed him.

More howls—not just the wind. The songs of night creatures were all around them, voices hungry and desperate out in the cold. The campfire cast shadows as big as mountains against the side of the tent, shapeless, but sure to be full of fangs and fur. As they began to shrink with the fire, one of them definitely looked like a dog.

A very big dog—not a shadow, but a silhouette. Just outside their tent.

Tears in her eyes, trembling against her man, Carrie prayed for a true savior, someone to lead her out of the woods.

And when she heard what sounded like a scream, she prayed all the more.

Carrie awoke to a kiss, then a scream.

Her husband had just planted one on her lips and rolled over onto his back to stretch when they heard a shrill cry, full of agony and torment. It sent the sleeping camp into action.

Carrie clutched her chest, lurching upright in her sleeping bag. Her breaths came so short and fast she thought she might hyperventilate. Her body ached from sleeping on the hard, uneven earth. Exactly when exhaustion had overcame her, she couldn't remember. Ripped from her grogginess by terror, she felt as if she'd barely slept at all.

Liam was on his feet, pulling on his jeans. He had slammed one foot into a boot before Carrie realized what he meant to do.

She wrapped her arms around his leg. "Don't go out there!"

He looked at her, his smile almost patronizing as he gently pulled her arms from his leg. "I'll be right back. I'm just going to go check it out."

"Fuck that!" Carrie scrambled out of her sleeping bag and threw on her shoes and jacket. "If you're going, I'm going." Not wanting to seem weak, she unzipped the flap and headed out into the rising sun.

The air outside was cold enough to frost her breath. She blew into her hands to warm them. A crowd was gathering around the remains of the campfire. A woman who looked to be about Carrie's age knelt beside it, the tattered remains of a sleeping bag crumpled at her knees. Blood covered the front of her jacket. Carrie didn't immediately recognize her; the woman kept keeling over and sobbing into the bag, hiding her face. When she came up for air, sucking in a gasp before bursting back into a snot-riddled wail, Carrie remembered her...

And nearly fainted. Liam caught her arm before she fell.

"Sh-sh-she had a boy." The memory of her own young son lying dead in his coffin flushed through Carrie like dirty water, polluting mind and soul. She covered her mouth with her hand and cried. "Said he was too old to be sharing a tent." She fell into her husband's arms. "He…he couldn't have been more than eleven."

Carrie stared up into Liam's eyes, searching for solace, but what she saw there made her recoil.

Nothing.

The man she had known and loved for the better half of her life seemed completely unfazed by the woman's sorrow. Had he hardened himself against grief and empathy, or did he just not care?

"Two others are missing," she heard someone say. Her eyes remained locked on her husband's.

"That older couple, the Farnsworths. Their tent's torn to shreds. Given the amount of blood, searching for them might be futile."

"We won't be searching for any of them."

The statement was made so calmly, so matter-of-factly, Carrie was momentarily stunned. When it had festered long enough to cause her blood to boil, fingers flexing in and out of fists, she slowly turned to face the speaker, his voice known to her and undeniable: their messiah.

She raised a finger, but before she could lash out at him, another launched his own complaint. An older gentleman with silver hair and a thousand-yard stare said through gritted teeth, "The hell we aren't." His right hand clamped over a dreadful wound on his left arm, just under a tattoo of a snake and the words, *Don't tread on me*.

Messiah didn't flinch. "It is exactly as I prophesized. The wolves have culled our herd, rooted out the non-believers." He nodded toward the man's wound. "It seems you've been given a second chance, Martin. Come, let's gather our things and walk the Lord's path together. We have many more miles to go."

Carrie stepped away from her husband, toward Martin. "Yesterday, you said we were close. Now we have many more miles?"

Messiah smirked. "The culling is not yet complete."

"A little boy is missing. Two other human beings too—good people who chose to follow you because you said you'd protect them. Promised them salvation. We can't just leave them out there. They may still be alive, and if so, they need our help!"

Messiah waved a hand dismissively. "Meh. They were non-believers. Blasphemers. Frauds playing at piety." He turned his back on Carrie and Martin. "They are exactly where they belong."

"That's some bullshit." Martin reached out and grabbed Messiah's arm. The crowd, all except Carrie and Martin, gasped. No one was permitted to touch their prophet. Like monsters kept away by the final flickers of a candle light in some old horror movie, they hovered close, at the ready, waiting for the dying of the light.

The contempt Carrie read in their upturned eyebrows and deep frowns caused her stomach to roil. Martin must have seen it, too. His hand fell from its grip.

Messiah raised his arms, an easy smile warming his face, complementing the dazzling twinkle in his swirling mud-colored eyes. "At ease, my brothers and sisters." He stepped toward the older man and clasped his shoulders. "Martin here has lost his way. I do believe we can help him find it again."

"The only way I'm finding is the one that leads me out of here." Martin scanned the crowd. "People died last night." He threw out a finger toward Messiah. "And *he* wanted it to happen. We're all going to die if we stay here. I'm leaving. Who's with me?"

No one stepped forward. Carrie glanced from face to face, each now set with a sort of cold resignation. But the contempt was still there, directed at Martin.

Are they all insane? Carrie turned to her husband for help. He, too, stared at Martin, the corner of his mouth twitching the way it always did when he was angry.

"Liam?" she whined, her mouth hanging open in worry and disgust. "We should go, too." She reached for his hand.

He pulled it away. "I'm not going anywhere."

She stared at him for as long as she could, looking for cracks in his steely armor. She couldn't figure out what hurt more: that in this, for the first time ever and despite everything they'd been through, he would not stand by her, or that she was experiencing this betrayal in front of a mob of strangers.

No, it was the former, and she thought throwing herself to the wolves might have hurt less. To top it all off, Martin was right. They were going to die out there, if not from wolves, then from exposure, or starvation, or any number of horrors she dared not think of. They would all die: her, Liam, Martin, Messiah, and all his followers, unless someone had the courage to break free from the madness and find help.

"I'll go with you," she muttered to Martin. She turned back to her husband, filled with sorrow and hope, the emotions in her voice unmistakable. "Please?"

He grunted and crossed his arms, all the answer he would give. Didn't she deserve more? Didn't she deserve better?

She straightened her back and composed herself, no longer willing to die following a madman or watch her husband commit suicide along with the rest of the lemmings. If the stubborn mule wouldn't do it for himself, she would have to do it for him, even if it meant going it alone or with a man she hardly even knew.

Just for a little while. He'll see. By the time I get back with help, he'll have come around. And then we can go home...together.

Carrie reached for Liam again, but he refused to budge. "I'll be back with help." She pulled a small circular object from her pocket.

"I have a compass. We can find our way back with this. I've been sneaking glances at it during bathroom breaks and whenever else I can, so I know the direction we've been traveling down to the degree."

Martin smiled. "Clever. Let's go."

They started away, Carrie unwilling to give Liam a third glance for fear her resolve would melt beneath his gaze. Her heart hitched in her chest. Leaving him hurt only second to losing her son.

Carrie set her jaw. She and Martin would leave those fanatics, find their way back to a more civilized world, and never, ever put their faith in any religion or false prophet again.

"You'll never make it," Messiah said. "Your only hope for salvation is with me."

Martin stopped dead in his tracks. His face went redder than the gash on his arm. Turning on his heel, he stormed up to within inches of the savior.

"You're no messiah, Jericho." He sucked in his mucus and spat a green glob into his former prophet's face.

Messiah slowly wiped it off with his sleeve. "Have it your way." He snapped his fingers.

Martin's feet burst into flames.

He screamed as fire crept up his torso. His skin radiated an orange glow just before the fire spread over it, consuming all. It seemed to burn within him as well as without, igniting his breath as it climbed his throat. The flame's heat intensified as it and Martin himself changed through reds, oranges, and yellows, to bright white, and finally to a brilliant blue.

The light was so bright it was blinding. Carrie clenched her eyes shut and shielded them with her sleeves. When she finally opened them again, the fire was gone. So was Martin. A small hill of fine gray ash smoldered where he'd stood.

All eyes turned toward Carrie. Messiah smiled and extended his hand. "May I see that?"

Carrie stood speechless, her mind struggling to comprehend what she'd just witnessed. Her mind slowly registered the weight of the compass in her hand. Without question, she passed it to Messiah.

"Thank you," Messiah said. The compass blinked out of existence. "I am all the guide you will need." He bowed and waved his arm outward. "Now, shall we continue our journey?"

"Yes, Messiah." Carrie stepped backward, her eyes never leaving her prophet's, her savior's, until she stood side by side again with her husband. Liam smiled at her warmly and held out his hand for hers. She took it, and on trembling legs, she took her first step as a believer toward the promised land, where her messiah's will would surely be absolute.

The Black-Jar Man

by Mark Steensland

Early in the morning when the clock strikes four
The Black-Jar Man will come creeping through your door
Quiet as a black cat across your floor
To take your soul away forevermore
— Traditional in the Ark-La-Tex region of the U.S.

So you want to know about the Black-Jar Man, hmm?

I'll tell you what I think: what you really want to know is if it's true. If that poem you heard is only something daddies use to scare their kids into behaving, or if there's some facts behind it. Well it's true, all right. As true as any story we tell each other. Which is to say, every story is true at some part. What good are they otherwise? How else do we learn what it means to be brave unless we tell stories about someone you think is weak getting up the guts to kill a monster? Now maybe in one story that monster is a dragon.

And in another, maybe it's a robot from outer space. Or maybe it's someone with an assault rifle leaning out the window of his hotel room. But if the hero wins, then those stories are telling the truth about how to do what's right.

Not this story.

The Black-Jar Man is about what happens when the monster wins. And maybe I don't have all the facts as straight as they really happened, but it's true, what they say about him. That before he became the Black-Jar Man, he was a planter named Peter Birchmoore. That he grew cotton back before the Civil War. That he was the kind who liked to discipline his slaves himself because he loved how the whip sounded when it hit bare skin.

The way it started, the story goes, was with him whipping a sixteen-year-old boy named Wesley. Peter's wife, Rose, who was seven months pregnant with their first child, was standing on the veranda with her maid, Jinny, watching. Not because she wanted to. No. Because Peter forced her to. Same as he forced all the slaves to gather in the yard outside their quarters and watch him whenever he whipped one of their own.

Now on this particular day, Rose decided enough was enough. And she dared to tell Peter so.

Peter froze like he'd been slapped, that whip dangling from his left hand, dirt sticking to the blood on the end of it, beads of sweat running down his forearm. He caught his breath for a moment, then slowly turned his head toward the veranda and asked, "What did you say?"

Rose realized too late what trouble she was in. But when she looked at poor Wesley tied to that tree, blood running down his legs, and then over at the group where his mother, Tayna, and Abram, his grandfather, were watching, she decided it couldn't possibly get any worse. So she said exactly what she was thinking: "It was only a cup of water."

"Taken without permission," Peter reminded her.

"He thought you said he could."

"And now he knows I didn't." Peter turned away from her, cast the whip to its full length behind him, then lifted his arm and faced forward.

"For the love of God, stop," Rose screamed.

"God is why I won't," Peter said through clenched teeth.

Rose buried her face in Jinny's bosom. The maid hugged her mistress tightly.

Peter cracked the whip again. When blood splattered back onto his white shirt like drops of red rain, he went into a frenzy, whipping faster and harder.

And just when Rose let go of the last threads of hope inside her, Jinny said, "Look, ma'am. Quick!"

Rose lifted her head and faced where Jinny was pointing: to the horse-drawn carriage turning in at the gate, across the cotton fields, 300 yards away. A wave of relief like she'd never felt before washed over her. "Reverend Welltris," she whispered with a smile, then repeated his name a second time, loud enough for Peter to hear her over the cracking whip.

Peter stopped and turned around again. When he saw the carriage, he quickly wound the whip up and approached Wesley. "You're lucky I don't greet my guests looking like this, boy," he said as he hung the whip on a hook in the tree trunk, then faced the group of slaves. "You got 30 seconds to empty this yard."

They moved forward fast. Two of them untied Wesley from the tree. Another pulled the gag from his mouth. Then four carried him to the slave quarters near the barn.

As he climbed the steps to the veranda, Peter shook his head at Rose. "I'll deal with your insubordination later," he said. "Until then, show some decency and put your tears away. The reverend will lose all respect for me if he thinks I allow you to cry for those animals."

Peter made sure the yard was empty, then entered the house through the side door.

Rose wiped her cheeks as she hurried around the porch and descended the front steps to greet the carriage. The driver jumped down, opened the door, lowered the step, and helped the old preacher out.

"Reverend Welltris," Rose said, wiping her eyes again and trying to smile. "Right on time. As always."

"Punctuality is one of the few things I have left, my dear," he said as he took her hand and grinned. But poor Rose couldn't maintain the façade. When fresh tears spilled down her cheeks, Welltris gripped her hands tighter and said he could come back the next day if she wasn't feeling well.

"No," Rose said. "Please stay. I need someone to talk to."

"That's what husbands are for, dear."

"Not when it's about them."

"Oh, I see," Welltris said as he glanced toward the house. "Is Peter here now?"

"Changing his clothes. And cleaning the blood off his face."

"Not his own, I'm guessing."

"Wesley's. I tried to stop him. But that only made him whip harder. Until he saw you at the gate. I daresay the boy would be dead if you'd been even two minutes later."

"You want me to speak to him?"

"I want you to speak to me. Tell me what I should do."

"What does your heart say?"

"That Peter is wrong. That all of this is wrong."

Welltris nodded grimly. "I think the war shall very soon prove you right."

"But until then?"

"What would you want if you were Wesley?"

"Hot water. Clean bandages. Brandy."

Reverend Welltris smiled. "Shall I help you with the tray?" he asked. Rose sighed in relief again and they went up the wide front steps into the house.

In the slave quarters, Wesley had been put onto a table, face down. Three women had cleaned his wounds, but the boy was pale from blood loss and his breathing was shallow. Tayna sat next to him, wiping the sweat from his forehead, then using the same cloth to wipe the tears from her own face.

As one of the women dipped her rag in a bowl of bloody water, she made eye contact with Abram and shook her head as if to say there was nothing left to do. But old Abram knew better. When he saw the pain Tayna was in, he turned away and pushed through the other slaves gathered around the table.

Down a short hall, he opened a door without knocking and stepped in. Bokor was on his cot, smoking his pipe as if he didn't have a care in the world.

"We need the black jar," Abram told him.

"Tayna send you?"

"I'm the one asking."

"And what do you have that I want?"

"Put me in it. Take some for yourself. Give the rest to Wesley."

Bokor laughed. "You think there's enough of you for that?"

"Please," Abram begged.

Bokor could see from the look on the old man's face he wouldn't stop until he got what he wanted. So he set his pipe down and stood up from his cot. He moved a chair against the wall and climbed onto it to open a secret panel near the ceiling. He didn't care that Abram saw where he kept the black jar hidden because Abram wouldn't be seeing anything ever again in a few minutes. He reached inside and took out a bone-handled knife and the black jar, about the size of something you might keep pickles in, except made from pieces of stained bone and black glass held together with a dark red mortar that might have once been blood. After he put the panel back in place, he followed Abram to the front room and pushed through the crowd to Wesley.

When Tayna saw the black jar and realized what was happening, she shook her head and screamed, "No, Daddy. Don't!"

"Hush, child," Abram told her. "I've had enough of this life. Let him work."

The other slaves backed away in fear as Bokor shoved him toward the table and said, "On the ground, old man."

Then Bokor crouched next to him and put the blade of his bone-handled knife on the old man's philtrum, what some call the cupid's bow, that little indentation between the bottom of your nose and your upper lip. Bokor sliced down with a quick stroke, cutting only enough to draw blood. Then he dipped his finger in the blood and smeared it on the inside of the black jar's mouth. Once he held the black jar under Abram's chin, the old man's life came out in a mist, like what you see from a block of dry ice in water. Out of his nose and mouth and into the black jar. As the mist got thicker and the flow faster, Abram's skin paled and shriveled, tightening until they could see every bone. His eyes sunk into his head and his lips peeled back. And when the mist finally stopped flowing, Abram looked like one of those mummies you see in a museum: nothing but a dry husk.

Tayna wailed.

Bokor smiled.

Then he touched the blood inside the mouth of the jar and dabbed a spot of it on his own lip.

Tayna grabbed his shoulder. "What are you doing?"

Bokor shook her hand off of him. "Collecting the price your pappy paid. A little for me. What's left for your son." He licked his lips as he lifted the jar to his chin, and he smiled as that electric blue mist came back out of the jar and went into his nose and mouth.

"That's enough!" Tayna lunged toward him again.

Bokor held the jar away from his face, breaking the flow. "What do you know about it?" Then he dipped his finger in the blood again and this time smeared it on Wesley's lip. The old man's life came out of the jar and went into the boy, and his skin grew less pale and his wounds stitched themselves up. Tayna clutched her face and cried tears of joy. When the flow stopped, Wesley's eyes snapped open and he took big, deep breaths.

Behind them, a tray loaded with hot water, bandages, and brandy crashed to the floor. Everyone whirled and saw Rose standing in the open doorway, her face a mask of terror.

She ran out screaming. Across the yard, past the whipping tree and the woodpile, up the stairs to the porch. She flung the side door open so hard the glass shattered. Jinny and Reverend Welltris rushed into the kitchen through the swinging door from the dining room and Rose went to her knees in front of them, crying.

Peter came down the servant stairs at the kitchen's rear. His blazing eyes found Jinny's. "What did you do to her?"

"Nothing, sir. She came in like this."

"Came in? From where? Wasn't she in the parlor with you?"

Reverend Welltris shook his head. "No. She'd gone to see Wesley."

Peter crouched and grabbed Rose by the shoulders, trying to peel her away from Jinny. "What did they do?"

"Black," Rose said. "A black…jar…"

At those words, Jinny sucked in a breath. Rose screamed in terror again and covered her face, completely hysterical.

"What are you talking about?" Peter demanded.

"Black magic," Rose whispered and collapsed into Peter's arms. He carried her out of the kitchen, through the swinging door into the parlor where he put her on a couch. Reverend Welltris tried to calm her down but she wouldn't stop screaming.

"I'll get a cloth for her face," Jinny said and hurried into the kitchen.

When she turned around to go back to the parlor, Peter stood there, blocking her way. "What is she talking about?"

"I'm sure I don't know, sir."

"I'm sure you do," Peter said as he stepped closer. He was glad when he saw Jinny shaking. "Been a long time since you've hugged the tree, Jinny."

She nodded and pushed tears from her eyes. "A black jar is a way of healing, sir. That's all. Nothing more."

"Then why is my wife acting like she's seen the devil?"

"Because the way it looks, I guess."

Before Peter could ask what that meant, Reverend Welltris slammed through the swinging door. "You better come quick."

When Peter returned to the parlor, he was relieved to discover Rose had stopped screaming. But then he saw she was staring at her hands because they were covered in blood. And so was her dress. And the couch. Enough blood to make a puddle on the floor.

When he rushed forward, Rose faced him, smiling. "Am I having the baby?"

Slowly, Peter lifted her dress and saw she had already had the baby. Jinny screamed. Reverend Welltris made the sign of the cross. Peter quickly covered the corpse with the dress again and said, "Get me a sheet."

But Jinny was frozen, unable to move.

Peter stood and slapped her across the face. "Get me a sheet, dammit!"

"Yes, sir. Sorry, sir."

Behind him, Rose started screaming again. Peter turned and saw she had lifted her dress and seen the baby. Then she passed out.

They got her upstairs into bed. But she wasn't doing well. She was as pale as her pillowcase. Her eyes were rolled back in her head. Her breath was shallow and ragged. Peter was worried she might never fully recover. That the death of her baby had somehow shattered her mind. He stared at Reverend Welltris, sitting at the side of the bed, holding Rose's hand, his lips moving in silent prayer. Peter shook his head in disgust. What good would prayers do? What good had they ever done? He walked to the divan at the foot of the bed and peeled open the bloody sheet to look at the baby again, then went down to the kitchen.

When Jinny turned from the stewpot and saw his face, her legs filled with ice water.

"Tell me what I need to know," he said.

"If I do, it'll be worse than a whipping for me."

"Worse than that if you don't."

Jinny knew what he meant, and so she told him about the black jar and how it worked.

"You really expect me to believe this voodoo nonsense?"

"I expect you can go see for yourself," she said.

Peter nodded, then got his Remington .44 revolver and went out to the slave quarters where he found Tayna at the table next to Wesley, petting his hair while he ate. She stopped smiling when she saw the gun in his hand.

"Stand up, boy," Peter said. "Shirt off and turn around. I want to see if what I heard is true." Wesley looked at his mother and she knew the boy had no choice but to do as told. "Well I'll be damned," Peter said when he saw the boy's back bore no sign of the vicious whipping he had given him. "That's good enough for me. Now tell me which one of you has it."

"Has what, sir?" Tayna asked.

"What did this for your boy. The black jar."

"I don't know nothing about that."

Without looking, Peter pointed the pistol to his left and pulled the trigger. A man collapsed to the ground, dead. "What about now?"

"Bokor, sir," Tayna said, frantic. "He got it. He got the black jar."

Peter went down the hall and kicked Bokor's door open. He entered, leading with the pistol. But when he saw the room was empty, he crossed to the open window and looked out. There he saw Bokor, running, a bag slung over one shoulder. He lifted the pistol and fired, but the shot went wide. Bokor stopped anyway and ducked down, using the cotton plants for cover.

Peter lowered his pistol, climbed out the window and headed to the barn. Bokor turned around and ran again, keeping down as low as possible. Then he heard the dog at his back and Peter saying, "Sic him, boy!"

Bokor looked over his shoulder and saw the cotton plants stirring in a line aimed straight at him. He ran faster.

Peter aimed the pistol and fired. The .44 ball zipped through the cotton to Bokor's left and kicked up a cloud of dirt less than ten feet away. Peter adjusted his aim and fired again.

This shot hit Bokor in the back of the arm. Bokor grabbed the wound and stopped running, then faced Peter and lifted his hands as high as he could. The cotton plants were still stirring as the dog approached. "I give up," Bokor shouted. "Call the dog off!"

Peter let the dog get a little closer, then put his fingers in his mouth and whistled the three-note command for him to return.

Bokor was glad when the plants stopped stirring, then started again, but in a line going away from him this time.

Peter returned to the slave quarters and grabbed Wesley by the wrist. Tayna screamed and tried to push Peter away, but he split her nose with the butt of his pistol and dragged Wesley through the door, outside, back to the tree.

"No, sir. Please."

"Don't fret, boy," Peter said, grinning. "In a minute, you won't have anything to worry about ever again." He tied Wesley's hands around the trunk, then faced Bokor. "Get on with it."

Bokor reached into his bag and took out the black jar along with the bone-handled knife. He approached Wesley, but the boy shook his head violently back and forth, making it impossible for Bokor to cut him. "Hold him still!"

Peter ignored the fact he was being told what to do by this animal and grabbed Wesley's head with both hands. He pinned it against the tree trunk. Bokor quickly cut him, then smeared the blood inside the mouth of the jar and held the jar under the boy's chin.

A scream pierced the air behind them: "Noooo!"

Peter looked over his shoulder at the slave quarters. The group had gathered in front again. By their choice this time. Several of them were holding Tayna back.

Peter faced forward. Whatever doubt he had was wiped away when he saw the mist stream out of Wesley's nose and mouth and into the jar. And when the boy's skin shriveled, Peter jumped back, swallowing the fear at the back of his throat. When the last threads of mist disappeared into the jar, Wesley slumped. Tayna screamed again.

In the upstairs bedroom, Jinny gasped when Peter pulled Bokor through the door.

Reverend Welltris rose from his chair next to the bed. "My God, Peter. What's happening? I heard shots. Who's that?"

"Someone who can do what you can't. Now shut up."

"How dare you, sir!"

"How dare you, sir. Inciting my wife to rebel behind my back. Get out." Peter used the barrel of his pistol to push Bokor toward the divan. "No mistakes. Understand?"

Bokor nodded, then opened the black jar and dipped his finger in Wesley's blood. As he moved his hand toward the baby's face, Peter grabbed his wrist. "You're not putting that filthy animal's blood on my baby."

"That's the way it works, sir."

Revered Welltris moved closer. "The way what works? What is this?"

Peter let Bokor's wrist go. Reverend Welltris gasped when he saw him smearing blood on the baby's upper lip. "Blasphemy!"

"I thought I told you to get out," Peter shouted, pointing his pistol at the old man until he was gone.

Bokor held the jar under the baby's chin. As the mist flowed, the baby stirred and coughed, then started crying like it had just been born. Jinny gasped and backed into the corner.

Peter grabbed the black jar from Bokor and pushed him aside. "Now both of you go, too."

Peter followed Bokor with the pistol as he moved to the door and Jinny exited with him.

Quickly, Peter put the black jar in a cabinet under the window, then picked up the baby and returned to the bed.

Rose's eyes fluttered open when she heard the baby crying. "What is this... I thought..."

"No, dear," Peter said. "It was a terrible dream. A nightmare. But it's over now."

Rose burst into tears of joy as she sat up and took the baby into her arms. Peter smiled at her and knew he'd saved two lives that afternoon.

Rose fed the baby, then banked him in with pillows close to her before they both fell asleep. Peter fell asleep, too, fully dressed, sitting in the chair by the bed. The flame in the oil lamp on the table guttered, moving the shadows on the walls. And then it went out, leaving only pale blue moonlight.

Outside, Tayna stared up at the dark window, then pulled the hatchet from the tree stump next to the woodpile and climbed the stairs to the veranda.

She opened the side door and entered quietly, her bare feet making soft swishing sounds on the wooden floor. She ascended the servant's stairs slowly, pausing to shift her weight when a step creaked. When she reached the master bedroom, she held the hatchet in her raised right hand, poised to strike, then pushed the door open with her left hand. ·

In the bed, Rose stirred, her feet thrashing under the covers. Tayna held her breath and waited. But Rose continued sleeping.

The baby snurgled and coughed. Tayna moved forward like a ghost, keeping her eyes fixed on Peter as she went to the side of the bed opposite where he was.

She stared down at the baby, savoring this moment where she could pay back Peter, not only for taking her son, but for every other thing he had done to her friends and family. She smiled as she covered the baby with one of the pillows and pushed down, muffling his frantic cries. She pressed harder.

Until: silence.

When Tayna lifted the pillow to make sure the baby was dead, Rose sat up and screamed.

Like a reflex, Tayna swung the hatchet down, burying the blade deep into the top of Rose's head.

Peter woke up, stumbling as he got to his feet, trying desperately to process the tableau in front of him.

Tayna yanked the hatchet out of Rose's skull and her body fell backwards, her head hanging over the edge of the bed on Peter's side, brains and blood splattering to the floor.

Peter screamed, frozen in place by the utter horror of what was happening. By the time he realized Tayna was jumping over the bed toward him, hatchet held high, he couldn't do much more than lift his hands.

She swung down, cutting into his palm. He roared in pain but still managed to grab her wrists and swing her around. Her feet crossed through Rose's blood on the floor and she slid back, smashing into the window, shattering the panes, turning the muntins into stakes which pierced her back.

She screamed and tried to stand, but her feet, still wet with Rose's blood, slipped out from under her and she fell back again, driving the muntins all the way through and out her stomach. She dropped the hatchet and Peter quickly kicked it away. Then he grabbed her hair and held her steady while he used a broken piece of glass to cut her lip. He tossed the shard aside and dipped his finger in her blood. He got the black jar from the cabinet and smeared the blood inside its mouth.

When Tayna saw what he was doing, she spit at him. But Peter only smiled and held the jar under her chin.

The mist flowed into the jar from Tayna's nose and mouth, and she paled and shriveled until there was nothing left.

Peter stumbled back to the chair and sat down heavily. He took another dip of blood from inside the jar and put it on Rose, then held the jar in front of her face.

Nothing happened.

He considered trying to stuff her brains back in her skull before trying again, but instead pulled the sheets over her body, smeared Tayna's blood on his own lip and lifted the jar to his chin. As the mist went into his nose and mouth, his eyes widened, blazing with a power he had never felt before. When the flow stopped, he turned his injured palm over, smiling when he saw it was completely healed.

He got to his feet, still holding the black jar, and retrieved his pistol from the nightstand.

The next morning, Reverend Welltris came back to the plantation. As his carriage rattled toward the main house, he searched for any sign of movement in the fields, but he was surprised when he saw none.

"Strange, don't you think?" he said, as he got out.

"Not as strange as that," said the driver, pointing to the front door, which was wide open.

Reverend Welltris nodded. "You better come with me."

Inside, they found Jinny on the floor, in between the kitchen and the parlor. Reverend Welltris made the sign of the cross as he crouched next to her. "Jinny? Can you hear me?"

Jinny grabbed his arm. "You got to stop him, Reverend," she said, wheezing. "Stop him before he takes them all."

"Stop who? Peter?"

"Yes, sir. He's out there with them now."

"Where's Rose?"

"Tayna killed her. And the baby. Then the master killed Tayna. With the black jar. He said he was saving me for last. Please don't let him."

"Let him what?" the old man asked. When she didn't answer, he peeled her hand off his arm and got back to his feet.

As they stepped onto the veranda from the kitchen, they saw Peter coming out of the slave quarters, a woman's body draped over his shoulder. Welltris gasped, but the driver motioned for him to keep quiet.

They waited until they saw Peter take the body into the barn, then quickly followed.

They soon discovered they were too late. Peter had already gotten them all. And lined them up like railroad ties down the middle of the barn. Reverend Welltris watched Peter carry the woman's body to the end of the row and drop it on the dirt with a strangely hollow thud. Then he said: "You'll burn in hell for this."

Peter turned around. When he saw Reverend Welltris and his driver standing in the open doorway, he smiled. "I know that," he said. "But I have to die first, don't I?"

"That can be arranged," the driver said.

Peter's smile grew by half. "By you?"

The driver nodded.

In one smooth motion, Peter drew his revolver and fired, hitting him dead center in the chest. He dropped to his knees and fell over, the look of surprise never leaving his face.

Reverend Welltris stared down at the driver's body, then turned and ran. Peter laughed and shot him in the back.

They say he's been keeping himself alive ever since then. Like a vampire drinking blood. Only he uses that black jar to take life from other people so he can keep his own going. Doing his best to put off meeting his maker.

So yes, the story's true. And I wish to God I could tell you someone finally stopped him. But they haven't. So you best watch yourself. You best hope he's not watching you, deciding yours is a life worth stealing.

Babylon Falling

by Brian Keene

Southern Iraq
March 2003

"We are so fucked!"

And they were.

Bloom coughed. Goggles protected his eyes, but they didn't prevent him from swallowing sand. Neither did his handkerchief, which was tied around his mouth and nose, and drenched with sweat.

He was perched atop an M-88 tank recovery unit, rumbling north toward Baghdad with an immense column of other vehicles from the 3rd Infantry. The convoy was nearly seven thousand strong. The M-88 held a two-man crew, and it was Bloom's turn topside. Myers stayed below, safe from the harsh desert conditions, bobbing his head to Led Zeppelin's "Kashmir." Myers played it over and over on a loop during the march.

"All I see turns to brownnnnnn," Myers sang, "as the sun burns the grounnnnnnnnd, and my eyes fill with sannnnnd, as I scan this wasted lannnddd…"

Bloom began to sing along, too. "Trying to find, trying to find where I've beeeee— ack!"

He choked as more grit blew into his mouth.

They'd left Kuwait City before dawn, driving past gorgeous luxury homes and seaside resorts unlike anything they'd ever seen back in the States. But soon, those faded from sight and the desert took over. The only thing for miles, other than camels and their nomadic herders, were massive power lines stretching across the horizon and oil pumps, thrusting into the earth. By midday, these disappeared too, leaving only the featureless brown desert. Even the lizards and birds inhabiting the wasteland vanished, hiding from the incoming storm.

In Iraq's late spring, hot winds swept in from the north, raising clouds of sand and dust several thousand feet into the air. The locals called these storms shamals. A media embed in Kuwait City had told Bloom and Myers that this particular shamal was the worst in decades, with winds whipping across the desert at over fifty miles-per-hour, burying everything under a fine coat of yellow and brown. The storm had interrupted bombing missions and ground combat, but not their advance. They were given orders to roll and roll they did.

Earlier that afternoon, their column had fallen under attack from an Iraqi artillery barrage, and one of the Paladin motorized howitzers caught fire and exploded. The crew escaped, but two of the soldiers were injured. One of them had suffered third-degree burns on his hands. Bloom cringed, remembering the smell, and the way the man's blistered fingers had resembled blackened breakfast sausages. Now, while shells were dropped on two Iraqi forward observation posts in retaliation for the attack, their section of the column had been ordered to wait.

Bloom took advantage of the delay. Myers replaced him at the gun, while he ducked inside. He wolfed down an MRE—Meal Ready to Eat (mixed with sand)—and then cleaned the grime from his face with a baby wipe, wincing as the alcohol came in contact with his red, wind-burned skin. Then he drank greedily from his canteen. Outside the M-88, Bloom heard artillery explosions rolling across the arid landscape. Soon, a report came over the radio that the opposition had been obliterated, and the lead forces were to hold their position to allow the rest of the division to catch up.

"We are so fucked," Bloom repeated, climbing topside to join Myers. "This goddamned sand is everywhere!"

"Could be worse." Myers's sounded tired. His laconic Texan drawl was even slower than usual. "Bad as these storms are, the temperature's only in the seventies. Imagine how this shit would be if it was mid-summer and a hundred and twenty!"

Bloom shrugged. "We'll be home by then. Won't have to worry about it."

Sharp and Rendell sauntered over; free for the moment while a mechanic unclogged the dust from their medical truck's engine. Sharp's pale skin and blonde hair were crusted with dirt, and when Rendell spat a wad of Copenhagen, Bloom noticed ugly blisters on chafed lips. A media embed trailed along behind the two soldiers, squinting against the blowing sand. His expensive sunglasses seemed to offer little protection.

"This sucks," Rendell moaned. "Why don't we just pave over this country and build some shopping malls?"

"That's how they'll know they're free," Myers said, nodding. "When they got a Starbucks and a Wal-Mart on every corner in Baghdad."

Sergeant O'Malley soon joined them, followed by Privates Williams, Sanchez, Riser, and Jefferson. O'Malley was older than the rest, and at thirty-two, a veteran of the first Gulf War. The younger men looked up to him. O'Malley was originally from Long Island. Like Myers, Sanchez hailed from Texas. Williams came from North Carolina, Jefferson from Mississippi, and Riser from Baltimore.

Shading his eyes with his hands, Jefferson surveyed their surroundings while another artillery explosion echoed across the plain.

"Look at it," he said. "This is Hell on earth, if you ask me."

"Can't be any worse than that garbage dump Bloom comes from," Myers said. "What's that city called? Trench-ton?"

Bloom punched him in the shoulder. "Trenton, asshole. And don't be talking shit about Jersey."

All the men laughed.

"What's going on back home?" O'Malley asked the reporter.

"Big protest in San Francisco," the media embed answered. "Martin Sheen and Sean Penn spoke at an anti-war rally."

Riser grimaced. "Does Martin Sheen think he really is the President? Somebody needs to remind him he just plays one on TV."

"What's Sean Penn famous for?" Williams asked.

"Fucking Madonna, apparently," Riser answered. "And that's all. He couldn't make a good movie to save his life."

"What about *Fast Times*?" Sanchez wiped his goggles on a clean rag. "He was pretty good in that."

"Oh, that took a lot of talent." Riser shook his head. "He played a stoned surfer. Not exactly academy award material, dude."

"My daddy was protested against when he came back from Vietnam," O'Malley said quietly, his eyes focused on the sand dunes. "He served with the 82nd, saw a world of shit. Did his time, made it through, and came home. Got off the plane at the airport and they spit on him! He was so shocked that he just walked away. He walked. I think that fucked with him in ways the war never did, you know?"

The others were silent, reflecting.

"I can't wait for one of these neo-hippie motherfuckers to spit on me," O'Malley continued. "Figure I owe them for him, and then some."

They waited for another hour, trying in vain to stay shielded from the shamal. With nothing to do, O'Malley gave them busy work. They checked and cleaned their gear—rifles, ammunition, body armor, helmets, Saratoga suits to protect against chemical agents, trenching shovels, sleeping bags, and gas masks. Their gas masks were to be within arm's reach at all times, and they'd been trained to don them instantly in case of attack; told there were nine seconds between life and death. So far, they hadn't needed to use them. They wrote letters home, tucked them away for safekeeping, and re-wrote their blood type on their helmets and sleeves.

The only thing they didn't do was sleep.

Eventually, the order came to move on. They proceeded on, into the shamal. The roads vanished amidst the storm, so they followed in the tracks of the vehicles ahead of them. The tanks and Bradley fighting vehicles could go faster, but the column moved at the speed of its slowest vehicle—a wagon train with everything from tanker trucks bearing fuel and water, to Humvees bearing young American soldiers. Radio chatter was kept to a minimum. Drivers focused on not driving off the roads.

The sandstorm's brutality increased. Topside again, Bloom wrapped his bandanna around his nose and mouth. He wished he had an asthma inhaler, some vapor rub, even an oxygen bottle—anything to make it easier for him to breathe.

They passed a hut, several unexploded cluster bombs from the previous Gulf War, and the wreckage of an Iraqi tank, before coming across a burned-out observation post. Lying amidst the carnage were the charred remains of an enemy soldier. Bloom wondered if the blowing sand would cover up the corpse before the man's companions found him.

They encountered no further opposition. Occasionally, they came across Bedouin women and children, who waved as they rolled past. Bloom wondered what they were doing out in the storm but decided they were probably used to such weather. He debated throwing the kids some hard candy but decided against it—visions of the children being run down by the next vehicle in the convoy while they scampered for the treat ran though his head. Visibility was worsening, and it would be easy for a driver to miss the children bent over in the path of the column.

The storm stayed with them, a constant nuisance. Word came back that there were three Iraqi regular army divisions ahead, but that one of them had already surrendered. O'Malley told them that the commanders didn't anticipate any serious opposition in the south. The troops deployed there were mostly made up of unpaid, unfed conscripts— more than eager to toss their weapons aside and stand down in exchange for a hot meal. The wagon train was supposed to be a psychological offensive—an effort to convince the enemy that resistance was futile. Bloom had heard the U.S. and British commanders even carried paperwork that allowed Iraqi commanders to sign and surrender their troops on the spot.

The winds reached seventy-five miles an hour. Riser cracked over the radio that they ought to rename the route the Hurricane Highway. This was greeted by laughter, and then a stern admonition to knock it off.

Bloom blinked the sand from his eyes and tried to focus. "We are so fucked."

He was very tired.

It was almost nightfall when they came across the old man.

He stood along the roadside, propped up by a tall, gnarled wooden staff. Shrouded in colorful robes, only his leathery hands and face were visible. He watched them pass. His expression was impassive. Several of the soldiers waved at him, but he did not return the gesture. Rendell shot him the finger, but this, too, earned no reply.

When Myers pulled alongside him, Bloom stared into the old man's eyes. They were black, like two drops of India ink, and despite the blowing sand, the old man did not blink. Indeed, he seemed almost comfortable in the storm. As Bloom watched, the old man dropped his staff and gestured at the yellow sky.

"The fuck's he doing?" Myers called out.

"I don't know." Bloom was mesmerized by the actions. "Having a heart attack? Praying to Allah?"

The old man's stare never left his. Their eyes seemed locked together. As the M-88 rolled past, Bloom's head swiveled around, unable to break the connection. The old man said something, but the words were torn away by the howling wind. As Bloom watched, he knelt, and with one bony finger, drew a symbol in the sand. Then, another vehicle blocked Bloom's view, and the old man passed from sight.

"That was weird," Bloom muttered.

The M-88 swerved suddenly, and Bloom had to grab on tight to avoid falling off.

"Yo," he shouted. "What the fuck, Myers?"

"Sorry! Almost nodded off there for a moment. I'm fucking tired."

"Want to trade off?"

"We can't stop, man. You know that. Besides, you haven't had any more sleep than I have."

Bloom knew his friend was right. Exhausted and covered in dirt, they were both operating on pure adrenaline. So were the rest of the convoy. He also knew that they probably would not stop all night, and even if they did, there would be little time for sleep. Instead, the commanders would have them working all night repairing the vehicles that had fallen victim to the storm conditions. If they slept at all, it would be in short shifts.

Suddenly, without warning, the sandstorm increased with a shocking intensity. Furious winds rocked the lighter vehicles, buffeting them from side to side. Bloom's bandanna was ripped from his face, sailing away before he could grab it. Blowing sand gnawed at his nose and mouth.

"The hell is going on out there?" Myers asked.

Before Bloom could answer, the sun disappeared behind the dunes. The sky was bathed in a strange orange glow as the fading daylight filtered through the swirling dust. Bloom shivered, watching as the vehicles in front and back of them took on a spectral quality in the billowing sand. The ones further away faded completely from sight. Within minutes, the last of the light vanished, plunging them into darkness. The vehicles in the column turned on their headlights, but they did little against the storm.

Bloom gasped as the truck in front of them disappeared into the dense cloud. Then came the lightning. Thunder boomed across the sky. To Bloom, it sounded very much like artillery shells. He coughed, trying to breathe. The sand was in his eyes and nose and ears, and the more he coughed, the more sand he inhaled. He sneezed out dust. His eyes began to water, washing out clods of dirt and leaving balls of grit hanging from his eyelashes.

Something pelted him on the shoulder. Then another—hard.

Jesus, he thought, *did I just get shot?*

A moment later he realized it was raining mud.

"Oh, fuck this! Myers, I'm coming down."

Abandoning the gun, he dropped down inside the vehicle, slamming the hatch shut behind him.

"Don't say anything," he warned. "It's only for a minute. Then I'll go back up."

"Couldn't say much if I wanted to." Bleary-eyed, Myers pointed to the radio. "Nothing but static the last ten minutes."

"You can't get a hold of anybody?"

"Nothing, man. Strangest fucking thing I've ever seen."

Myers tapped his fingers to the drums on the "Kashmir" loop.

Bloom began to sing along again. "I am a traveler of both time and space—"

"Hey, who sings this?" Myers asked him.

"Led Zeppelin."

"Well, then shut up and let them."

Bloom punched him in the shoulder, grabbed a baby wipe, and cleaned more sand from his face.

Myers focused on the road. Bloom could tell that the combination of the sandstorm, fatigue, unfamiliar terrain, and now blackout conditions were working against him.

"You okay, Myers?"

"I can't keep my eyes open. I'm driving while standing up and I'm still falling asleep!"

"Let me take over."

"We can't stop, especially now. We'll get rear-ended."

As if to illustrate his point, the truck in front of them suddenly swerved back into view, veering off the path and vanishing again into the blackness.

Myers gasped. "Where the hell are they going?"

"They probably nodded off. Now let me drive!"

"I'm okay," Myers insisted. "Just chill and help me watch ahead of us."

It was a long and dangerous night. The storm and fatigue drained the caravan in a way the Iraqi forces never could. Drivers fell asleep at the wheel and veered off their route. Soldiers behind them fought through on foot to wake the drivers and get them moving. Then another driver in the convoy would fall asleep, and the whole ordeal started over again. Traveling off-road, they'd lose sight of the vehicles in front of them and turn off in other directions.

The radios worked sporadically. There was mostly just the hiss of static, occasionally interrupted by a snatch of confused conversation or barked orders. The commander of an Abrams tank radioed that he was lost, couldn't see the rest of the convoy, and was almost out of fuel. Others were dispatched to find him, but nobody could locate him. Then the commander stopped responding.

Rendell wondered over the radio if their night vision goggles would help.

"NODs can't see through sand—" O'Malley's curt reply was cut short by an explosive whine of feedback, and the radio went dead.

"The fuck is going on?" Bloom asked.

"Look at that!" Myers pointed out the window.

The tip of the radio antenna glowed with a ball of blue energy. Bloom grabbed the handset to ask if anyone else was experiencing the phenomena and got shocked.

"Ouch!" He sucked at his tingling fingers. "What the hell is that?"

Myers shrugged, gaping at the phenomenon. "Static electricity? St. Elmo's Fire? Who knows?"

"How are we supposed to fight a war in this shit?"

"One thing's for sure. The Iraqis ain't gonna be putting up a fight tonight."

Bloom fumbled in his pocket and produced a squashed pack of gum. "Want some?"

"No thanks. What I want is a smoke."

"Can't help you there." He unwrapped the stick of gum and chewed it happily, his parched mouth relishing the burst of flavor. He turned his attention back to the desert. He couldn't see anything. Blackness had swallowed up the entire column. He shivered. "It's cold in here."

"You shouldn't be cold. You've got five layers of dirt on you to keep you warm."

Bloom didn't reply. He wrapped his arms around his shoulders as another chill passed through him.

"Bloom?"

"Yeah?"

"It'll be okay. You'll be back in Trench-ton before you know it."

That was when the desert disappeared from beneath their wheels.

Bloom couldn't see anything other than darkness. It wasn't just black— it was the absolute absence of light. His face felt sticky. Wetness ran into his eyes. He placed a hand to his forehead and gingerly felt the edges of the wound. Myers moaned from somewhere to his left. Outside, the wind howled, rocking the M-88 back and forth.

"Myers? You okay?"

"Can't see…"

Bloom sighed in relief. At least he wasn't blind.

"I can't either," he whispered. "Must be the storm. Where are you?

"Over here."

Carefully feeling his way, Bloom crawled towards the voice. His palm flattened down on what felt like glass—the window.

"We're on our side. What the hell happened?"

"Don't know," Myers coughed. "The ground just disappeared. Maybe the storm blew us over."

"Somebody must have seen us wreck. Help's probably on the way."

His hand closed around Myers's leg.

"Quit feeling me up, or I'll make you my bitch."

"Fuck you, Myers. You okay?"

"Yeah, nothing's broken at least. Must've banged my head when we rolled. Got one hell of a headache."

"Me, too. My forehead's bleeding." Bloom wiped more blood from his eyes.

"How bad?"

"I can't tell. Not too bad, I don't think. I'm still conscious."

They sat quietly for a moment, letting their eyes adjust to the darkness. After a few minutes, they still saw nothing. Bloom had the uncomfortable impression that the blackness was pressing in on them, wrapping them in an embrace.

"This is no good," Myers said, finally. "Where's the night vision goggles?"

"I don't know. Everything got tossed around when we crashed. I told you we should have stowed everything like O'Malley said."

"Hang on."

There was a rustling sound. Then, Myers's lighter flared to life, illuminating them in its tiny circle of light. Bloom gasped. The darkness seemed to surround the flame, as if it wanted to extinguish it.

"Let me see." Myers's fingers probed his head, appraising the damage. "You're okay. It's not deep. Scalp wounds bleed like crazy though."

"Think we should put that out?" Bloom nodded at the lighter. "What if there are hostiles in the perimeter?"

"Fuck 'em. I need a smoke." He shook a cigarette out of the crumpled pack. "Besides, something just doesn't feel right..."

"The darkness?"

"Yeah. You feel it, too?"

Bloom nodded.

Outside, the wind shrieked in response, pounding the vehicle.

"I don't think help's coming," Myers said. "Not tonight, at least."

"Try the radio."

"Already did. It's dead."

"We are so fucked."

"Would you please quit saying that?"

"I can't help it!"

They crawled through the wreckage, salvaging what they could. When they were outfitted, Myers extinguished the lighter.

"You ready?" he asked.

"Let's do it."

They crawled outside into Hell. As they plunged again into the darkness, stinging sand lashed at their exposed skin, chipping the lenses of their goggles. The wind roared in their ears, and it was impossible to breathe, let alone speak. They communicated in sign language.

In the distance, they saw Sanchez and Riser struggling against the storm. Bloom and Myers found it hard to identify the two men at first and had to watch carefully before they were sure. Bloom tried shouting, but the gale tore his voice away. He raised his arms over his head and waved. Barely visible, even from only a few yards away, the two soldiers made their way toward them. Wading through the sand, the four reached each other.

"What happened?" Myers shouted above the winds.

"We wrecked," Riser yelled. "One minute the road was there, and the next—fucking gone!"

Myers nodded. "Does anybody else know where we are?"

"Our radio's busted," Sanchez hollered. "How about yours?"

Myers slid his finger across his throat in a slashing motion.

Sanchez frowned. "Shit!"

"Well, what the hell do we do now?" Bloom coughed. "I don't see the rest of the convoy!"

"You can't see anything out here," Riser answered. "Our truck is toast! Let's head back to yours and take cover 'til this blows over!"

They waded back to the M-88 and slipped inside. Myers pulled the door shut behind him, partially muting the wind. They sat clustered together in the feeble glow of a chem light, shaking the dirt out of their ears, nostrils, helmets, and boots. Riser removed his Kevlar vest, and sand poured from it.

"Shit," Sanchez muttered, banging his handheld GPS against his leg. "This thing's on the fritz too. Can't get any readings that make sense."

"It's this storm," Bloom said. "I've never seen anything like it."

Riser dumped the dust from his boots. "I don't think anybody has. This shit is biblical, man."

They all stared at him.

"Think about it," he said. "We're in the cradle of civilization! It may be Iraq now, but this was Sumeria, wasn't it? This was fucking Babylon! This is where it all started."

"If that's the case," Myers said, "then I sure do wish God would send us a burning bush right about now."

"Fuck that," Sanchez replied. "I want him to send a couple Chinooks to fly our asses out of here."

"I just want to go home," Bloom said quietly. "I miss Jill."

"She your girlfriend?" Sanchez asked.

He nodded.

Riser yawned. "Me, too. All I want to do is go to Camden Yards, catch the Os, and drink a few cold ones. God damn, a cold beer would taste good right about now!"

Sanchez fumbled with his wedding band. "I miss my wife."

"I need a smoke." Myers searched his empty pockets again.

They sat in the darkness. All four men were disoriented, dirty, and exhausted. Outside, the storm continued, showing no signs of abating.

It was a long time before any of them slept.

When Bloom awoke, his tongue felt like beef jerky. His lips were cracked and raw. His puffy eyes itched, and he dug at them with balled fists. Then, he slowly opened them and looked around.

"Jesus!"

His shout woke the others. The entire bottom of the M-88 was covered in a layer of sand. They had fallen asleep sitting up, and while they slept, it had had piled up to their waists, obscuring everything. It was like sitting in cement, and they struggled to get free.

"Hey!" Sanchez glanced around. "Where's Riser?"

Frantically, they began digging with their hands, calling his name. Riser didn't answer. They found him seven inches down. His mouth, nose, eyes, and ears were filled with sand.

"Oh shit…" Sanchez ran his hand over his crew cut. "Riser."

Myers knelt, checking his pulse. "He's dead."

"You think so?" Bloom choked. "Sorry. This just sucks. Fucking Riser."

"He was short," Sanchez said. "Thirty-nine days and a wake up and he would have been out of here. He said when I got out, I could come to Baltimore and he'd show me around. They've got crabs there, supposed to be good—"

His sobs cut off the rest.

Bloom turned away, tears streaking through the dust on his face, as well.

Solemnly, Myers closed the dead soldier's eyes. "Rest easy, brother."

Later, Bloom and Myers ventured outside, while Sanchez stayed behind to guard the vehicle—and their fallen comrade.

The sky was clear. The piercing blue was broken only by a few wispy clouds. The wind had vanished, and the temperature was beginning to soar. No trace of the storm remained, except for the sand. Large dunes covered everything, obscuring their surroundings. The M-88 lay half buried on its side.

"No way we're getting that thing out of there." Bloom kicked at the desert in frustration.

"At least we got out. If that storm had kept up a few hours longer, we'd have been shit out of luck."

"Myers," Bloom began, hesitant. "Did you notice something last night?"

"You mean other than the weather?"

"Remember that old man, the one along the roadside? The storm didn't get really bad until after we passed him."

"What do you mean?"

"He said something—something in their language, and then he drew some funny symbols in the sand. Like he was doing magic or something."

Myers snorted, and spat a wad of mucous and dirt.

"Bloom, what the hell have you been smoking? Man, if your number comes up for a random piss test, you're looking at a dishonorable on your DD-214."

"I'm serious. That storm wasn't natural. And what about all that shit with the radios? That blue light? The darkness?"

"It was nighttime. Of course, it was fucking dark. That don't make it magic. We've got enough trouble without inventing more."

"Forget it."

They explored the terrain in a steadily broadening circle, looking for anything that seemed familiar.

"Where the fuck is the road?" Bloom sat down on a dune. "Shouldn't there at least be tracks from the rest of the convoy?"

Myers shrugged. "Got covered up, I imagine. I don't see nothing that looks familiar. No buildings. Not even a tree."

"What's that over there?"

The sun glinted off a flat piece of metal. They approached it curiously.

"That's the roof of a truck," Myers said. "How the—"

"Shhh," Bloom silenced him. "Listen!"

Dim, muffled pounding came from somewhere beneath their feet. A voice called out from beneath the desert.

"Somebody's alive in there!" Myers began digging at the sand with his hands. "Go back to the truck! See if you can find the shovels, and bring Sanchez!"

"On it," Bloom said, dashing away.

"Hang on," Myers shouted at the ground. "We'll get you out!"

Bloom and Sanchez returned with a compact shovel and an empty coffee can. The three men dug in frantic silence, their bodies drenched with sweat.

Bloom knocked on the roof of the vehicle. "Hey down there! If you can hear me, we're digging you out!"

They kept at it, but their determined efforts quickly turned to frustration. For each scoop of sand they hauled away, more poured into its place.

"This ain't working," Myers moaned.

Sanchez stood up. "Hang on."

He ran back to the M-88 and disappeared inside.

"What's he doing?" Bloom asked.

"I don't know. Maybe he got heat stroke."

The burly Texan reappeared a second later, holding a fire axe over his head.

"Stand back," Sanchez warned, then swung the axe downward. There was a shriek of metal, and sparks danced over the sand. The trapped voice grew silent. He brought the axe down again, ripping a hole in the roof. He swung a third time. A fourth.

Five minutes later, Sharp stared up at them through the hole. His expression was a mixture of relief and sadness. Relief that he was saved. Sadness that Rendell, lying next to him, had met a fate similar to Riser's. During the night, when the air inside the buried truck grew thin, Rendell had fallen asleep and never woke up.

Having rescued Sharp, they grieved for their fellow soldiers. Exhausted and hot, each gulped greedily from their canteens, until Myers advised them to conserve their water. Since the others were privates, and he was a specialist, and there were no sergeants or corporals to be found, command of the rag-tag squad fell to him.

"I think we need to face facts," he said as they huddled around him. "Either they don't know we're lost, or there's nobody left to find us. Either way, I don't reckon we'll get rescued anytime soon. We've got to make our own way out."

"Shouldn't we just wait here?" Bloom asked. "Dig some trenches and defend our position?"

"We could," Myers said. "But the way I see it, we're better off trying to find civilization—or at least a road. Even if they are looking for us, that storm messed everything up. They don't know our location, and neither do we. The radios are busted, so we can't call anybody, and we've only got enough rations for a day or two. I say we hoof it. Head due east and eventually we've got to come across a road or a village. Maybe even another convoy or platoon."

"What about Riser and Rendell?" Sanchez asked. "We just gonna leave them out here?"

"Yeah, unless you feel like carrying them over those dunes. Look, I know it sucks. They were my friends, too. Hell, Rendell and I went through basic together. But be realistic. We can't carry them. And we ain't doing them no good if we die out here, too."

They moved Riser's body to the medical truck and then kicked sand over the roof to camouflage it better.

"We'll be back," Sanchez said to the ground.

"Count on it," Sharp added, quietly.

As they crossed the first dune and stared out across the vast desert plateau, the opening chords of "Kashmir" ran through Bloom's head. He hummed along, until he found it was smarter to save his breath.

They began to walk.

By midday, the desert gave way to palm trees and mud.

Bloom cheered, celebrating the change in landscape. "This is more like it!"

"What—this?" Sanchez scowled. "It's a fucking swamp, Bloom."

"Yeah, but at least there's no sand. The mud's hard packed.

Sharp paused, wiping the sweat from his brow. "This looks like Nassiriyah."

"Can't be," Myers replied. "I thought so too, at first, but we're too far west."

Trudging onward, they came across a rugged, narrow path winding through the mud.

"Anybody recognize this?" Myers asked.

Sharp and Sanchez shook their heads.

"Yeah." Bloom rubbed his calves. "It's a goat track."

"That's very helpful," Myers said. "Wherever we are, this path has been used recently. Look at the tracks."

He pointed at a pair of tire treads, baked into the ground.

"Not one of ours," Sharp said. "Too small."

There was a scuffling sound behind them. They whirled, raising their weapons in unison. A lone Iraqi man, barefoot and dressed in tatters, faced them. Two women in black robes, carrying bundles on their heads, and a boy and a girl in brightly colored rags, rounded the hilltop behind him. They all gasped in surprise.

"Are they civilians or militia?" Sharp asked.

Myers grunted. "Hard to say. The women and kids are civilians, but the guy could be wearing civvies to throw us off."

The man smiled a toothless grin and mimed drinking from a bottle. Slowly, Bloom shook his canteen to show that it was empty.

"Speak English?" Myers asked.

The man stared blankly, still smiling. Then he held out his hands and gave them the thumbs-up sign. The women and children joined him.

The man spoke. "Good... America."

Myers laughed, and after a moment, the others joined him, lowering their weapons. The young boy looked at the soldiers and said something barely understandable—"chocolate." It broke Bloom's heart not to have any to give him.

Myers walked forward and shook hands with the man.

"Thank for liberate us," the man said in halting English. "You great army."

"You're welcome." Myers paused, then rummaged in his pack and brought out two packs of MREs. He handed them to the man, who looked at the gifts with puzzlement.

"Food," Sharp said, and then mimed eating. "Meal Ready to Eat."

"I thought we were here to make friends," Sanchez said. "Ain't gonna do it giving them those things."

The man turned and said something to the others. Then they all bowed in gratitude. The little girl ran up and hugged Myers around the legs. He shooed her away in gentle embarrassment, then spoke again.

"Can you tell us where we are? Is there a town nearby? Town?"

The man thought for a moment, then nodded.

"Al-Qurna," he said, pointing down the road. "Eden."

"How far?" Myers asked.

"Eden," the man repeated, "Al-Qurna."

"Al-Qurna," Sharp mused. "I remember seeing that on the map."

One of the women whispered something in the man's ear. He seemed to consider her request for a moment and then nodded. She stepped forward to Myers.

"We thank you for your help," she said in English. "My husband, his American is not so good. Mine is better."

"We're glad we could help," Myers said, smiling. "But why didn't you just tell us you spoke English to begin with?"

"Is not my place. That is my husband's choice."

Myers laughed. "If I tried that on my wife back in Nacogdoches, she'd likely whip me."

The woman smiled.

"Three miles that way," she pointed down the road, "is Al-Qurna. Is believed to be Garden of Eden, where Adam came to pray to God. Today it is, how you say—destroyed? Paving stones are broken, the walls full of bullet holes. The eucalyptus we call Adam's tree is dead. Every generation is taught that this was true Garden of Eden and this was Adam's tree, where he first spoke to God. Now is ruined."

"What happened to it?" Bloom asked.

"Saddam," she answered.

At the name, the man spat on the ground.

"The Ba'ath party, they built shrine," the woman said, "for pilgrimage of tourists. After last time Americans come here, Saddam punished Al-Qurna for supporting you. They drained the water. Now the walls and floor of the shrine are cracked. The garden is mud. Children fight with dogs there. But village elders will help you. Seek for them. Just do not go in the shrine. It is no place for uniforms and weapons."

"I understand," Myers assured her. "We'll be respectful."

Bloom gently asked, "Do you believe it's really the Garden of Eden?"

She was quiet, and Bloom worried he had offended her. Then she nodded.

"I am Muslim, and I believe. No harm shall come to you there, from any Muslim. The Koran say 'if the Muslims capture them and take them to a place that has been prepared for them, they should not harm them or torture them with beatings, depriving them of food and water, leaving them out in the sun or the cold, burning them with fire, or putting covers over their mouths, ears and eyes and putting them in cages like animals. Rather they should treat them with kindness and mercy, feed them well and encourage them to enter Islam.' The village elders are Muslim, so this they believe, too."

"I hope you're right," Myers said.

She smiled. "In Al-Qurna, you shall find rest."

"I liked her quote from the Koran," Bloom said as they approached the village. "Reminded me of the way my Grandma used to quote the Bible."

Before the others could reply, gunshots rang out, followed by a woman screaming. Four more gunshots echoed in rapid succession, and then silence.

"What the—"

Four white SUVs roared over the hill and slid to a stop behind them. The tires gouged trenches in the mud. As the Americans pulled their weapons, nine figures dressed in black uniforms, their faces covered with black scarves, leapt from the vehicles, brandishing rifles of their own.

"Fuck," Myers screamed. "It's the Fedayeen!"

"Hold your fire," a voice called.

The old man who they'd passed on the road before the storm, stepped out from behind one of the vehicles.

"Hold your fire," he said again. His English was clear, and though he spoke softly, they could hear every word. "If you shoot, your friends die."

There was a commotion behind him, and several of the Fedayeen pushed forward, shoving O'Malley, Jefferson, and Williams ahead of them. The three were bound and had been beaten badly.

"Drop your weapons," the old man said calmly, "or they die, and then you join them."

Cursing, Bloom considered their options. They were easily outnumbered. Myers must have realized the same thing, because he reluctantly ordered the others to lower their rifles.

Bloom put his hands up and turned to Myers. "Just remember the part of the Koran the woman quoted to us."

As their hands were bound behind them and their rifles were collected, the old man smiled at him.

"Here, we do not read the Koran. Our book is much older. Come, we will show you."

Bound, gagged, and beaten, the Americans were brought to a building in Al-Qurna and then herded through an underground passage in the basement beneath it. The complex beneath the village was staggering in its size. The prisoners soon lost all sense of direction as they were shoved down a maze of winding passageways and tunnels.

Finally, they came to a bunker built out of white sandstone. They were crammed together into a tiny jail cell with a red door and a rusted grate window that looked out on what could only be an interrogation chamber. Aside from the bloodstains on the floor and a pile of dried feces in the corner, the only other thing in the cell was a coffee can for a toilet.

The men stood together in a tight knot as the door slammed behind them. When the bolt clicked into place, they realized that Jefferson was still outside

"What are you going to do with us?" O'Malley demanded through split lips. "I'm in command of this squad and I demand to know!"

The old man peered through the bars in the window.

"What we are doing? Electric shocks. Cigarette burns. Pulling out of fingernails, castration, rape, cut off your eyelids, your lips, hang you by your limbs from the fan in ceiling. Beating you with cables and hosepipe. Or maybe Falaqa, yes?"

"What's Falaqa?" O'Malley asked.

"We beat the soles of your feet with a metal rod."

"That doesn't sound too bad," Sanchez muttered. "I got calluses."

"We will cut them off first," the old man said.

Williams stepped forward. "Hey, douchebag. Ever hear of the Geneva Convention? You can't treat prisoners of war this way. They'll try you for war crimes!"

"But you are not prisoners of war," the old man answered. "You are sacrifices."

He nodded at the guards, and they immediately shot Jefferson in the back of each kneecap. As he collapsed to the ground, shrieking in pain, they pumped more bullets into his elbows, his hands, his legs, and finally his face. Gore sprayed across the alabaster sandstone.

O'Malley gripped the bars, unable to look away, while the others cursed and screamed. Bloom closed his eyes, turning away.

"That is one sacrifice," the old man told Williams. "Now, let us see about your mouth."

Before deploying to Iraq, the men had learned all about the Fedayeen. The name meant 'those ready to sacrifice themselves.' They were Saddam Hussein's most trusted paramilitary unit. Their duties included assassinating his enemies, and the capture, imprisonment, and torture of anyone deemed a dissident. The majority of their recruits were composed of criminals, pardoned in exchange for their service. One of their endurance drills was to survive on snake and dog meat. Their training included urban warfare and suicide missions. They reported directly to Saddam's eldest son, Odai.

"I want to speak with Odai," O'Malley shouted. He was strapped to a chair next to Williams, who had been tied to a gurney. Both men had been injected with a pharmaceutical grade of speed so they wouldn't pass out from the pain.

Ignoring him, the old man wiped blood from Williams's chin.

"This doesn't have to happen," O'Malley continued. "I demand that you let me talk to Odai. He's in charge!"

"No," the old man said. "Odai has been in hiding since the start of the war. The Fedayeen report to me, now."

"Okay…" O'Malley paused. "Then talk to me. Tell us what you want."

"I want you to be still," the old man said. "It is not your time to scream yet."

He nodded at two of the guards, one of whom was smoking a foul-smelling cigarette. The two stalked toward O'Malley and forced his mouth open. As he struggled, the smoking guard snuffed his cigarette out on O'Malley's tongue. O'Malley shrieked. Calmly, the guard lit another cigarette and then repeated the process. O'Malley's tortured cries turned to moans.

"Much better," the old man said, and with a yank of the rusty pliers, pulled another tooth from Williams's ruined mouth.

His gurgling scream echoed throughout the cells.

Bloom closed his eyes again and tried to think of home. Summertime on South Clinton Avenue. His father's extermination company. He was going to work for him when he got out. Jill, with her long, blonde hair. The week before he'd shipped out, they'd gone to see Linkin Park in concert. Afterward, they'd done it in the back of his parent's car…

Williams's shrieks, O'Malley's moans, and the old man's laughter shattered the visions.

"Leave them alone," Sanchez pleaded. "Stop it! O'Malley, hang in there, man."

O'Malley tried to answer, but the cigarette burns on his tongue made him hard to understand. He bunched his muscles, pushing against the restraints binding him to the chair, but the leather straps were stronger.

"Hey!" Myers rattled the bars of the cell.

The old man paused, dropping one of Williams's molars to the floor.

"You can't do this," Myers said. "It's not human."

The old man nodded. "Correct. Is not human."

He turned back to the quivering soldier and wrenched out the last tooth. Williams convulsed on the gurney, blood running from his mouth, but this time he made no sound. He was beyond sound. The old man appraised his handy-work. Satisfied, he selected an ice pick from the tools laid out on the table next to him.

"Now, we take your eyes, yes?"

Williams did not scream, so the others screamed for him.

The old man turned to the guards and cocked his head toward O'Malley. Then he turned back to the prisoners.

"His eyes, too," he said.

His gnarled fingers reached out and held Williams's eyelid open. Slowly, hypnotically, he waved the ice pick back and forth in front of the soldier's contracting pupil. Then, he jabbed it forward. At the same time, the two guards extinguished their smoldering cigarettes in O'Malley's eyes. Both men shrieked.

Myers turned away and vomited.

"You motherfuckers," Bloom shouted. "Oh, you motherfuckers are so fucking dead when I get out of here! You are so fucking dead, you sons of bitches—"

He stopped mid-ramble, spying something hovering in the air, directly above the old man. Something formless and dark. It looked like a cloud, the size of a baseball. Colors for which there were no name swirled in the blackness.

The old man looked up, smiled, and then glanced back to the men in the cell.

"You see? It begins. He is coming."

Calmly, he plunged the tool into Williams's other eye. Williams's back arched up off the gurney, and this time he screamed so loudly that something tore in his throat. Blood poured from his mouth and eyes, pooling onto the floor. His mouth gaped like a fish as he continued to scream, but all that was generated was a tiny mewling whimper.

Then he was still.

"Why?" Bloom sobbed.

"We summon Kandara," the old man explained. "You are in Iraq. This was once Babylon. All of the great gods came from here. Dagon and Baal— all these belonged to us first. And there were others—Ob and Apu, Meeble and Kat—who came from elsewhere but resided here for a time. This is where magic was born. There are many books, much knowledge. You have bookstores in America where you can buy them in paperback. All this came from our lands."

"Magic..." Bloom's voice trailed off.

"Yes," the old man said. "Kandara is demon—what we call Djinn. There are many Djinn. Some control animals or humans. Some grant wishes and others destroy dreams. Kandara is great among the Djinn, and powerful. He commands the desert winds. You think the storm last night was bad, yes? Kandara will show your friends what bad storm really is! Even now, the rest of your army drives north. Kandara will go to meet them, and there he will destroy them. The desert will swallow even their bones."

"This motherfucker is crazy," Myers whispered.

"And you are the next one, I think," the old man answered. "Kandara must be summoned with pain, fed with suffering and anguish. Each of you feeds him until he is whole. When the last one is sacrificed, then may he be controlled, to obey the torturer's commands. The rules of summoning tells us this. The one who causes the most pain, the most suffering—this is the one that will bind Kandara to him, and Kandara will grant his wishes. And I wish for you to be gone from our lands. I will command him to destroy your 3rd Infantry. They will not reach Baghdad."

He wiped his bloody instruments on Williams's gore-stained uniform, and then gave orders to the guards. Williams and O'Malley's bodies were dragged away, and two Iraqi's approached the cell, their weapons drawn.

"Now you," the old man said to Myers, "and if the rest of you resist, we shoot."

"You're going to kill us anyway," Sharp said. "What does it matter?"

"Maybe yes, maybe no. We see how many more Kandara need. Maybe I not need to kill you all. He is getting big already, yes?"

Still floating in the air, the black cloud had tripled in size.

Bloom stepped forward. "Take me instead. Not him."

"Bullshit," Myers said calmly, and grasped his friend's shoulder. "You've got to get back home to that girl of yours. What's her name?"

"Jill," Bloom sobbed.

"Right. Jill. You get out of this and when you two have some rugrats, you name one after me, okay?"

He smiled, but Bloom said nothing.

"I need you to be strong for me, Bloom," Myers whispered. "Please."

Then they took him out of the cell.

The thing in the air swelled again. When Bloom glanced at it, he could see two small red dots in its center.

They blinked at him.

Myers was strapped naked to the gurney, and then a thin glass rod was shoved into his flaccid penis, via his urethra. After the tube had disappeared inside, the old man grabbed the organ with both hands and began to wring it like a dishrag, shattering the glass. Myers bucked against the restraints, grunting and hollering in the same breath.

The old man snarled, and one of the soldiers began to pummel the prisoner in the kidneys. Again and again the savage blows landed, until Myers's bladder let go. He howled in agony as the bits of glass were ejected with his urine.

"Listen," Sanchez whispered in Bloom's ear, "we've got to make a break for it! I've got my hands loose."

"How? Myers—they…Myers…"

"Get it together, man! Ain't nothing we can do for Myers or any of the others, except make these bastards pay."

"They'll shoot us if we try it," Sharp whispered.

"And they'll torture us if we don't," Sanchez said. His words were masked by Myers's screams.

In the torture chamber, three guards struggled with a hand-truck, on which sat a massive, industrial-sized battery charger. When they reached the gurney, the charger was plugged into an outlet. The room's single light bulb dimmed as they applied the first shock to Myers's nipples.

"I ain't going out like that," Sanchez continued. "When they open that door again, I'm rushing them. If you guys are with me, cool. If not, I'll try to do what I can for you."

"Fuck it," said Sharp. "I'm with you."

Sanchez began to undo the ropes around Sharp wrists. "Bloom? You in?"

Bloom stared in horror as Myers began to smoke and char. A long, keening wail came from his throat as his teeth shattered from the electricity jolting through him. After a horrifying second, Bloom recognized what Myers was saying.

"Trying to find, trying to find where I've beeeeeeeeeee—"

Myers was singing "Kashmir," just like aboard the M-88.

"eeeeeeeeeeeeeeeeeeeeee—"

Simultaneously, they applied the jumper cables to his testicles and slashed his bulging throat with a box cutter.

"eeeeeeeeeeeeeeeeeeeeeeeeeeeeeeeeeeeeennnnnnnnnnnnnn."

With his final breath, Myers hit that perfect Robert Plant wail that he'd always sought.

"Bloom?"

"I'm in," he snapped, so fiercely that both Sanchez and Sharp took a step back. "Goddamn it, I am so in!"

"Quick, let me see your wrists. Don't let them see us, though."

Above the gurney, Kandara took shape. Much bigger than a baseball now, its arms and legs were clearly visible, as were the malevolent red eyes, glowing like cinders in an otherwise featureless, obsidian face.

"You hear that, you fuck?" Bloom screamed at the creature. "I'm in!"

"Okay," the old man answered, as Myers's body was disposed of. "You can be in next."

Everything happened very quickly. Despite his time in the country, Bloom had yet to experience real up close and personal combat. The only fighting he'd seen had been done from far away—bombing runs and artillery strikes. He wasn't sure what to expect. He thought perhaps time would slow, like in a movie, and that everything would transpire in slow motion.

There was the click of the bolt on the door being thrown, and two guards entered, reaching for him. Then—chaos. Sanchez and Sharp were shouting, and Bloom was surprised to find himself shouting as well.

"Jersey in the house, you motherfuckers!"

They rushed forward, desperately grappling with the armed men. Even as Sanchez wrestled the rifle away from one of them, there was a loud explosion, and Sharp's stomach disappeared. He gasped, choking on his own blood, and then toppled onto his enemy, crushing him to the floor. The Iraqi struggled beneath him. Sharp clawed at the man's throat.

Bloom snatched a fallen rifle from the floor and glanced around. The other two guards scrambled, and Sanchez opened fire, mowing them down.

Bloom charged into the torture chamber. The old man backed toward the exit, his hands raised in fear.

Kandara swelled, unmoving.

The door opened and two more guards ran in, spraying bullets indiscriminately. Sanchez lurched as rounds slammed into him, destroying flesh and bone. He slumped against the wall.

Crouching, Bloom fired back, the rifle jerking in his hands. The heavy staccato of automatic gunfire and the stench of cordite filled the room. The two guards fell beneath the barrage.

"Don't you fucking move," Bloom hollered at the old man. "Get away from that door!"

Cringing, the old man glanced up at the Djinn and began chanting. Bloom squeezed off one controlled shot at his feet, and the old man stopped.

"Lay down."

Bloom motioned toward the gurney with the barrel of his rifle. The old man complied, his bones and joints creaking audibly as he clambered atop it. Bloom lashed him down tight, smiling when the old man winced in pain.

He crept toward the door and listened. Silence. He opened it and peeked outside into the underground tunnel. More silence. They were alone, for now. He shut the door again and bolted it.

"I'm guessing that thing, that genie or whatever the fuck you called it, isn't full grown yet, since it didn't try to stop us."

"It is not bound to me yet," the old man babbled. "Only by causing the most pain can it be bound. Let me go, and I will see that it does not harm you."

Bloom's laughter sounded like the bark of a dog.

"I bet I can cause a lot of pain," he said. "Let's see just how much."

He tapped the old man's arm, searching for a vein. Then he emptied one of the speed-filled hypodermic needles into it.

"Don't want you passing out on me. We're gonna be here a while."

He picked up the box knife and got started.

Above him, Kandara trembled in ecstasy.

It took Bloom a long time to find a radio that worked, and even longer to contact the coalition forces. By then, he was hopelessly lost in the underground maze. While he'd been locked in the room with the old man, chaos had descended on Al-Qurna. He was stunned at the aftermath. Everywhere lay signs of the Hussein regime's fall—abandoned posts and equipment, shredded files, even the bodies of dead officers, gunned down by their own deserting troops. One room, behind a locked door that Bloom had to kick in, held row upon row of wooden shelves, lined with metal boxes. In each box was a plastic bag, containing the remains of previous Fedayeen victims. Some of the bags had identification cards stapled to them. Others did not. One held only a smashed skull. Another, a severed hand. A third contained the desiccated remains of a newborn infant whose limbs had been removed. After that, Bloom stopped searching, afraid he'd come across what was left of his friends.

Deeper in the tunnels, he found two recently dug pits. Dozens of bodies had been thrown into the mass graves, in such haste that their killers hadn't even taken the time to cover them up. Most of the dead were women and children. Among them, Bloom recognized the woman who had helped them along the road. Tears rolled down his cheeks.

"Eden," he whispered.

He wept for her and he wept for his friends. He wept for Riser and Rendell, buried in the sand while they slept. He wept for O'Malley and Jefferson and Williams and Sanchez and Sharp. He wept for Myers.

He wept for himself.

Finally, he found an exit. Sunlight greeted him, shining down upon his face. He went outside to meet it, his tears drying in the heat.

"Oh, let the sun beat down upon my face…"

Humming a snatch of Led Zeppelin, he waited.

Eventually, he heard the hum of the rotors, and rose to his feet. Two Chinook helicopters buzzed toward him. He waved them down. Several soldiers disembarked, barking orders and securing the area while a medic checked on him.

"You're gonna be okay," the medic assured him. "What's your name?"

"Bloom. PFC Don Bloom, 3rd Infantry."

"The 3rd? Man, you're a long way from the rest of your company, friend. Lucky, too!"

"Why's that, sir?"

"Way I hear it, they're heading into some shit. Looks like you won't be with them when it hits. I'm talking major shit, right outside of Baghdad. Saddam's got the Revolutionary Guard heavily entrenched around the city. Looks like it's gonna be a big battle."

"They'll be okay." Bloom grinned. "I sent reinforcements to help them."

He passed out before the medic could ask him what he meant.

Beneath their feet, in a white sandstone dungeon hidden under the desert, the remains of something that had once been human lay scattered across the room. It was no longer recognizable as the old man. Bloom had taken his time and as he'd promised, he'd been very thorough.

The desert winds howled as Kandara raced north toward Baghdad.

Express

by Edward M. Erdelac

Manning the day security desk in the lobby of The Sturgill Building mainly consisted of pointing out the directory sign to visitors and keeping the panhandlers from harassing the suits on their smoke breaks. It was a cushy gig. Most people knew where they were going when they came through the revolving door, and the stinginess of the corporate types was known far and wide among the downtown tramps, so all but the most addlebrained beggars knew it was useless to hit them up, and stuck to the park and the tenderhearted out-of-towners.

Dion Wilkes had been here six years now. He'd started on nights. In the beginning, the change had been jarring. You could doze through most of the night shift if you set an alarm to remind you when to get up and do your checks, and you could let the bums sleep in the doorways as long as they were packed up and gone by the time the cleaning crew left in the morning.

His promotion to days had been a hassle at first; there weren't as many opportunities to screw around. But he soon learned the perks. No rounds to check, so you could actually plunk your butt in the chair and never move 'til quitting time. Sure, some Fridays he got called upstairs to escort somebody out through the front door for the last time. That kind of sucked. They always let them go on a Friday or before a holiday break. He didn't know the psychology behind that, but he had heard it softened the blow. The people he walked out always seemed on the verge of crying, like they were bewildered refugees staggering away from the site of a bombing. They clutched their boxes of personal items, family photos, and the kind of goofy toys and knickknacks office workers decorated their cubes with to fly some desperate personal flag of individuality, something to fool themselves into thinking they were anything but what they were.

Dion didn't keep anything on his desk. He brought his coffee in a thermos and took it home at the end of his shift. He didn't leave anything of himself in this joint, aside from a fart in his chair and the occasional booger rubbed off surreptitiously under the desk.

Those final Friday dead man walks sucked, but they were as rare as the panhandlers during office hours. End of the month was Dion's least favorite time, and today of course, his relief had called in sick. He was pulling a double.

The top floors of the building were occupied by C.D. Holdings, one of those big companies you heard about on the news whose names popped up all over the place, on car dealerships, baseball stadiums, construction sites, and protest signs. What they actually did, Dion couldn't say. They made a lot of people miserable, for sure, because every end of the month a recurring cast of sad looking people wandered up to his desk and asked to speak to somebody about their rent or their mortgage or their business loan. These he'd send to the directory. They would drift over there, blink at the placard, and invariably take the express elevator that bypassed the intervening floors and went directly to C.D. Holdings' corporate offices up on fourteen, usually after meandering back to his desk to confirm which elevator they were supposed to take.

Some of them clutched thick manila envelopes stuffed with cash or yellow folders bursting with reams of receipts and wrinkled checks. When he called up to C.D., the snooty, attractive receptionist with a head full of race car red hair that didn't fool anybody, the one who click-clacked past his desk every morning and evening and never said hello, and seemed to take personal offense at the sound of Dion's voice, would tell him to keep whatever offering the sad sacks brought at the security desk and she'd send somebody down to get it at lunchtime.

He got to know their faces if not their names; the jittery old Korean lady trying to hold onto her late husband's corner grocery store, the skinny hipster in the ratty scarf who'd had a bad experience once and now didn't trust his rent check to the mail, the overweight mother in the tube top with a tattoo of the name "Bruce" in cursive over the arch of her left breast, dragging her frenzied toddler by the wrist, there to tearfully ask somebody in charge for more time.

Only one of these did Dion memorize the name of, and that was Dr. Verman Kind, the owner of The Mystic Scion Bookstore downtown.

Dion didn't know what Kind was a doctor of. It surely wasn't medicine, or if it was, he'd go see a vet before he'd step foot in any office of his. Kind was a compact little German man of indeterminate age, Dion guessed somewhere between forty-five and sixty, pale, without a scrap of visible body hair. He squinted up at you with beady, bloodshot eyes from behind a pair of square Ben Franklin-type glasses, and spluttered demands in his thick war criminal accent. He dressed like one of those steampunk nerds, always in a black bowler and three-piece suit with striped pants and a voluminous black velvet cape (so big, maybe it counted as a cloak) over a silky, brocaded vest and a shirt Dion expected a pirate would run you through to the hilt for. He carried a black case, and always walked swinging a shiny black cane with a fancy silver star-shaped handle.

Always, except for today.

Today, Dr. Kind came through the door (never the revolving door), with a little black terrier scurrying ahead of him on a silver leash.

Dr. Kind's relationship with C.D. Holdings was tempestuous, and Dion knew the details of his drama by heart because Kind repeated it to him every month, angrily punctuating his narrative with repeated, sharp raps of his cane on Dion's desk.

Somehow, several months ago, C.D. Holdings had acquired ownership of the building his weirdo occult bookshop had occupied for a number of decades, and they had raised his rent beyond "agreeable rates," no doubt with the intention of pushing him out so they could level the place and install some garish, soulless monolith like The Sturgill Building itself.

Every month since, Dr. Kind had come to renegotiate the terms of his lease with the powers that be, and every month he emerged from the express elevator loudly and flamboyantly declaring his hatred of C.D. Holdings and its moronic administrators in expressive curses both German and English.

For once though, Kind did not accost Dion at his post, but made straight for the express elevator.

"Hey Dr. Kind!" called Dion, in his authoritarian voice, which was basically an imitation of his father. He stood up as Kind walked by. "What's with the dog?"

The terrier was a Scotty, a sharp-eared, long nosed, stubby legged little thing hidden somewhere in a mass of drooping black hair, like a dirty mop that had come alive and broken free of its handle.

Dr. Kind drew up short and stiffened.

Dion came around the desk slowly. "You can't bring him in here."

"He is an emotional support animal," Kind snapped in his clipped tone. "I was prescribed him by my therapist, for my anger. You will notice I have stopped carrying my walking stick. Also under the advisement of my therapist."

Well, God bless modern psychiatry, Dion thought, as he came over.

Kind dug in his inner coat pocket and drew out an unevenly laminated letter written in an illegible hand which he thrust out disdainfully.

Dion took it and made a point of looking it over, though he truthfully didn't know its worth. He thought there was a difference between service dogs and support animals and where you could take them, but he was alone at the desk and didn't feel like getting into it with the excitable German.

"You see to what personal depths my exasperating dealings with this *verdammt* company and its brainless capitalist drones have reduced me to? *I*, Verman Kind, Third Order Ipssissimus of The Inner Temple, Dweller On The Threshold, who have in my time, bent the primordial forces of life und death to my will? *I*, Verman Kind, mouthpiece of The Great Sultans of The Outer Dark, to whom devils attend und angels sing und beasts beyond mortal imagining answer? No more!" Kind declared, thrusting up his finger. "Today, I tell you, it ends!"

He was really in a rare mood today. Let the receptionist upstairs deal with him. Dion wasn't in the mood.

"He's cute," Dion said, smiling down at the pooch. "What's his name?"

"Feck," said Kind, curling his lip.

"Hey Feck!" Dion said. The dog panted up at him. "Okay, Doc. As long as he's housebroken, I guess it's okay."

The dog looked up at him and wagged its tail.

"Und now," said Kind, "unless you wish to forestall the imminent hour of my liberation from this cathedral of mundanity further…"

"By all means," said Dion, stepping aside and letting Kind and his dog make for the express elevator. "Good luck, Doc."

He watched Kind mash the button and mutter in guttural German as the progression light of the descending elevator flickered above the red double doors. Beside him, the terrier rolled on its back and wriggled on the cool marble floor.

When the door opened, he practically dragged the dog inside. He spun on his heel and dropped his case. Dion watched him stoop down to retrieve it as the doors closed.

Fifteen minutes later Dion was about to head out to lunch when the stairwell door banged open and Dr. Kind swept out, a disturbing grin of heretofore unseen glee smeared across his pale face, his long black opera coat swirling behind him. He deposited something in one of the bronze trashcans that sent the little revolving lid spinning, then strode for the front door, chuckling, laughing loud enough to turn heads by the time he was outside.

It wasn't until he was eating a pastrami sub at the lunch truck across the street near the end of his break that Dion realized he couldn't remember seeing Dr. Kind's dog.

Maybe the dog had gotten tired on the stairs and Kind had scooped him up. Maybe Dion hadn't seen him under his big Dracula cloak.

But why had he taken the stairs at all?

It was a mystery he pondered all the way back to his desk and promptly forgot about when he pushed in an earbud to listen to the game.

At the top of the third inning his phone lit up.

"Security desk," he muttered, picking up.

"Security, this is Mr. Pressman on the fourteenth floor."

Dion sat up a little straighter in his chair.

Walter Pressman was the silver-haired bigwig that occupied the top floor corner office of C.D. Holdings. He was the resident one percenter. The King of Castle Sturgill. Somebody had told him once that Pressman had a standing edict not to lay eyes on anybody outside of his personal assistant and immediate staff. People literally hid behind doors when he passed. To be addressed directly by him, even over the phone, was like getting a summons from the burning bush.

"Yes sir?" Dion asked, trying to keep the shake out of his tone. A rich asshole like this was, in his way, as volatile as crazy old Dr. Kind. Except this particular lunatic could cost him his job if he said something to offend him. Dion's lunch dropped down into his lower intestine. Jesus, had Dr. Kind's mutt taken a dump upstairs? He would catch hell if he had.

"Are you familiar with the employees of C.D. Holdings? Do you know them by sight?"

"Sure. Yes sir. Some of them."

"Have any of them passed by your desk recently?"

Dion looked around, trying to think of who had passed his desk in the last half hour. Hell, truthfully, they all looked alike to him.

"Um," said Dion.

"My receptionist perhaps? Ms. Deacon?"

Dion thought hard. He had not seen the fake red head since she'd come in this morning. Come to think of it, there had been almost no crowd at the lunch truck. He just figured he'd beat the rush.

"No sir, Mr. Pressman. I haven't seen her since she came in this morning."

"What the fuck is going on down there?" Pressman demanded. "The floor is empty. None of the staff has returned from lunch. They were due back hours ago."

Dion opened his mouth, attempting to form a reply, unsure of what the man wanted to hear, but Pressman snarled.

"Never mind! I'm coming down!" Pressman hung up.

Dion threw out the remains of his sandwich and stowed his earbuds, even wiped the surface of the desk down. He watched the lobby clock tick off the minutes. Five. Ten. Twenty. He waited tensely for the phone to light up again but got bored. Pressman wasn't coming. Evidently his staff had finally turned up. Maybe it was his birthday and they'd been hiding or something, jumped out to yell surprise.

Man, some cake would be good about now…

The rest of Dion's shift was pretty quiet. But he noticed something weird.

A couple more end of the month stragglers showed up and made their way upstairs. None of them came back down. Whenever they did go up, he watched the elevator light climb to fourteen and just sit there until it was called again.

Nobody ever came back down.

It got to be quitting time.

He stared at the red doors of the express elevator. Nobody emerged.

Was everybody up there working late?

The other offices emptied out. Still nobody came down from fourteen.

The cleaning crew showed up, chattering in Polish. Half of them made for the elevators to start on the offices, half went to the supply closets to get the spare trash bags for the lobby cans and the floor waxer.

Dion watched a couple of the guys head to the express elevator. He watched the light count down from fourteen. They stepped inside the empty elevator, still talking. The doors closed behind them.

Somewhere down the hall the waxer whined to life.

Up went the express elevator.

And then a woman screamed. There was a loud bang.

Dion ripped out his pepper spray.

One of the cleaning ladies was backing away from the overturned bronze trashcan by the door, shaking her head. She didn't spare a look at Dion, but went wailing and running down the hall, shouting to be heard over the floor waxer.

Dion stared at the trash that had spilled out from the can.

He came around the desk and sprinted over.

Lying on the floor among the garbage was a little black dog's foreleg, one end bright red with blood like a paintbrush.

Dion nearly went shrieking after the cleaning lady.

What the hell was going on?

He thought about Dr. Kind, and about how he'd taken the stairs back down from fourteen.

What the hell had happened upstairs? Had the little old German gone batshit and machinegunned everybody? Why had he thrown his dog's leg in the trash?

Dion went to the gun locker under the desk and fumbled the combination three or four times with sweating hands.

Jesus, he should just call the cops.

But what if it was nothing?

He couldn't call the cops unless he knew there was a reason to.

The gun locker popped open with a buzz and he stared at the Glock inside. He would have to fill out a shit load of paperwork just for opening this thing.

Well, he was committed now.

He took it out, flipped off the safety, thought better of it, and flipped it back on. He had fourteen floors to ride before he knew if he had to bust a cap in anybody.

He crossed the lobby to the elevator and called it. It seemed like forever before the numbers counted down to one and he heard the ding.

As the red doors began to slide open, he suddenly jumped to the side.

Nothing came out. No bomb went off, no people fell out, no gang of Uzi-toting Europeans spilling suitcases of bearer bonds emerged. *What the hell were bearer bonds, anyway?*

Dion peered around the corner.

The elevator was empty, nothing out of place.

He stepped inside.

The doors closed behind him, and the car began to ascend.

He turned to watch the progress on the lighted panel. The inner doors of the elevator were dripping with blood. That's not to say it was spilling down the door like paint. Somebody had written or drawn something in dark red blood on the doors. It was a big crude circle full of geometric patterns and squiggly little symbols and words in a language he didn't recognize, like a psychopath had gone buck wild with a Spirograph in here.

He was so surprised at the bizarre sight he forgot to flip the safety off his Glock.

The elevator whisked to the fourteenth floor and dinged. The bloody circle on the doors flashed bright red for just a second, or else Dion imagined it. The doors slid open, the circle breaking to pieces like a puzzle and receding into the door housing.

He didn't understand what he was looking at.

A long round tunnel stretched out before him. It glistened wet and radiated heat. It looked like a cave, the floor and ceiling prickling with weirdly translucent black stalactites or stalagmites or both. Which ones stuck up and which ones hung down?

All around the very threshold of the elevator door was a soft, rubbery gray substance that quivered and dripped a clear, syrupy fluid. An overwhelming, chemical stink like laundry detergent wafted into the car.

Dion peered down the dark tunnel as the whole length of it undulated. The sharp objects shivered, and the puckery seal around the doors went rigid and made a wet, slurping sound.

Dion had stood in high winds before. In the winter the wind blew hard through the downtown area off the lake and pulled your clothes tight. But he had never felt a wind attack him in the opposite direction. That was, it didn't blow toward him, it sucked at him, so strong he had to stumble back and grab the safety railing.

He dropped the Glock and watched it go flying down that dark wet hallway.

He was pulled right off his feet, and one of his shoes followed the pistol.

The air rushed violently from his lungs, faster than a sneeze. His nostrils dried up and he was treated to the sight of his saliva escaping his mouth in a burst of steam. His joints and fingers prickled, and he found himself unable to hold the rail.

He was drawn from the car, into the grasp of something, several somethings, that slithered in knots from the dark tunnel. They tangled around his feet, curled up his legs, tightened around him in the light of the elevator like bumpy red snakes.

No, not snakes.

Tongues. He knew, as his joints swelled painfully and he gulped for nonexistent air, that they were tongues.

They dragged him out of the elevator, over the black, sharp things.

He saw the lift doors close, cutting off the light. They receded quickly into the distance. They were the size of a stamp before he could think to scream.

The sharp things ripped him open like a fallen water skier dragged though jagged coral, flayed the flesh, shredded the flesh to the muscle, scraped the muscle to the bone.

He went where the others had gone; where Dr. Kind had sent them.

Over the teeth and through the gums. Something his mother used to sing to him as a kid at lunchtime.

He didn't have time to remember the rest.

Witches' Night

by Owl Goingback

April 30, 1974.

"Bullshit. I don't believe you." Paul Roberts reached the top of Barker's Hill, trying to catch air on his bicycle. The thirteen-year-old imagined he was legendary stuntman Evel Knievel, sailing his Harley-Davidson motorcycle over a row of parked school buses. But then his back wheel slipped on some loose gravel and he almost went down, fishtailing to keep control of the bike. The other boys laughed and hurled catcalls at him.

"I saw it the other night," Howard Baker replied, topping the hill but not attempting to catch air. Howard was overweight and the rusting frame of his old bike would probably snap like a twig if he tried to jump it. He was the biggest kid in seventh grade, blaming his size on overactive glands and not from all the pasta and baked goods his mother cooked.

"Liar. You did not see *The Exorcist*." Paul slammed on his breaks, bringing his bike to a sliding stop. *The Exorcist* was the biggest movie of the year, at least to Paul and his fellow horror loving friends. The movie had been released nationwide in theaters on December 26, but hadn't yet been shown in the small town of Logan, Missouri.

Howard pulled to a stop beside Paul, breathing hard from peddling up the hill. "I'm telling you; I saw it."

"Liar. You did not already see *The Exorcist*." Eric Henderson rode up beside the other two boys, having caught air perfectly at the top of the hill. Eric was thin and muscular, a regular jock compared to the other two boys.

"I'm not lying," Howard said, his voice taking on a familiar whine. "My sister took me to see it."

"Okay. You saw it," Paul said. "Where?"

"Where what?" Howard asked.

"Where did you see the movie?"

"In a theater," Howard answered

Eric laughed, snorting out his nose. "Of course, you saw it in a theater, dipshit. Which one?"

"I…I. It was…" Howard stammered, seeming at a loss for words.

Paul and Eric smiled at each other, knowing they had caught their friend in another fib. Howard had a habit of stretching the truth, especially when trying to impress the others.

"I saw it in St. Louis," Howard finally said.

"Really?" Paul didn't believe him. "You drove seventy miles one way, on a school night, to see a movie? And your mom was okay with that?"

"My sister took me, so it was okay." Howard looked around nervously.

"Which theater?" Eric asked.

"Uh, ah…" Howard stammered. "I don't remember."

"You saw the biggest horror film of the decade, and you don't remember the name of the theater?" Eric asked.

"Okay, you saw it," Paul patted Howard on the shoulder. "We believe you."

Howard visibly relaxed, smiling.

"How does Regan die?" Paul asked, grinning. He squeezed Howard's shoulder, holding him so he couldn't pull back.

Howard's smile melted like ice cream on a warm summer day. He stammered, "What? Who?"

"Regan. The girl who gets possessed. How does she die?"

"She…she gets staked through the heart."

Paul burst out laughing. He had read the book and knew the ending. Nobody got staked in the story. "You're such a bullshit artist. I knew you were making it up. You haven't seen *The Exorcist*."

Eric also laughed. "Staked? She's not a vampire, dumbass. She was possessed by the Devil."

"We were going to see it, honest, but my sister had a flat tire on the way," Howard said, making up a second lie to cover the first.

Paul let his hand fall off his friend's shoulder. "Sure, you did."

Neither of the boys wanted to make a big deal out of catching Howard in another lie. He might be a constant fibber, but he was still their friend. And he had the biggest collection of comic books and monster magazines in town, which made him a valuable member of the group.

As a matter of fact, Howard's bedroom was their preferred meeting spot. His room was decorated with monster movie posters and Aurora model kits. He also had his own television, so they could watch Creature Features, Dark Shadows, and old Beach Party movies. His parents both worked late, so they usually had the house to themselves.

"Let's go get Sally," Paul said, changing the subject. "She should be home by now."

"Her dad isn't home, is he?" Howard asked, nervously.

They were all frightened of her father. Ben Freemont was a former army soldier and probably the toughest son of a bitch in Logan. Everyone steered clear of him, even the cops, especially when he was drinking. The man was a mean drunk.

Ben had served two consecutive tours of duty in Vietnam, earning a chest full of medals and a face full of scars. Rumor was he had been captured during his second tour, spending six months in a tiger cage, finally managing to escape by killing two VC guards with his bare hands.

Whatever had happened to him over there must have been really bad, because he spent nearly a year in a hospital after returning stateside. And then, every three months, a long black car would stop in front of Sally's house, and two men in dark suits would go inside to check on her father. The three of them would talk in whispers in the back room, talking so low that his wife and daughter could never hear what was being said.

Sally had once shown the boys a patch that came off her father's uniform, probably the coolest patch any of them had ever seen. It featured a human skull wearing a beret. Underneath the skull were the letters MACV

SOG. None of them knew what the letters stood for, but Sally said one time she asked her mother about the two men in the black suits. Her mother told her the men were CIA agents and she should never ask about them again.

Sally's mom, Edna, was the complete opposite of her husband. She was really nice, like Sally, but there was a quiet sadness about her. She rarely smiled, like she was afraid the happiness would slip off her face and run away. And, like her daughter, she always seemed to be sporting new bruises.

Reaching the bottom of Barker's Hill, they cut through the neighborhoods behind the high school, crossed the rickety old footbridge spanning Lost Creek, reaching the city limits sign marking where Logan ended and the county began.

Code enforcement didn't exist beyond the city limits, and the houses they now passed all needed painting, roof repairs, and general maintenance. Junk cars silently rusted in yards choked high with weeds, old tires stacked like rubber totem poles beside them.

Leash laws were also nonexistent in this area, so they all rode with their heads on a constant swivel. They were especially on alert for a large German shepherd that loved chasing kids on bikes. Paul had lost the seat of his favorite blue jeans to the dog's fangs, and Howard had once received several puncture wounds in the calf of his left leg. But luckily, the shepherd was nowhere to be seen.

Sally lived in a clapboard house at the end of the dirt road, its fading white paint almost gray. Two massive oak trees took up most of the front yard, casting their shadows over much of the property. The trees were a welcome addition during the hot summer months, but a pain in the backside when their leaves started falling in autumn. By mid-October, there were usually dozens of leaf piles waiting to be stuffed into giant jack-o'-lantern trash bags.

Paul spotted Sally sitting on the front porch reading a book, feeling a nervous little flutter deep down in his stomach. He had known Sally ever since the first grade. She had always been part of their group, but in the past few months he started thinking of her less and less as one of the guys.

Maybe it was because Sally had filled out in all the right places. She was still thin, a bit on the boney side, but there was now a softness to her that hadn't been there before, making it awkward when they wrestled or played Twister. He felt his face flush on more than one occasion when their bodies touched. He wasn't sure if she had noticed. If she had, then she didn't tease him about it.

Sally closed the book and looked up as they rode into her yard, her smile framed by long blonde hair cascading down to her shoulders. It was a school day, but she had already changed into her play clothes: a pair of faded denim bell-bottoms, Pink Floyd t-shirt, and white sneakers.

The boys all said hello, dropping their bikes in the front yard.

Sally stood up, brushing the dirt off the back of her pants. "What's up, guys?"

"Nothing much," Paul answered. "We're going to ride over to the Rexall Drug Store to see if they've gotten any new magazines. Might stop off first at the Dairy Queen for a shake. You want to go?"

"Sounds like fun. Let me go put this up, and we'll go." She started to take her book inside the house.

"What are you reading?" Howard asked, always the nosey one.

Sally turned back around, a sly grin unfolding on her face. She held the book facing her, so only she could see the title. "This? This is a book about magic."

"Magic?" Eric asked. "You mean tricks, like Houdini?"

She shook her head. "Not tricks. Real magic."

Howard laughed. "There's no such thing as real magic. It's all an illusion, done with smoke and mirrors."

"Not smoke and mirrors," she said. "Real magic, ancient knowledge handed down for centuries."

She turned the book around so they could all see the front cover. There was no title, or author's name, just a black cloth cover with a large white pentagram painted on it. "Spells. Chants. Forbidden things."

"You mean witchcraft?" Paul asked, staring at the book.

"Where did you get that?" Howard asked, his eyes getting bigger.

There weren't any real bookstores in Logan. The drugstore had racks for magazines and comics, and stocked a few paperbacks, but the selections were rather slim. And the public library refused to carry any titles about the occult, not even horror novels.

"I bought it at an estate sale a couple of weeks ago." She slowly stepped down off the porch, her voice dropping to a mere whisper. They circled around her, like football players in a huddle. "Do you guys know what day this is?"

"It's April 30th," Howard said.

She looked from one boy to the next, studying their faces. "April 30th. That's right. But do you know what tonight is?"

"April 30th night?" Howard asked. Eric punched him in the arm. "Ow. Why did you do that?"

"Because you're being a moron," Eric said. "Stop interrupting."

"But she asked—"

"Are you finished?" Sally gave Howard a look that cut him off mid-sentence.

He nodded.

"Tonight is Walpurgisnacht, Witches' Night, a time for real magic, when the boundary between the world of the living and the world of the dead is thinnest."

"You mean, like Halloween?" Eric asked.

"Yes, like Samhain," she replied, using the original Celtic name for the celebration.

"A second Halloween. Cool," Howard said. "We can go trick-or-treating."

Eric punched him in the arm again.

"I've never heard of it," Paul said, staring at the book she held.

Ever since *The Exorcist* had come out the media had been flooded with things about the occult. There were stories about covens and cults, witches and demons, and deep dark stories of the Catholic church. Sally had been fascinated by it, much more than the rest of the group, almost to the point of being obsessed. She had gone to new age shops in the city in search of black magic and occult items, hiding her new possessions behind the bottom drawer of her dresser so her parents would not find them. Paul knew her secret because she had shown him the items a few months earlier. He didn't like the occult stuff, but figured she was going through a phase. And who was he to complain about such things when he loved monsters and all things horror? But the monster movies were all fake, and Sally had been trying to get hold of real occult stuff.

"Walpurgisnacht isn't celebrated much here in the United States," she continued, "but it's really big in Europe, especially in Germany. It's a night when witches and warlocks gather on the highest peak of the Harz Mountains to do magic. Dates all the way back to the old ones."

"Old ones?" Eric asked.

Sally nodded. "Pagans and witches, gods and demons."

"I don't believe in that stuff," Howard said. "Not really."

"Just because you don't believe in something doesn't mean it's not real. Tonight is a night for witches, and for ghosts. The boundary between the two worlds will be thinnest. Doors can be opened, allowing the dead to…"

She stopped talking. Stepping back, she looked at them for a moment before speaking again. "I will prove to you that real magic exists. Tonight."

"Tonight?" Paul asked.

Sally nodded. "There's no school tomorrow; your parents won't mind if you stay out a little late. Just tell them you will be at Howard's watching movies." She turned to look at Howard. "And you can tell your folks that you'll be at Paul's."

"Where will we really be?" Eric asked.

She smiled. "We'll be in the old Catholic cemetery."

"The cemetery, at night?" Howard gasped. "Why the cemetery?"

"Because tonight we will be asking favors of the dead," she said. "And if you're talking to the dead, then you need to go where they are. Now, you—"

They heard a vehicle coming down the road, the engine revving loudly as if the transmission was stuck in second gear. They all turned to look and spotted a beat-up green pickup truck coming their way, swerving back and forth across the dirt road, a cloud of dust billowing behind it. It was Sally's dad, and he had been drinking again.

"You've got to get out of here," she said, a look of absolute terror coming over her. "I'm not supposed to have visitors. He'll kill me."

"What should we do?" Howard asked, his voice becoming a whine. "He'll see us for sure."

He was right. If they rode out of the front yard onto the road, they would be spotted.

"Quick. Run," Sally said, pointing at the far side of the house. "Around the house and out the backyard, there's a hole in the fence. Cross the field to the woods. Stay low."

Sally and the boys took off for the side of the house, cutting around to the backyard. Paul and Eric grabbed their bicycles, running with them, but Howard left his bike lying in the weeds. In the terror of the moment, none of the others noticed he had forgotten his bike.

They cut through the overgrown backyard to the hole in the fence, racing across the open field. They stayed low, trying not to be seen by Ben Freemont.

The pickup slowed, turning into the gravel driveway. It was at that moment Paul noticed Howard did not have his bike.

"Howard, your bike!" Paul yelled.

Howard looked at him. "What?"

They reached the edge of the open field, ducking into the woods and stopping. Sally ran up behind them, also stopping.

"Your bike," Paul repeated. "Where is your bike?"

Howard pointed back at the house. "In the yard."

Sally looked shocked. "You left your bike?"

"You said run," Howard answered. "So, I ran."

"Moron, she meant get your bike and run," Eric said.

"I'll go back and get it," Paul said, dropping his bike.

Sally put her hand on his chest, stopping him. "No. You can't. It's too late. You'll get caught."

"I'll go," Eric said, also letting his bike drop. "I'm the fastest. I won't get caught."

"No," Sally said, genuine concern in her eyes. "Don't. You don't know what my father's like when he's drinking. It's not safe."

"But he'll see the bike," Paul said. "You'll get in trouble."

"Maybe he won't see it," Howard said. "The grass in your yard is really tall."

Just then they heard her father call out, his voice angry and slurred. "Sally. What the hell is this? Get your ass over here."

Sally's complexion went pale as alabaster, tears forming at the corners of her eyes. "I've got to go."

"No. Wait," Paul tried to stop her. "I'll go with you. I'll say it's my bike, my fault for coming over. I'll cover for you."

She shook her head, a trembling smile touching the corners of her mouth. "It won't do any good." She reached down and took his hand, touching the tips of his index and middle finger to her lips, lightly kissing them. "Just be there tonight, at the cemetery. Be there for me."

She let his hand fall, then turned away and ran back toward her house and the drunken fury awaiting her. Paul watched her go, feeling his heart break. Had he been older, stronger, braver, he could have done something to protect her, could have been her knight in shining armor, but he was none of those things. He was just an eighth-grade boy, and her father was a trained killer of men.

"Come on, let's go. Before he sees us." Eric grabbed Paul's arm, turning him away from Sally's house. Paul reached down and grabbed his bike.

"What about my bike?" Howard whined.

"Forget it for now," Eric said. "We'll get it later, when her dad isn't around."

The three of them turned away from the house, following a path through the woods. They walked in silence, for they knew what kind of hell Sally was about to endure. But there was nothing they could do about it. Not even the cops would intervene.

The sun was setting when the boys arrived at the front entrance to the old Catholic cemetery, just west of the town of Logan. Howard rode his older sister's pink bicycle, much to the amusement of the others. There was a noticeable chill in the air, so all three of them wore blue jeans and jackets.

Reaching under his jacket, Howard pulled out the rubber werewolf mask he had been hiding the whole trip, slipping it over his head and growling.

"Dude, seriously?" Eric said.

Howard took off the mask. "What? Sally said tonight was like a second Halloween, and how many chances do I get to wear this thing?"

"I don't know. How many?" Eric asked.

Paul looked at Howard, shaking his head. "You probably wear that stupid thing every day. Heck, you might even sleep in it."

"Take it off before Old Man Sharkey sees it and calls the cops on us," Eric said, his voice serious.

Howard took off the mask, stuffing it back under his jacket. Old Man Sharkey lived in a two-story brick house atop the hill on the opposite side of Cemetery Road. He had a pair of military binoculars and was always on the lookout for kids messing around in the cemetery at night.

"Do you think Sharkey saw us?" Howard asked. "Do you think he called the cops?"

"You know he did," Eric teased. "Deputy Harding is probably on his way here right now. Going to arrest you and throw your ass in a cell."

"That's not funny. My parents would kill me if I got arrested."

"That would be the least of your problems," Paul said, joining in on the teasing. "From what I hear, those guys in jail get really lonely. They would just love a sweet young thing like you."

Eric grinned. "Yeah. You'd be somebody's bitch."

"No. I wouldn't," Howard argued. "I'd kick their ass if they tried to touch me. I know karate."

Both of the other boys laughed openly, knowing Howard was telling another fib.

"Karate. Since when?" Eric asked.

"Since last summer. I took a course at the YMCA in Warrenton." Howard struck a pose, doing his best Bruce Lee impersonation.

Paul and Eric cracked up.

Howard lowered his hands, looking around. "Where's Sally? Figured she would be here already. This was her idea."

They all looked around, but didn't see any sign of her or her bike.

"Maybe she's already in the cemetery," Paul suggested. "Let's go in."

They rode their bikes through the open gates, following a graveled path up the hill to the oldest section.

The old Catholic cemetery was only about twenty acres in size, surrounded on three sides by dense forest. In the center of the cemetery stood a large metal cross that always seemed to glow at night, no matter how dark or cloudy. On the back side of the graveyard, in a small clearing behind the last row of headstones, stood a five-foot marble statue of a young girl in an old-fashioned dress. The statue was so lifelike some of the older teenagers swore that it moved, especially late at night after a few beers or some weed.

They spotted Howard's bike leaning against the statue. A blue burlap bag with a white drawstring cord sat on the ground beside the bike. Sally stood in the shadows just beyond the statue, in the middle of a patch of bare dirt. She held the large black occult book open in her hands, quietly reciting words out loud.

"Hey, Sally!" Howard called.

"Shhh… Keep it down. We don't want the whole world to know we're here," Paul warned, suddenly aware of how quiet it was in the cemetery. Quiet and very creepy. Maybe conducting an occult ceremony on Witches' Night wasn't such a good idea. By the light of day, it didn't sound so bad. But now, darkness fast approaching, it sounded like the dumbest damn idea in the world.

Sally turned to face them, stepping out of the shadows. She wore a sleeveless black dress and shoes to match, the lightweight material moving ghostlike in the evening breeze. It was the same dress she had worn two years ago on Halloween. "I was afraid you wouldn't come."

Paul felt his pulse quicken. Standing in the clearing, the black dress billowing around her pale white frame, the setting sun turning her blonde hair the color of fire, Sally was absolutely stunning. It took a moment for him to find his voice. "We promised to be here."

Howard cleared his throat, destroying the magic of the moment. "If what you're saying is true, then how do we summon these ghosts?"

Sally closed her book and tapped it. "With this."

"The book?"

She nodded. "With what I found in it."

"What did you find in it?" Paul asked, his curiosity aroused.

She pulled a folded piece of paper from between the pages, carefully unfolding it. The paper was old and yellowed, looking like parchment. On it were handwritten words, the lettering thick and coppery brown.

"What's that?" Eric asked, leaning forward to get a better look.

"I found it in the book," she said. "I guess the previous owner left it there. Maybe they left it for someone like me to find. It's a spell."

"A spell?" Paul said, a chill walking down his spine. He suddenly felt as if they were all standing on the edge of a deep dark pit about to step off.

"What kind of spell?" asked Howard.

Sally looked into Paul's eyes, as if only talking to him. "It's a spell to open the doorway between the worlds."

Eric laughed. "Someone is pranking you."

She held the paper up for all to see the writing. "If so, then they went through a lot of trouble. The spell is written in blood."

Howard snorted. "Bullshit."

"Look for yourself," she said.

Howard stepped forward to take a closer look at the paper, but he didn't take it from her. Maybe he was afraid to touch it, just in case it really was written in blood.

"It does look like blood," he said, looking around at the rest of them.

"But you can't be one-hundred-percent sure," Eric added.

"I'm sure," she said. "Someone left this spell for a reason. They want us to open the doorway tonight and let the spirits through."

"Sally, no," Paul said, his voice a whisper. "You don't know what you're messing with. Something bad could happen."

She turned to look at him, lowering the paper. And it was then he noticed the fresh bruises on her right arm. A set of four dark stripes just above her wrist, finger marks. She had tried to hide them with makeup, but the bruises were still darkening and showed through the concealer. There was another set of bruises around her neck that he had mistaken for shadows in the fading sunlight, and more along the inside of her thighs.

"Something bad has already happened," Sally said. There was a slight quiver to her voice, as if she was on the verge of tears. She took a deep breath, quickly regaining her composure. "This couldn't be any worse."

"Gee, I don't know—" Howard said, about to back out.

"I'm in," Paul said quickly, not really understanding why he did it. Maybe because Sally had let her armor slip, and he had seen the frightened, abused girl beneath it.

"You're in?" Eric asked, as if not believing his ears.

Paul shrugged. "Sure. Why not? Unless you guys are chicken."

Sally smiled.

Paul had ended any and all debate by throwing out the word "chicken." None of them wanted to be branded a coward.

"Sure, why not?" Eric said, seconding the decision. "We don't have anything better to do."

"So, what do we do?" Howard asked.

Sally set the occult book on the ground, referring to the piece of parchment paper. She picked up a stick that was lying next to the burlap bag. "First, it says to draw a pentagram on the ground."

"A pentagram?" Howard asked. "I thought that was for werewolves. I don't want Lon Chaney showing up here tonight."

"Relax, it's not just for werewolves," Eric said. "Besides there's no full moon."

She ignored their banter, using the stick to draw a large five-pointed star in the dirt. When done, she tossed the stick aside and walked back over to her bag, removing a zippo lighter and three red candles set in glass vases.

Walking back over to them, she handed each boy a candle. "They're supposed to be black, but this is all we had so I guess they'll do. They're leftover from Christmas." She lit all of their candles with the Zippo. "Now, each of you pick a point of the star to stand."

Moving slowly so the flames of their candles wouldn't blow out, they each chose a point of the star.

Sally walked back over to the statue, dropping the lighter into her bag and removing the final item. "We're supposed to make an offering."

"A what?" Howard asked.

"An offering to the spirits," she answered. "A sacrifice."

"I say we offer Howard," Eric suggested.

"Screw you," Howard replied.

Paul's heart skipped a beat as Sally straightened up and turned back around to face them. In the palm of her left hand she held an orange and white ball of fluff, complete with tiny legs and a tail. A ball of fluff that made a tiny mewing sound.

"Sally, no!" Paul said, horrified. "You can't sacrifice a kitten."

"It's okay, Paul. This poor thing has pneumonia. The whole litter's infected. Daddy was going to put them down in the morning, so they don't suffer no more. We'll just end this guy's pain a little sooner."

Putting down an animal with country folks usually meant shooting them, especially if you didn't have money for an expensive vet bill. Howard had to do it two years ago with his beagle, Chips, after the dog got hit by a car while playing on the road.

"Okay." Paul nodded. "If it's sick, I understand. It's not right to let it suffer." He looked at the others. "Okay with you guys?"

"How are you going to do it?" Howard asked. "None of us has a gun."

For the first time that night Paul saw Sally's confidence slip a little. She probably hadn't thought about how to kill the sacrifice. But before anyone else could say anything, Paul answered, "I'll do it."

"You?" Eric laughed. "You got sick dissecting a frog in biology class."

He turned to face Eric, feeling his face flush with embarrassment. "Yeah. But I'm not going to dissect the kitten. I'm going to snap its neck like my grandma does when she kills a chicken for Sunday dinner. Quick, easy, and painless."

"I doubt painless," Howard mumbled.

Sally walked forward, placing the kitten in Paul's hands. Never had a cat felt so warm and so alive as that poor little thing, and he felt like a monster for what he agreed to do. The kitten raised its head and tried to look at him, but its eyes were glued shut with mucus.

Sally moved to the center of the pentagram, taking a stand with her legs slightly apart and her left hand raised to the night sky. Holding the piece of parchment paper in her right hand, she read what was written on the page.

"Oh, spirits come onto us this Walpurgisnacht. Come through the portal and be among us. Oh, Satan, great Dark Lord, I beg you to open the doorway and let the ancient ones pass into this world. On this Witches' Night I offer you this sacrifice of flesh and blood, and ask that you pull aside the veil that separates the world of the living from the world of the dead."

As Sally spoke, Paul noticed the air behind her ripple like heat waves over a fire. Tiny molecules of darkness began to swirl about and bump together, the movement slow at first but quickly becoming frantic. The shadows behind her became a few shades lighter, more gray than black, the boundary between two very different worlds becoming thinner, forming a doorway.

Paul was spellbound by the sight, unable to look away. Sally's voice seemed to fade into the background as she read words off the parchment page, in an ancient language he didn't understand. He suddenly found it difficult to breathe. A strange buzzing filled his ears.

The patch of moving air grew wider, more turbulent, like steam above a large cauldron of boiling water. The veil between the worlds grew even thinner. Beyond the rippling air, Paul could suddenly see dozens of humanlike shapes. The shapes took on definition. They were people, but they were not flesh and blood. Nor did they belong to the world of the living. They were shadow people, spirits, perhaps even demons, huddled together in a group, summoned by Sally's words, waiting for a magical portal to open.

And then what? What would the shadow people do once the gateway fully opened and they were allowed entrance into the world of the living, entering a cemetery where four teenagers performed a ceremony calling upon dark powers they knew nothing about? Paul had seen enough horror movies to have a sudden suspicion that what they were doing would not end well. Maybe this was why ancient people erected bonfires on Samhain and Walpurgisnacht eons ago. They built bonfires to keep the shadow people out.

But Paul's sudden suspicion came a moment too late, and he heard his name frantically being called. Hearing his name broke his stupor, causing the buzzing in his ears to dissipate and his mind to clear. He looked at Sally.

She stood with both arms by her side, fists clenched. She screamed at him, her voice frantic, "Now, Paul. Now. Make the sacrifice!"

He looked down at the kitten, but the thing he held no longer had the face of a tiny sick cat. Instead, the little ball of orange and white fluff had a human face, complete with bloodshot eyes, scars, and the unshaven stubble of a beard. It was the face of Sally's father.

Paul screamed and let go of the kitten, watching in horror as the human-faced monstrosity fell to the ground at his feet.

Sally yelled again. "Paul, pick it up. Do the sacrifice. Kill it. Now!"

The other boys stood motionless, holding their candles and watching him. They were too far away, the night too dark, for them to know what was going on. They didn't see the cat with the human face lying in the grass at his feet, or the evil smile that suddenly unfolded on Sally's face. A vengeful smile.

"Go on, Paul," she said, speaking in a voice only he could hear. "Do it. He deserves it. Do it for me. Kill him."

Slowly, he bent over and picked up the kitten, holding it in the palm of his left hand. Ignoring the human face, he reached his right hand around the back of its head, thumb and fingers on opposite sides of its face. Feeling the human beard stubble made his skin crawl, and he realized that he was about to kill more than just a kitten. The sacrifice being offered to the dark gods this night was Sally's father.

Paul let his right hand fall limply to his side. "I can't."

Sally looked at him in stunned disbelief. "Paul, you must."

He shook his head. "I'm sorry. I can't do this."

"Please. You have to," she begged, fear edging its way into her voice. "You don't know what he's done to me."

"I know." He looked into her eyes. Tears rolled down his cheeks. "We all know."

"Then why won't you do it? Why won't you help me?"

"Because we're just kids, Sally. And this is not kid's stuff."

As he spoke, the boiling patch of air behind her began to slow and become less frantic. The shadow people grew dimmer, the veil between the two worlds growing thicker and more solid. As it did, a pair of humanlike arms shot out from the darkness of that other world and grabbed Sally around the waist from behind.

"Paul, noooo—" Sally's eyes went wide in terror; she reached both hands out to him in desperation.

Paul ran toward her, leaving his place in the pentagram, reaching out with his right hand to grab her and pull her back. Their fingertips briefly touched, a feeling of electricity shooting up his arm and into his heart.

And then she was gone, snatched by one of the shadow people into the land of the dead. A sacrifice had been offered to the dark gods this unholy night, and a sacrifice had been claimed.

"Paulllll…" Her voice stretched out into a long cry of agony and despair, fading away into nothingness as the door between the two words closed.

He looked down, and saw that the tiny sick kitten he held once again had the normal face of a cat. It was spared from a ritual death, and would soon be spared from pneumonia by a trip to the local veterinarian.

Howard and Eric walked up and stood beside him, staring at the place where Sally vanished. None of them spoke.

The boys slowly rode down the hill to the front of the cemetery, leaving the book of magic and Howard's sister's bike hidden in the forest. They knew none of them would ever talk of this night. They also knew horror movie marathons were now a thing of the past. Scary movies were no longer fun when you knew real horrors existed in the universe.

As Paul rode away from the cemetery, he wondered if the world where Sally now resided was any more, or less, horrific than the one she had left behind.

Biographies

The winner of both a Bram Stoker and World Fantasy Award, **P.D. Cacek** has written over a hundred short stories, seven plays, and six published novels. Her most recent novel, *Second Lives*, published by Flame Tree Press, is currently available from Amazon.com. The sequel, *Second Chances*, will be released from Flame Tree Press, November 2020.

Cacek holds a bachelor's degree in English/Creative Writing Option from the University of California at Long Beach and has been a guest lecturer at the Odyssey Writing Workshop.

A native Westerner, Cacek now lives Phoenixville, PA. When not writing, she can often be found either with a group of costumed storytellers called The Patient Creatures (www.creatureseast.com), or haunting local cemeteries looking for inspiration.

Kenneth W. Cain is an author, editor, and graphic designer. His most recent short story collections, *Embers* and *Darker Days*, were published by Crystal Lake Publishing along with the novella *A Season in Hell*. *From Death Reborn*, his next novel, is forthcoming from Silver Shamrock Publishing, where he served as editor of the anthologies *Midnight in the Graveyard* (nominated for the Splatterpunk Awards, the Indie Horror Book Awards, and the This Is Horror Awards) and *Midnight in the Pentagram*. He has also edited *Tales from the Lake Volume 5* for Crystal Lake Publishing and *When the Clock Strikes 13* for In Your Face Books. In 2017, he was awarded the Silver Hammer service award as an Active member for the Horror Writers Association. Cain enjoys sports, having played in various adult leagues, painting, fishing, wildlife, and tie-dyes. He resides in the suburbs of Philadelphia with his family, where he continues to write in the dark.

Catherine Cavendish first started writing when someone thrust a pencil into her hand. Unfortunately, as she could neither read nor write properly at the time, none of her stories actually made much sense. However, as she grew up, they gradually began to take form and, at the tender age of nine or ten, she sold her dolls' house, and various other toys to buy her first typewriter.

She hasn't stopped bashing away at the keys ever since, although her keyboard of choice now belongs to her laptop.

The need to earn a living led to a varied career in sales, advertising and career guidance but Cat is now the full-time author of a number of supernatural, ghostly, haunted house and Gothic horror novels and novellas, including *The Malan Witch*, *The Garden of Bewitchment*, *The Haunting of Henderson Close*, and the Nemesis of the Gods series. Her short story "Euphemia Christie" appeared in the Silver Shamrock *Midnight in the Graveyard* anthology and another short story of hers is due to appear in their new *Midnight in the Pentagram* anthology. A new novel – *In Darkness, Shadows Breathe* – is due out in early 2021. She lives in Southport, in the U.K. with her longsuffering husband and black cat and can be found at www.catherinecavendish.com as well as the usual social media.

Tim Curran is the author of *Skin Medicine, Hive, Dead Sea, Biohazard, Monstrosity, Skull Moon, The Devil Next Door, Clownflesh,* and *Dead Sea Chronicles*. His short stories have been collected in *Bone Marrow Stew* and *Zombie Pulp*. His novellas include *The Underdwelling, The Corpse King, Puppet Graveyard, Worm,* and *Terror Cell*. His short stories have appeared in such magazines as, *Splatterpunks, Weirdbook,* and *Inhuman,* as well as anthologies such as *Ride the Star Wind, Eulogies III,* and *October Dreams II*. His fiction has been translated into German, Japanese, Spanish, Russian, and Italian. Find him on Facebook.

Stephanie Ellis writes dark speculative prose and poetry and has been published in a variety of magazines and anthologies. Her latest work includes the novella, *Bottled*, published by Silver Shamrock, her short story, "Milking Time" in Flame Tree Press' *A Dying Planet* anthology and the novelette, *Asylum of Shadows* from Demain Publishing. Her poetry can be sampled in the Horror Writer Association's *Poetry Showcase Volume 6*. She has collected a number of her published, and some unpublished, short stories in *The Reckoning*, her dark verse in *Dark is my Playground*, and flash in *The Dark Bites*, all available on amazon. She is co-editor of *Trembling With Fear*,

HorrorTree.com's online magazine. She is an affiliate member of the HWA and can be found at https://stephanieellis.org and on twitter at @el_stevie.

Edward M. Erdelac is the author of twelve novels including *Monstrumfuhrer, The Knight With Two Swords*, and the acclaimed Judeocentric Lovecraftian weird western series *Merkabah Rider*. His short stories have appeared in dozens of places including *Sherlock Holmes and The Occult Detectives* and Star Wars Insider magazine. He lives in the wilds of Los Angeles with his wife, three kids, and three felines and maintains a blog, Delirium Tremens, at http://emerdelac.wordpress.com. He can be spotted skulking about Facebook and Twitter but seek him not there; you may not like what you find....

A life-long resident of New York's haunted Hudson Valley, **JG Faherty** has been a finalist for both the Bram Stoker Award® (The Cure, Ghosts of Coronado Bay) and ITW Thriller Award (The Burning Time), and he is the author of 7 novels, 11 novellas, 2 collections, and more than 75 short stories. He writes adult and YA horror, science fiction, paranormal romance, and urban fantasy. He grew up enthralled with the horror movies and books of the 1950s, '60s, '70s, and '80s, and as a child his favorite playground was a 17th-century cemetery. Which explains a lot. Follow him at www.twitter.com/jgfaherty, www.facebook.com/jgfaherty, and www.jgfaherty.com.

Shannon Felton was born in Riverside, California. After serving in the United States Army and spending several years in Germany, she and her family relocated to the Phoenix area. There, Shannon began to pursue her love for writing and soon published her debut novella, *The Prisoners of Stewartville*, among other works. You can find more news and information by following her on Twitter at @ShannonNova3.

Robert Ford has written the novels *The Compound*, and *No Lipstick in Avalon*, the novellas *Ring of Fire, The Last Firefly of Summer, Samson and*

Denial, and *Bordertown,* as well as the short story collection *The God Beneath my Garden.* He has co-authored *Rattlesnake Kisses* and *Cattywampus* with John Boden. You can find out more about what he's up to by visiting robertfordauthor.com

Owl Goingback has been writing professionally for over thirty years, and is the author of numerous novels, children's book, screenplays, magazine articles, and short stories. He is a Bram Stoker Award Lifetime Achievement Recipient, a Bram Stoker Award Winner for Best Novel and Best First Novel, a Nebula Award Nominee, and a Storytelling World Awards Honor Recipient. His books include *Crota, Darker Than Night, Evil Whispers, Breed, Shaman Moon, Coyote Rage, Eagle Feathers, Tribal Screams,* and *The Gift.* In addition to writing under his own name, Owl has ghostwritten several books for Hollywood celebrities. He has also lectured across the country on the customs and folklore of the American Indians, served in the military, owned a restaurant/lounge, and worked as a cemetery caretaker.

Amanda Hard's dark fiction and poetry have appeared in numerous publications including *Lost Signals* and *Tales from the Crust* (both from Perpetual Motion Machine Publishing), as well as *City in the Ice* and *Idolators of Cthulhu* (both from Alban Lake Press), Ruthless Peoples Magazine, and parABnormal Magazine. She earned an MFA in Creative Writing from Murray State University in Kentucky, after studying literature and fiction writing as an undergraduate at the University of Evansville, in Indiana. A former professional dancer and magazine editor, Amanda now works as a freelance journalist, covering vaccine advocacy and integrative medicine. She is a member of the Horror Writers Association and lives in the cornfields of southern Indiana with her husband and son.

Michael Patrick Hicks is the author of several horror books, including *The Resurrectionists, Broken Shells: A Subterranean Horror Novella,* and *Mass Hysteria.* He co-hosts Staring Into The Abyss, a podcast focused on all things horror. His debut novel, *Convergence,* was an Amazon Breakthrough Novel

Award Finalist in science fiction. He is a member of the Horror Writers Association.

In addition to writing his own works of original fiction, Michael is a prolific book reviewer and manages the High Fever Books website. His reviews have also been published by Audiobook Reviewer and Graphic Novel Reporter, and he has previously worked as a freelance journalist and news photographer in Metro Detroit.

Michael lives in Michigan with his wife and two children. In between compulsively buying books and adding titles that he does not have time for to his Netflix queue, he is hard at work on his next story.

Laurel Hightower writes a mix of horror, thriller and noir. Her debut novel, *Whispers in the Dark*, was published by JournalStone on December 7, 2018. She is also a guest contributor for DeadHead Reviews, and one third of the InkHeist Podcast team, along with Shane Douglas Keene and Rich Duncan.

Laurel grew up in Lexington, Kentucky, and after forays to California and Tennessee, has returned home to horse and bourbon country. She counts the likes of Kelley Armstrong, Neal Stephenson, and Stephen Graham Jones as her influences, as well as Stephen King and R.A. Dick, not just because *The Ghost and Mrs. Muir* was such an excellent book – who couldn't love that pen name?

Social media:
Twitter: @hightowerlaurel
Facebook: **https://www.facebook.com/laurelhightowerky**
Website: **www.laurelhightower.com**

Brian Keene writes novels, comic books, stories, journalism, and other words for money. He is the author of over fifty books, mostly in the horror, crime, and fantasy genres.

His 2003 novel, *The Rising*, is credited (along with Robert Kirkman's *The Walking Dead* comic and Danny Boyle's *28 Days Later* film) with inspiring pop culture's recurrent interest in zombies. Keene's books have been translated into German, Spanish, Russian, Polish, Italian, French, Taiwanese, and many other languages. He oversees Maelstrom, a small press publishing imprint specializing in collectible limited editions, via Thunderstorm Books.

He has written for such Marvel and DC properties as *Thor, Doom Patrol, Justice League, Harley Quinn, Devil-Slayer, Superman, and Masters of the Universe*, as well as his own critically acclaimed creator-owned comic series *The Last Zombie*. Keene has also written for media properties such as *Doctor Who, The X-Files, Hellboy,* and *Aliens*.

Keene also hosts the popular podcasts *The Horror Show with Brian Keene* and *Defenders Dialogue*, both of which air weekly on iTunes, Spotify, Stitcher, YouTube, and elsewhere.

Several of Keene's novels and stories have been adapted for film, including *Ghoul, The Naughty List, The Ties That Bind*, and *Fast Zombies Suck*. Several more are in-development. Keene also served as Executive Producer for the feature length film *I'm Dreaming of a White Doomsday*.

Keene's work has been praised by *The New York Times, The History Channel, The Howard Stern Show, CNN, The Huffington Post, Bleeding Cool, Publisher's Weekly, Fangoria, Bloody Disgusting,* and *Rue Morgue*.

His numerous awards and honors include the 2014 World Horror Grandmaster Award, 2001 Bram Stoker Award for Nonfiction, 2003 Bram Stoker Award for First Novel, the 2016 Imadjinn Award for Best Fantasy Novel, the 2015 Imaginarium Film Festival Awards for Best Screenplay, Best Short Film Genre, and Best Short Film Overall, the 2004 Shocker Award for Book of the Year, and Honors from United States Army International Security Assistance Force in Afghanistan and Whiteman A.F.B. (home of the B-2 Stealth Bomber) 509th Logistics Fuels Flight. A prolific public speaker, Keene has delivered talks at conventions, college campuses, theaters, and inside Central Intelligence Agency headquarters in Langley, VA.

Keene serves on the Board of Directors for the Scares That Care 501c charity organization.

The father of two sons, Keene lives in rural Pennsylvania with author Mary SanGiovanni.

Todd Keisling is a writer and designer of the horrific and strange. He is the author of several books, including *Devil's Creek*, *Scanlines,* and *The Final Reconciliation*, among other shorter works. He lives somewhere in the wilds of Pennsylvania with his family where he is at work on his next novel. Share his dread:
Twitter: @todd_keisling
Instagram: @toddkeisling
www.toddkeisling.com

Allan Leverone is the *New York Times* and *USA Today* bestselling author of twenty-four novels and five novellas, as well as countless short stories. A former Derringer Award winner for excellence in short mystery fiction, Allan lives in Londonderry, New Hampshire with his wife of more than thirty-five years, three grown children and three beautiful grandchildren. Connect on Facebook, Twitter @AllanLeverone or at AllanLeverone.com.

Chad Lutzke has written for Famous Monsters of Filmland, Rue Morgue, Cemetery Dance, and Scream magazine. He's had dozens of short stories published, and some of his books include: *Of Foster Homes and Flies, Stirring the Sheets, Skullface Boy, The Pale White, The Neon Owl* and *Out Behind the Barn* co-written with John Boden. Lutzke's work has been praised by authors Jack Ketchum, Richard Chizmar, Joe Lansdale, Stephen Graham Jones, Elizabeth Massie and his own mother. He can be found lurking the internet at www.chadlutzke.com

Graham Masterton is mainly recognized for his horror novels but he has also been a prolific writer of thrillers, disaster novels and historical epics, as well as one of the world's most influential series of sex instruction books. He became a newspaper reporter at the age of 17 and was appointed editor of *Penthouse* magazine at only 24. His first horror novel *The Manitou* was filmed with Tony Curtis playing the lead, and three of his short horror stories were filmed by Tony Scott for *The Hunger* TV series. Four years ago Graham turned his hand to crime novels and *White Bones*, set in Ireland, was a Kindle phenomenon, selling over 100,000 copies in a month. This has been followed by ten more bestselling crime novels featuring Detective Superintendent Katie Maguire, the latest of which is *The Last Drop of Blood*. In 2019 was given a Lifetime Achievement Award by the Horror Writers Association. A new horror novel *The House of 100 Whispers* will be published in 2020. He has established an award for short stories written by inmates in Polish prisons, Nagroda Grahama Mastertona "W Więzieniu Pisane" which will be presented for the fourth time this year. He is currently working on new horror and crime novels, and is writing new horror stories with Dawn G. Harris.

Kenneth McKinley was born and raised in the small town of Bronson, Michigan. He grew up in the time of heavy metal mix tapes, VCRs, and library cards. Ever since that magical moment when he wandered into the adult horror section of the public library at the age of 11, he has always dreamed of being a writer. With his critically acclaimed debut, "The Glimmer Girls," in the ghost story anthology, *Midnight in the Graveyard*, he could finally realize his dream.

Kenneth graduated from Ohio State University and owns Silver Shamrock Publishing. He is a member of the Horror Writers Association and the Independent Book Publishers Association. He resides in Michigan with his wife, Kathy, and their four children. Kenneth is currently working on his next novel.

William Meikle is a Scottish writer, now living in Canada, with over thirty novels published in the genre press and more than 300 short story credits in thirteen countries. He has books available from a variety of publishers including Dark Regions Press and Severed Press and his work has appeared in a large number of professional anthologies and magazines including among them a story in the previous Silver Shamrock anthology, *Midnight in the Graveyard*. He lives in Newfoundland with whales, bald eagles and icebergs for company. When he's not writing he drinks beer, plays guitar, and dreams of fortune and glory. Seek him out at williammeikle.com

Tim Meyer dwells in a dark cave near the Jersey Shore. He's an author, husband, father, podcast host, blogger, coffee connoisseur, beer enthusiast, and explorer of worlds. He writes horror, mysteries, science fiction, and thrillers, although he prefers to blur genres and let the story fall where it may.

Brian Moreland writes a blend of mystery, action-adventure, thriller, and horror. His books include *Shadows in the Mist, Dead of Winter, The Witching House, The Devil's Woods, The Seekers, Darkness Rising* and *Tomb of Gods*. Coming January 2021, he'll be releasing a new novella, *Savage Island,* through Silver Shamrock Publishing. Follow on Twitter: @BrianMoreland

James Newman lives in North Carolina with his wife and their two sons. Since the release of his first novel *Midnight Rain* in 2004, Newman has thrilled readers with fiction that speaks with a Southern twang and an occasional streak of pitch-black humor. His published works include *The Wicked, Animosity, Ugly as Sin, Odd Man Out*, and the collections *People Are Strange* and *The Long N' Short of It*. He has also co-authored several fan-favorite collaborations such as *The Special* and *In The Scrape* (both with Mark Steensland), *Dog Days O' Summer* (with Mark Allan Gunnells), and *Scapegoat* (with Adam Howe). *The Special* was recently adapted as a feature film by B. Harrison Smith, director of *Camp Dread* and *Death House*.

Azzurra Nox was born in Catania, Sicily, and has led a nomadic life since birth. She has lived in various European cities and Cuba, and currently resides in the Los Angeles area. She has a B.A. Degree in Letters – Classical Studies and an M. Ed. in Secondary Education. She's always been an avid reader and writer from a young age, entertaining her friends with ghost stories. She loves horror movies, cats, dancing, and a good rock show. She dislikes Mondays and chick-flicks. For more info on her writing go here: https://azzurranox.com/books/. She's also the founder and curator of the lifestyle blog The Inkblotters: https://theinkblotters.com/ where she shares her love for makeup, movies, books, music, traveling, and skincare with her readers. You can follow her on Twitter @diva_zura or Instagram at @divazura. Her latest works are "Good Sister, Bad Sister," appearing in *Betty Bites Back: Stories to Scare the Patriarchy*, "Fragile Fruit," co-written with Erica Ruhe appearing in Running Wild Anthology of Stories Book 2, and her anthologies as editor, *My American Nightmare – Women in Horror Anthology* and *Strange Girls – Women in Horror Anthology*.

Jason Parent is an author of horror, thrillers, mysteries, science fiction and dark humor, though his many novels, novellas, and short stories tend to blur the boundaries between these genres. From his EPIC and eFestival Independent Book Award finalist first novel, *What Hides Within*, to his widely applauded police procedural/supernatural thriller, *Seeing Evil*, Jason's work has won him praise from both critics and fans of diverse genres alike. He currently resides in Rhode Island, surrounded by chewed furniture thanks to his corgi and mini Aussie pups. www.authorjasonparent.com

Charlotte Platt is a young professional who writes horror and urban fantasy. Charlotte spent her teens on the Orkney Islands and studied in Glasgow before moving to the north Highlands. She lives off sarcasm and tea and can often be found walking near cliffs and rivers, looking for sea glass. Charlotte was shortlisted for the Write to End Violence Against Women Award 2017, placed second in the British Fantasy Society Short Story Competition 2017 and presented the pitch for her upcoming novel *A Stranger's Guide* at the London Book Fair 2019 Write Stuff competition. She can be found on Twitter at @Chazzaroo.

John Quick is the author of several novels, including *The Corruption of Alston House*, also available through Silver Shamrock. He lives in middle Tennessee with his wife, kids, four dogs, and a cat. You can find him on Twitter and Instagram @johndquick.

Armand Rosamilia is a New Jersey boy currently living in sunny Florida, where he writes when he's not sleeping. He's happily married to a woman who helps his career and is supportive, which is all he ever wanted in life...

He's written over 150 stories that are currently available, including horror, zombies, contemporary fiction, thrillers and more. His goal is to write a good story and not worry about genre labels.

He not only runs two successful podcasts...

Arm Cast Podcast - interviewing fellow authors as well as filmmakers, musicians, etc. The Mando Method Podcast with co-host Chuck Buda - talking about writing and publishing. But he owns the network they're on, too! Project Entertainment Network.

He also loves to talk in third person... because he's really that cool.

You can find him at https://armandrosamilia.com for not only his latest releases but interviews and guest posts with other authors he likes!

Wesley Southard is the Splatterpunk Award nominated author of *The Betrayed, Closing Costs, One For The Road, Resisting Madness, Slaves to Gravity* (with Somer Canon), and *Cruel Summer*, some of which has been translated into Italian, and has had short stories appear in outlets such as *Cover of Darkness Magazine, Eulogies II: Tales from the Cellar* and *Clickers Forever: A Tribute to J.F. Gonzalez*. When not watching numerous hours of ice hockey, he spends his free time reading and drinking copious amounts of Diet Dr. Pepper. He is also a graduate of the Atlanta Institute of Music, and he currently lives in South Central Pennsylvania with his wife and their cavalcade of animals. Visit him online at www.wesleysouthard.com.

Mark Steensland first learned how to scare people at the age of four during a drive-in screening of *Rosemary's Baby*. Although he was supposed to be asleep in the back of the family station wagon, he stayed awake, secretly listening. When the doctor on screen announced Rosemary's due date as June 28th, he sat up and proudly exclaimed, "That's *my* birthday!" giving his parents and siblings a shock from which they still have not recovered. Over the years that followed, he became obsessed with Aurora monster models, *Dark Shadows*, *Famous Monsters* magazine, and Rod Serling's *Night Gallery*. His first professional publication was as a film journalist, in Jim Steranko's *Prevue* magazine. Numerous bylines followed in *American Cinematographer*, *Millimeter*, and *Kamera*. As a director, his short films (including *Lovecraft's Pillow*, *Dead@17*, *Peekers*, *The Ugly File*, and *The Weeping Woman*) have played in festivals around the world and earned numerous awards. His first novel--*Behind the Bookcase*--was published in 2012 by Random House. His most recent book is *In the Scrape*, a novella co-written with James Newman. He currently lives in California with his wife and their three children.

Mark Towse is an Englishman living in Australia. He would sell his soul to the devil or anyone buying if it meant he could write full-time. Alas, he left it very late to begin this journey, penning his first story since primary school at the ripe old age of 45. Since then, he's been published in the likes of *Flash Fiction Magazine*, *Cosmic Horror*, *Suspense Magazine*, *ParABnormal*, *Raconteur*, and his work has also appeared three times on The No Sleep Podcast and many other excellent productions. His first collection, *Face the Music*, has just been released by All Things That Matter Press and is available via Amazon, Dymocks, B&N, etc.
https://twitter.com/MarkTowsey12
https://marktowsedarkfiction.wordpress.com/
https://www.instagram.com/towseywrites/

Tony Tremblay is the author of the novel *The Moore House* (Haverhill House Press). He has also penned the short story collections *Blue Stars And Other Tales Of Darkness*, and *The Seeds Of Nightmares* (both from Crossroad Press). Tremblay has worked as a horror reviewer, a television host, and is co-founder of the NoCon convention held annually in Manchester, N.H. He currently lives in New Hampshire.

Cameron Ulam is a Speech-Language Pathologist residing in a southern suburb of Cleveland, Ohio. An alumna of Kent State University, she received a master's degree in Speech-Language Pathology in 2015 and currently works with children on the autism spectrum to support the development of communication skills. Cameron writes primarily within the genres of horror and speculative fiction; her stories have appeared in audio format on multiple podcasts, including the "Creepy" and "Scare You to Sleep" podcasts. She also has published work in other horror anthologies, including the "It Calls from the Forest: Volume Two" anthology by Eerie River Publishing. Cameron is currently working on a few short, speculative fiction pieces, as well as her first full-length horror novel, which she is looking to complete by the winter of 2020. Cameron is an avid lover of cats, watercolors, podcasts, and all things terrifying; you can often find her hoarding vintage horror novels from the shelves of her local thrift shop. Find out more about Cameron's latest publications on Instagram/Twitter @ *Ulam_Writes* or check out her website, Cameronulam.com.

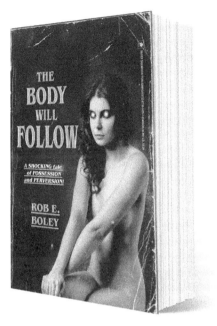

Lightning Source UK Ltd.
Milton Keynes UK
UKHW011426130422
401514UK00001B/6